# The Seer

JORDAN REECE

Copyright © 2015 Jordan Reece
All rights reserved

Cover photo courtesy of Can Stock Photo and taden
Cover by Joleene Naylor

ISBN-13: 978-1-9833-8173-7

# CONTENTS

| | |
|---|---:|
| CHAPTER ONE | 1 |
| CHAPTER TWO | 14 |
| CHAPTER THREE | 27 |
| CHAPTER FOUR | 41 |
| CHAPTER FIVE | 61 |
| CHAPTER SIX | 74 |
| CHAPTER SEVEN | 88 |
| CHAPTER EIGHT | 106 |
| CHAPTER NINE | 122 |
| CHAPTER TEN | 139 |
| CHAPTER ELEVEN | 156 |
| CHAPTER TWELVE | 170 |
| CHAPTER THIRTEEN | 188 |
| CHAPTER FOURTEEN | 199 |
| EPILOGUE | 208 |

# Chapter One

Jesco was out on the grounds with the children when the police carriage turned down the flowered lane of the asylum. Errant branches scraped along the bright black sides as the autohorse drew it on, shoes making merry clips on the cobbles.

They had been watching the aviators, the handful of othelin children who were recovered enough from spot-flu to be outside in the garden. The pale blue sky was full of bulbous shapes in every color, and they were sketching what hung suspended high above while Jesco minded them. The arrival of the carriage took their attention away from paper and pencil. No face could be seen within the carriage, as the glass was darkened. One could look out, but not in, which Jesco had explained to them many times from personal experience.

"Is it a body, Mr. Currane, sir?" asked a girl.

"It may be," Jesco replied as the carriage rolled past them to the main building. The scratching of the branches gave off as the autohorse pulled into the driveway circle. The grounds always had a riotous look despite the dedicated ministrations of wizened Phipps and his assistant. Vine roses crept up the windows by night to shine their blushing faces into the rooms at morning, and cheery purple holidays took frequent rambles over the stepping-stones. The lane was ever in danger of being crowded out by the lines of shaggy trees stooping over it, the petals of their white flowers drifting down all summer to swathe the cobbles in snow. The happy disorder of it all had been Jesco's first impression of Cantercaster Asylum when he was delivered to it at the age of eight, and though he had been beaten in body, tormented in spirit, and terrified from skin to marrow in the back of the wagon, his heart was kindled at the mutiny of form and explosion of color. He had never seen such a thing in all his life, and surely it could not be such a bad place when it was so lovely. It was a child's logic, but it proved true.

Soon a nurse was stepping quickly down the path and calling for Jesco, who excused himself from his small company of artists. They whispered in his wake as the nurse took over his duty. His excursions from the asylum fascinated them one and all, and often the evening-time stories they requested were not The Bolging Hare or Tales of a Girl Pirate but of his participation in the mysteries of murder. The cases in which it was not a mystery had no need of his involvement.

Ideally, he would have had more time to recuperate since the last case. He was up and walking, but he was well aware that if he pushed too hard, he would land himself back in his wheelchair in short order. Yet he would not dream of sending the police carriage away without him. Jesco was very limited in the work he could do, and to be part of investigations out in the world excited him. In one way, and one way only, was his seer skill valuable. In every other way, it was a detriment that constricted his life to these grounds where his environment could be controlled.

The carriage had stopped at the entryway to the asylum. It was Sinclair who had come for him, a junior detective to whom the ignominious tasks of an investigation fell. A nervous fellow with flapping cheeks, he was holding open the door of the carriage so that Jesco's chair could be pushed inside. The new attendant had brought it out. Pawing at the ground, the bay autohorse settled and stilled. They were in almost every fashion a real horse, from appearance to mannerisms, and only by looking directly into the eyes was the truth revealed in the faint glimmer of tiny springs and gears and circuitry, which extended into a whirring, revolving infinity.

"Greetings," Jesco said as he came to the carriage. He liked Sinclair, who had always treated him politely though some others at the station did not. The chair was now inside, and the attendant as well to engage the brakes. After a click-clack, he ducked out, inclined his head to Sinclair and Jesco, and retreated to the entryway.

At first glance, Sinclair did not seem suited to investigating homicides. He was too much of a gentleman. In all the cases that Jesco had worked with him, the man was as wide-eyed and aghast as an innocent to have happened upon the scene of a crime. Better suited to robbery, perhaps, or simply filing papers at the Fourth Street Station, yet despite his shock he worked hard and no one had transferred him. He looked down to Jesco's hands and said, "Good, good, you've got the gloves on already. Then we shall go."

Jesco entered the carriage and took a seat. Sitting down across from him, Sinclair called, "Second destination, ho!" From the bowels of the autohorse came a symphony of metallic sounds, which muted when Sinclair shut the door. The carriage lurched and curled gracefully around the driveway, returning to the lane and the scratching of branches as they passed down it to the road.

"They're staring at us," Sinclair said about the children, who watched unabashedly from the garden with their sketches forgotten. "Always, always, they stare at us. Do they know what you do, the little ones, or do they think that I am arresting you once or twice a month?"

"They are well aware of what I do. It is the one-way glass that draws their eyes," Jesco said. "They're from farm country, many of them, and a glass of this kind is beyond their kenning." He had once lived in a place such as that, where advancement did not penetrate and the tales of it were deemed nonsense or devilry.

"And are they all othelin like you?" Sinclair queried.

"Othelin, yes, but not all like me. I was the only seer in that party."

"What are the rest?"

"Kineticists, manipulators, and telescopics."

The horse turned smoothly at the corner and merged into the traffic there. "I hope this day has found you well," Sinclair said formally.

"It has," Jesco said. "But not so well for another, I presume."

Sinclair blanched at even such an oblique reference to the deceased. "No, not so well. Not so well at all."

It was best to approach the issue gently, which Jesco had learned over time would win him the most information from the junior detective. Theolodus Sinclair did like to chat, if one only found the right route to encourage his words to flow. "When did this case come to the attention of the force?"

"At dawn," Sinclair answered readily. "A tramp made the discovery in an alley and came to the station, where he caused quite a commotion. It was first assumed to be ravings induced by alcohol, but he was so specific and insistent that two patrolmen were dispatched to investigate. One stayed there when it proved truth; the second hurried back to the station to alert the detectives."

"Has the scene been disturbed?"

"Fortunately, no. For love or money, few but a drunken tramp will trespass into Poisoners' Lane in Wattling."

Poisoners' Lane! Along the riverside in Wattling had long been a site of great industry and crushing poverty entwined, but the factories and tenements alike were now silent. The water was beginning to clear years later without fresh deposits of chemical waste dumped into it, but people had not returned to live there. The ground was poisoned, the bricks and wood and metal of the buildings, with kolymbium. Alchemy was the science of weak minds, resting upon its dubious laurels with phrenology and astrology and homeopathy, but likewise so powerful that it had arrested several city blocks in the matters of life entirely. The greatest devastation had been on Poisoners' Lane itself. The half-life of kolymbium was very long indeed, and no one in Jesco's lifetime would ever be able to dwell there.

"Is it safe for us to investigate?" Jesco asked in concern.

"Yes, not to worry," Sinclair said. "We consulted the chemist on retainer as soon as we learned that it was not a tramp's morbid fantasies. Safe to study the . . . scene, safe to take what evidence we may find, so long as it has not been there long." His hanging cheeks drained of what little color they had regained. "As to the body, should it appear to have been there for some period of time, she suggested that we not let it linger overlong with the coroner. It should be examined and removed to the facility at Pine Cross post-haste. They have the means to deal with it there."

"Did you see the tramp yourself?" Jesco asked. "Did you find him suspicious?"

"I spoke with him for more information immediately upon the return of the patrolman. I do not think he would report a man in whose departure from this world he was responsible."

"Ah, but he wouldn't be the first, would he? The Praying Mantis was such a sort: killing his victims, and then reporting the remains so that he might win accolades for finding them. That was before I began to assist, but I have heard of him in the station."

Sinclair considered this as he glanced out the window to the shops. "The Mantis Man, yes, he had cold eyes. So cold, cold and flat, like twin lakes of ice beneath an overcast sky. I remember him well. His last strike happened in my third year at the station. His lips all a'tremble, he wrung his kerchief and looked like he was in the straits of utter misery as he relayed to us what he had found. But his eyes caught me again and again, those icy eyes that all his distress did not touch."

This was one of the reasons that Sinclair had gotten the promotion. For all his delicate nature, he was keenly attuned to subtle incongruence, and that was a necessity in a homicide detective. The Praying Mantis had created his first discovery in his boyhood years and basked in the newspaper articles about his bravery. A cry! A most terrible cry he had heard in the night, but where others shrank in their beds, this brave son of a railroad engineer girded himself with blade and boots and sought it out in his nightdress. But too late, too late had he come to save the woman in the woods, whose body was blackening within a fire.

This had happened in the small town of Switch, and the unsolved murder obsessed all of western Ainscote for months. Then it faded, pushed into the background behind fresher crimes. The Praying Mantis moved far away from Switch, supplied himself with a new identity, and let Time carve him into a man. It was not until he was well into his thirties that he did it again, murdering a woman and dumping her body into a lake just before it froze over. In the spring, this clerk of haberdashery was in the news for spying something curious in the water and paddling a boat over to see what it was. A torso! That was all that remained. Once again, he basked in the attention of his gruesome find, and nobody connected the balding man who sold pins and bobbins to the son of the railroad engineer two decades in the past and hundreds of miles away.

Yet again he moved, changed his identity, and waited for Time to transform him. Sinclair had encountered him in his elder years, enormously fat and reeking of cigars, a respectable man of business with a wife and a son at university. Without the junior detective's diffident assertions that all was not as it appeared, the murderer might have gotten away with it for a third time. Now the Praying Mantis in his dotage resided in a cell within Crofthollow Prison, and guards regularly relieved him of contraband in the form of articles about his crimes. The murders he had committed had only been a means to experience his true thrill of gaining attention, and that was the greatest atrocity of all.

Sinclair was also remembering the crimes of the cold-hearted murderer, and murmured, "Thrice! Thrice it turned out that he had done this. I cannot fathom it." The carriage slowed, stopped, and picked up speed. He returned to the case at hand. "The tramp's eyes were clear. A fallen man, a despairing man, but I believe him to be an honest man. He was much too intoxicated to be cunning. He was taking Poisoners' Lane as a shortcut to reach the Archangel Micalo Indigent Home on Selbie Road. His aim was only for a cot to sleep the sunlight hours away. It's a penny for a cot by night and a half-penny by day. If he had aught to do with this, it would be to my astonishment."

Jesco trusted the detective's instincts and they fell into silence. The scenery out the glass grew grimmer as the carriage came to Wattling, which was the poorest area in all of Cantercaster. Children in rags played in the lanes, wet from a recent rain, and drunks sagged against walls with bottles pinched between their thighs. A fellow in dirty but fine clothing came in ecstatic paroxysms to the carriage, where he pounded on the sides and ran alongside it with his feet kicking up the water from puddles.

# THE SEER

He shouted incoherently. Jesco caught a glimpse of his maddened eyes, which could not see in but that did not matter. The man was clearly soaring high upon the wings of rucaline, and he was seeing what was not there. Recoiling from the window, Sinclair said, "It cannot be weeded out, the twists and turns that bring that damned hallucinogenic here."

"I know very little about rucaline. But they are brought to the asylum now and again, people ruined by it," Jesco said. "They're placed in another ward, so I do not often have dealings with them." Sometimes he saw them strapped into wheelchairs, ostensibly being taken out for a pleasant stroll through the garden, but they were drooling, slant-eyed, and unaware of their surroundings.

Less shrinking in the matter of drug trafficking than he was with murder, Sinclair said, "Once, just once, can hook a soul upon rucaline forever. It is an evil made manifest. Grown in Brozzo to the south, and in the Sarasasta Islands, those lace flowers. The growers take care to keep their farms well hidden in the forests. The properties of the drug are in the seedpods, like opiates, but the effect is not at all similar. Picked, treated, and smuggled here in small cakes, they are shattered and sold and snorted. One small cake is worth many thousands of dollars since each individual dose is so miniscule. And never the same, its strength, and the strongest can relieve a person of all sensibilities permanently. The body lives on but the mind has vacated. The Drug Administration does what it can to staunch the flow of rucaline into the country. But where one head is cut off, three more sprout in its place."

The autohorse clipped faster down the road and the drugged man fell away. Jesco looked out the back window to see him sprawled in a puddle and laughing with insanity. He had done all of that running without shoes, and was oblivious to his lacerated feet. "I wonder what he sees," Jesco said, for all he saw was a pathetic sight in a man of means, his clothes torn and stained, laying helpless in an area famous for its proliferation of pickpockets.

"He sees grandness, and that is why he does it," Sinclair said. "They are brought into the station to dry out in the tank, weaving tales of knights and dragons and glory, maidens or gentlemen fair, cracking their knuckles on the bars and walls of the cell and believing them dastardly assailants. They are heroes in their own minds for the length of the intoxication, and they love themselves for it and believe themselves to be loved. This is why they cannot find temperance. They wish to stay within these fantasies forever. It is an endless loop of flying high, coming down and remembering how they acted without comport, and desiring to fly high again to forget how their conscience pricks. This goes on and on until they die or else stumble into a bolus dose that destroys their sanity."

Grimmer still was the scenery out the glass. "A rich man's delight, rucaline," Sinclair said. "The rest keep to opium." Such a den was outside: a squat gray establishment hunkered down between taller buildings and with bursts of fake poppies around the door to indicate what one could find within. There was a room within the brothel Jesco patronized on occasion that was for the smoking of opium. Though curious, he had never entered it, and Collier warned him not to create a problem where there was none. For Collier's sake, Jesco would avoid it. That beautiful man knew much more about opium from working there than Jesco did from his sporadic visits. Leave opium to the sick and broken for pain relief; there was no need for Jesco to have it.

The traffic had ended. Now the carriage was passing through slums peopled only by shadows. This was the dead zone. All was silent except for the dulled sounds of the autohorse's hooves and the rattling of the wheels. Although they had the assurance of the chemist, nervousness filled Jesco to be nearing Poisoners' Lane. It had been fifteen years since anyone called this area home, fifteen years since those terrifying articles appeared in the newspapers of the bodies in the streets and the tenements, still sitting at tables over meager meals and sagging in corners. One did not feel sick upon exposure. One did not feel sick at all, and then hours later, Death suddenly came knocking. The Church had taken advantage of the fall of thousands, blaming it upon demons, but Science fingered the true cause. Jesco was ten years old at the time, one of many children in the asylum crying out in nightmares of bodies strewn everywhere like paper dolls, streams of foam leaking from their lips and their eyes staring into whatever lay beyond.

But there were no bodies now. The carriage bumped and turned through the silent streets, ever held in shadow from the abandoned, looming tenements. They could not be knocked down without freeing even more kolymbium, and still it would be sunken in the earth so that nothing could be built here again. The buildings stood as a graveyard, and once a year patrols of street officers swept through to peep in windows and make sure no one had broken in and perished. The fear of the dead zone was so extreme that they rarely found anyone save those intentionally missing, who had had the goal of ending their lives by dwelling in an emptied apartment until the poison overtook them.

Sinclair was looking at him in concern, although Jesco's remembrances of that childhood fear had made only a small divot in his forehead. "Are you well?" The eyes of the junior detective slid to Jesco's gloved hands.

Jesco shook his head to dismiss the worry. "I am not in thrall. It is simply strange to be in this haunted place that I've heard about since childhood."

Sinclair saw the truth of it and returned to gazing out the glass. "It was the worst of the worst even before the poisoning, a squalid place, no sanitation, no clean water, no insulation or ventilation in many of the buildings. I heard about how they slept here, three to a bed and two *under* a bed, rented for eight hours and then it was three more to the bed and two underneath. Then the same again in another eight hours. There could be fifteen people living in the smallest of rooms, forty in a larger one, and that house, that house there, it must have held hundreds." He motioned and moved aside so that Jesco could look. They were passing a huge, centuries-old house with two floors. Hints of its former grandness remained in the stone quoins, the columns and pediment about the front door, and the oriel windows. When first built, it had been the home of a very rich person. Now it was a cracked and smudged disaster with shattered glass.

"Only to see it in its heyday. The gardens had to have been splendid," Sinclair said wistfully. There were no gardens now. Nudging up on either side were cheaply constructed tenements, each shrugging a deferential shoulder towards the once fine mansion. "This used to be the belle of the river. Called Wadalabie in olden days, before industry took root here."

Amused, Jesco said, "Are you a man of history, Sinclair?"

"A man of insomnia. A book of history cures it." He smiled as Jesco chuckled. "Many lords and ladies kept summer homes in Wadalabie. Did you know some of the earliest photographs were taken here? A collection called *Place of Dreams* showed it in all its finery: mansions and stables, and paths of white stone going down through fields of flowers to the river. A boat ran between Wadalabie and Rosendrie, where they could travel to shop. A short and pleasant trip on calm waters. But those lords and ladies died in time, and left their homes to their children, and some of them leased out those homes or sold them. And then the Industrial Revolution swept through Ainscote, and it transformed this place entirely. Wadalabie to Wattling, mansions to tenements, stables to textile factories, and no trace left of those paths or flowers." He looked once more to Jesco's hands. "Have you seen things like this, how time changes the world? You must."

"Yes." It was why Jesco had to be so careful about what he touched.

The carriage made another turn and slowed. They had arrived at their destination. Then Jesco was stepping out after the junior detective, and into Poisoners' Lane where the alchemist had wrought his destruction in one of these very buildings.

It was the grimmest place of all. Along either side of the narrow gray road were tall brick buildings, all of them coated in grime. They were eyeless, as the windows had been removed and sealed up with bricks to discourage anyone from going inside. The doors were sealed in the same way, making every building wholly faceless. Above, the sky seemed only to be a reflection of the road beneath in its gray flatness. No trees pierced the rooftops and no birds flew overhead. All that existed within this claustrophobic lane was itself. The rest of the world felt miles away. Even the river, as close as the far side of the buildings to Jesco's right, made no sound.

There was another police carriage parked in the road, and a voice hailed Sinclair from an alley. Jesco breathed shallowly to take less of the air in this place into himself. Over twenty thousand people had died here almost simultaneously. Should ever there be a place ripe for spooks, this would be it. Failing to quell his anxiety, he followed Sinclair to the alley. The patrolman Tokol was standing at the end of it, a newspaper rolled up in his fist. Despite being of the same age as Jesco, he still looked like more of an overgrown boy than a man. Greeting Sinclair warmly and ignoring Jesco, Tokol moved aside to let them pass.

"And a good day to you, too," Jesco said loudly, forgetting his resolve to take in as little air as possible while he was here. Embarrassed, Tokol grunted a hostile good day. Jesco did not have to inquire to know that Tokol accepted Church teachings that what he did was obscene, but that placed the boyish officer in a quandary. The police relied on seer skills to assist in solving crimes. He resolved the matter by pretending Jesco did not exist, which was why Jesco took a special delight in reminding the officer that he most assuredly did, had every right to be here, and that his word was not only admissible in court but preferred.

The alley was piled with a tall heap of long beams on one side. Rags and bits of paper were trapped in the heap, and nails protruded from the rotting wood. The ground was carpeted in layers of trash, so trodden upon that it lay mostly flat, and it reeked of mold. Fresher trash was present in a few sheets of newspaper, which Tokol had discarded.

More beams connected the buildings on either side, one so low that Jesco had to stoop to pass beneath it. The purpose of the beams was beyond his kenning. Jesco was no student of architecture, but from the way the buildings leaned, he guessed that they were holding them at bay so that they did not collapse upon each other.

Also within the alley was a duo of his least favorite detectives in Steon Ravenhill and Laeric Scoth. Ravenhill had no animosity toward Jesco, but he had grown increasingly incompetent over the years. Now fifty, he was a man who drowned the horrors of his work in ale and smelled suspiciously even now at mid-morning. His wife had left him recently, and he had fallen apart further in her absence. Stubble-cheeked, slumping, and slovenly with stains on his lapel, his oily, graying hair hung in lusterless locks from too long without washing.

Scoth was his protégé and partner. Twenty years younger and unmarried, he cut a fine, straight-backed figure in his spotless uniform and trench coat. Even the wind skirted around him rather than muss his thick brown hair. He patronized the same brothel as Jesco, who had seen him once in the dining room with a male prostitute, and again in the back garden. Scoth hadn't noticed Jesco on either occasion, and Jesco hadn't waved. Everything about Scoth irritated Jesco. In fairness, everything about Jesco appeared to irritate Laeric Scoth. The first murder case they had worked together was a disaster, Scoth a newly minted detective absolutely certain that he knew who was responsible for the dead woman in the garden, and Jesco blasting his certainty to shreds with one touch of the woman's skirt. Scoth had never forgiven him.

Another street officer was posted to the far end of the alley, and that was one who loathed Jesco even more than Tokol did. She studiously looked away when she noticed Jesco observing her. He did not repeat his boisterous greeting, because now he could see the body.

The man was naked and laying flat on his back, his arms raised over his head. Fair-haired, pale skinned, and with unnaturally light blue eyes, his natural pallor had been enhanced by death. His only color was in the smears of blood on his chest, and grains of dirt from the alley. The rest of him was ghostly white, even the slug of his tongue, which was visible in his gaping mouth. His head was tilted to the side and he stared unblinkingly at the filthy bricks.

"There was a case I had," Ravenhill mumbled, and the smell of spirits grew heavy around him. He weaved a little on his feet. "Young fellow got drunk and was leaping roofs. He fell into an alley and right onto a post dumped at an angle there. Speared him straight through the groin and he bled out in minutes."

The man before them was also relatively young, somewhere in his twenties. Scoth's eyes were fixed to the body. He had always been resentful that his powers of observation flagged in the face of a seer's abilities, and he did not acknowledge Jesco. Sinclair crouched down by the head, a kerchief pressed daintily to his nose and mouth.

"I don't think he was leaping roofs here," Jesco said.

"Is that your professional opinion?" Scoth asked acidly.

"It is my unprofessional opinion," Jesco said, "seeing as you haven't supplied me with anything for my professional one."

He was a very strong seer, but he could not read from flesh. Ravenhill looked up to the buildings on either side like he was gauging them for distance. Someone going at a run *could* have leaped them, but the chances of a person getting drunk, wandering into Poisoners' Lane, scaling a building, and disrobing to leap roofs was infinitesimal. The man had not gored himself upon a beam either. None of them were bloody over their heads, and the two deep punctures in his chest looked like the work of a blade.

"We shouldn't stay here long," Ravenhill rumbled.

"Then let's do this swiftly," Scoth said. "He was not murdered in this place. That much is clear. There isn't enough blood. He was struck low elsewhere and dumped here sometime last night."

"How do you know it was last night?" Jesco asked. It was not to aggravate the detective but true curiosity. "You can't conclude that by insect life or lack thereof in this place."

Aggravated anyway, Scoth did not look like he was going to answer. But then he saw Sinclair's interest, and deigned to respond. "He is not decomposed, indeed, he has barely begun to bloat. The tramp did not find him by scent. I would say that this man was alive and well less than twelve hours ago, and only sometime after that did he meet his fate."

"Perhaps this was a mugging," Ravenhill said, drawing down his eyes from the rooftops. "No one around here to act as a witness."

"What pickpocket would lurk about in this part of Wattling?" Scoth asked.

"Said yourself the body was dumped. So that's what happened. This fellow is strolling about the streets outside the dead zone, minding his own business, and a pickpocket comes up and demands his money. Happens all over Wattling every day and night. Then the fellow fights him but ends up on the wrong side of the blade."

"What pickpocket would bother to drag the body over here?" Scoth pressed. His aggravation at Jesco was gone, and he was struggling mightily to contain it with his partner. "Let the body fall and walk away, that's what a pickpocket would do. And I hardly think this fellow was strolling about the streets naked. That means the pickpocket dragged him all the way over here and stripped him as well. Why? What was significant about his clothing?"

Ravenhill blinked slowly.

"This was done in cleverness," Sinclair said, getting back to his feet and speaking through his kerchief. "The murderer knew that the police would bring a seer, so he removed every article of clothing to ensure the skills of one such as Mr. Currane would be nullified."

Removing a pointer from the inner pocket of his trench coat, Scoth extended it. He slipped it beneath the arm of the deceased and examined it. Then he let the arm fall. "That is not the skin of someone dragged over several city blocks. Also, look at the size of him. He was a big fellow, tall and well muscled. To pull him so far would have been slow work even for a strong man. And if he was going to go this far, why not go thirty more feet to the river and dump him in? He would not have emerged for days, and the current would have borne him away."

Scoth peered down the alley to the river, and then back to the road. "I think that he was brought here from that direction, dragged by his feet from the road and down this alley. And I cannot see how this would be the work of a pickpocket. This fellow ran afoul of some other kind of mischief."

"Perhaps *he* was the pickpocket," Ravenhill said, content in his hypothesis that the unlawful alleviation of funds had something to do with it. "Tried to rough up some big bloke a few blocks away, and the big bloke gave him what-for, final-like. But the big bloke, see, he isn't clear as water with the law. He couldn't come to the station and give an honest tale without us finding out about him. Got to get rid of the body, so he pulled it over here and left him in the suit his mama first saw him in. Should have the patrolmen walk the blocks outside the dead zone, ask if anyone saw two men having a squabble, or one man dragging another away. Should visit all the saloons and brothels and opium dens, too."

Reminded of the poison all about them, Jesco said, "Surely this debate could take place in the station. If there is no clothing for me to read, then why did you send for me?"

"Let you read the bricks and trash and things," Ravenhill said.

"If he was murdered elsewhere, then he will not have imparted any of his thoughts, feelings, or sensations to this alley. I can do nothing."

Scoth had gone into his trench coat again. He withdrew a small evidence bag. Now it was Jesco's turn to be aggravated. The whole conversation was unnecessary if there had been something left on the scene. Undoing the drawstring, Scoth said, "This was stuck to a nail near the head of that beam just over there, a bit of fabric. It could have come off the deceased's clothing, or his assailant's."

Jesco had to refrain from snatching it away. Swallowing down on his temper, he removed his gloves and tucked them in his pockets as Scoth said, "It may have nothing to do with this-"

"I shall be the judge of that," Jesco said tightly. Attaching a clasp to the end of the pointer, Scoth put it in the bag and pulled out a torn white scrap. It was dirty. He hesitated as he looked at Jesco, like he didn't know what to say.

Jesco didn't wait to hear the next jab or hypothesis. The jabs were childish and all of the hypotheses irrelevant. He pinched the scrap between his fingers, and stepped aside within himself.

# Chapter Two

-he was-

-he was Taniel-

She was sitting in the chair, his mother, gray and wasted and talking fooleries to no one. If only her Da hadn't died, if only her Ma had remarried, if only the little boys hadn't succumbed to cholera, if only she hadn't had to drop out of her petty school to pulp rags into paper, if only Taniel's father wasn't lost to opium, if only her hands worked . . . if only . . . if only . . . if only-

He was Taniel and he was *sick* of her dreams of that pawned silver bracelet he was *sick* of her dreams of Taniel in a robe at university he was *sick* of her dreams from the first one to the last one and that was all she did, sit in her chair and tell him these dreams full of air . . .

That was all she ever told him, weeping in her chair, weeping against his back in the tiny bed with her putrid breath puffing over his shoulder, *we lost so much, Taniel, our family has lost so much-*

He had said that he was going to work in the cotton mill and instead of yes, you are the man of this family . . . instead of yes, you will bring home money and we will eat . . . instead she moaned like she was breaking inside and said the demons, the demons blighted us, you are too good for mill work, you should be studying for university! I saw you, I saw you in your scholar's robe at Nuiten, I saw you clipping by with books-

He was so famished that he could cry . . .

Jesco was looking into a dim and inhospitable room, cracks in the walls caulked with newspaper, and the walls themselves were slick with dampness as a thin fire snapped and twisted. It appeared that the walls were smoking, but no, it was fog, fog seeping from the saturated pogo. Pogo was good for nothing.

The smell in the air was enough to make a person choke. It was sewage coming from the yard, the lavatory having overflowed. A woman was sitting upon a chair. Wrapped in layers of ragged clothing, she wept as a boy sat in the corner with a sullen expression. They lived in the Mowe now, and the Mowe was the worst street in all of Wattling. Nothing green or sweet could grow in the Mowe. Even the sun shrank away from the warren of dilapidated tenements.

The boy was nine, and with a black eye compliments of Yudo's gang from walking down their alley. Taniel had only taken it since he was being chased by two of the boys from the 45. There was no cohesive Mowe Street gang, nor had he succeeded in forming one, but none of it mattered because he had gotten a job. So his mother could spin her dreams to the demons who plagued them, rather than spinning them to Taniel, and he was going to earn some *money*. The mills wouldn't take children under the age of ten, and when Old Lady Marro had asked why he wasn't working yet, he told her the reason and she laughed. She asked him if his age was printed upon his person and called him stupid.

At first, he'd been mad. Then he knew that he *was* stupid. He had gone to a mill just that day and told the Boss Man that he was ten and the Boss Man told him to show up at six in the morning sharp. One day soon Taniel was going to have coins in his pocket, and one day he would get back at Marro for disrespecting him, too.

This bleak story wasn't giving Jesco the information he needed. He nudged and it sped up. Now Taniel was within the cotton mill, his plans to strike back at that old woman forgotten. From dawn to dusk he worked with the other children, hustling down the avenues between the spinning-frames. He was pleased with his employment because the mill-owner supplied them with a hunk of bread at lunch, and once a week, butter scraped across it. Not full of air, his bread and butter and pay, but his mother still wept at how he was working in a cotton mill when she had seen him at a university. When he could not even read! When he could not trespass the roads about his home to get to school! When-

Jesco nudged, pushing the timeline closer to where the scrap of cloth belonging to this angry boy ended up speared upon the nail in the alley. Although Jesco retained the understanding that he was in the alley in some future point, the detectives all about him and a man's body at his feet, all he saw before his eyes was the past. To and fro the boy went, home and the mill, the mill and home, and then, and *then* he came to the mill one day at dawn and Jesco sensed that this day was what he was seeking.

# THE SEER

The boy was now ten, and his hand was stinging. He had slapped his mother just minutes ago when she draped the filthy bed sheet around him and said in excitement, *see, see, now you are a scholar! Doesn't it feel fine! Go to school today, Taniel, go to school!* Her words had made a wild panic rise in his body. His stomach emptied to that grinding ache of hunger that grew sharper and sharper and then it shriveled to a point beyond pain, when he just wanted to sit in his corner and look at nothing, think nothing, *be* nothing . . . He had his work and it filled him with food but she would fill him with letters and that pain would come back . . .

*Go to school!* She smiled and her eyes glowed brightly with her dreams. In fright and rage, he'd slapped her. She did not slap him back but fell stunned to the bed as he let the sheet drop to the floor.

At the mill, he did his work with the slap never straying far from his mind. It had felt *good* to strike her, and if she dreamed at him again, so would he slap her again to wake her up!

He ate his bread at break but it did not sate his hunger. It was his mother's fault for talking about school. Part of him was still panicking, and he wanted to fill his stomach until it burst. That would make him feel better. He ate the last crumb of his bread and schemed to get more from the kitchen. Oh, it was easy, too easy!

It was a half-day and there was little else for him to do until dismissal. He took himself to the kitchen and offered to check the traps. The three women who were in there gave him the job with gladness, hating to do it themselves. One was washing dishes and two were still awarding themselves a break in the corner although the whistle had blown. He busied himself and they swiftly forgot him to work and chat.

Going from trap to trap, he let himself into the pantry. Oh! There were special soft rolls in the Boss Man's basket for later, cheese and butter and ginger candies. Did they count the rolls? Taniel didn't know. But he could not resist the temptation. Buttering a roll with his finger, he shoved it into his mouth. He took a chunk of the cheese and gobbled that up, too. Two of the ginger candies went into his pocket for later.

Someone was coming. He heard footsteps and a woman coughing. His heart pounding that he might be caught in the Boss Man's food, he bent down solicitously to a trap with a mouse in it.

It was still alive, its leg caught under the bar. If not for those footsteps, he would have pressed down on the bar to make it squirm and squeak. The dust and spilled flour in the pantry made a tickle in Taniel's throat and he coughed. The woman outside was still coughing as well.

Jesco wanted to pull away. He was himself, standing apart; he was the boy, feeling sick and frightened. Taniel was on his hands and knees now, coughing violently on the floor of the pantry as the mouse stilled.

Something crashed and Taniel turned. The woman who had been washing the dishes had fallen just outside the open pantry door. Blood was coming out of her nose, froth from her lips, and she was staring right at Taniel with her brown eyes open wide in terror. The ring of white contracted as her facial muscles relaxed, the terror ebbing to a distant stare that pierced through him.

It was the flour and dust, the boy reasoned, and the cotton fibers. The kitchen was not the cleanest place and it was getting in their lungs, coating them and keeping out the air. He scrambled to his feet and ran across the pantry, where he leaped over the woman and fled from the kitchen. The two women in the corner were doubled over and hacking so hard that they shook.

Downstairs in the opening room, where the bales of raw cotton were removed from their bags, Taniel could hear a storm of coughing. One man was struggling to come up the stairs as Taniel passed by. He looked up to the boy and spoke through froth. "Help! Help-" Then he collapsed and Taniel ran on.

The lappers were doubled over and coughing when they should have been cleaning the cotton. The card hands were down on the floor, twitching and their fingers splayed out. The Boss Man had collapsed on his desk in the office. What was going *on*? Taniel's throat was tickling fiercely and he swallowed as he dashed through the mill, trying desperately not to cough. It was the same in every place he passed, the machinery forgotten, men and women and children bent over and coughing, falling to the floor, bleeding and frothing and crying out weakly for help, laying still and staring, staring at nothing . . .

Demons. Demons! It was the Last Day that the Church spoke of, and to which Taniel had paid little heed. Demons were assailing the mill to collect the sinners. They would be taken to hell and just this morning, dear angels on high, just this morning Taniel had slapped his mother! Just *seconds* ago he had planned to torture that mouse!

The demons were coming for him. He could feel them on his heels, slavering with hunger for this sinner boy, and he was going to burn in fire for eternity if he did not go faster than they did.

A few people like him were coughing as they ran, most of them children. Terrified, Taniel turned to the door that would carry him out into the street. So did a girl, a hint of crimson edging from her nostril as she ran alongside Taniel. Then she fell, bumping into him. He staggered but was not knocked off his feet. Sunlight was bright out the dusty windows and if he could just get outside, this demonic affliction would no longer mark him as its own . . .

# THE SEER

*Angels watch over you*, Jesco thought as he watched the frantic, sprinting boy. It was a useless platitude when this event had played out long ago. It was not uncommon for seers to lose their minds and terrible things, *terrible* things had Jesco seen through his ability. Things that made him weep in the night and now he would add this demon-fearing boy to his store of memories, the girl who hadn't made it to the door, the hundreds of mill workers wracked with coughing as they fell.

Taniel made it to the door and beheld a horrific sight. It was not just the mill that the demons had overcome. Bodies were everywhere in the lane, people dodging them in horror only to fall in turn. The boy ran along the road as a horse drawing a wagon crumpled. The driver fell from his perch with a cry and even birds were falling out of the sky . . .

The boy had not been baptized. He recognized that this would save him, and wheeled sharply into the alley. He only had eyes for the mucky water at the far end, which was not safe to drink but surely the angels would not begrudge Taniel's oath to fealty with soiled water when his heart was theirs in whole. The demons had come to collect but they would not collect him just so long as he got one finger into that blessed water!

The tickling became unbearable and he coughed. Then a fusillade of coughs broke from him, each one spurring the next to be worse, and his pace slowed. The river . . . the river . . . the boy listed like a ship upon a stormy sea as he ran, and then he fell, his small body striking the heap of beams. Nails pierced through his shirt and scored along his side, drawing blood as more leaked from his nostrils. He lay in the alley's filth and stared in agony at the river where salvation waited . . . he just had to get up and go a little farther and he crawled on his belly like a baby as the scrap of his shirt ripped away on a nail . . .

"No," Jesco said quietly after the dying boy vanished. The detectives were all staring at him, and he felt like he had been run over by a carriage. Knees shaking and head throbbing, he put out a hand to the grimy bricks to steady himself. Then he jerked away before touching them and went into his pockets for his gloves.

"Nothing to do with this murder?" Scoth asked about the scrap, which he took from Jesco.

"That is from a death during the Great Poisoning." No longer did Jesco feel any aggravation for the detective or the street officers. Being in thrall often did that, especially if what it showed him was something grave and terrible.

"The things that you must see," Sinclair said somberly. His flabby cheeks wobbled as he looked around anew at the alley. "The Great Poisoning indeed."

Since it had nothing to do with this case, Scoth let the scrap fall to the mat of trash. Ravenhill looked up to the beams and said, "We should let him have a feel at the garbage under the body."

"But this man was not killed here," Scoth reminded him.

"Well, he could check a few things at least. Just in case."

"It's not as easy as that," Jesco said in a winded voice. "They cost me, each and every one. Only give to me what you truly feel may bear a relevant memory."

"I didn't know if this one would be relevant or not," Scoth said. His tone was strained and defensive. "And we can't stand about doing that here at any rate when it takes the seer so long to perform a single reading."

Jesco did not react to the criticism. The boy had fallen just a few feet shy of where they were standing today. Parliament had had to form disposal teams, which went through every affected street and building to gather the bodies. As it was not safe to burn them, and it was worried that putting them in a mass grave would eventually deliver the poison to the groundwater, they were piled in sealed wagons and driven all the way to the sea. There they were loaded onto ships, which set sail for Palamin Atoll. Formerly a prison island, it had been many years since it was used for that purpose. The contaminated bodies were dumped there and covered in horan salts to make them unpalatable to sea birds that might consume them and spread the contamination.

That was where Taniel's body had gone, to be tossed into the heaps and left to rot. His dreaming mother had no doubt been taken there, too, and everyone down to the horse in the road and the mouse in the trap.

The detectives were talking. Jesco tried to listen, but the thrall had drained him of a good measure of his strength. Sinclair was the only one who remembered that Jesco's abilities did not come free, and he offered to fetch the chair. Scoth shook his head. "That wheelchair can't be gotten around the pile of beams. Return him to the asylum; he's of no more use to this investigation."

"You're welcome," Jesco said, his temper reawakening despite his tiredness and the horror of the thrall. The detective did that to him.

Scoth looked offended, but Jesco didn't wait to hear what he had to say. Turning on his heel, he stumbled away from the naked body. Sinclair came with him. A breeze whistled through the alley and fluttered the pieces of newspaper that Tokol had dropped. He'd also discarded the rolled-up pages that he had been holding earlier. Upon the mat of trash, the pages were bright against the dimness of its trodden brethren.

A sheet flapped against the pile of beams and flew up into the air. Sinclair sighed and called out, "Patrolman Tokol, a word of advice. One must preserve the sanctity of the scene of crime, not contribute one's litter to it . . ."

The junior detective stopped abruptly and stared at the pile. Curious, Jesco did the same. The clouds over the dead zone were parting here and there, and the light had caught upon a silver gleam within the rotting wood. Seeing it as well, Tokol hurried over.

"Did you find something?" Scoth called.

"I don't know," Sinclair said, motioning aside the patrolman. Eager to rectify his errors by being overly helpful, Tokol covered his hand in a kerchief and put it between the beams. He pulled out an object hanging from a chain. It was a silver open-face timepiece, and a fine one. On a plate between the numbers, it was carved with wheat growing tall under a sky full of clouds and floating flowers.

The timepiece was clean, very clean, unlike everything else in Poisoners' Lane. Tokol held it in the palm of his hand as Sinclair and Jesco took a look. Ravenhill and Scoth quit the body and came their way to see.

"This has not been here long," Sinclair said. "It must have been hanging from a trouser pocket and gotten its chain caught on a nail in these beams."

"And the chap didn't notice?" Tokol asked in amazement. "*I* would notice if something lifted my watch."

"Dragging a body and you might not have," Scoth said, coming to Jesco's side. The detective's eyes were alight at this new discovery, far more than they had been with the scrap of Taniel's shirt.

Jesco had gone almost too far in that thrall, and he was struggling to keep hold of himself and his time. They had been the same age at the Great Poisoning, Jesco and Taniel. But Taniel had lived in meanness from the day he was born and until Jesco was six, he had worked the fields of his family's farm in the loving pack of his brothers and sisters. Singing as they planted, singing as they harvested, and fragments of those songs still came to him in dreams. Until his fingers upon the hoe became a dangerous thing, and the bed he shared with his brothers at night, and the fork with which he ate, he had been innocent of the ways of cruelty. And then he was remanded to the asylum, where he relearned what it was to be treated kindly. But Taniel . . . at no point had he had a measure of grace . . .

There was renewed excitement all around him at the timepiece. Unable to relinquish the pickpocket story to which he had fastened himself so strongly, Ravenhill said, "Maybe they were fighting over this."

"Hardly worth a fight to end in murder, I should venture," Scoth said, taking the timepiece from Tokol. He held it up by the chain and the clock rotated below. "This is very fine craftsmanship, no doubt, but there are no jewels within it. This would fetch no large sum of money."

"I've seen a bloke kill another bloke over a couple of pennies," Ravenhill said querulously. "This is worth a decent amount. People would kill for it."

"Shall I then?" Jesco asked.

"We'll take this back to the station for now," Scoth said, not looking at him. "The chemist can tell us if it's picked up too much kolymbium. But it doesn't penetrate metal as deeply or as quickly."

Ravenhill had become sulky at how his partner was not entertaining his hypothesis as much as he would like. "Perhaps it doesn't have anything to do with the murder anyway. Just another waste of time like the fabric."

"I could handle it and tell you all you need to know," Jesco said. He was bleating into the wind for all the attention they paid him. Scoth stared at the timepiece like he was trying to summon some latent seer skills within himself rather than solicit Jesco for them, and Ravenhill was taking a surreptitious sip from a flask. Then he paused and spat it out into the alley. Mournfully, he dumped out the rest just in case it was gathering any poison.

"Tokol, get Amatu and you two bag that body," Scoth ordered briskly. "Load it up in the second carriage and we'll ferry it to the coroner. You two should do a fast but thorough inspection of this alley from one end to the other. Bag anything you could conceivably construe as related to this case, and do the same on the road here in both directions. After that, clear out. I want the two of you to be leaving this place in no more than an hour."

"Yes, sir," Tokol said.

"Get started." They moved aside so that Tokol could go down the alley and relay his orders to Amatu. Next, Scoth addressed Ravenhill and Sinclair. "After we drop off the body at the coroner, we'll take this timepiece to the chemist for testing and make sure it has not imbibed too much to be handled. Then we can examine it properly. This carving in the middle is quite distinctive, and the maker could lead us to the buyer . . ."

"Or I could do it," Jesco said in frustration, already with a glove removed.

At last, Scoth spoke to him. "Haven't you had enough for the day? There are other seers who-"

"Who have been driven mad, or refuse to use their skill altogether for fear of what they will see," Jesco snapped. Losing his patience, he snapped the timepiece away from the detective.

-he was-
-he was-
-he-
-was-
-gone-

When Jesco opened his eyes, he was no longer standing at the end of the alley. His feet were swaying and his arms were tucked across his chest as Scoth carried him to the carriage.

He had pushed too far. He'd known that he was in danger of doing that when the police carriage first turned down the lane of the asylum, and he had promptly done it anyway from pique. Scoth was grim above him and the timepiece was nowhere to be seen.

Sinclair held open the door to the carriage. Grunting, Scoth got Jesco inside and upon a seat. "The next time," the detective said in irritation, "you feel like showing off how marvelous your abilities are, wait until you are stronger so that I can be amazed."

"The next time," Jesco said in the same acid tone, "you feel like requesting my assistance, do a better examination of the crime scene so that you present me with the real clue before a red herring. That would amaze me in turn."

Scoth's lips tightened and his eyes flicked outside the carriage to where Ravenhill was fidgeting. Jesco understood from that look that Ravenhill had been the one to inspect the alley and miss the timepiece. Removing a pad of paper and pen from his uniform, Sinclair said, "Should I stay in the carriage and write down anything Mr. Currane has to say about the timepiece, sir?"

"No, I'll do it," Scoth said, pulling out his own paper and pen. "Help the officers get that body out of the alley and into the compartment. We should not tarry here."

Jesco's legs were numb. He fumbled clumsily for his pocket, but his glove was not in there. "Did you see where my glove fell?"

Scoth sat down across from Jesco and covered his hand in a kerchief. He pulled the glove from his trench coat and offered it. When Jesco leaned over to take it, he nearly fell out of the seat. The second thrall had left him boneless.

The detective moved swiftly to catch him. "Would you be better served by your chair?"

"Yes. There's a belt and a latch that can be fitted around my hips."

"As I recall."

They had worked very few cases together and the last had been a long time ago. For him to recall a detail so minor was a surprise to Jesco. Scoth dropped the glove upon his lap and turned to the chair, which was facing the wrong way for Jesco to get in. The brakes kept Scoth from turning it. He bent down to unlock them as Jesco struggled to get the glove on.

Days. It was going to be days before he could walk again. But that was why he lived in the asylum, where his meals would be fixed for him and an attendant would help him to the lavatory and anywhere else he had to go.

Scoth was triumphant with the brakes and turned the chair; Jesco failed with the glove and had to endure the detective putting it on for him. They worked together to get him into the chair, Scoth's hands digging around Jesco's sides for the halves of the belt. Once snapped into place, the detective retook his seat and picked up the pad of paper and pen.

He looked at Jesco as voices echoed in the alley. Ravenhill wasn't being of any assistance. Through the window, he could be seen leaning upon the autohorse and yawning. Jesco did not envy anyone having Ravenhill as a partner, even Laeric Scoth.

The detective's expectant posture bothered Jesco. Only the timepiece mattered to him. "The fabric belonged to a boy who worked in the mill there," Jesco said. "His name was Taniel, he lived on the Mowe with his mother, and he was ten years old when he died."

"But it has nothing to do with this case," Scoth said.

"None," Jesco said, defeated at how this boy had interested no one in his life, or even in his death save a peeping seer. All of the information from the second thrall had crashed into him at once, and was in a complete tangle in his mind. He closed his eyes to sort through it.

"Should we do this later?" Scoth asked.

"A woman," Jesco said. "I saw a woman."

"A *woman*? It had to be a strong woman to drag that man's body."

"I didn't say that I saw her dragging anything. I saw the face of a beautiful woman with red hair. She was in her forties or so, and weathering time well. This timepiece is tied to her somehow. I believe . . . I believe it was a gift. A gift that she gave to a man, a much younger man." He opened his eyes, but saw the man before him.

"Her son?" Scoth queried.

"No." Jesco couldn't ferret out their relationship, but it hadn't been a familial one. "It was within a case, this timepiece. I saw her face as the man opened it and touched the clock. She was smiling . . . yet he was not pleased to receive it. This gift was not what he wanted. He was . . . he was pretty. Not handsome, but pretty. Soft, weak features . . . black hair hanging to his shoulders. Twenties, early twenties."

"Whose memory was this? The man's?"

"Yes. I think the timepiece was new at that giving, and the person to make it imparted no memories. That's common with something that one has done many times. Just a job, a routine, not thinking or feeling anything much as it is performed. But the recipient of the timepiece flooded it with anger, this young man. He held it only for a few seconds. I didn't get his name."

"Would you recognize his face?"

"I would recognize both of them in an instant. She gave this gift to him in a grand drawing room. I would recognize that as well. I have no sense of the time . . . but the clothes they were wearing, those are fashions that one might see today, or not too far in the past. The furniture in the room is crafted of cherry wood, and there is much decorative glass and flowers."

Scoth looked in dissatisfaction at his notes, which he had recorded in precise print. "Is that all?"

"This was not an object much handled," Jesco said. "Its first impression was of that anger at its unveiling. After that, it was kept in its case."

"He didn't wear it because he didn't favor it," Scoth murmured as he wrote. "He rejected it. He wanted a more expensive piece, do you think? With jewels?"

"He wanted something else entirely, although I cannot say what. This gift was meant as . . . a goodbye. A severing of their relationship, however it was. Occasionally after that scene in the drawing room, I saw him opening up the case and touching the timepiece briefly. Always he was angry when he did it. This was no fleeting aggravation but more akin to rage. Behind him . . . behind him at these times was a shabby room with peeling wallpaper and a spindly wooden table."

"But it is not a woman's body in this alley," Scoth said. "He was furious at her. Perhaps this raging man could not strike out at her, but selected a person important to her in some way." He scratched out a line on the pad. "Conjecture. We have far too little information from your visions to draw any conclusions-"

"I would like to get through this before my total collapse, which is most assuredly on the horizon." Sleep was calling, and it would be many hours before Jesco awoke. "Once again, the lid of the case opened. The man with the black hair looked a little older. A few years had passed since the giving of the gift. And he was thinner. In the first scene, he was quite well nourished. In this one, it was like he had not eaten well in a long time. It was not the face of a gaunt man, but one in need of much better meals. This time, the anger in his eyes was matched with hope. He lifted the timepiece and spoke to a woman. Equally thin, and with straggling blonde hair. He said that he had her now. Not the blonde, but that beautiful redhead who gave the piece to him. The blonde looked worried and told him not to involve himself. He threw her an angry look and returned the timepiece to the case as the blonde fretted that he was going to get himself killed. He didn't know what he was dealing with when it came to these people."

"So vague," Scoth said. "It seems like you are telling me a tale of blackmail. But how did this timepiece end up at the scene of a murder?"

"That I cannot say. Of the last two contacts with the timepiece, I could make out very little. The first was of the case being opened, a finger tapping on the clock face, and all I could see was a chandelier above. I heard male voices going in and out, but no words."

"And nothing of the person tapping it?"

"The touches were much too brief, and the case was almost instantly closed again. And in the second, I can tell you even less, for it was very dark. The timepiece was being held under some thin cover and . . ."

Jesco paused. Scoth said, "Go on."

"These are impressions only, nothing I could offer as testimony in court. The timepiece was in the possession of a male, but it did not feel like the angry, black-haired man. This was someone else, someone older. He was . . . excited. Angry, a little frightened. His blood was racing. He wanted to be far away from where he was, yet something was thrilling him at the same time."

"Was this in the alley?"

"I cannot say with surety. But I read nothing in the timepiece after that, so I would suppose so."

"This man could have had the timepiece within his trouser pocket, which would explain the darkness and how you do not have more than impressions since it was not against his flesh. And as he dragged the body down the alley, he brushed against those beams. A nail snagged the chain. It dragged the timepiece from his pocket, and it swung between those beams and got caught. He may have not known it was gone when it was night and his mind was occupied with the body. This had to be what happened!" Scoth wrote furiously in his pad. "When he realized it was gone, if he has, he did not even know where he lost it. We almost missed that timepiece by day; how could he see it by night?"

The carriage rocked as the two street officers stuffed the bagged body into the compartment beneath the floor. Then they hurried back to the alley to begin their sweep of it for evidence. Ravenhill climbed into the carriage and took a seat as Sinclair leaned out the door and called to the autohorse, "Fourth Street Station, ho!" He closed the door and the carriage began to move.

Jesco was fading away into oblivion. His eyelids drifted down until he was looking at the world through a minute crack. Ravenhill said, "He see anything of importance?"

"This whole case may hinge on a timepiece left by accident in that alley, and little enough could the seer read from it," Scoth said.

*You son of a harpy*, Jesco thought with well-worn loathing, and succumbed to sleep.

# Chapter Three

He dreamed of angels and demons, delicate fingers slipping protectively over his shoulder as claws with fire at their tips scored deep gashes into the night sky. As winged armies stormed forth, shrieking and chattering in fury, Jesco awoke and stared up to the ceiling of his room in the asylum. It was a child's nightmare, but that scrap of fabric in the alley had allowed him to touch the mind of a child, and in that mind fantasy and reality stood not as flip sides of a coin but side by side, their arms around one another. Jesco did not have those dreams on his own merit any longer.

He was too weak to turn, so he was trapped in his head until Gavon came to prop him up. That would not be for some time still. The light was gray. It was closer to night than it was to morning. Up on the wall, his star twinkled. That had been a gift from Collier. It was not a true star but a fragment of *telaza* held in a glass pocket within a star made of golden-dyed metal. In his childhood, Collier had been an Asqui roamer from Lotaire, just one more of those great waves of poor that moved with the seasonal tides through Ainscote. West they went in spring to pick the early greens at the industrial farms; then south as the days lengthened where they spread out to toil amongst fields of berries and vegetables and grains. In late summer, farm owners bid on lots of roamers to pull in the harvest. Those calloused hands so desirable in the autumn months found no work in winter, sending the roamers east to the mountains where they cut through Modello Pass in their wagons for the warmth of Lotaire beaches. They spent their earnings, drank and lazed, and in spring, they returned to Ainscote again.

Collier's father had lost him one winter in a card game to a whoremonger. He had only been fourteen at the time. Outright slavery was illegal in Lotaire, but people could be put in bondage for up to thirty years. Whoremongers circled the poorest Asqui communities like vultures, seeking prey in comely children on the edge of puberty.

Two days after the card game, Collier found himself in a different sort of lot. Naked and inspected like cattle, he was bid upon by brothels' proxy buyers. When an old man representing a Lotaire brothel grasped his chin and demanded to see his teeth, Collier obliged and then spat in his face. It was his pride that caught the eye of another buyer, this one who purchased for the best Lotaire-owned brothels in Ainscote. That was a stroke of luck. Ainscote regulated its brothels, and took a dimmer view of bondage. A citizen of Ainscote could not be put in bondage at all; one coming from Lotaire or Brozzo had his sentence reduced automatically upon setting foot in the country. Fifteen years was the maximum, and his work was compensated commensurate with free laborers in his trade. It paid back his bondage swiftly, and if he made enough before those fifteen years were up, as often happened, the law required him to be released. After that, he was considered a full citizen and could go where he pleased.

Sold to The Seven Temptations, which supplied a finer crust of prostitutes to its clientele, Collier spent four years in training. Reading and writing, elocution and charm, he was not allowed a client of his own until he reached his majority. By then, there was nothing left of the dirty, hard-handed roamer boy in the poised young man in a fashionable suit, nothing but old stories and songs from Lotaire, and the folk remedy of a *telaza* to ward away nightmares.

It didn't work, but Jesco liked it up there. He could not have a man with his condition, or live in a house like a normal person, and that had once pained him greatly. He had fallen in love with Collier at their first meeting and lived in torment for months that someone else would pay his debt to the brothel and steal him away. But Collier set him right, and gently. The intricacies of his ownership left him three-quarters part in control of his future, and he did not want to be one rich person's plaything as he earned the last quarter and won his freedom. He loved Jesco as a client, and Jesco had to separate the whole of his heart from Collier since one did not pay for a heart returned.

And truly, he did not want Collier to see him this way. Helpless in bed, unable even to roll over, let alone feed himself or walk. Whenever Jesco went to the brothel, he was at his best. It was expensive, though. Jesco could not just roll about on any old bed when the sheets and blankets and pillows held memories, as did whatever Collier wore. An evening there had to be carefully prepared, his condition forefront in the brothel's mind. Of the money he made through his consultant position with the police force, a third of it went to the brothel. Another third went to his sister Isena, and the last third to the whirly-gigs on his counter and desk. He took them apart with great pleasure to see how they worked.

The bell of the local church struck five reverberating gongs. Otherwise, the world was still asleep. Five had been Jesco's rising time as a boy, his father liking to say that a good farmer rose with the cry of the cockerel, and a better farmer rose before it. Six days a week Jesco had slipped yawning from his bed, and on the seventh, he was granted his oblivion until the cockerel cried. That was the day they went to church. It had been many years now since he'd attended a service, even though the church with the bell was only a quarter of a mile from the asylum. To accept that he was not evil for his abilities had sundered him forever. Still, he missed the hymns and the incense, and the exciting stories of angelic and demonic wars that he and his siblings had acted out with sticks for swords.

Memories assailed him, both his own and those belonging to others. His heart thumped hard and sweat broke out on his brow. He stared fixedly at his star and breathed deeply to center himself. It was a mind trick that the nurses had taught him from long experience with seers. The flood of memories could not be stopped, and to try to stop them would make them even more desperate to be seen. He had to permit the clamor. But part of his mind he claimed for himself to see the star. The rest of it was stormed by fire and sickness and every form of cruelty, all of it dodging this way and that to turn him away from his star. He fastened himself to it like a rock within a tempestuous sea, noting each flicker cast upon the wall around it, the shafts of iridescent light stretching into the gloomy gray of his room.

The flash of blades crowded it out. Many times he had felt the cold intrusion of metal in his gut, his throat, his back . . . there was always a moment of disbelief within the person receiving it. Pierced all over, Jesco jerked from shock in the bed. He refocused on the star, fighting to see it around the blaze of a setting sun as a man ran full bore to the edge of a cliff and leaped . . . Air rushed up around Jesco, who gasped as the world fell away beneath him. But he kept his eyes trained to the beams of starlight within the sun . . .

The room returned. It was like attempting to focus on a single voice in a crowd at a party, and the price of not doing so was his sanity. The weaker memories drifted away as his concentration on the star grew. One could not predict which way it would shine, and the small game of guessing pushed away a handful of the stronger memories. Better ones slipped into the vacuum left behind. It was not only ugly things he saw. No, there was the fish-raft going down, two children clinging to the boulder that had cracked their flimsy little voyager, a man and woman upon the shore diving into the furious torrents and swimming out to save them . . . the star burned upon those four wet heads, the adults churning their arms against the hungry water, each with a clutching child until they dragged themselves wearily onto the grass . . . There was the old woman from a century ago who pulled a wagon through a park and filled the mugs of the homeless with hot soup . . . There was Jesco drowning within the world . . .

Like a dousing of cold water, it released him. His eyes were burning. He had not blinked. To the Lotaire people, this twinkling rock was a piece of a fallen star to shatter upon the earth. It was something of a higher divinity than angels and demons bound to this planet. To Jesco, it was a touchstone to who and where and when he was.

It had been two days since Poisoners' Lane, and as the minutes slipped by, he gained the strength to turn his head. Yes, there were his fingers too, and he kicked his left foot. These were good signs. Today he could sit in his chair, which pleased him. It was very dull to lie in bed all day, needing someone to prop him up, spoon mash into his mouth, wipe his chin, and embarrassingly, change his padded underwear. Foolish to push so hard in the alley! That was an act of pure temper, and the only one it ended up hurting was Jesco himself. Laeric Scoth had just gone on with his day.

As the light within his room turned from gray to pink, Jesco worked his way up to a sitting position. His chair was parked beside his bed, and as the pink became yellow, he got into it and rolled to the lavatory where he took care of himself. By the time the attendant came in, Jesco was white-faced in the doorway, too fatigued to ferry himself any further.

To the attendant Gavon, patient and nurse and doctor alike were all of five years old. He was good-hearted but slow-witted, fit for the duties of a junior attendant but never one to rise higher than that. Jesco had disliked him at first, but now he saw the comfort in a man who was incapable of thinking deeply about anything. The embarrassment about being changed was only on Jesco's side; Gavon had no more embarrassment about changing him than he would a baby's diaper. It was just something that had to be done, and that was all there was to it. To a person capable of empathy, of placing himself in Jesco's shoes, the shared shame would have been acute.

"There now," Gavon said in surprise. He was so tall that the top of his head nearly brushed the lintel. "Didn't think to see you up and about on your own."

"Up and about and needing a proper shirt," Jesco said.

"Right, or you'll give the ladies a scare, won't you?" As he spoke, the man opened the closet and whipped a shirt from the hanger. He came to the chair, took off Jesco's nightshirt, and helped him into the other one. Doing up the buttons, Gavon said, "Do you want trousers then, or just your drawers under a blanket?"

"Tears of angels, I'll take my trousers," Jesco said in indignation, holding out his hand for them. "Once a man starts going around in naught but his drawers and a shirt, he might as well just give up entirely."

The attendant was oblivious to his tone. "A message by telegraph arrived yesterday evening from the station. Wanting work from you. Artwork, not the other kind. The sketch artist will be coming this afternoon."

"Fine, fine," Jesco said, lifting his feet minutely so that Gavon could pull on his socks. All Jesco had to do was sit there and describe faces as the sketch artist did all the work.

"A nice morning to spend in the drawing room after breakfast. Should we take your toys along then?"

Five years old indeed. "These are whirly-gigs," Jesco said, as he had many times before. "Very expensive. They aren't for children."

"And your tool case," Gavon said unflappably, hitching it to the handle of the wheelchair. He scooped up a canvas bag and dropped in some of the whirly-gigs like they were blocks and balls.

"Careful, careful," Jesco warned. The attendant hitched the bag to the second handle, its contents clanking against the bar of the seat. The nurses always covered their hands when touching Jesco's things, lest he pick up on their memories later on, but Gavon didn't always remember to do that. However, he imparted nothing at the times he forgot. Jesco found it quite strange. It was as if Gavon had sprouted fully formed upon this earth when he walked into the asylum for his first day of work three years ago. Nothing made an impression on him, so he left no impression on anything else.

"I like that one you got," Gavon said, rolling him out to the wood-paneled hallway. It was blindingly bright from the sun shining through the windows. "The one that changes color with the day."

"It's a weather-catcher," Jesco said. It was one of his favorites, and so complex within its casing that he fretted every time he took some bit of it apart that he would never get it back together. "Centralized with the Mothership Aviator and attuned to every weather-catcher in all of Ainscote. With a few turns of the pointer upon the map, I can tell you if it's going to rain all the way north to Surren or south to Port Adassa."

# THE SEER

Despite Gavon's considerable height, the explanation soared straight over his head. "I like how it changes color all the time. I come in your room and it's got a little sun on the front piece, telling me it's going to be a nice day. Or raining and it'll have sleet coming down at an angle. Snow for snowing and clouds for gloomy weather."

"Yes, I like that, too," Jesco said kindly as he was wheeled into the dining hall. Gavon left him at the private table that was just for Jesco, and went into the kitchen for his personal tray and utensils. The othelin children chattered to one another at a long table, the newest arrival watching them in a mix of wariness and longing to join in. That had once been Jesco. The pack of children that he had grown up with here had transferred to other asylums, were living on their own, or had taken work far away and were given housing by the companies to hire them.

At another table, a nurse was spoon-feeding a baby in a high chair. Abilities usually made themselves known between the ages of five and eight, with one exception in infant Nelle. She had been left on the asylum doorstep in a basket. The examination was over and done with in a moment when she wailed and shattered a window. Everyone within twenty feet of her had nosebleeds. In order to spare the glass and protect general health, the doctor had had to fit her with a special collar. It delivered a small zap when she cried. Now a little over a year old, she was the darling of the asylum with her big black curls, chubby thighs, and tinkling laugh. Even the mental patients smiled to see her toddling down the hallways and in the garden, and a fair number of them avoided the othelin patients for all they were worth.

Gavon delivered Jesco's meal and started to fix a napkin in his shirt. Batting him off, Jesco said, "I'm well enough to feed myself, thank you."

"That's a good spirit you've got in you this morning," Gavon said cheerfully. "Well then, I'll go and say hello to everyone and come back to wipe you off in a few minutes." He lumbered away.

After eating, Jesco was taken to the drawing room. It was a beautiful space full of small tables and comfortable chairs, a library of books along two of the walls and a grand view of the garden through the bay windows. Gavon set up a tray for Jesco to work upon and left him to it, only coming by now and then to check on matters and bring lunch.

Jesco deconstructed and reassembled for long hours, and then an attendant opened the door to the drawing room and threw him a significant look. The sketch artist entered a moment later. Another woman was with her, one that Jesco didn't know.

Lady Memille Ericho hailed from a proud old Ainscote family, never to sit the throne in its time of monarchy but ever in the wings as advisors. The fall of the kings and the advent of Parliament seated them high in government and university chairs. The luster had worn off the rose in the intervening decades, other old families and new upstarts to the scene commanding more power, but the good Lady Ericho carried herself from a time in which everyone in the land knew her surname. She was nothing but a sketch artist, the branch of her family fortune having been shaken of its leaves, but her posture was rigid, her manners and dress impeccable, and the roots of her nobility without question. Striding into the room with her long blue dress swishing about her ankles, she gave Jesco a curt nod. The attendant was already bringing over a chair, which she took as she motioned for a table. He supplied it in a snap.

Her features were too severe to be called pretty, yet her very aura drew attention. "Greetings, Mr. Currane. I trust my call has not been too soon."

"Not at all, my lady," Jesco replied, putting away most of his whirlygigs. "I hope you are well, and your husband."

"Quite well, thank you."

The second woman was the complete antithesis to Lady Ericho. Ink smudges on her fingers and chin, her light brown hair askew in its braid and her dress soiled at the hem from a puddle, she had a threadbare satchel over her shoulder where the lady carried her art supplies in a polished case. For all the mess of her, or perhaps because of it, she had a friendly and approachable attractiveness. A plain gold band was around her fourth finger.

No sooner had the attendant brought the table than the lady laid her sketchpad atop it. "I have been assigned a junior sketch artist temporarily. This is Ms. Tamora Squince. Ms. Squince, bring over a chair and table for yourself." There had been the slightest emphasis on *temporarily*, like she was relieved that their partnership was not going to be a permanent one.

"'Allo, just Tammie then, Jesco. Neat things you got there," the junior artist said in the broad dialect of south Ainscote. She snagged a chair leg with her foot and jerked it over. Dropping her satchel to it, she looked around for a table.

"Mr. Currane has two accessories to a piece of evidence in the Poisoners' Lane case, as I was informing you in the carriage," Lady Ericho said frostily. Tammie shoved over a table, transferred her satchel to it, and plopped down in the chair. As elegant as Lady Ericho was in her movements, everything planned and executed with precision, so was the younger woman sloppy. Sketchpads and pencil cases splashed over her table, a drawing working its way free and fluttering down to the carpet by the wheelchair.

She waved her foot for it but came up an inch short. "Ach, can you reach it?"

"I can't touch it," Jesco said, stuffing down laughter at how much this had to be trying Lady Ericho's patience. Sliding down in her seat a little further, Tammie stamped on the corner of the paper and drew it back. She stuffed it into her sketchpads at random and opened up a pencil case. One promptly rattled down the small mountain of pencils inside, hit the table, and rolled off.

"Have there been any new developments in the case?" Jesco asked Lady Ericho as Tammie flailed about to get herself in order.

Looking steadily away from her companion, Lady Ericho said, "The body discovered in the alley was taken to the coroner, where it was determined that he died from two stab wounds to his chest. Both were killing blows. His photograph was taken-"

"I took it," Tammie said. "Got a liking for photography."

"That aside," Lady Ericho said, "the photograph has been widely disseminated and identifications gathered."

"He had more than one?" Jesco asked.

"No, but more than one person claimed him as a missing relative. Detectives Ravenhill and Scoth performed interviews all through yesterday of those claiming the deceased. Some were simply misunderstandings, and others purposeful in the hopes that claiming him might win them monetary restitution." So upright in her chair that she didn't press on its back, Lady Ericho gave a minute nudge to her pad so it was in the perfect position. Tammie continued to tidy a variety of messes upon her table. "However, there remain names upon the list that have not been eliminated. As to the timepiece, it is still under examination. There is an insignia upon an inner plate, presumably inscribed there by its maker, but it matches none of the most recognized clockmakers in Ainscote. An expert is set to come tomorrow for his opinion."

"In other words, it's a whole lot of not much," Tammie said, at last ready to work. She was oblivious to the cold eye of the lady upon her. "Nothing really they've found since you were brought back here. Fleets of patrol clip-clopped all over those roads around the dead zone there, looking for the place where that chap was stabbed and asking everyone to take a look-see at his photograph. Trotted it into every opium den and saloon and inn and grocery and brothel around that area. I did some of it myself yesterday evening since I live over at the Byway near Wattling. Found myself standing in a crowd of the prettiest ladies and gents you ever saw at The Spanker. Never been in there before, but it was police business and the prosties were quite nicer than I expected-"

Lady Ericho cleared her throat. "Shall we begin?"

The angry man who had disliked his gift of the timepiece was the more interesting of the two in Jesco's visions. He described the fellow as Lady Ericho's pencil whisked over the paper in confident angles and curves. That weak but pretty face took shape. Jesco worked off the most recent image he had of the man, so it was thin as well.

A hand extended to his weather-catcher, which was the only whirly-gig that he had not returned to the satchel. He gave off on describing the man's hair to move it away and said, "You must not touch it without gloves, Tammie, or you could impart memories to it. Then I will not be able to touch it bare-handed ever again."

"What if I wrap up my hand in a scarf, will that do?" Tammie offered. "I've never seen one of those up close. Do you know how much they cost?"

He knew because he had paid for it. Exasperation piercing through the frost, Lady Ericho said, "Ms. Squince, please contain your curiosity! We must get these done and back to the station. Prepare yourself to draw the redheaded woman."

"Mine won't take as long," Tammie said, leaning down to rest her head upon her arm as she stared at the weather-catcher in fascination. "I'm going to use my book of pieces and that never takes as long as from the raw. Should we do that other woman, too? The blonde that the man was talking to?"

"Only if Mr. Currane's strength will hold. She is not as relevant to this inquiry as the others." Lady Ericho's eyes flicked in distaste to the long, narrow book that Tammie was now dumping out onto her table. She rifled through the thick pages, each of which had drawings of noses, chins, and eyes upon them.

So aggravated was the older woman that when her drawing of the man was finished, she excused herself to get some air. Tammie instantly pushed the book of pieces over to the edge of her table and said, "You have a good recollection for faces."

"Impeccable, due to the visions," Jesco said. "I just don't have the talent at art to render them in drawings myself."

"Good for that, because then people like me would be square out of a job." She flipped to a picture of eyes. There was a dozen in a long line. "Just point and I'll put it together."

Each pair of eyes was drawn upon a card, and as he pointed to the one that most resembled the redheaded woman's, Tammie removed it from the book. Then she turned to noses, and on they went until she had a face made of cards upon her table. Cocking her head as her pencil flashed over the sketchpad, the junior artist said, "She's a pretty one."

"More than pretty," Jesco said.

"You took a liking to her then?"

"Not my type."

"More mine," Tammie said, and they smiled at one another in perfect understanding.

It had never seemed appropriate to speak to Lady Ericho about anything other than the face while she was amidst its creation, but Tammie was far more casual and quite at ease with talking and working at once. "It was a mess at the station all morning, and I'm sure it still is now. Every grease-haired clodhopper on duty because the Shy Sprinkler has done it again, dribbled letters late last night all about the Parliament building with threats to break in and unload his snapper powder on them all. It's a bug-killer, but it's no good for people neither. Have you heard about this case? It's been going on for some time."

"No, not a word," Jesco said.

"They're doing their best to keep it out of the news. Worried it's going to encourage people to do more of the same every time Parliament votes something off-ways from how you like it. This is the fourth time the fool has done it, waits for Parliament to have a session and says he's coming to kill, but he never shows. The seer they're using on that case can't tell much from the letters. The fellow wears a mask and costume when he composes them, he must wear a pair of gloves too, come to think of it, and he's got a massive amount of liquor in him besides so it skews everything. All those rich, bewigged gavel-holders are fit to be tied that he'll muster up his gumption at last, however, stop talking big and actually show with murderous intentions. The building's security has been tripled. You can't breathe there without a guard staring up your nose and they've got every station in twenty miles on alert. But on alert for what? No one knows what he looks like. It could even be a she. Scoth got into a huge row with Captain Whennoth about it, office door wide open and the two of them having a good, healthy holler about it as I came in this morning."

Enjoying the gossip that he never would have gotten out of Lady Memille Ericho in ten thousand years, Jesco said, "What exactly was the fight about?"

"The way that Detective Laeric Scoth sees it, he works homicide and there hasn't been a homicide for him to work when it comes to the Shy Sprinkler. He's got done deal homicides on his desk that need his attention and plenty of them: Mr. Dead in the Alley, the woman murdered and dumped in the sewer last month, the necktie killings and all those unsolved faces in the pictures behind his desk that keep him working all night long. So he doesn't know why anyone's trying to get him involved in helping out with the Shy Sprinkler case when at this point that man is just a big talker and a menace to people's sense of safety."

Her pencil swerved merrily around the paper. "Now, the way that Captain Tacker Whennoth sees it, he's got the whole of Parliament breathing down his neck to catch this man, and he can feel the whole of the country breathing down his neck if he doesn't. Can you imagine the headlines if that loon pulls it off? Can't keep *that* out of the news. It's the captain's station closest to the Parliament building, and its welfare is in his purview. It's his head that will roll if he misses an angle and the Shy Sprinkler chugs his bug-killer over everyone. So he wants every pair of feet in his station flooding the streets to look for suspicious activity, visiting the companies that manufacture the poison, doing everything they can to nail the culprit. Cases like this one here can wait, he said. I saw Scoth take a pace past the door right then, and to my reckoning, he was three ticks away from a personal explosion. It isn't Mr. Dead in the Alley's fault that his case isn't as shiny as the Shy Sprinkler, Scoth said, and the dead man's got every right to have a detective working his case while it's still hot.

"The captain didn't like that. Do you know who Mr. Dead in the Alley is? That's what he shouted. Mr. Dead in the Alley is some dolt who went chasing after a married woman with a jealous husband, or dodged his tab at an opium den. No one does that and lives to tell about it. Maybe he acted up in a brothel somewhere, took liberties with a prostie that weren't discussed beforehand. The ladies at The Spanker told me that that happens every week, men paying for the front door but taking a dive at the back, or breaking out handcuffs or plugs or nipple clamps by surprise since they didn't want to pay the extra to see Madam Zostra. Only the Madam there handles those things, and with a bodyguard hidden in the corner behind a screen to make sure all the play stays respectful. Any of that kind of behavior on a regular prostie will get a fellow kicked straight out of The Spanker, and if he gets an attitude, he'll receive a fist to his face or a crop across his back until he goes off. He'll get more than that if he dares to come back. Or maybe Mr. Dead in the Alley got drunk in a dancehall and in the face of the security there to keep order. The captain suggested that, too. He was just a nobody who got himself poked in the chest, and the case can wait. The Shy Sprinkler is plotting to take out the most important people in all of Ainscote."

Now she was adding color to the picture of the woman, a pink flush to the cheeks and red to the hair. "That made Scoth tick down to boom. He flat-out refused to take point on the Shy Sprinkler case or have anything at all to do with it until the man actually murders someone. The captain told him to pack up and get out of the station since he couldn't follow orders. Scoth came flying out on a wave of wrath and plopped himself down at his desk to look over the latest identifications that have been coming in for Mr. Dead in the Alley. He was calling the captain's bluff and the captain let it be called. He saw Scoth there for the rest of the morning and didn't say a word to remove him."

"An exciting day," Jesco said, thoroughly entertained by the garrulous junior sketch artist.

"One of those arguments that you can see both sides, to my mind. But if I ever get myself murdered, I'd want Scoth on the case. He's a veritable bloodhound. I don't know how he stands to always have Death looking over his shoulder with that sad line of pictures. He had a brother or cousin murdered when they were lads, they say at the station, and that's why he's got such intensity about everything. Unsolved case. Having a bad morning all the way around with Detective Ravenhill so drunk that he passed out in his chair, and then he woke up and got reassigned to investigating poison companies. He didn't throw a fit about it. Didn't care. So Scoth doesn't have a partner for the time being. Not that Ravenhill is much of a partner, but don't go around telling people I said that or I'll tell them that you said it first. He needs a bump on the backside to retirement. Any time he talks to me, I have to hold my breath or risk getting drunk on the fumes."

After Jesco picked out the cards for the blonde, Tammie constructed the face from them and started work on a fresh page. Lying upon Lady Ericho's abandoned table were the completed pictures of the black-haired man and beautiful older woman. They were almost exactly the people in his visions. "Where did you receive your schooling?" he asked.

"I grew up in Flanders, a little place far southeast of here that's just above the Squasa Badlands. I've been drawing since I was supposed to be doing my chores as a girl, and I was accepted for the two-year program at the Cantercaster Institute of Art when I was eighteen. My parents were fit to be tied. I had a proposal from a lordling with a squashed nose that would have given me a title, but that world is gone, eh? Titles should have gone down with the kings but they can't bear to let go of what once made them important. That aside, even if *he* had been a *she*, and the title still meant something grand, I just couldn't wake up next to someone with a squashed nose everyday. It's such a distraction. Every time he came around, all I could see was the great, bulbous cauliflower of his nose. When he breathed, it sounded like he was whistling with the air forced in and out of those two tiny slits for nostrils. I told my mother that I would be in prison for his murder within days of our wedding from having to listen to his nose whistle, and all she had to say about it was that lords and ladies are sent to a nicer prison than commoners so I should marry him anyway. I just wear this-" she gestured to her ring, "to dissuade strange folk into coming up and offering themselves, as has happened too many times especially when catching a carriage." Erasing the curve of a cheek, she redid it as Jesco looked out the window. Lady Ericho was taking a brisk constitutional around the garden paths.

Redoing the cheek, Tammie said, "How long have you been stuck here in this asylum?"

"Since I was eight," Jesco said. "It isn't an imprisonment. Here my needs can better be served." He turned his hands over in explanation and nodded to the chair.

"Does your family come to see you? Are they understanding? A lot aren't, as I've heard."

"My oldest sister comes to visit every few months, and brings her children."

"Just a sister out of a whole family?"

"Yes." It was a painful topic for Jesco, who fell quiet as she drew. Being a seer and a child of the angels was incompatible with divine teachings, and the Church had a strong hold on the farm communities still. His ability aligned him with the plagues of the earth. They had tried to drive it out of him when he was six, the prophets of the church in his hometown of South Downs. By hand, by lash, by paddle, by hunger, by thirst, they strove to return him to the angels and finally gave him back to his parents in defeat. The dark king of seersight had laid a hand upon Jesco, and it would be best if they just . . .

To their credit, his mother and father did not kill him. But they were simple folk without a letter between them, and they were terrified of their son who writhed and screamed and slept for days only to wake up and do it all over again. They locked him in the attic and mourned him in the community, their poor son fallen to fever and swept away before a doctor could be summoned.

Two of his older brothers, Lyall and Novani, unlocked the door on occasion to beat him bloody and spit on him. His father showed his love through a belt when he was drunk. Almost twenty years later, Jesco could recall with perfect clarity his mother's thin, pale face framed by the gap in the door where she gave him food and drink. *Jesco? Are you being a good boy? Are you praying? Wear out your knees in prayer and the angels will hear . . . they will not turn away the penitence of a child . . .*

They had. But luckily for him, whispers about his faked death and imprisonment were spreading, and at last they landed in the ear of someone in the South Downs police force who had sympathies for othelin. Jesco was freed, and brought to the asylum.

Tammie was now adding color to the blonde woman. Awkwardly, Jesco said, "My family was, and is, very religious. But my eldest sister married a man of science and he convinced her that I was simply an aberration of genetics, not a child of demons. Rafonse died a few years ago in a carriage accident, but Isena still comes to see me. Rafonse is the one who got me interested in whirly-gigs. He worked for a company that sold them."

Giving him a sympathetic nod, Tammie pressed no further. "Well, I won't ask exactly what you paid for that weather-catcher, because then I'll want one and I've got too much claim on my coin already. I've got a rough notion of that price tag and it's a flincher." Adding a final dash to the last sketch, she held it up for his opinion. "Is that the woman you saw in your vision?"

"It is." Tammie had captured her well, all the way down to the nervous expression.

"I don't recognize any of the three, not that I would, but hopefully someone will if Scoth is still employed and working on the case. Strange, this murder. Strange all the way around. I can't make head or tails of anyone dragging a body to Poisoners' Lane of all places. You couldn't make me go into the dead zone for any reason under the sun and stars." She put the drawing on the empty table and packed her things haphazardly in the satchel. The door to the drawing room opened and Lady Ericho came in. Giving a crisp nod to the three pictures, she stowed them in her belongings.

"Mr. Currane, it has been a pleasure," she said formally.

"As always," Jesco returned with a polite bow.

"I hope to see you again on another case soon." Taking up her case, she returned to the door.

"Until next time, Tammie," Jesco said.

"I'll be back before you know it, just as long as the fine citizens of this country keep murdering each other, and we both know they will." Tammie smiled brightly. "Take care of yourself until then, Jesco, and get a fast rolling start should you come across someone with an agricultural sprayer over his shoulder, asking if you're a member of Parliament. He's up to no good."

"Ms. Squince!" Lady Ericho said in aghast. "Don't make light of a madman!"

Tammie threw Jesco a wink on her way to the door, and then Gavon ferried him to dinner.

# Chapter Four

He was tottering around with his cane by the next day, and as fit as any man the day after that. Gavon was reassigned to other patients and the children hammered at Jesco for details of his latest case. He gave them only what was in the newspapers, since the case was unsolved, but the fact of the man being naked scandalized and titillated them enormously and they did not inquire much further. The story of poor Taniel caught them up in horror. Jesco took some comfort in that. The boy had not faded away entirely into the mists of time. Now his sorry life and sorrier demise was engraved in the minds of fifteen othelin children who reenacted his desperate flight in the garden until an unnerved nurse told them to stop coughing and squashing flowers in the throes of death.

His pay came in the post and was duly allotted to his three interests in life. Rafonse had been secure in his financials, but his untimely death left his wife in a fix. The house was not quite paid for; Jesco's two nephews attended an expensive, private academy and his niece was due to start there as well once she was old enough. With the money that Jesco sent, Isena didn't have to return to South Downs with her children to live with their parents. Their education would cease at once, were she forced to do that. Teachers in farm communities only held school through the summer season, and the basics of reading, writing, and figuring were all that was supplied.

Many of the othelin within the asylum had no one. Their families had turned their backs for good. To have the love of a sister, two worshipful nephews and a little niece made Jesco rich among his company. He had a few roots whereas they felt severed. That pain had been his own from ages eight to eleven before Rafonse pushed Isena and Jesco back together, and he did not speak of them too often lest he hurt someone inadvertently. But when his family visited, Jesco could hardly contain himself. This, this was his beautiful and loving sister, and they had the exact same shade of brown hair atop very different faces. These, these were his nephews Bertie and Alonzo, and Bertie was the top of his class while joking Alonzo was an echo in appearance of Jesco himself as a boy. And this tiny, golden-haired one at their heels was his niece Gemina, and she could count to one hundred and loved horses both biological and auto-mechanical alike.

He wrote a letter to them upon his personal store of paper and pen that had no memories, tucked the money inside, and folded it into three before placing it in an envelope. The money would become new academy uniforms and keep the roof over their heads, food in their bellies and wood in the fireplace when it was cold. He was sure to have a letter in return from Isena within a week or two, thanking him and telling him all the latest in their lives. A nurse would read it to Jesco, and then he'd add it to the box of letters under his bed.

That was the most important third of his pay. The rest was for play. Whirly-gigs were a massive expense, and he was also storing up for another trip to The Seven Temptations. It was well worth the cost. Brothels were abundant in Cantercaster, but many were squalid institutions where lust was to be dispensed of as swiftly as possible. He had seen that for himself in his initial venturing after love, in which he hadn't known any better at eighteen but to walk in and see what was there. His youthful, undiscriminating nature had brought him to Hole in the Wall, which was exactly that, and it frightened him straight out the door with his lust flagging for all the wrong reasons. No part of his body did he want to stick through a hole in the wall, leaving it at the mercy of the invisible person on the other side. That failed first attempt led him to Carrot and Stick, and again he left unsatisfied. No, he did not want to be strapped to the wheel for a handsome man to flog him, or to grovel about in a dog collar shining his master's boots with his tongue. From there he wandered into The Oily Toe, and at last he put together that a brothel was advertising its particular services by its name and outward appearance, and to these things he had to attend.

And so he landed at The Seven Temptations, which was dedicated to luxury in every form. It was not a place for a fifteen-minute frolic. There was music and dancing in the ballroom, drinks and food in a fine dining room, and countless little living rooms in which to read or chat. Three times a year there were grand parties, and he had paid a mint to reserve Collier as his date for the last one. It had been a night of fortunes, the ballroom transformed into a sea of black-swathed tables with psychics stationed at each one to read cards and palms and birthdates, foreheads and chicken bones and dice. At one table the cards revealed that Jesco would die a solo adventurer in the Northern Ice; at another, his forehead showed a propensity to grand romantic gestures and a love of staying at home. The psychic reading the chicken bones had been blind and that had Jesco and Collier in fits of merriment. The man waved his hands over the spilled bones and claimed to see their vibrations with his third eye. Yet his lack of sight in the first and second ended in him knocking over a glass of wine.

A few men and a woman had come over to visit in their time in the ballroom. They were also clients of Collier's. He was gracious to them but turned down their overtures for companionship, and then he and Jesco had a wonderful meal before retiring to the special room where he would not be triggered into visions while making love.

It had been one of the most perfect nights of Jesco's life. In the morning, he wanted to invite Collier for a day about town. The autohorse races, the whirly-gig shops, tea at Obokin's . . . but that was not who they were to each other, and not what they could do unless Jesco arranged for it with the brothel and paid out the nose for the privilege. The perfection gained a slightly sour note. All of their closeness was really an illusion. Still, he wanted to save up for another party, but that would mean not seeing Collier at all for long months.

As Jesco went back and forth on it, an attendant found him to report a carriage had arrived. He put on his gloves and took hold of his wheelchair to steer it from his room. He was in no great hurry to get back into it, and resolved to keep his temper this time.

Assuming that it was a police carriage, he was baffled when he went out to the driveway. This was someone's personal carriage, an older model that was gray. It was well tended yet humble, and the windows were plain glass and showed no one inside. The autohorse was huge and dusty black. It turned its head to look at Jesco and a recording began to play. "Mr. Jesco Currane, please report to Saliwan Bank." That was on the same street as the police station.

Gavon hurried out with a sack. "Take your lunch along with you now." He pressed it into Jesco's arms like an indulgent mother. "There are cookies."

Once the wheelchair was within the carriage, Jesco took a seat and let Gavon close the door. The man's hand had barely withdrawn an inch when the carriage jerked into motion. This autohorse was programmed to waste no time.

There were no curtains over the windows, and the fabric of the two seats was worn. Jesco looked out to the trotting backside of the giant autohorse. For such a simple carriage, such a big horse was unnecessary. This one looked like it had the strength to pull two carriages. The police station had many carriages and autohorses, all of them clearly identified except for those used in undercover work. Jesco knew those. This was either a new purchase by the precinct, or something else was going on here.

Several blocks passed away, the autohorse swishing its tail impatiently when it had to slow for traffic. Jesco became aware of how odd this carriage was on the inside. The ceiling was a little lower than it appeared to be from the outside, and it was covered in a glossy wooden panel. As well were there wooden panels at the four corners, extending from the ceiling down to the seats, and passing below them. The frames around the windows were thick and wide, giving Jesco the impression that he was traveling within two carriages: a shabby one that hadn't been new since he was a boy, and one refurnished by a clumsy decorator who missed the threadbare fabric to reframe the windows and attach a new panel above. Jesco was heedful when the carriage rocked not to touch any part of it with the bare skin of his face. There were memories here to explain this oddness, but he needed his ability for other things.

He was full of curiosity by the time the autohorse turned onto the road that would take them to the bank. Never before had the police sent for him without an escort. With the Shy Sprinkler's latest prank, perchance, no one could be spared. He glanced out to the station as he rolled past. Nothing looked amiss, nor was there anything amiss at the bank coming up. The carriage slowed and stopped, and for several moments, he sat there in confusion.

Then the door opened, and Laeric Scoth climbed in. "Third destination!" he shouted to the autohorse, and then he slammed the door and took the seat across from Jesco. The carriage lurched into movement and merged with traffic, bearing them away from the bank.

"Good day," Jesco said.

"Good day," Scoth said grumpily. He tucked a slim pocketbook into his trench coat and withdrew his pad of notes. Silence stretched out between them while he read.

"Care to tell me why I'm here?" Jesco asked.

Scoth looked up. He had beautiful brown eyes, or he would if there were ever any lightness in them. "Didn't the horse tell you?"

"The horse just said we were taking a trip to the bank."

The detective sighed. "Damn thing. The recorder keeps tripping at the same point and cutting off the message."

"Be that as it may, I still have no idea where we're going, or why I came to the bank instead of the station."

"I knew the line would take ruddy forever, and it did." Scoth's eyes fell away and pages flipped. "We identified the victim. Hasten Jibb, twenty-seven, man from Chussup."

"Where is that?"

"Five miles, six, just outside the western edge of the county. He worked as a courier for a company called Ragano & Wemill, also in Chussup. We're off to interview his mother and his superior at his workplace. See if we can't piece his last day together."

"Who identified him?"

"It was a coincidence. We distributed his photograph to the other stations. One of the couriers from his company happened to see it over the front desk at Station Eight while dropping off a package. One hundred percent positive that it's Jibb, and said he hasn't shown up to work for days even though he's always been regular." Scoth looked weary, his eyes red-rimmed and bags beneath them.

It was nearly lunch, and Jesco was getting hungry. He opened the sack and withdrew the meal that the asylum had made for him. There was a tomato and bacon sandwich wrapped in wax paper, a covered mug of water, two apples and a hunk of cheese, and another wrapped package of sugar cookies. As he took out the sandwich, he noticed the detective's gaze touch upon it before returning to his notes.

The man hadn't slept or eaten or done anything but chase down this case and make sure his hair was perfectly coiffed. Leaning over, Jesco offered half of the sandwich. "I'm fine," Scoth said.

"Then you wouldn't be leering at my lunch," Jesco said. "They pack too much at the asylum anyway."

The detective took the sandwich and held it for a few beats like he was still trying to think of a reason to refuse. Jesco took a big bite from his half and crunched on it loudly. Scoth gave him a dirty look, surrendered to the good smell of the sandwich in his fingers, and took an equally big bite.

"Is this a new police carriage? It's odd," Jesco commented.

Scoth shook his head and swallowed hard. "It's mine. All of the police carriages have been requisitioned for another case."

"The Shy Sprinkler?"

"How did you know?"

"I met the junior sketch artist."

"There are two, but you can only mean Tamora Squince. The second can't string a coherent sentence together." The detective looked around the carriage with a discerning eye. "What in this do you find odd?"

"All of the extra panels. If your aim was to make it look nicer, you should have had the seats reupholstered."

"That was not my aim," Scoth said.

Whatever his aim was, it didn't matter to Jesco. He wished Sinclair were also in the carriage. It was uncomfortable being alone with Scoth. "Has there been any progress on the Shy Sprinkler case?"

"Not to my knowledge, but it isn't my case. My concern is how this man," he said, indicating his pad of paper, "came to be dead in that alley."

"Perhaps he was delivering something in the area and ran afoul of a miscreant," Jesco said. "Someone who wanted to steal what he was delivering."

Flipping a page back and forth, Scoth said, "But why kill him for it? Just sneak up behind him, give him a thump, take the package, and run off."

"Jibb could have fought."

"The coroner found no signs of a fight. His knuckles weren't bruised from delivering blows, nor was he bruised from receiving them; there was nothing on him but the stab wounds and very minor scraping from being dragged a short distance."

"He was caught off guard. Or sleeping in the nude. Then there would have been no need to strip him."

"But why was there a need to move his body? Was he killed at the home of a friend who wished not to be implicated?" Scoth waved away the idea and went back to the previous possibility. "This miscreant approaches him in the road, stabs him to death, takes the package if there is one and strips him naked, wraps him up in something so he doesn't trail blood everywhere, and drags him into the dead zone? And then unwraps him and moves him into that alley? And no one saw this? The streets about the dead zone aren't thick with traffic at night, but they're hardly unoccupied."

"A carriage," Jesco said. "They'd think something odd about a person dragging a body from one street to another, but not a carriage going past."

Scoth did not disagree. "And the location . . . was he left where he was because his murderer thought that no one would look in an alley in Poisoners' Lane? Why not move the body deeper into the alley than where we found it, or kick trash over it? Or dump the body in the water?" Scoth was speaking more to himself than to Jesco. "Tramps go through there regularly, even though they shouldn't. Did the murderer want him to be found? Or not want him to be found?"

"If someone wanted him to be found, then just dump him in the road," Jesco said. "No need to go into that alley at all."

"Someone wanted him to be found, but not immediately," Scoth ventured. "But why would you kill a courier, steal his things, and want the body to be discovered? Jibb had to be in the area on personal business. It makes no sense otherwise, unless this is a message."

"A message?"

"Murders can be messages. There were two street gangs put down in my first year as a detective, gangs that selected innocent people and killed them, marked them up with the opposing gang's insignia and left them to be discovered. To get the opposing gang in trouble, to settle an old score or start a new one, which was carved into the flesh of the body . . . the victims had nothing more to do with it than being in the wrong place at the wrong time. This could be Hasten Jibb's end, to prove a point to someone that had little to nothing to do with the man himself."

"Are your cases usually so muddy?" Jesco asked.

"We don't all have your gift of seersight."

Jesco had been planning to offer a sugar cookie, but at that sarcastic dismissal, ate both of them. They did not speak again as the carriage rattled along through the many neighborhoods within Cantercaster. It was a bright day, and too windy except for the most diehard aviators to be up and about. The gusts of air ruffled the locks of the pedestrians and trembled the carriages. This one was heavier than it looked, and the wind failed in its challenge and parted around it.

Ragano & Wemill was a solid brick building of two floors. About the door was a flurry of signs listing methods of delivery, weights, and costs. Bicycle, horse, autohorse, it was a bustling business and evidence of that was everywhere. Office workers passed behind many of the windows, walking at a fast clip and some outright running. The door swung open and shut every few seconds, customers going in and out with packages, couriers in green jackets bolting to the bicycle racks on the sidewalk or to the stables across the road. In the building's driveway, a heavier delivery was being loaded into a wagon by a half dozen couriers. Already hitched, a sturdy white autohorse waited with its chest flap open for a destination card.

The carriage pulled over to the curb and halted. Scoth opened the door and let himself out, holding it for Jesco to disembark and closing it behind him. A courier shot past them on his bicycle, shouting, "Pass!" With a thump-thump, he rocketed off the sidewalk and swerved into the road. The satchel over his back was stuffed to the brim.

"Stay out here," Scoth ordered.

"Why?" Jesco asked.

"It's a madhouse in there. Someone knocks into you on accident and you'll be seeing nothing to do with our situation." The detective went up the steps to the front door and vanished inside, a clot of couriers coming out with their arms laden and calling to those at the wagon.

For several minutes, Jesco waited beside the carriage and watched all of the activity. Bicycles were jerked from the racks and returned to it with a clatter; couriers bickered about the way to Amon Hollow; a man dropped a stack of packages going up to the door and swore heartily as they bounced down to the sidewalk. The chest flap was closed on the autohorse and a sole courier took the driver's seat on the wagon. The autohorse pulled into the road and clopped away. Over at the stables, it was nearly as busy. Real horses finishing their shifts were being brushed and put away for feeding; fresh mounts were brought out and saddled. One was spooking at a scrap of paper on the ground, its nostrils flaring as it stamped a hoof. A groom spoke sharply and the horse quieted. Then the wind fluttered the paper, which was trapped beneath a rock, and the horse stamped again.

It was a very exciting place to work, and Jesco thought of the dead man who had once gone up and down these steps with a green jacket and satchel. But the image that came to mind more strongly was of his corpse, still and staring upon a carpet of trash.

The door opened and Scoth came out with a thickset older man. The buttons of his jacket were under great strain from his extra bulk, and he had a file tucked under his arm. Gauging from the style of jacket, he was not a courier. It was green, but had red trim. Running a hand through his thinning hair as the breeze tossed it about, the man looked over the railing as he followed Scoth down the steps. Then he shouted at a boy crashing the front wheel of his bicycle into the racks. "Ho, there! You! If I find a popped tire on any bicycle today, it's coming out of your paycheck!"

"Sorry, sir!" the boy yelled, kicking down the stand. A limp satchel over his shoulder, he ran for the steps, squeezed by Scoth and the man with a polite nod, and went inside.

"Endrick Wassel, this is Jesco Currane. He is helping with the case," Scoth said when the two got to the carriage. "Mr. Wassel was Hasten Jibb's supervisor."

The man glared over his shoulder to two couriers aiming for the rack. "Ho, there! Mind yourself! Mind those bicycles more; I can replace you faster!" They hit the brakes and brought them to the racks at a crawl. Wassel turned and said, "The crash, all day long I hear the crash of them hitting those racks. They think it's grand fun, but I daresay it won't be so fun when I dock them all a penny per crash I hear. So, this is better then. We can talk out here. Office is being repainted-" he explained to Jesco, "- and there's no place to talk in there without someone running into you every minute. Let's keep this quick, eh? I've got a meeting in ten minutes."

"How long did Hasten Jibb work here?" Scoth asked.

Jesco assumed that the file was related to Hasten Jibb's employment, but the man answered without needing to check. "Eight years and a little more. Odd chap but regular, and I'll put up with odd for regular. He got the job done and that's all I care about."

"How was he odd?"

"Just odd. Odd is odd." Seeing that this was not a sufficient explanation, he elaborated. "Jibb didn't make friends out of the other couriers. They go out and get a drink after a shift; they stand about in back between jobs and have a lark. He never did that with them, just wanted to be on his own. It was like they weren't worth his time. We've got some very pretty women here and he never showed a whit of interest in making their acquaintance."

"What about the men?" Scoth queried.

"Got some strapping men here as well and he wasn't interested in making their acquaintance either. They certainly wanted to make his, a lot of the women and a few of the fellows. Jibb was a handsome chap. He worked his way up to Golden Circle two years ago and the smile on his face when I gave it to him . . . first smile I'd ever seen on him."

As they didn't understand courier parlance, the man hastened to clarify. "The newest couriers work Iron. Cheap jobs taking cheap goods to cheap places. Some of them are far out so they spend the day biking only two or three deliveries. Do a good job on Iron and move up to Brass. Then they spend their days doing business strips. We got contracts with over a hundred companies and they love our Brass boys and girls. Iron made them strong and Brass teaches fast. When Leggato Music Limited tells Mr. Customer that a wagon will be at his house tomorrow morning with his brand new piano, then that piano had better be there tomorrow morning as promised. If we can't provide excellent service to both Leggato and the customer, well then, Leggato will just hire its own couriers to deliver and dump us on the curb."

He gave a foul look to another courier on a bicycle, but that one dismounted and walked it the last steps to the rack. Pleased, Wassel said, "Do good on Brass and move up to Silver. Those are for our companies and private citizens who have paid for preferential treatment. They want their money carted to the bank for deposit, or their messages carried from one office branch to another lickety-split. And at the top is Golden Circle. You're working with the richest of the rich there. They expect strength, speed, honesty, and discretion, and they'll tip for it. Jibb was odd indeed, but he had those things."

"Do you keep a list of his jobs?" Scoth asked. "We're especially interested in the jobs that he had on the day he died, anything that might have carried him near or within the Wattling area."

The supervisor looked at him incredulously and opened the file. "We'll deliver just about anything to anywhere for the right price, but I can't think of the last job that took one of our couriers to *Wattling*. Nothing but slums and grime, Wattling, and I very much doubt our Golden Circle clients have family or business there." He shuffled through the paperwork. In minute print, each shift and its jobs were catalogued. "This file has the work he did for the current year . . . if you want back years, I'll have to get a secretary to dig them out of the basement."

"We'll start with the current," Scoth said.

"Here we go, his last day. Yes, it was his regular trip to Lord Ennings over in Kevor Heights." Wassel looked up with an expression that could only be described as preemptive indignation. "Am I to understand that this conversation is privileged between us?"

"Nothing is privileged within the context of a murder investigation," Scoth said. "However, should the lord be determined to have no connection to this case, his private information will remain private."

That satisfied the supervisor. "Lord Shooster Ennings is . . . a man of mercurial moods. He owns seven homes scattered about the area, all of them filled with the finest in art and furniture and which he is constantly moving about as fancy takes him. We are contracted with him for that reason. Jibb had a monthly appointment to take an autohorse and covered carriage to whichever residence the lord is currently residing within, and to move whatever the lord deemed necessary." Squinting at the miniscule print, the man said, "It says here that Lord Ennings had nothing to move between his homes that day, but he wished Jibb to place several pieces of jewelry within his bank vault in Corder. Jibb did so and returned to the office."

*Jewelry*. Jesco shot a look to the detective, who kept his attention on Wassel and said, "I'll need the bank information."

In umbrage, Wassel said, "You can be sure that the jewelry is there! We don't promote couriers to Golden Circle to steal and ruin our image. I've got a tick here that indicates the bank gave him a receipt. That will be in another file, if you want to see it."

"I am not accusing the deceased," Scoth said. "But he was in possession of jewelry that someone else might have had a keen interest in acquiring."

With a grunt, the supervisor returned to the notes. "It says here that he got back late in the day. But that wasn't surprising. Lord Ennings has kept our couriers late before as his mood and decisions change, and Jibb also had to swing wide for Corder." He closed the file. "I know the rest of it since I saw him when he was here. There wasn't anything left for Golden Circle, but a Silver job had come in and all of those couriers were out and about. None of the Brass knows that circuit so I couldn't use them. I asked Jibb. Figured that he might be insulted, but he had no problem running the package. He had to take his bicycle; the autohorse was needed for something else. It's a lovely area, though, Melekei, fancy homes and not far. The package had five of those whirly-gigs inside, so it was marked fragile all over. Going to old Mrs. Daphna Cussling for her grandchildren and she likes her deliveries sharp. She doesn't care if it's dinner or almost bed; she just wants that knock on the door and she'll slip the courier a personal if she's pleased. That was Jibb's day, and he never showed up the next. And I know those whirly-gigs made it or else Cussling would have stomped in here days ago and rapped her cane on the counter."

"He had to take *his* bicycle, you said?" Jesco asked.

"Couriers serving Silver and Golden Circle often buy their own bicycles. Lightweight and speedy. Nothing wrong with the company bicycles, but it's something to show off and they don't have to come back and return it at the end of the day. They can ride whatever they want as long as they wear the green jacket. Jibb pedaled about on a sapphire blue Fleetman, rode it into work and locked it up in the special rack out back when he didn't need it. He must have been saving up his personals since he worked Iron to afford a Fleetman, or else he was slipping courier work on the side." Primly, Wassel said, "Ragano & Wemill doesn't approve of that, but it's hard to stop."

The detective and supervisor traded information and then they parted, Wassel going up the stairs quickly to make his meeting and Scoth opening the carriage door. Jesco climbed in. There was nothing here for him to touch, since all of Hasten Jibb still at his workplace was a file that he had never handled himself.

Once the carriage was moving, he said, "What did you make of that?"

Scoth scribbled a note into his pad. "What did you?"

He wanted Jesco's opinion? Jesco tugged at his gloves and said, "It wasn't a job that led Hasten Jibb to Wattling, although he wasn't necessarily killed there. He couldn't have been murdered too far away, though, could he? He died in the night and was found early in the morning. The comment about the jewelry was interesting. I wonder if the timepiece was something he lifted from it. Perhaps he deposited some of the jewelry but kept the rest for himself."

"Would a man risk his livelihood and his freedom for a timepiece like that?" Scoth returned. "That wasn't going to make him rich. Why not take a finer piece, pawn it, and run?"

"Maybe he did, and was keeping the timepiece for himself. He took his money and headed off into Cantercaster, where he ended up in Wattling. You need to get a list of the jewelry that Lord Ennings gave to Jibb and another list of what ended up in the bank vault."

"Is that what I need to do?" Scoth queried testily.

"You're the detective, aren't you? Apparently you need some reminding of that fact since you're asking for my wholly unqualified opinion instead of giving me yours."

"It's never a bad idea to get another person's perspective on a tricky case."

That settled Jesco down. He had misread Scoth's reason for asking. In a way, it was almost an apology for how Scoth had acted in their first case with the dead woman in the garden. With less tartness in his tone, Jesco said, "I didn't hear anything that seemed all that relevant to how he died. If he was going to steal the jewelry and make a run for it, why bother to deposit anything? And I would think he would run farther than Wattling, and not return to the office and take on that second job to Melekei. So if it has nothing to do with the jewels, nor is the timepiece something that belongs to Lord Ennings, and the whirly-gigs were delivered, then he was doing something unrelated to his job after work ended for the day. What caught you in all of that?"

"That he didn't make friends of the couriers."

"What does that mean?"

"Maybe nothing. I just find it elucidating about his character. He considered them not worth his time, if the supervisor was interpreting the situation correctly. Yet Hasten Jibb worked as nothing more than a courier. How was he any better? Did he fancy himself a long-lost prince beneath that green jacket? Where did he find his friends if not through work? Where did he find his lovers, since he wasn't chasing any of the women there? Or the men? Why did he hold himself apart, or was he just very shy and awkward in social situations, and it was misattributed to being aloof?" Scoth tucked the pad of paper and pen into his trench coat. "We'll speak to his mother now. The bank will be closed by the time we get there. That will have to be done another day, as well as visiting Lord Ennings and the old woman with the whirly-gigs."

A hard wind blew past, flapping cloaks and trousers on the passerby. "I had wondered if he was in Wattling to visit a brothel there," Scoth said. "Some places cater to very odd tastes that can't be found elsewhere. Yet if he found his fellow couriers beneath him in matters of love, would he be the sort to visit a Wattling prostie? It seems like he wanted to associate himself with richness. He bought the most expensive bicycle on the market and was thrilled to be assigned to Golden Circle. This man would patronize a finer establishment."

"If he had a very odd taste, then he couldn't satisfy it there," Jesco said. "But he would wait until he had a day off, to my reckoning. He had had a full day at work, and another scheduled for the next day. Wattling is a long trip to make there and back. I wouldn't do it."

"In the throes of lust, a man will do just about anything," Scoth said. "Here we are."

The autohorse was pulling over in front of a shabby home. It was narrow and had two stories capped by a round roof. Identical houses stretched right and left on both sides of the street. They looked like long lines of thumbs in beige and brown, and there was barely a foot of space between them. However, when compared to Wattling, this was the height of luxury. Most of the homes were tended if humble, although the one where Hasten Jibb once lived had been treated with a slapdash hand. It needed to be repainted, and the garden was weedy.

"She's been informed, hasn't she?" Jesco asked, loathing to be the bringer of bad tidings, and pitying the poor old woman who would sob to receive them.

"She's been informed," Scoth said. "Her name is Guiline Jibb."

A white-haired woman opened the door to them. She was dressed all in black. Looking far more annoyed than grieved, she listened to Scoth's introduction and jerked her head to welcome them in. She clipped down the hallway to the kitchen, Scoth and Jesco going after her. There was a framed photograph on the wall of the woman in her younger years, seated upon a chair and with two boys posed behind her. Each had a hand on her shoulder. The younger was Hasten Jibb.

Pans clattered in the kitchen. As they entered, the woman hung a pan upon a hook and said, "Sit at the table then, I can't stop my day for you."

"We are very sorry for your loss," Scoth said. "I assure you that I'm going to do all I can to bring your son's murderer to justice."

They sat down. Mrs. Jibb banged a teapot on the counter and filled it with water from a pitcher. "That's life, isn't it? It gives and takes away. It took my husband when he ran off; it took Dochi when his heart gave out. Twenty-two years old, a strapping lad, and dead on the sidewalk. He worked for Lord Calvert, the only one that the lord trusted with his show dogs. Huge brutes, Kavenyork breed, but just big loves, Dochi said. Stand tall and let them see you won't be knocked about, and they won't knock you about. He went with Lord Calvert to the show over in

Oppentown, and the lord had Dochi guide the best dog through his tricks for ten thousand people. Second place. Second place!"

Having banged the full teapot onto the stove and thumped a mug onto the counter, now she was lifting a cloth from a bowl to check the rising dough inside. Even that she somehow did loudly. From there, she checked a pot on another burner upon the stove. Letting the lid fall with a resounding crash, she said, "The lord was giddy with that red ribbon, upped Dochi's salary and said he would up it again once he was holding the blue. Dochi was going to be known as the finest dog trainer in all of Ainscote had he lived. All of those lords and ladies would have been fighting tooth and nail to have him out to their manors to train up their dogs in agility. And he said, Mother, when I've gotten rich off those fools, I'm going to buy an autodog so I don't have to clean up so much *hair* anymore. Kavenyorks have a coat so thick that you could sleep on it in winter, and they shed in great sloughs the rest of the year. Hair on his clothes, hair up his nose, hair all over this house from him trailing it in." She laughed.

This was not what Jesco had expected from a woman who just lost a son days ago. Even Scoth seemed taken aback as Mrs. Jibb went on. "Just *hair*. I'd tell him that we would have been those lords and ladies going silly over dogs, but my great-great-grandmother was a lord's bastard on a prostie. She made good, that prostie, but she didn't get a title out of it, nor did the baby. But that's how close we were to manors and champagne and Kavenyorks. Dochi was going to get us there." Three bowls landed on the counter, the lid was jerked from the pot, and a ladle crashed inside. Liquid splashed everywhere.

"We're here to talk about Hasten," Scoth said.

"Got himself killed. I told him that he would get himself killed, riding around on that stupid bicycle. Who do you think is going to win in a crash between you and a carriage in the road? Who do you think is going to win if you get sued for mowing down a pedestrian on the sidewalk? Bicycles don't belong in roads and they don't belong on sidewalks and I don't think they belong anywhere. I just hate them. But no, he never listened to me."

Alarmed to hear this, Jesco looked at the detective. His voice gentle, Scoth said, "Hasten wasn't killed in a bicycle accident. Someone stabbed him. Were you told that?"

"Oh, yes, the officer made mention of it." Filling the bowls with soup, she slammed them down on the table and went to a drawer for spoons.

"Did Hasten have any enemies? Was anyone bothering him?"

She clattered about the utensil drawer. "How would I know? He came in at the end of the day and had his dinner, went upstairs to his room and closed the door. He always left early to have breakfast over at Shining Water, so I hadn't seen him in the morning. He wasted his money dining there. You get a red jacket for an owner in your company, and *then* you eat there. Anyone can have a green jacket. You have to be someone first. Dochi only ate there when Lord Calvert's son invited him, to talk dogs and training with friends of his who were interested. That's what put Shining Water in Hasten's head. He thought he was making some connection just by being there with his waffle and eggs and that's not how it's done. Connections are for lunch and dinner, and you have to know someone to *make* a connection. A waste! But he took after his father, spitting image, went about things the wrong way and wouldn't change course for anything."

"You don't know what he did on the day he passed?" Scoth asked as she laid out the spoons and took a chair.

"I got up and he was gone with his bicycle like regular. Went about my day, visited with the ladies, did the shopping, and I came back in the afternoon to make dinner. He came home and was acting queer."

"Can you tell me more about that?"

"He took his satchel up to his room rather than putting it on his hook by the door, and I had to call three times before he came down for dinner. He gobbled up his food and went back upstairs." She had not been interested then in what was bothering her son, and it didn't appear that she was interested now. Sipping her soup, she said, "I did the dishes and took to the parlor to do some mending and listen to music. He came downstairs and left without a goodbye, fit to be tied about something."

"How do you know?"

"I saw his face. Mad or upset about something as he went by. He had his satchel on again, his work clothes still, and I heard him get on his bicycle. Then he rode off and never came back. Exactly like Dochi, just left and didn't return. Is there something wrong with your soup?"

"A querulous stomach," Jesco lied. Because some people still found a demonic cause to his power, Scoth had introduced him as a police consultant until they had a better guess of the woman's most likely reaction to the truth.

The soup before Jesco was of uncertain color, scent, and description, its surface pimpled by mysterious chunks of meat or vegetable underneath. He had not brought his own utensils from the asylum and could not risk the spoon touching his lips or tongue. Nor could he wipe off with a napkin.

Displeased with him, the woman turned to Scoth. He ate a spoonful to placate her and said, "Thank you. This is good." There was something quite subtle in his eyes that made Jesco think it was not good.

# THE SEER

"I like to see a man with a healthy appetite," she said to Scoth. "I could put a whole roast chicken in front of Dochi and come back ten minutes later to a heap of bones and him in the cupboard looking for something else to eat. Never picky."

After taking a second and third sip of the soup, Scoth brought out a photograph of the timepiece. "Mrs. Jibb, this was found near your son. Did it belong to him?"

She looked at the photograph and shook her head. "He didn't own a timepiece, that one or any other."

Scoth put it away. "Was he ever in trouble?"

"What do you mean?"

"Trouble with women or men, trouble with opium, trouble of any kind. Did he run with friends who had some trouble?"

"That boy never ran with anyone. I told my sons from the time they were small: you don't have anything to do with these common folk. You've got the blood of lords and ladies in your veins! All of this is beneath you. So you talk proper and use your manners, act like lords until the world gives you your due. Lord Calvert saw the grandness in Dochi. He didn't scuffle about on break with the grooms in the stables but read a proper book in the corner, said please and thank you to the maid who brought him food and drink, always rushed to get the door for the lord's wife and to wish her a fine day. He made sure his clothes were spit-spot and a cut above anything you'd find in any closet on this block. He could mingle with the rich at that show and not stand out with nasty street dialect or behavior."

Jesco could only feel sorry for Hasten Jibb, who was neither the favorite son while he lived, nor very much mourned in his death. His mother could only keep bringing the conversation back around to her beloved Dochi. She cast Jesco another peeved look for not touching the soup and turned her full attention to Scoth. But then she grew peeved with him as well, because he was just as stubbornly bringing the conversation back around to Hasten. "Is it possible that Hasten stole this piece?" he asked.

"Stole?" she exclaimed in outrage. "Hasten was not a thief! I taught my boys to be respectable."

"I'm just trying to figure out how this arrived at the crime scene."

"It came some other way than in Hasten's pocket! I didn't raise a criminal in this home!"

"He doesn't mean to offend," Jesco said as the old woman swelled up. She looked like she wanted to yank the bowl of soup away from Scoth. "We only want a clear picture of your son to help with finding the person who deprived you of him. Hasten sounds like he was an honest fellow."

"Yes, he was! Honest!" Mrs. Jibb cried. "He wasn't half the man that Dochi was, but he was *honest*. If he had ever found a wallet in the street, he would have returned it with every cent intact. I've got money squirreled away and he knew where, and never did a dollar of it go missing even when he was so keen to buy that big, stupid blue bicycle." Now she preferred Jesco and turned in her chair to face him. Given a scornful shoulder, Scoth had another sip of his soup and winced.

"Was he interested in anyone?" Jesco asked. He had accompanied detectives on enough investigations to know what the most common questions were. "Did he ever mention a person special to him?"

"He didn't have those interests." She nodded fiercely when Jesco's brow furrowed at the thought of a man in his twenties having no interest in romance and sex. "It's true! Because of the illness he had, the Gelerm fever. He was in the hospital to have his tonsils out and somehow contracted it in his recovery. He was eight then, and it neutered him in head and body. A boy forever, unable to father a child, unable to even know what it was to desire a woman. So no, there was no one special. The doctors said that he would look like a regular man when he grew up, but he wouldn't ever understand what the fuss was all about. Then he did grow up and they were right. He looked every bit a man, but he wasn't. The prettiest woman in all of Ainscote could stroll past him and he wouldn't notice. I asked the doctors all those years ago: what good is a son like that? Generations raise generations, but all that work and I'll just be raising a dead end. That's what the fever left him, a dead end. The doctors pointed out that some of the greatest inventors and healers and poets were people without children, but Hasten wasn't going to be the greatest of anything, so what was the use of him?"

"I've never heard of the Gelerm fever," Jesco said, pitying Hasten all the more.

"It's rare as hen's teeth, more rare than that, and nobody could establish precisely how he got it. Someone had to have gone through the hospital in the early stages of infection, perhaps a visitor, left the germs around and a doctor or nurse transferred them to Hasten. It almost killed him and Dochi was just distraught to see his baby brother in isolation."

Before she could get started on Dochi, Jesco asked, "How did he get the job at the courier company?"

"I wanted him to go into dogs, pick up the torch, if you will, but he didn't like them much. He didn't follow up on Dochi's connections and I told him that he was being a fool to let those slip through his fingers. But he wanted to do it his own way. A lot of the boys and girls around here do a stint as a courier. He was bound and determined to work Golden Circle and make his own connections. But what are those? Here's your package; thank you, here's a dollar. Being a dog trainer gets you right into someone's home. A courier only ever sees the front doorstep."

From what the supervisor had said, Hasten saw a lot more than the front doorstep with Lord Ennings, but Guiline Jibb had not been a confidante of her son's. Since he had not done things her way, she could only disparage him. Quietly, Jesco said, "Do you have any idea, any idea at all, who would want to hurt your son?" He hoped that Scoth was going to step in soon, but the detective appeared content to let Jesco ask.

The woman stared down to her soup and trailed her spoon through the surface. Her clashing and clattering and excitement had passed. Now her shoulders slumped and she looked old and drawn. "No. He kept himself to himself and had ever since he was a small boy. He got up early, worked hard, and slept the night away. He wasn't lazy. He wasn't a thief. He wasn't a fighter. He was missing a little . . ." she paused to tap on her forehead, "upstairs since the fever. Just a smidgen, not so much he stood out. A bit of him was still a boy in that man's body. He didn't stir up trouble; he didn't want any part in trouble. He just wanted to ride his bicycle all around and read those penny tales about pirates and battles in the high seas, save up for nice clothes. That's all I can say about Hasten."

With the same quiet, Scoth said, "Does your family know anyone in the Wattling area?"

Her pepper rose once more. "*Wattling?* That cesspool? We're descended from lords, Detective, not risen from rabble. We don't have any people in Wattling."

"Can you think of any reason he would have been there? Or in the surrounding communities?"

"No! We don't know anyone who lives over in that area. It had to be a courier job that took him there."

They already knew that it wasn't. "Would it be all right if we took a look at his room?" Scoth asked.

She escorted them upstairs and left them to it. Great clashes and clangs and whistles rang out from the kitchen below as they looked around a very small bedroom. The bed was made, and Scoth opened the closet door to a neat rack of clothes. Drawing his finger down the sleeve of a shirt, he said, "Hasten had good taste."

There were stacks of penny tales upon the table under the window, each one weighed down with a decorative rock. Jesco wanted to touch something that Hasten Jibb had used on the day of his death, but he had left with his bicycle and satchel, and dressed in the same clothes that he had worked in all day. What had he done for the short time he was in here? He had not rested upon his bed, unless his mother made it up. It didn't seem likely that Mrs. Jibb would remember which plates and utensils he used in his last dinner either. Jesco could always try the knob to the front door, but the problem with that was he would not only get a flood of memories from Hasten, but also his mother and brother and everyone who had ever lived within this house or even just visited it. Another problem was that one only touched a doorknob for a second or two at a time. All of the memories within doorknobs were fragments.

Scoth went through the closet, looked under the bed, and examined the table. "He lived lightly upon this world."

"He might have sat in that chair," Jesco said.

"And he might not have, and if he did, he was wearing his trousers. That's an old chair. You'll be flooded." Turning around in place, Scoth skimmed the sparse features of the room. "Something to upset him happened in the afternoon. He came back from the job with the lord and the bank just fine, or Wassel would have mentioned it. Jibb was happy enough to spot the Silver job, ride that package over and maybe collect a personal for his trouble. But then he came home in distress. What happened between Melekei and here?"

Deciding that there was nothing clearly related to the case for Jesco to touch, they said their goodbyes to Mrs. Jibb and returned to the carriage. The wind had picked up speed but still the carriage didn't rock as all the others did on the drive to the asylum. Scoth took notes of what they had learned from Hasten's mother and rubbed his face tiredly. "Guess I brought you out for nothing."

His tone was gruff and unpleasant. Jesco gave him the benefit of the doubt and said, "It was better for me to come and have there be nothing to touch than the other way around."

"Still, just a waste of a day for you."

Curious at what the detective was truly getting at, Jesco said, "I take pleasure in my work, and I do not consider it a waste just because we did not learn as much as we had hoped."

It was quiet within the carriage, and all that could be heard outside of it was the roar of the wind. Jesco looked out the window as the detective dozed in his seat. He kept forcing himself back to wakefulness and losing the battle, and his spurts of sleep were restless. But he had denied himself too long the rest that he needed, and it persisted in overcoming him again and again.

By the time the autohorse turned down the flowered lane of the asylum, the wind was approaching violence. They were winds from the Shorgum Sea, and they were the advance guard of a storm. Branches scraped all along the sides of the carriage on the way to the building, and Scoth woke just as the autohorse stopped. He looked even more tired for his rest than he had without it.

An attendant came out at once to help with the chair, the wind even shaking the thin fabric of his disposable gloves as he changed his grip on the bars to bring it down to the ground. He rolled it inside fast, the wind pushing at him with such ferocity that both he and the chair went off course and nearly hit the wall.

All that was left of Jesco's lunch was one apple and the hunk of cheese, which he offered to Scoth. Scoth shook his head and Jesco gleaned that it was not personal but automatic. He placed them next to Scoth and went to the door of the carriage.

"I'll try not to call on you unless I have something firmer on this case," Scoth said uncomfortably.

Jesco wondered what he would see if he touched a belonging of the detective's. "It's not only those on the police force who care what has happened to the victims. The seer does, too. I walk with them. I walk with them as they were when living. I know them as I know myself, and I want to bring them justice just as much as you do. If not more, because for a short time, I *am* them."

The detective looked at him with an inscrutable expression, almost as if he were trying to see Hasten Jibb within Jesco. "They walk with me," Scoth said in a whisper.

"Be kinder to yourself, Laeric," Jesco said, and got out of the carriage. Scoth called to the autohorse and closed the door. The carriage went around the drive. Just before it turned onto the lane, Jesco caught a glimpse of the detective through the window. He had the cheese at his lips.

# Chapter Five

"I see 'um," the boy said, his eyes fixed to some far-off point. He was the new one, and he was in thrall beside Jesco's private table in the dining hall. The nurses and attendants were busy and had not noticed. Jesco was eating quickly, having received a message that he was going to be picked up for further investigative work on the Jibb case. The message had also told him to have a bag packed for several days.

Nine-year-old Sfinx had rather the opposite problem of Jesco's. His thralls concerned the future, he had no way to guide them, and there was no way at all to protect him from it. Luckily for the boy, the thralls were random occurrences that came upon him once or twice a week. He remained marginally aware of his true surroundings while in thrall, and when Jesco did not reply, Sfinx repeated, "I see 'um, sir."

"What do you see?" Jesco asked.

"What's here and what's not. The asylum, see, it's not here. It's gone. Ripped down and carted away. You're dead. I'm dead. Everyone here is dead. There's a house here now, with a great big picture box on the wall. The pictures are moving. They're telling a story about a dragon. A man and woman are sitting on the couch, and they're wearing funny blue trousers. I see 'um. The house rattles a little 'cause the flying tube full of people is passing over." His look became more distant still. "The house is gone. They're dead. Their children are dead, and their grandchildren and their great-grandchildren. Now this is a street. It's full of shelled carriages that move on their own, no horses or autohorses, and there are dozens of people going into shops for the holidays. I see 'um. Shops on the first floor, apartments on the second floor, little colored lights strung everywhere in the trees and everybody is talking and laughing. But then it's quiet. Real quiet. You never seen anything so quiet, sir, so quiet when it shouldn't be quiet at all. The buildings are crumbling. Curtains hang out the broken windows. Some places are just heaps of rock, and the street is cratered. Nothing grows. Nothing moves but shadows and it's always dark." The boy's head turned so that he could see something, and he said fearfully, "No. Something *is* moving out there."

He fell silent to stare at it. Jesco motioned to an attendant, who set down a tray and came over. The woman put her hands on the boy's shoulders and said kindly, "All right then, love, leave Mr. Currane to finish his meal."

"And then it's green," Sfinx said as he was steered away. "Green grass and blue sky and white clouds, and little yellow flowers growing in bunches. Everywhere you look, it's beautiful. A woman with dark skin and a red gown appears from a shaft of light like an angel. She's walking through the grass and picks a flower, and then she laughs to the heavens."

It was odd to listen to someone foretell what would happen in this very place hundreds and thousands and tens of thousands of years in the future. Jesco thought about it over the last of his eggs, profoundly relieved to have his own problem and not the boy's. It was likely just as odd for people to listen to Jesco tell them of the past. He had witnessed ancient times through artifacts, touched inadvertently or with reason.

"Ach then, you're a precious thing, aren't you!" He looked up to Tamora Squince, who was scooping up Nelle into her arms. The girl crowed as the junior sketch artist spotted Jesco and came to his table. He set down his fork and pushed back his chair. In good cheer, she said, "Sorry to interrupt your meal, Jesco, it's just that you and Scoth are dropping me off at the train station to catch a ride to Hooler."

"Not a problem," Jesco said, picking up his suitcase.

A nurse came to take Nelle. Brushing back her hair, which was loose today and hanging almost to her elbows, Tammie smiled at a table full of patients. They looked away from her stonily. "Who put sand in their drawers?" she asked as the two of them walked out of the dining hall. "It isn't because I'm wearing trousers, is it? It's not such a rare thing to see a woman in trousers anymore."

"They're here for mental problems, not othelin issues," Jesco replied, "and some don't like to have to share space with those like us."

"Oh, for the love of angels! Like talking to tiny green fairies that nobody can see is somehow preferable to what you do? Sometimes I marvel at people, and not the good kind of marveling. I marveled a bit at Captain Whennoth this morning, if you catch my drift."

"Caught it."

"He told Scoth days ago not to use any of the police carriages since they're in use for the Shy Sprinkler case. Scoth solved it fine and dandy by using his own personal carriage. Today the captain tried to requisition that as well, but he can't, of course, since it doesn't belong to the station. But he needs it, he complained, and pulled the official police business angle on someone who works in the police business! Scoth said no, but at my suggestion he kept the peace by offering to drop me off. That spares a police carriage the errand. The captain had to content himself with that. And how can he work with Scoth for all these years and still mispronounce his name so regular? It's not Scoth what rhymes with moth; it's Scoth like both. You'd think the captain had just met him."

At the far end of the hallway, Scoth's carriage was waiting in the driveway. The door was open, and Jesco's chair was already inside. "I'm off to Hooler for a week to work on all the missing cases in that county and the ones surrounding it," Tammie said. "They want age-progression pictures. An eight-year-old girl snatched twenty years ago doesn't still look eight years old, does she?"

"How can you guess what a girl will look like after twenty years?" Jesco asked.

"If I'm lucky, I'll have a photograph of her at eight to work from. Then I'll get photographs of the siblings and parents, anything they can give me. If I'm unlucky, I'll just have a drawing at the time of the disappearance to work from and nothing else." She opened the door for him and they stepped out into the sunshine. Heavy clouds were building at the horizon, a deep gray mass that shifted and stirred with the wind. Scoth nodded from the autohorse, where he was busy at the chest flap rearranging the destination cards.

"That's going to be a blisterer," Tammie said about the impending storm. "Kind that rips the carrots right out of the ground if it doesn't drown them first. How long do you think you're going to be gone, Jesco?" Forgetting what he was, she attempted to take his suitcase to load it into the compartment. He drew back and so did she, remembering.

He loaded it in beside two much smaller bags and they stood together, waiting for Scoth to finish with the autohorse. "I have to take extra things," Jesco said. "My own utensils, plates and cups, sheets and a blanket."

"That's a pain in the arse."

On the contrary, he was excited to be taking a trip. "Do you know where I'm headed?" He asked it loudly enough to make a point to Scoth that the message had been absent that information.

"Crikey, don't you tell your own seer where he's going?" Tammie asked Scoth blithely. "Don't hold it against him, Jesco, the station is in a bloody conniption and I could barely hear myself think when I first got in. The usual nonsense going on, and the press got hold of the Shy Sprinkler case, Parliament is yelling their fool heads off and sending representatives daily to ask for updates, and on top of everything, that prat Patrolman Stamax came in all puffed up 'cause wouldn't you know it? He broke the bicycle theft ring operating in the area. Everyone's got six things to do with only two hands and there he is wanting accolades for the sorriest trio of red-faced boys you ever saw, thirteen years old, fourteen at most, bawling at the top of their lungs and pleading to not tell their mums and dads or they'll get the whippings of their lives. But you still don't know where you're going, do you?"

"I do not," Jesco said.

"North to Vasano. The expert gave his opinion on the timepiece. He recognized the insignia as belonging to the late clockmaker Wotalden Seele. The initials were something different since Seele used different names for different lines of his creations. Richest of the rich want something only for themselves, not something lesser folk can buy. This was one of the cheaper lines. Still nice though, and worth a pretty penny. He didn't make anything too common; his pieces were usually very special."

"Did you meet the expert? How do you know all this?"

Tammie motioned to Scoth. "He told me on the way over. For a while it was like pulling teeth, but he's like most quiet folk, if people like me just keep yammering about something stupid, eventually he won't be able to stand it anymore and he'll throw in something smart. That gets a conversation going. Did you hear that, Scoth? You didn't know what you were messing with when it came to me. It was all by design."

Incredibly, Scoth chuckled at the horse. Tammie grinned. "Take that as a lesson, Jesco. Pick something nice and stupid for your carriage ride. I'll get you started on the way to the train station. Have you given your autohorse a name, Scoth?"

"Yes," Scoth said, closing up the flap. "Horse."

"Horse the Autohorse? It's like you didn't even try," Tammie said as they loaded into the carriage. "Some people get all clever, call their horses Widget or Gears. You know what would be very clever of you since you like to name things what they are? Call it Otto. Sounds just like auto, and you've played it. That's what I would name an autohorse if I had one."

"Being a detective must pay very well for you to have an autohorse of your own," Jesco said. He wouldn't have made such a comment with only the two of them, but Tammie's ease had embraced all three as the carriage rolled away from the asylum.

"It was an inheritance that paid for it," Scoth said mildly.

"You had a great-aunt or great-uncle leave you a chest of gold?" Tammie asked, impressed. "My great-aunt Corstina tied herself in knots over which of the nieces and nephews should inherit her sixty-five piece teardrop flatware set that was really just sixty-four pieces because my father swiped a dinner knife while he was playing pirates with the lads and lost it. She held that over his head for forty years. But none of us wanted her flatware so all her worries were for nothing. It just gave her some excitement in her last years to think of the family fighting to the death over her dinged-up, rusty cutlery."

"From my parents," Scoth said. "They died within weeks of one another and I sold their properties."

"That was a lot of properties or a couple of quite fine ones. Well, don't keep Jesco in the dark. Tell him the update on the case just like you told me," Tammie prompted. "He went to visit that rich and crazy lord."

"Shooster Ennings?" Jesco asked.

"The very same," Scoth replied. "He gave me a list of the jewelry that Jibb was told to take to the bank. Then I went to the bank and cross-checked-"

"How can you skip the best part?" Tammie exclaimed. "Jesco, that old coot has a mansion packed with junk from floor to rafters! All the windows are blocked and some of the doors as well, and there are only narrow passageways for a person to walk. Part of it collapsed behind them as they were going through it and the lord said off-handedly to never mind, he has a tunnel to get back that way. Millions of dollars, this man has, and there he is bending down to crawl through a freakish tunnel surrounded on all sides by the mess, and there's Scoth crawling along behind him and afraid the whole thing is going to collapse and squash them both to death."

Scoth raised his eyebrows to indicate that Tammie was telling the truth of it. "What constituted the mess?" Jesco asked.

"Everything under the sun and moon," Tammie said. "Tell him!"

"Paintings, stacks of books, musical instruments, and whirly-gigs he means to repair," Scoth said. "Tools, molding furniture, chewed heaps of suits and gowns, children's toys, it was a graveyard of fineries and home to no small amount of mice and their droppings."

"But Scoth assured me that he has had a bath since yesterday," Tammie said, wrinkling her nose. "Sickening. And every room in that mansion is that same way, and the lord's got a bunch of other mansions and I'm sure they're in that condition as well. He pays Ragano & Wemill to shuffle it all around as takes his fancy. This month he might want the paintings all together in this house; next month the whirly-gigs in his place that has a workshop. But Hasten Jibb didn't steal any of those jewels."

"Lord Ennings gave him a small, decorated box containing three necklaces of pearl, ruby, and sapphire, two emerald rings, and an intricate wooden bracelet," Scoth said. "I showed him the photograph of the timepiece and he did not recognize it as his."

"But he asked to have it should no one ever claim it," Tammie said, "to contribute to his collection."

"At the bank, I was admitted to inspect the goods in his name," Scoth said. "It was all there: the box, the necklaces and rings and bracelet. Jibb delivered it intact. The senior bank clerk who oversaw him said that he was in good spirits. They had a laugh about the delivery, the clerk joking that the lord was just going to send Jibb back in a few weeks to collect the jewelry and move it somewhere else."

"It doesn't sound like Lord Ennings has anything to do with this," Jesco said.

"I never had the sense that he was hiding anything. He was sorrowful about Jibb, and agitated at the inconvenience it presents him in finding a new courier that he trusts. The relationship between the lord and Jibb was strictly professional and quite amiable; he had nothing to gain by killing someone who always did as the lord wished and without complaint."

"He's not all there in his head, not even by half, but he's no murderer," Tammie said. "And then Jibb had the Silver job in Melekei, and Scoth went to see that old woman, too. Jibb delivered her whirly-gigs in the afternoon and she was happy to see him. It's been a couple of years since he's come by her place since moving up to Golden Circle. She gave him a glass of lemonade and five dollars. Makes me think I'm in the wrong profession. Nobody tips me for a drawing."

"Was Jibb still in good spirits by that time?" Jesco asked.

"He was," Scoth said. "Mrs. Daphna Cussling said they had a drink and a chat about the whirly-gigs she'd purchased, and he helped her get down her box of tissue paper and ribbons so she could wrap them up as gifts. She called him the boy who never grew up. She didn't know about his fever, but she could tell that he was immature. Yet it was a harmless immaturity, he was polite and responsible with his work, and she liked him very much. After their visit, he rode away on his bicycle. It was late afternoon. She showed no signs of deception and had no reason to harm him, nor is she physically capable of doing so herself. She is frail from age and has heart trouble."

"Husband thinking that the courier was flirting with his wife?" Tammie guessed.

"Widowed," Scoth said. "Her cook confirmed Jibb's visit, and brought in the lemonades for them. All was well."

Something had happened between that late afternoon in Melekei and the evening when Jibb arrived at home in Chussup. "Did Mrs. Cussling see which way he rode off?" Jesco asked.

"She didn't, but the cook did as she went out to pick herbs from the garden for dinner. He turned left down the road, which was the normal route he would take to either get home or return to the office. Nothing was amiss at that point."

"But something was soon after."

"Mrs. Cussling lives at the farthest edge of Melekei. He would have passed through the whole of the city and a few miles of farm country before he pulled into Chussup. I tried to retrace the most likely route he would have taken. It leads through many streets of fine homes and shops, no dangerous territory, and there were plenty of couriers about on bicycle and horse. I stopped at the east gatehouse that he would have had to pass through to leave Melekei. The guards took no special notice of a man in a green jacket that day in their logbook. They tend to wave couriers on."

"Then what is the point of having guards?" Tammie said.

"Melekei is a home for the financially comfortable. It isn't couriers they want to watch for but beggars and troublemakers. Anyone who looks a little suspicious has his or her particulars noted, and passed on to the other gatehouses and the police force. They've had a real problem with people coming in to beg and steal. Hasten Jibb drew no attention to himself going in or out that day."

The autohorse delivered them to the train station, where Tammie waved enthusiastically from the platform until the autohorse pulled away. The silence in the carriage was not as awkward as it usually was, and Scoth volunteered what information he had about the clockmaker. "Seele is deceased, as of a year ago. Wasn't married, no children. His shop was passed on to his nephew and niece and they run it still."

"The man could have made a thousand identical timepieces," Jesco said. "Are you going to track down each purchaser?"

"Remember, though, Seele did not create for a mass market. He also did custom pieces. This timepiece could have been made for one specific person, and never did he make another like it again. When we get there, don't say where exactly we found the timepiece save Wattling. We don't need anyone getting twitchy about Poisoners' Lane and refusing to examine the piece."

"Do you have it with you?"

"It's in my luggage. It isn't contaminated; I had it checked over thoroughly."

Being so close to it still made Jesco nervous. "If I never have to return to Poisoners' Lane, it will be too soon."

"Quite."

It was well into the afternoon when they arrived in Vasano. A thin splatter of rain had fallen, wetting the roads. The shops in this city had brightly colored walls and red roofs. Some were downright garish in peacock blues and pumpkin orange, which made the clockmaker's shop stand out all the more when the autohorse arrived at it. Wedged between a forest green grocery and a butter yellow tailor's, it was a simple white building with faded green trim and small windows filled with timepieces on display. Over the door was a sign that said SEELE and nothing more.

Something about it made Sfinx come to Jesco's mind. Today it was a clockmaker's shop; tomorrow it might be burned to the ground; in a year, it could be an empty field and in a hundred years, a farm. It was a melancholic ability to see the ages, and a beautiful one at the same time. A place could be ruined and remade, ruined and remade again. Nothing was attached to time but change. Getting out after the detective, Jesco followed him into the shop.

It was cluttered yet tidy, every conceivable surface crowded in clocks but everything dusted and arranged neatly. There was a proliferation of ticking and dinging, tapping and cuckoos. A track ran along the ceiling, and from the cars of an upside-down train hung antique timepieces. The clock part was hooked close to the car like each was cargo, and the chains stretched down. They went in a circuit around the shop as the train whistle made merry toots.

A man with a thin mustache and glasses balanced atop his head was working at a counter in the back. He had not heard them over the ruckus, and only took notice of them when they stepped up to the counter. Wiping his fingers upon a rag, he said, "May I help you?" Scoth laid out a succinct explanation while Jesco gazed at the shop. The train had come to a crossing and stopped, its chains waving in the air. He only looked back once the timepiece was handed over the counter.

The man was named Phineus, and he had worked with Wotalden Seele for many years. Jerking his head casually, his glasses tumbled off his crown and landed directly upon the bridge of his nose. He turned over the piece and said, "Oh, yes, Seele designed these for Kyrad Naphates about nineteen, twenty years ago. It was right about the time I began here as his assistant."

"She wanted more than one?" Scoth asked.

A hint of a blush touched the man's cheeks. "Quite a few were in that first lot, and she ordered several more lots of them since then. In fact, I just received another order about six months ago, but I had to inform her that Mr. Seele had died. She sent back a bouquet in his memory and a personal note."

"Do you know what she did with so many timepieces?"

His cheeks stained redder and redder until Jesco feared he might burst. "Mrs. Naphates has many . . . friends. I believe she gives them to those whose company she finds most . . . entertaining."

"Would this entertainment be of a sexual nature?" Scoth asked. It was the only reason that this man could be so embarrassed.

"Do not misunderstand: it is nothing improper! Her husband died of a heart attack weeks after their marriage long ago. He was very old; she was only in her early twenties then. A person has needs, man or woman, and she never remarried," Phineus said in a rush. "She just has . . . more needs than most. But I will never believe that she is in any way involved in a murder! She is a lovely woman, very considerate, and she changed Naphates Mines that she inherited from her late husband for the better."

"You feel quite strongly about her," Scoth said.

He nodded with sincerity. "All the mines were fighting every regulation the government tried to lay on them. People were dying but what did those rich men care? Why should they care as long as they got their money? She broke that wall and accepted the regulations. No little children put to work! Proper ventilation and roof support! Inspections twice a year! If the inspectors find something dangerous, she fixes it up lickity-split. And she pays good wages! A working man, a working woman, they can support their families on what they make and send their children to school. She came up from nothing, a family of miners, so she's seen it from both sides. My family hails from that area, and people will fight for a chance to work for her. She's fair as a summer day, and I don't just mean in her looks."

"Does she, perchance, have red hair?" Jesco asked.

Phineus beamed. "Yes, the most beautiful red hair. She lives in Rosendrie. I just read a small piece in the papers that she has put herself forth for a position as liaison with the Parliament Committee of Mine Safety."

Suddenly, Scoth jumped for Jesco and pushed his head down almost all the way to the countertop. Jesco struggled, crying out in surprise, and then realized the train was passing directly overhead. The chains on the timepieces were trailing through Scoth's hair. Phineus stepped back in alarm as Jesco was released. The train chugged on and whisked the timepieces away.

"Just chains," Phineus squeaked. "Nothing to worry about."

"He is a police consultant with special abilities," Scoth said.

Phineus lost his startled look. "An othelin, eh? Here, then, just a second." He went to the wall, lifted a teacup hanging there, and flicked a switch. The train on the ceiling halted. "I pushed to remove the chains, but Seele liked how it looked, and his nephew Jon-Jakob doesn't want me to change anything. But we've always fielded complaints from our taller customers swatted in the head over and over with those chains." He was also tall, and rubbed his head thoughtfully. "Will you be wanting her old order forms? I can give those to you."

"I would be grateful," Scoth said as rain hit the windows.

"Thank you," Jesco muttered to Scoth after the man disappeared into the back. Only the angels and demons knew the history in all of those chains attached to the antique timepieces.

Scoth wrote the woman's name in his pad of paper, along with Rosendrie. "That's close to Wattling. Just a few miles south." He took out the drawings of the red-haired woman, thin man, and nervous blonde, along with a photograph from the coroner's office of the deceased Hasten Jibb. Putting them in a line on the counter, he looked at the redhead. "I want to confirm with him that this is Kyrad Naphates."

"And then we'll go to Rosendrie?"

"Unless you can think of somewhere better." His eyes flicked to the windows, where raindrops were streaking down the glass. "We won't make it there today. There's an inn at Keepsie where I've often stayed on investigations, and we can make that in a few hours."

Phineus returned with the order forms. "Here. You can keep them. Jon-Jakob doesn't design timepieces. This shop mostly does repairs now, and sells the already existing stock. That timepiece won't ever be made again."

"Do you recognize any of these people?" Scoth asked.

Phineus nodded immediately about the redhead. "That's Kyrad Naphates there. You won't see me proven wrong about this: she's no killer, and she's not involved in any way with someone who is. She doesn't have the title, and she does have quite an appetite for entertainments, but she is a lady. Once you meet her, you can't help but to like her." He skimmed over the rest of the pictures. "No, I've never seen these other people."

It was raining furiously by the time they left the shop. Jesco got straight into the carriage; Scoth went to Horse to program it for the inn. When he climbed into the carriage himself, the hard strikes of the rain on the roof had turned to raps of hail.

All the traffic on the road faded away at the change in weather, and the autohorse pulled them on at a fast pace. Chunks of ice bounced over the pavement. It was too loud to speak, so Jesco debated with himself about how and why Hasten Jibb had gotten to Poisoners' Lane, and what the connection was between him and the timepiece.

"We should have something to eat. It's well past lunch," Jesco said once the rain and hail abruptly stopped. Scoth made a gesture to indicate he was fine. "What do you and Ravenhill do? Just keep working until you pass out from hunger together?"

"I grab something here and there. We could wait until we get to the inn." Scoth gazed out the window. Then he heaved a sigh and lifted one of the panel additions along the back window. Jesco stared in amazement at the array of buttons. Pressing one, Scoth said loudly and clearly, "Food." He put back the panel and sank into his seat. "We'll see if that works."

"What were all those?" Jesco asked.

"Some additions I made to the carriage and autohorse. If it goes well, the autohorse will stop at the next inn or restaurant it comes across."

"And if it doesn't?"

"We'll go off the road and stomp through someone's field, or land in a river somewhere."

When the autohorse pulled over, it was at a grocery. Scoth got out, the rain restarting as soon as he was on the sidewalk, and returned with a random assortment of food. There was jerky and bread, cheese and fruit, two bottles of fizzy drinks, and candy. They ate well as the carriage moved along, reset for the inn in Keepsie. A piece of jerky pinched in his fingers, Scoth went through the order forms. "This Naphates woman has ordered close to a hundred of these over the last two decades."

"He's so certain that she has nothing to do with it."

"They're always certain," Scoth said gruffly. "If I had a nickel for every person that was certain someone they liked had nothing to do with it, I could buy a second autohorse."

"What would you name that one? Otto the Autohorse?"

It was almost a smile, but the detective bit it back fast. "Horse Two."

The storm came and went in spurts, but it was building. Jesco could feel it in the air, a heavy anticipation that something stronger was brewing. It was going to last for days, according to the forecast. The sky was a sweep of dark gray from one end to the other, and as evening got underway, it became even darker. "I remember storms like these from when I was a boy," Jesco said. "I lived on a farm. They smashed the crops flat."

Scoth didn't say anything. Jesco asked, "Where did you grow up?"

"Why do you want to know?"

It was hard to imagine somber Laeric Scoth as a boy. "So that I can know you."

After a moment of silence, Scoth said, "Korval. You've never heard of it. No one has. It's an out-of-the-way town along an eastern branch of the Razille River."

"How did you get all the way to Cantercaster?"

"A lot of the towns and villages farther out have no official police force. It's a passel of mayor's sons and rich merchants' daughters strutting about in uniforms to maintain order, and creating as much mayhem as they profess to restrain. They don't know the first thing about an investigation. I wanted to gain a true education of crime and justice, so I applied to every university with a program for law enforcement in Ainscote."

"How many did you get into?"

"One, but the best one, in my opinion. Nuiten. That was how I got to Cantercaster, and I stayed."

When the autohorse reached the inn, Jesco stepped out into torrents of rain and was soaked in the time it took him to reclaim his suitcase and run to the front door. Scoth was a step in front of him, his lighter bag thrown over his shoulder, and he opened the door for Jesco in a hurry. They entered a warm foyer with cushioned chairs beside a fire, and a high ceiling with carved wooden beams.

Sheets had been laid down inside for wet travelers, and they walked atop them all the way to the counter. The innkeeper sent out a girl to board the autohorse in the barn and gave them a cheeky grin. "One room then?"

Startled, Scoth said, "Two, please."

They had dinner in the side room, the waiter giving Jesco a curious look when he used his personal utensils, and then went upstairs to locate their rooms. They were directly across from one another. After unlocking his door, Jesco hesitated in the doorway and called out, "Did you go to Shining Water the day that you visited the lord and the woman with the whirly-gigs?"

Scoth was in his room and closing his door. Cracking it wider, he said, "No."

"Jibb went there every morning, his mother told us."

"It didn't sound like he did anything there but eat."

"The staff would know for sure, though. Perhaps he made a connection there. A bad one. If Rosendrie turns out to be nothing . . ."

"I'll add it to the list," Scoth said. "Will you be all right in there? I won't come in tomorrow morning and find you in thrall from the sink?"

"I can take care of myself, thank you," Jesco said.

"Better than you did in the alley, at any rate."

It stung, but it was a fair dart for the detective to throw. "It can be hard at times to work with people who can't stand me for being a seer, Scoth. You were talking to the others like I wasn't even there, and I lost my temper."

Scoth cocked his head like he couldn't quite remember the particulars of the incident. Then he grimaced. "It was being there. Trying to direct an investigation in that poisoned place, remembering every minute or so that that kolymbium was sinking into us. My mind was in twists. It wasn't anything to do with you." He nudged the door back and forth. "I can't speak for the rest, but I stand you just fine."

The door clicked shut and his shadow vanished from the crack beneath it. Jesco went into his room, wishing that he had been more professional in the alley. To be in Poisoners' Lane had put them all on edge. He was looking into a tidy, snug room at the inn but seeing that mat of trash and low-hanging, nail-studded beams superimposed upon it. And the body, naked and punctured . . .

Though his mind was with Hasten Jibb, he fixed up the room for himself. His sheets, his pillow, and his blanket went on the bed; his spare towels covered the sides of the sink and the top of the nightstand. It was not until the room was made as safe as it could be that he dressed for bed. Once within it, he doused the lamp with his hand covered, and rested in the darkness.

It was not truly rest when the corpse appeared every time he closed his eyes. Reaching down to his bag, he searched through the contents and pulled out his star. He leaned it against the lamp and stared at its twinkling.

Scoth was such a handsome man. The thought crowded in with the star and Jesco let it stay. Peace overcame him and he fell asleep.

# Chapter Six

It should have taken one day to reach Rosendrie, but the storm made it two. Roads were washed out, invisible beneath roaring rivers that could not be safely forded. Scoth was forced to reconfigure the destination cards to a route on higher land. It took them miles out of their way, yet travel was swifter there.

The autohorse clopped on indefatigably through rain and hail and lightning alike, yet still came to a sudden stop on the high road. Cursing under his breath, Scoth went out to see what was wrong now. A tree had fallen, blocking their way, and an hour was spent in taking turns with a small axe to chop it apart and push it down a ravine.

Otherwise, the trip was surprisingly pleasant. Jesco took a page from Tammie's book, modified it, and just talked like he didn't expect Scoth to reply. The asylum gave him a wide variety of stories, from little Nelle and her collar to the ruined rucaline patients, the nurses and attendants and their lives, the out of control foliage always threatening to drown the building and its grounds in flowers. There had been the day when Jesco was fourteen that an aviator fought a battle with the wind and lost, bringing down her balloon in the garden. And then there was the night when a mental patient tried to burn down the asylum and sent them all out into the streets, coughing from the smoke and in their pajamas, and some in less than that. Jesco had been confined to bed at the time and too weak to even climb into his wheelchair, let alone steer himself out. He'd been deeply touched at how ten people from nurses to patients came hurtling into his room to help. His asylum family was good to him. Not one person had perished in the fire, everyone making sure that everyone else got out.

It was that story which provoked more than a nod from Scoth, who said, "I didn't believe you boarded with the criminally insane."

"We don't," Jesco said. "That patient had no record until that point, and he was removed at once to a more secure setting."

"They go to Linvus Institute in Glensporra, the dangerous ones. I've caught a few who ended up there: a woman who murdered both her mother and her daughter; a man who liked to catch old folks, tie them up, and set them on fire. There was some debate over Mantis Man, if that was where he should have gone instead of Crofthollow Prison."

"What do you think?"

"Four walls and a locked door was as much as I cared what happened to him."

"But if you were the judge?"

Scoth considered it. "If I were the judge, I would have called it for Crofthollow just like how it went. There aren't any medications to make him better. There isn't a head doctor alive with a cure. At Linvus, they would try. It's a waste of time and energy. His mental disorder is severe and unfixable, and he will always present a grave threat to those around him. At least locked up in Crofthollow, he's surrounded by men who pose just as grave a threat to him. But you've seen into them, haven't you?"

"What do you mean?"

"You've seen into their minds, people like that." Scoth shifted in his seat as hail tapped on the roof of the carriage. "You've been them, briefly. I know what they do; I know why they do it; but I can't feel it."

"You don't want to feel it," Jesco said. Indeed he had ridden about in those darkened souls now and then, and they made him shiver.

"But how do they feel?"

"They feel . . . free. Freed from the bonds of love and friendship, of the happiness and sorrow those ties can induce. None of these things they understand in any more than the shallowest of contexts. They know that these matters are important above all else to people, yet not to themselves. And because they are free, they are superior. This is how it is in their heads. They are proud to be who they are, of their remove from regular human affairs. They feel no qualms at stealing a purse, or setting someone on fire. People exist for them to take things from, you see, and they cannot empathize with the distress of their victims since they feel no distress themselves. People aren't real to their perspective. No more real than animated dolls, there to be manipulated at leisure."

"Please go on," Scoth said when Jesco stopped.

Jesco called up the strongest memories that he had experienced. "Let me say it this way: what frees them also binds them. It leaves them with a void, and they seek to fill it. There was a man I walked within, a very attractive, charming man who hated the strictures of work yet loved to be surrounded by fineries, so he pursued rich and gullible women who could give him what he craved. He lived about a hundred years ago."

"What was it about an honest day's work he hated specifically?"

"Being told what to do, being expected to do things. Not being in control. To not be in control makes them rage. And they are toddler-like creatures in some regards: they can't stand to wait for what they want. They want it now. Why can't they have it *now*? They want it, they deserve it, and that means they should have it at once. He wasn't going to work hard and save up for years when he had another way to accomplish his goal. A short cut."

"So he chased those rich women."

"It was irrelevant to him that some were married, or even married with small children. It was irrelevant that others were decades older and uninterested. People really were just dolls for him to play with. He worked obsessively at wriggling into their lives, and then he drained them. If one of his women ran out of money, he simply moved on and found another. If one caught on to what he was doing, he was enraged to be confronted. He felt their riches were his due. He left behind him ruined marriages, broken children, empty purses, and blithely did it all over again until he was old. Then the last woman had him evicted from her home, leaving him with no one and nothing. No longer could he enchant anyone with his looks, and he had to go to a poorhouse. Even in his last years, he was trying to finagle extra food and goods for himself. Stealing from the weak and dying, and getting beaten by younger men who caught him at it. A sorry life. Many of them end up like that. Alone and penniless, with a wide swath of destruction behind them."

They passed a sign welcoming them to Rosendrie. The loveliness of it could not be concealed by the gray sky and streaking rain. Every home upon the blocks was stately; every road was paved and braced by white sidewalks. As Jesco enjoyed the prettiness of the place, Scoth tidied up the paperwork of timepiece orders and said, "I was in court to testify against a murderer a year ago. I said nothing more than the truth and he stood up so violently that the chair tipped over behind him. He pointed a finger at me and shouted *how dare you? How dare you?* He had to be muzzled for the trial to continue. That was what he meant, I suppose, from what you said. How dare I confront him about what he had done when he could do whatever he wanted? He had that right."

"That's generally how a mind like that works." After Scoth tucked the file away, Jesco said, "We weren't in Poisoners' Lane in our first case with that woman dead in her garden."

"No, we were not. You were just being a pompous little prick."

"I thought the same of you."

It had grown easier between them, and Scoth again had one of his almost-smiles that waned before it waxed. "And now we're older and wiser, and still pricks, eh?"

Jesco laughed. "Yes, still pricks."

"I learned not to hang so much of myself upon one hook there. A detective has his pet theories, but a seer can blast them from the water with a thrall."

He looked over expectantly, a teasing quirk to his lips, and Jesco said, "And I learned that detectives have egos as we all do, and to be more gentle when declaring a murderer."

"You were so ruddy pleased with yourself, and all I could see was my entire education in the criminal process falling to pieces at my feet. You saw what I could not."

"It was no comment on your education."

"But I would have happily placed the wrong man in cuffs, and testified to land him in prison. To have my judgment proven so misguided was a shock. You can undermine everything. If only every detective could do as you do . . . but I would not have your vision, even so. The burden of sight at those crimes . . . I am heavy enough without it. I understand why those with seersight refuse to work with it lest they lose their sanity."

The rain stopped. The autohorse was now leading them down a lovely lane lined with cherry trees. Pastures stood beyond them, soaked and crumpled from the deluge with standing pools in the lowest points. Avenues wound away from the road here and there, and all of them led to tall manors in the distance. They put to shame the first homes that Jesco had seen in Rosendrie. Those were only fine; these were masterpieces of architecture and wealth.

"Perhaps this woman killed Jibb, and sent a strong servant or two out in a carriage to dump the body," Scoth said. "They might not have known that they were within the dead zone when they pulled Jibb into the alley."

"Why doesn't the government put up a fence around those blocks?"

"They did that several times, and posted guards to walk the perimeter. But those guards walked off the job in fear, and people stole the boards and bricks or knocked them down. It was seen as a waste of money when it kept happening. So they hung some signs at the roads leading into the poisoned area, warning to go no further, and that's all. Luckily, that part of Wattling is off most of the main routes."

Jesco hadn't seen those signs, but he had been within the police carriage and talking to Sinclair. "I suppose the people who live there remember well what happened, and stay away without encouragement. It's plausible that the person to dump the body might not have known where he was. It was night. But would a servant have owned that timepiece?"

"Kyrad Naphates does appear to give them out quite readily." The autohorse turned down an avenue, its feet splashing loudly in puddles. "We shall soon find out."

At the end of the avenue was a driving ring centered about a fountain. It was overflowing from the rainfall, the small basin on top dripping down to the wider basin beneath, and that in turn seeping into the large one on the bottom. From there, it splashed down into the pool and dripped over the side to the pavement. Lights within the water dyed the streams a purplish cast. The purple became yellow, and then green.

The manor was a flawless construction, white and with a pale yellow trim. The windows ran from floor to ceiling, and the curtains were pulled back to reveal beautiful rooms on two stories. The porch was generous, as were the balconies, and several chimneys puffed smoke into the air.

The front door opened as Jesco and Scoth got out of the carriage. A butler stepped out in a pressed black suit and inclined his head in polite bewilderment. "Forgive me, gentlemen. I was not informed that we were expecting anyone."

"I am Detective Laeric Scoth with the Cantercaster Police Force," Scoth said. "We would like to speak to Mrs. Kyrad Naphates. Is she home?"

"The police! May I see some form of identification?"

Scoth showed his badge to the astonished butler, who ushered them in and left them in a drawing room with a promise that he would return at once. On a side table was a weather-catcher just like Jesco's. It showed a tapering rain. Beside it was a clock, which Jesco passed over with indifference until something drew him back. The second hand was passing over a carving identical to the one on the timepiece. Wheat reached up to a cloudy sky, which was strewn with flowers. "Scoth, look."

The detective took note of it. Footsteps returned down the hallway and the butler peered in at them. "Mrs. Naphates will receive you in the great room."

He led them through lighted corridors, each bearing nooks that held paintings of pastoral scenes. Through an open door was a second, larger drawing room full of cherry wood furniture and decorative glass. No one was in it now, but that was where the timepiece had been given as a gift.

The butler pushed open double doors and admitted them to a cavernous room holding a dozen people. Several were crowded around a billiards table, shouting and laughing and too engaged in their game to notice the new arrivals. A servant came in from a side door, her tray loaded with drinks, and aimed for the table.

Two men were reading upon armchairs, one lazily turning a carrel full of books with his foot. It squeaked with every rotation. Both of them were good-looking fellows, one dark and one fair, and Jesco looked back to the billiards game. The four people there were uncommonly attractive as well, the men young, muscular, and dressed impeccably, and the woman equally lovely in her blue gown.

The butler was taking them to the far corner, where people were sprawled upon couches and chortling. Kyrad Naphates was among them, sitting in a careless posture upon a voluminous golden armchair. A wine glass was cradled in the palm of her hand, the stem hanging down between her fingers. She was older than Jesco had seen from his visions, and a tad heavier, but still radiant. A few locks of her hair hung over her breasts and the rest tumbled over the armrest and spilled down like a living flame. Her dress was long and white, and bore a golden belt that sparkled in the light.

Looking away from her companions, she beckoned to Scoth and Jesco with ringed fingers. Her expression was mild and puzzled. "The police, you say?" she asked as they came close. She motioned at the man upon the closest couch to move aside. He did so at once and she gestured for them to sit down. Putting aside her wine, she said, "How may I help you, gentlemen? Would you care for any refreshments?"

"No, thank you," Scoth said after he and Jesco had taken a seat. "Mrs. Naphates-"

"Please! Call me Kyrad."

"Kyrad, we are investigating the murder of a man named Hasten Jibb. Would you happen to have known him?"

"Hasten Jibb? No. I know no one by that name." She waved to the butler. "Three fizzy drinks." He bowed and turned on his heel.

Scoth proffered the photograph. It showed only Hasten Jibb's face, but he was clearly dead in the shot. Kyrad took it from him and squinted. Then she laid it upon her lap, straightened in her chair, and reached for the side table where she withdrew a pair of spectacles from the drawer. "Old age," she said mournfully. "The cruelest cut of it is that you still feel perfectly young, but your body disagrees." Putting on her glasses, she took another look at the photograph. "No! I've never seen this face in my life. And he was murdered? I am sorry to hear that, but why would I be drawn into your investigation?"

"Something was found at the crime scene; something that we traced back to you," Scoth said, and traded the photograph of the dead man for a small box.

She opened the lid. "One of my timepieces! But I never gave one to this man. He is a stranger to me."

"Can you give me your whereabouts nine days ago?"

"I was here, of course."

"Can anyone verify it?"

She gestured to everyone in the room. "And my staff as well. I caught a cold about two weeks ago, and spent most of it flat on my back in bed. It was only five or six days ago that I started to feel human again. A terrible inconvenience as I am looking to get chosen for a committee position in Parliament. They'll have their vote soon and I was hoping to visit more of them in person to state my case. And then this storm descended so I will have to hope my record stands on its own since I could not. It may go to one of the two others trying for it, and in Alf Udusa's case, that would be a damn shame. He'll fight to undo every regulation he can." Touching the timepiece, she grew agitated. "I have given out many of these as keepsakes, but that does not mean that those I give them to necessarily keep them."

"To whom do you give them?" Scoth asked.

She snapped at the men upon the couches and they relocated themselves farther away in the great room. After she returned the timepiece to Scoth, she said, "I like to enjoy myself, Detective, and so I surround myself with lovely people. They stay with me a little while, and then they move on."

"Are they prostitutes?"

"Yes. I contract with several escort agencies for their finest. Not just in looks, but in elocution and intelligence. And none can be in bondage to the work; I find that distasteful. Some stay with me for years; others last only a few weeks."

"And all of them receive timepieces?" Jesco said.

"No, angels above! I would have handed out six times as many if I did. I give them to my special ones. The ones who please me most in our time together receive a timepiece, and of the most special ones, I give them the timepiece and also a boost. Some are happy to be escorts, true, but others wish different careers. Halowel Flowers, have you heard of it? Straick Halowel was one of my boys many years in the past. Darling, just darling, quick with numbers, keen for business and good at botany, so I set him up with a little flower shop once he left here and he has built it into an empire. I like to do that, give a boost to those who know what to do with it. I've put a few through university, and placed two or three in newspaper positions. Lowly ones, yes, but it's the boost they need and they have to decide what to do with it from there."

Scoth brought out the picture of the nervous blonde woman. Kyrad looked at it and shook her head. Then he showed the picture of the black-haired man and she leaned over to take it from him. "Do you recognize him?" Scoth asked.

"He bears a strong resemblance to a young man I had here, oh . . . five years ago, or six. Tallo. Tallo . . . Quay, I think it was. Yes, Tallo Quay! He was from Ipsin. This could very well be him, but he's much thinner in this picture. He worked as an escort for Sunset/Sunrise at the time. They hadn't recommended him to me, but I saw him at a party there and brought him home. It was a mistake, as I quickly learned." The butler dropped off a fizzy drink for each of them and took his leave.

"And then what happened?" Scoth prompted.

"He was a delight at first. But then he began to hint at how he would like a boost into a theater." She looked around the room to her escorts sternly. "They are being paid well enough to keep me company. I owe them nothing more than that, payment and fair treatment. But Tallo was a pushy sort of fellow, only pleasant when he was going to get his way. And, frankly, I'm a pushy sort myself. I cut him down to size quite sharply when his hints became outright demands. No, I was not going to introduce him to the directors and producers and playwrights in my social circles, and he showed some nerve one evening after a play we attended. We went backstage and he did it himself, made his introductions and described himself as my dear friend and a burgeoning actor seeking roles. Then he looked at me to confirm how gifted he was. I was enraged. He was in my home to look attractive and entertain me in bed and out; he was my employee and I was not his. He had an impeccable memory and could memorize a script in a day, but in the little plays they throw for me here, he had no expression. No talent for anything but saying the words. And even had he been in possession of stunning talent, I would have withheld the recommendation simply for his presumption."

Remembering the long-ago conflict was agitating her. "He grew sulky and sullen after I chastised him. I gave him a few days to sort himself out, but he had no intention of doing so. He didn't want to return to the escort agency, nor did he want to be here if there was no grand gift of a theater boost at the end of it. I pitied him: he came from a pathetic background, hungry and cold and cowering from his drunken father. He didn't know how to behave any better, but I wasn't going to pay him and his agency to put up with it. I wouldn't give him a boost to a theater company, but I did give him a timepiece on his way out the door. I figured he would sell it and make his way in the world somehow."

Here was another piece of the puzzle, but it didn't fit with any of the other ones. Her agitation fading, Kyrad sipped her fizzy drink and considered the picture. "We all have dreams and we all have strengths, is that not true? And they do not always align with one another."

She looked at Scoth, who said, "That's very true."

"Tallo's dream was to act; however, it was not his strength. One of the hardest parts when turning from child to adult is reconciling the imbalance, should it exist. I took stock of myself at nineteen and my only strengths were beauty-" she passed a hand over her face, "-and a raw intelligence without much education. My family was all miners, and I worked in the mines myself from a young age. But I realized that I could capitalize on my strengths to better my position, and I did. I could marry a Joe Pick-Ax, have his children and struggle as all the women of my family struggled, or I could play a game with the wealthy older men who were interested in bedding me. As you can see, that is what I chose. But I was not going to entertain them for a night and be discarded. I was savvy enough to make a marriage with a rich, sick old fool who wanted a pretty young thing on his arm and my entire world changed. You must play the cards you're given in life, not waste your time longing for the cards given to someone else! But Tallo refused his hand."

"Could Tallo have been angry enough to seek revenge upon you?" Scoth asked.

Soberly, Kyrad said, "I want to think better of him, but yes, I could see him feeling spitefully towards me. It would be easier for him to be angry than to reconcile his own imbalances."

"How would he hurt you, if he could?"

"Tell naughty stories, I venture, of the time we spent together. Tell everyone about the insatiable older woman and her many young escorts. But what audience this would find is not large. I am not so well known by the populace of Ainscote that many would care what I do and whom I do it with. And since what I do is hardly scandalous, and whom I do it with are adults who give their consent, I can't see these stories being of much note. And it's no secret in Rosendrie what I do, but when I give such hefty donations to the schools and city hall and the fire department and the widows-and-orphans charity and plenty more . . . well, let's just say that people will overlook almost anything when you are giving them money."

Carefully, Jesco drank from his bottle of fizzy drink. Kyrad was a keen observer and said, "You did not let that touch your lips or tongue."

Realization instantly glimmered in her eyes. "You are a seer, are you not? Yes? Could I offer you some object to prove my innocence?"

Surprised, Jesco looked at Scoth. The detective had not expected this turn in conversation. "I do not know that it is necessary at this time-" Scoth said.

She cut him off. "I have told you all that I can about Tallo Quay, and I would like to not be suspected in the murder of that other man. Let's cut straight to the quick of this and have it be done. There must be something of mine that would show a seer that I have spoken nothing but the truth. Clothing? I was in bed at the time of this murder . . . does it matter if they have been washed since then? Could you touch my blankets or pillow?"

Scoth raised his eyebrows at Jesco. It was his decision. Gesturing to Kyrad's hand, Jesco said, "Do you have pieces of jewelry that you always wear?"

She extended her hand. The ring on her smallest finger was too tight, and wholly unlike the finer pieces she wore. It was a plain silver band with a dull blue rock caught in the clasps. "This one was my grandmother's, and she gave it to my mother. Then my mother gave it to me. It's only ever fit upon my small finger, and lately, it's grown too tight even for that. I can't get it off and should so that I can have it resized. But you mustn't think I have put it on to hoodwink you." She tugged at it hard to demonstrate. The ring did not budge.

"I would be able to tell if you had," Jesco said. This old ring would lay him low with all its history, but it would have the answers.

"And I must have reassurance that this will be private, should you see business matters. I am aboveboard, more or less, but there are still things that would not be advantageous for everyone to know about."

"Your business matters are not of interest to this investigation," Scoth said. "We're only here concerning Hasten Jibb."

"I can nudge the thrall to more relevant matters," Jesco said. "Scoth, would you be willing to get my wheelchair from the carriage?"

"For after your thrall," Kyrad said, and gestured to two of her escorts. They came over and she instructed them to bring the chair inside.

"You are well-versed in seersight," Jesco commented.

"I was not educated much in childhood; I remedied that condition as soon as it was possible after my marriage. I couldn't bear to have my ignorance be a permanent condition." Kyrad winced at her ring. "I pity you for what you are about to see. Nudge away from my bedchamber as much as you can."

Jesco did not need to touch the ring to be certain that this woman was innocent. But his feelings were not evidence. Moving his fizzy drink to the far side of the table in case he collapsed, he scooted to the edge of the sofa and removed his glove. Kyrad splayed out her fingers so that he would not bump any of the bejeweled rings. The friendly hubbub in the room was stilling as the escorts gleaned that something different was going on.

Thunder rumbled over the house. The storm had not spent itself in full, and the light out the windows was dimming. Jesco pressed his finger to the ring.

-he was-
-he was-
-she was-
-she was watching him die-

She was sitting upon a hard wooden chair beside the bed, and he was taking his last breaths. The only color in him was in the bright red of his hair, what of it hadn't gone gray. Mine dropsy, she had known it was mine dropsy when he started to cough months ago. She hadn't needed the doctor to confirm it.

Twenty years and five children and he was still a stranger . . . *that woman* had taken the best of him and the strumpet had had the nerve to show up on the doorstep, begging to be let in to say goodbye. Goodbye from her and goodbye from their son . . . he had fathered a son upon her and the boy was a redheaded, sniveling creature born of betrayal upon her hip . . . much too old to be carried, much too old to be sniveling, she would have slapped her children for sniveling at his age . . .

Jesco was looking at Kyrad's grandparents. The man upon the bed was taking rattling breaths, each at a longer and longer distance from one another. The woman was named Amena, and she was watching him. Her mind drifted to her long-dead grandmother, who could remember a time when this land was without mines. Scant memories, since she had been small, but she remembered the golden fields of wheat belonging to their family, and how her lunch pail was full on the flowery walk to the schoolhouse. It was all a dream to Amena.

Rattle, rattle, rattle. He had stood so tall and proud once, and now he was a shriveled husk under the blanket. There were footsteps in the hallway belonging to the children . . . Faugnas and Alastasia were arguing in whispers about *that woman* since she had come back . . . Alastasia wanted to be merciful and Faugnas did not . . . Faugnas understood that the cuts of meat on his plate had been thinner over the last years for the money going to *that woman* and her child . . .

This had all happened long in the past. None of it had anything to do with the case at hand, and Jesco pushed away from it. Amena's memories pushed back, demanding their due, and there was so much of her in this

ring . . . at the funeral when *that woman* dared to show with her ill-begotten brat, the vicious slap Amena delivered to the gasps of the mourners and the boy wailing like he was two and not six or seven . . . at the weddings of Faugnas and Silvestre where she stood proud . . . at the home of Alastasia in a heated argument, the daughter defiant that the sniveling brat was her half-brother and now he was a man and Amena could not dictate who entered Alastasia's own house . . .

But Amena did not have to enter it again.

She had meant to give the ring to Alastasia as her elder daughter, but it passed to the younger in Livina. Sweet but silly, her daughter Livina, yet Amena preferred her now. It moved from hand to hand and he was-

-he was-

-she was-

-she was-

Livina was getting out! Out from this dirty air, away from these dirty people and dirty mines, oh, she was going to the city! Where every day was a festival and the shops never closed . . . Mama was not happy that she was leaving, but Livina was so happy to get away from the tide of anger washing from wall to wall in their tiny house . . . *some man is going to get you in trouble in Cantercaster and don't think you can come back here . . .*

The train stopped at Vellen Station and she stepped out and into her future. Time skipped, since Livina did not always wear the ring. Her job at the slaughterhouse forbade jewelry, so she only wore it now and then on her days off. The city was not all that she had thought it would be but there was Colton, her brooding poet who wrote such fearfully dark verses and always looked so far beyond where anyone else could see . . .

When Jesco saw her next, her face was tight. Colton had blown away with the wind, but he had left something behind in Livina's belly. She would not take drake root to rid herself of it. He would come back . . . oh, he would come back and see her with their beautiful child and the darkness in him would turn to light . . . then she was standing before the door of that cramped house she had been so thrilled to leave and her mother was staring silently at her and the baby . . . Mama was going to send her away and then she and Beri had nothing . . . *was he married . . . no, Mama . . . may as well come in . . .*

The sting of relief through Livina pierced the ring and left its mark, and pierced into Jesco and left a mark upon him as well. Relief to have a home, gratitude to be forgiven . . . Mama was a harsh and angry woman but she took in Livina and when Mama held Beri, when she dandled him upon her knee, something had grown softer in her. She was not as Livina remembered . . .

# THE SEER

He pushed. Livina married a miner who raised her son as his own and gave her two redheaded daughters . . . Kyrad grew up in front of the ring and he sped it along until she was a young woman in a nightdress before a bathroom mirror . . . in disgust to climb into bed with that old man . . . he grunted and slobbered and snored but it was a trade, life was a trade, and she would trade on this so her back didn't break in the mines and the dropsy didn't take her . . . he was in poor health and not going to live more than a year and after that, after that she was free and she would *never* chain herself and her fortune to a man . . . how she loathed chains . . .

They hated her.

They wanted to take Naphates Mines away from her . . . not the role of a woman, a widow, just sell to us, sell and live in prosperity, buy wardrobes full of pretty dresses and let us do the dirty work . . . They came to her, one man after another with their fists already closing over her business but only to leave empty-handed. She would not sell so they pushed their sons at her . . . so young, so beautiful, so alone, so naïve . . . in the conviction that through marriage they could gain what she would not give.

But they were *her* damn mines now.

The boys, she loved her boys, she took in a girl here and there and loved that too, there was Jasper, Yannis, Stansen, Gorman, Hylo, Sulla, Ames, Tallo . . . Jesco experienced the giving of the timepiece from her perspective and she was smiling but filled with annoyance at this bratty man-child who would not face his reality like she once had . . .

She had no respect for that.

She was sick in bed and they came to her in ones and twos to keep her company. To read the news, to tell jokes, to warm away the chills . . . Jesco nudged and nudged to center himself at this period of time, but it held nothing more than what she had told them. While Hasten Jibb was being murdered, Kyrad Naphates was sniffling and coughing as the escort minding her for that night brought in medication and stayed at her side. It was the woman at the billiards table, who was named Rallie and she was one of the sweet ones . . . not sweet as was her job but genuinely sweet-hearted . . . *tell me what you'd like to do that you never have been able to . . . I want to see the ocean . . . you've never been? Not ever?* . . . All she wanted was the sea and Kyrad loved her all the more for it. They'd go in early summer, the two of them and a handful of the boys, rent out the top floor of . . .

Jesco pushed away from the scene, which was intimate though not sexual. There was no trace of Hasten Jibb anywhere within Kyrad's ring, not his face, not his name, nothing at all. Jesco turned to the courier company but neither was there Ragano & Wemill here. She used a different service.

He was growing weary of trying to keep his focus, overwhelmed with Amena and Livina still clamoring in the background, there were beds and babies and parties and boardrooms and illnesses and dinners and there was that sniveling, redheaded brat with his mouth wide open in a shriek to see his mother slapped . . . there was Mama stepping aside to let Livina and Beri enter . . . *Mama, I made such a mistake never mind that what is his name? Beri? Beri after my father? Oh, Livina! Let me hold him* . . . there was handsome Vangelis with his cuffs and paddle and Kyrad had waited all day in those dull financial meetings to enjoy this . . .

. . . angels above, was she going to enjoy this . . .

. . . she had been a very bad girl . . .

He took his hand away from the ring and went limp. They were waiting for him, Kyrad and Scoth and two of the escorts, and he collapsed with a flurry of hands shooting out to break his fall.

"There is nothing for us here," he said to Scoth, and blacked out.

# Chapter Seven

He came to in the carriage. A drumbeat of rain was striking the roof, and a heavy and furious torrent obliterated the world through the window. It was evening. The carriage shuddered in the wind, and no wind until now had been strong enough to do that. Jesco was Kyrad was Amena was Taniel and all of them quaked with the rocking of the carriage.

A man was sitting beside the wheelchair. Worry had folded his brow into two parallel tracks. His hair was wet and flat and Jesco stared at the detective, who he had never seen before in such disarray. A panel was lying on the seat, and a light flashed red above the buttons along the wall.

"It's not her," Jesco mumbled, his words coming out mashed. He was looking at the world sideways with his head bent. His neck could sway from side to side, but not hold up his head. The thrall had left him limp.

"I know," Scoth said. "I knew that before you touched the ring. A guilty party would not have been so swift to offer herself to a seer. We just needed the proof."

Home. Jesco had heard Scoth repeating *home* as his senses were returning. *Home. Destination home.* But what came out of his mouth was his previous remark, his brain looping upon it. "It's not her."

"I know, Jesco," Scoth said, and hearing his first name broke the loop. "Tallo . . ."

"Yes. The next step is to track down Tallo Quay of Ipsin."

"Home . . . why were you saying home?"

The carriage swayed violently in the wind. Scoth kept his voice calm, but there was growing panic in his eyes. "The storm is getting vicious. It isn't safe to travel. My home is much closer than the asylum, so I changed the autohorse's destination."

Jesco slipped into a whirling confusion of memories that were not his. The star shining in his mind's eye was stormed and he was drowning within hundreds of individual histories. Then he saw Rafonse among them, and that was Jesco's own history. He launched himself at the towering bear of a man just as he had done as a boy. The friendliest fellow in the world, that had been Rafonse, and his arms closed over Jesco's back as the big man roared his welcome. There were a great many bones in the human body, but not one of Rafonse's bore a scintilla of meanness or spite. He was not a handsome fellow to the objective eye, but five minutes in his company and he became radiant.

Isena was quieter in her greeting, but her husband's joy always seeped into everyone around him and she was no different. Jesco was firmly in his own memories now, and he walked with them down the lane away from the asylum. He was twelve, giddy with excitement, and in his room were his brand new whirly-gig and tool case that they had given him for his birthday. There was a street fair several blocks away and they were going to buy a poof of pink cloud candy wrapped upon a white stick . . . listen to the music and wander through the shops . . . his brothers hated him but Rafonse was his brother-in-law, his new brother, and he liked Jesco just fine . . .

The carriage. Home. Scoth. The memories receded and Jesco said, "Your hair is a mess."

"You aren't looking so put together yourself," Scoth said. Some time had passed since they last spoke. It was dark outside the window and the detective no longer looked so alarmed. The storm had not abated in the slightest, but the autohorse was slowing. They had arrived at Scoth's home.

Little of it could be seen through the window save a tall, shadowy structure. The horse stopped and Scoth got out. Light blossomed within the doorway and he returned to the carriage. For a moment, he stared at Jesco and the chair in puzzlement. Then he retreated and came back with boards, which he leaned from the ground up to the open door of the carriage. Turning Jesco to face away from the house, he rolled the chair to the top of the boards and lifted it onto them. Then he rolled Jesco down to the ground and pushed him into the house. The bags were deposited beside him. Pulling out the planks, Scoth closed the door and ordered the autohorse to go to the stables with the carriage.

Jesco could only see his legs beside an umbrella stand. The chair turned and went forward. "Where . . ." he muttered, losing the strength to even keep his eyes open.

"I'll set you up in the spare bedroom," Scoth said.

"I can't touch the sheets. You have to make it up with the things in my bag."

"All right."

"But you can't touch them."

The wheelchair stopped and Scoth said, "How am I to make the bed?"

"You have to make it with your hands covered."

Scoth muttered a stream of vile oaths. Some time later, Jesco was lifted from the chair. His head tilted and his cheek touched a cool, smooth fabric.

-he was-

-he was-

-he was Laeric-

He was walking into The Seven Temptations and there was Collier . .

Jesco was laid in the bed and the thrall ceased. "You know Collier. So do I."

"How did you . . ." Scoth swore again and said crossly, "Get out of my mind."

That was the last Jesco knew until morning, when he opened his eyes to a strange bedroom. It did not look like it had been intended in its construction to become a bedroom at all. The ceiling was high and the windows along the wall behind the bed were massive, filling the room with a weary gray light. Bookcases stood tall along the walls, crammed with books from end to end. Even more books and sheaves of paper were laid atop the uneven rows.

Jesco's suitcase was beside the bed, as was his wheelchair. It was quiet outside of his room, and he assumed that Scoth was still sleeping. Rain pattered down and streaked the windows. He shifted in the bed and was startled that he could shift. It had been an intense thrall; however, he had not worn himself out in the days beforehand. His recovery would not take long, and the thrall from Scoth had been exceedingly small. His arms felt weak but he could move them with relative ease; his legs felt weaker but he could flex his toes and make tiny kicks. Control of his bladder had stayed with him, yet it was not going to remain that way if he didn't find a lavatory. He recalled that he had packed for disaster, and he got hold of his suitcase to take care of the problem. Tucking the soaked pad into a bag and tying the handles, he set it down and dozed.

. . . she had been a very bad girl . . .

He woke up aroused. Whether it was his or hers, he couldn't say. There was nothing to be done about it in any case. He distracted himself

by thinking about Tallo Quay, who had had something in his possession that he was going to use against Kyrad Naphates. It couldn't have had anything to do with her admirable drive for bedsports. She had made very good points that she was not so important that the whole country would take an interest in her sexual activities, nor was there anything scandalous when her partners were all consenting adults from escort agencies. Also, it made little sense that Quay would wait several years to reveal his stories. He had been up to something else, and Hasten Jibb must have inadvertently gotten involved.

There were footsteps upon the stairs, a steady thumping from Scoth coming down to the ground floor. Jesco scooted up in bed and pulled up his knees so that his erection was not as evident. The door opened.

Scoth at home was wholly different from Scoth at work, and just as appealing in a different way. Dressed in battered work trousers and a long-sleeved white shirt, his hair was as rumpled as a wind-scathed sea. Stubble covered his cheeks and a screwdriver was protruding from his pocket. "Came to see if you were interested in eating yet. Or if you needed anything else."

The presence under the blanket twitched. "I could do with some food. There are-"

"Plates and utensils in your bag and not to touch them," Scoth finished. Wrapping his hands in rags, he came forward and removed those items from the suitcase. "Might be a queer breakfast, or it's late enough to be almost lunch, I suppose. I just keep odds and ends around."

Jesco wouldn't expect anything different from this man. "Whatever you have will be fine." As Scoth straightened, the screwdriver almost fell from his pocket. "What is it that you're doing?"

"Working on some things upstairs. You want a book to read to pass the time? I can't drive you back to the asylum yet. The roads are flooded."

"I can't read."

Scoth looked at him incredulously. "I've seen you read street signs just fine. You mean you can't touch the books? Just wear those gloves you have and fumble a bit to turn the pages."

"Yes, I know my letters, but no, I can't read a book," Jesco explained. "It happens with those who have strong seersight. Reading the author's words will conjure a thrall in me if they wrote with strong emotions."

Scoth stared in amazement from him to the books. Then he shook his head and retreated to the door. "Everything in the world is a bloody menace to you."

The money set aside for a new whirly-gig was going to have to be rerouted to The Seven Temptations. Jesco argued with the lump under the blanket and lost. It did not flag until it had reassurance that its needs came first, and it had been so long since the last visit . . . No, it really hadn't been *that* long. Perhaps it was a little of Kyrad's insatiableness still within his mind.

Breakfast arrived and it was as promised, a hodgepodge collection of odds and ends rustled up from the kitchen. Scoth thumped back upstairs as Jesco ate. Then he slid down in the bed to rest. From many recoveries from thralls, he had learned to estimate how long each would take. By tomorrow, he would be upright. Neither running nor walking fast, but he would be able to get around with no more assistance than a cane.

He was dozing when he became aware of thumping on the stairs, and his eyes stayed closed as the sound incorporated itself into a hazy dream. Then his mind roused and he woke to Scoth in the room. The detective was setting a gigantic whirly-gig upon a side table. It looked similar to a phonograph, its most notable features being a large golden horn attached at its base to a black spinner. Jesco rubbed at his eyes as Scoth fiddled around with it.

Unfolding a collapsible music rack beside the horn, he went to the bookshelves, perused the many options there, and pulled out a thick green book. That was placed upon the rack. From behind the horn came an extension of slender black tubes that stretched down to the book and joined up above it at a flat black disk. Flicking switches and repositioning the book, bringing down two metallic eyes that opened and shut, Scoth stepped back.

The pleasant voice of a man filled the room. "Autohorse Races." The black tubes moved with mechanical clicks and opened the cover of the book. The first page was blank. Working just like real fingers, they turned it to the next where the title was repeated, followed by the author and publishing house.

"I've never seen one like this!" Jesco said. "Did you make it?"

"More like I just stuck a bunch of whirly-gigs together," Scoth said, looking at it with something akin to pride. "It reads me books when I'm busy. The only thing it can't do is fetch itself another book when it finishes the one it's reading."

Up the stairs Scoth went once more, and Jesco listened to the voice and the clicks of the mechanical fingers turning pages, and many thumps and crashes and taps from upstairs. The rain tapered outside the window but did not cease, and strengthened by afternoon. Every angel in the heavens was weeping upon the world, as a nurse had said when Jesco was young, and it seemed like there was a divine sadness in how the sky poured inconsolably.

It was almost evening when the phonograph came to the last page of the book. Closing it, the fingers retracted and the machine turned off. Jesco could take no more curiosity about the noise from upstairs, and some strength had come back to him. He dressed himself and stood up, wobbled yet held, and started for the door. It helped to hold on to the furniture. Halfway up the stairs he felt like he might fall, so he sat down heavily and rested his gloved hand upon a bar of the railing. The clattering stopped and Scoth appeared at the landing. Embarrassed, Jesco said, "I'll make it."

"Could have just called for help." Scoth came down, wrapped his hands under Jesco's armpits, and pulled him up step by step. Dragged into a room, Jesco was lifted to a chair.

It was a workshop filled with tables, whirly-gigs both whole and disemboweled all over them. There were tools for wood and metal along the walls, strips of horsehair in multiple colors hanging from a bar, and clusters of jars filled with nails and screws and washers on a bench. What slim light the sky was offering came down through giant skylights in the ceiling, where they caught upon strings of crystal and reflected over everything. Scoth went to a corner of the shop that was further lit by lanterns and bent down to pick up screws that had been dumped all over the floor.

"What do you do in here?" Jesco asked.

"Make a huge mess most of the time," Scoth said as he dropped a screw in a jar. "It was my mother's, a lot of it. She had a gift."

"What did she do?"

"Made things. She couldn't see a machine without wanting to improve it." Looking to a pale blue, mechanical bird hanging from the ceiling, its beak open in a silent cry, he said, "That was hers. I hated that thing. She would put destination cards in its chest and send it flying around to find me with reminders about my chores. When I kept coming home late from school, she sent it downriver where I was larking about and had it yell at me. She'd coded her scolding to the map. I ran home real quick, my friends laughing their fool heads off."

"She must have been young when she passed."

"She was, and so was my father. They did almost everything together, so it was fitting that they just about died together, too. She had a weak heart, and he couldn't keep going without her."

"Did you never want to return to Korval to work there?"

"No. Money buys justice in little towns. It does that everywhere, but in some places, it's much more blatant. And when money isn't involved, well, then it just depends on the victim how much interest is going to be shown."

"Was that what happened to your brother? Or was it a cousin?"

Scoth stopped picking up screws to give him a puzzled look. "No brothers or cousins to speak of. Why would you think that?"

"I'm sorry. It was station gossip that you lost a brother or cousin."

Annoyed, Scoth returned to his clean-up job. "It was Ravenhill running at the mouth over his cups, and as usual, he got it wrong."

Thinking of Ravenhill's insistence that a pickpocket had dragged Hasten Jibb's body to Poisoners' Lane, and wishing fervently that he had never brought up the gossip, Jesco said, "He's not doing well lately, is he? He's worked too many bad cases."

"Nothing to do with his cases, or not much," Scoth replied. "They don't walk with him. Ravenhill's lazy, they warned me when I got assigned to him. He'll sew up a case with any thread at hand. Black thread, white thread, good thread, bad thread, he'll use anything and figure it's done. He was better than that once. But now . . . now he's just wanting to get back to the card tables and a glass of gin, some fun with a prostie girl."

"Is that why his wife left him?"

"His wife is a good woman. She knows about the prosties; she has a prostie man at a place that she visits herself. You play with your body but you leave your heart at home, that's always been their understanding about it. And you patronize a quality establishment where you won't be trotting home an infection on your personals. She kept up her end of it and he didn't. Twice he gave her infections of different kinds, and there isn't going to be a third time. She won't be back. And all he thinks is that she's the one being unreasonable." Scoth put the last of the screws in the jar and set it on the workbench. He eyed Jesco warily. "Did you already know all that from your thrall on me?"

"All I saw was you going into The Seven Temptations."

"Honest?"

"Honest. And it was nothing new to me. I've seen you there twice before."

Astounded, Scoth said, "I never saw you there. Why didn't you come over and say something?"

"We've admitted to being pricks. That should answer your question."

Scoth ran his hand through his hair and made it even messier. "You could touch the things in that room and peep on myself and my whole family if it pleased you."

"I could, but I'd rather not be in a wheelchair for weeks."

"You could see my deepest, darkest secrets laid out in front of your eyes, experiencing them just like you were me. I thought at first that Kyrad didn't know how much privacy she was giving up when she offered her ring, but she knew damn well. She knew and did it anyway to clear herself."

"I sincerely doubt that your deepest, darkest secrets could be anywhere near as shocking as the things I have seen in my life."

Turning off the lanterns one by one, Scoth said, "What do you do with all of that private information? Those are people's souls laid bare before you."

"All of it comes at a great cost to me. I don't watch for entertainment, and I try to steer away from memories that aren't relevant. And for what I do see anyway . . . I keep it to myself, the most private things. Because they are usually memories of pain, and I don't want to tell anyone. I'm quite regularly sorry that I know them myself."

They went downstairs, Jesco's arm over Scoth's shoulders, and made it to the spare bedroom without disaster. "Should we head for Ipsin?" he asked as Scoth settled him back in bed.

"Should but can't for another two or three days. The only place I'll be going tomorrow is to the market and on foot, and maybe the station the day after that to write a report of what we've learned. I've been to Ipsin once before and it'll be a damn mudslide at the moment. You're stuck here, sorry to say." He removed the book from the phonograph and returned it to its shelf. Then he scanned the shelves for another one.

"Would it be all right if I came upstairs to watch tomorrow?" Jesco blurted.

"Sure. Wear your gloves and you can take apart the pile of clickers if you like. I want those gears inside." He took another book from the shelf and brought it to the phonograph, though he didn't turn it on to read.

"What are you making with them?" Jesco asked.

"A shooter, or I'm trying. Attaches to the arm, make a fist for the ignition, blasts out a projectile. Like a tiny cannon. So far I've just succeeded in shooting myself in the shoulder, so I can't say that I'll be wearing it out in the field any time soon."

Jesco laughed and Scoth actually smiled. It was a small smile, a flash of white teeth and a sarcastic cant to his eyebrows at the shoddy workings of his invention, but it was the most that Jesco had ever seen from him. Then he went to get dinner, and brought it in upon two plates for both of them to eat together.

The next morning, Jesco got upstairs without trouble, and stripped a collection of old clicker cameras for the gears. It was not easy to do in gloves but still happy work. Afterwards, Scoth dressed his arm in a black holder with a cylinder that stretched down his forearm, and a strap that extended around his palm. He made a fist and rounds of pellets flew out to score dents into the wall. Jesco's cheer was cut off by a yelp, Scoth ripping the shooter from his arm. The cylinder had grown very hot with each successive round and was scorching him.

There was little evidence of the thrall by the next day, Jesco tired but getting about without assistance. Scoth went to the station and returned in the evening with a furious expression. "Look at this!" he snapped, throwing down a newspaper in front of Jesco, who was sitting at the kitchen table to eat.

"I can't," Jesco said, and Scoth snatched it away.

"Owner of Naphates Mines is under investigation of murder," he growled. "It was published in the Rosendrie South Press just this morning."

Shocked, Jesco said, "But she isn't under investigation! I cleared her. Who was the source for the article?"

"Doesn't name the person and it's a right piece of yellow journalism. It says that investigators went to the home of Kyrad Naphates to question her about the brutal murder of Hasten Jibb. It insinuates that he was one of her prostie boys."

"He damn well wasn't! That poor fellow couldn't have faked it if he had tried. What else does it say?"

"It goes on at length about how she's aiming for that position in Parliament and how this is going to hurt her chances. They won't want someone accused of criminal activity, someone involved in an open investigation. It even says a seer was brought to her home! But not that you found her innocent. And here . . . here it says that the detectives on the case refused to comment. How was I supposed to comment when no journalist ever approached to ask me a thing?"

Jesco had lost his appetite. Pushing his plate aside, he said, "The source had to have been one of the escorts, but why?"

"Or a servant. She has plenty of both. Someone at that house spoke to this journalist who wrote it, Noran Gordano. He made sure to note that Parliament will be taking their vote on the liaison position next week. Do they want a criminal in their midst?" In disgust, Scoth tossed the paper into the rubbish bin.

"I wonder if the servant or escort approached the journalist and sold the story," Jesco said. "Netted himself or herself a pretty penny and likely trounced Kyrad's chances in the process."

"Do you need to return to the asylum for anything, or can you go to Ipsin with me tomorrow?" Scoth asked. "I need to track down this Tallo Quay!"

Jesco paused to think of anything he could need from the asylum. "No, I've got my belongings with me, and I've already sent a portion of my pay to Isena for the month. I can go to Ipsin tomorrow."

"Who is that? Isena?"

"My older sister. She was widowed a few years ago. I send her money."

"Decent of you."

"She's all the family I have, she and her children. The rest of them believe I'm a demon's child."

Grumpily, Scoth sat down with his own plate of food. "I'll take you back after Ipsin. Good to get rid of you. I eat far too regularly when you're around."

"How you suffer."

"And Tammie's back from Hooler. She said to give you a kiss, but I won't."

"How I suffer. Saving them all for Collier? Why don't you have a man of your own?"

"I did. He said I was married to the job and quit me. Can't hold that against him. Why don't you have a man?"

Jesco held up his hands. "Who would have me but a prostie? Who wants to make a partner of a man who has to live in an asylum, who can't touch anything but flesh without gloves, who can't even go out to eat or drink without complications?"

Scoth neither agreed nor disagreed, and changed the subject. "They're pulling back on the Shy Sprinkler case. Nothing's been found. The captain is taking heat about the unsolved necktie killings and wants me to focus more on those. I'm only going to finagle a few more days on Jibb before he starts coming down harder. I put him off with Ravenhill, who will be continuing that investigation for now."

"I didn't get called in for that case. Was a seer not needed?"

"No, those killings don't call for a seer. I know damn well who did it but we just can't locate him. We didn't call you in for the Tesoola Park case either."

"What's that one?"

"Mother and little daughter taking a walk some time back, middle of the day, and someone or more than one someone shot them both in the back with arrows. And then pulled the arrows out and strolled away. They were killed almost instantly. No motive, no witnesses, no leads, no evidence, nothing. Just two dead bodies on the ground side by side, the mom holding the girl's arm. That one keeps me up a lot of nights. It was like game sport for someone, but instead of hunting deer in the forest, he went to the park and hunted people."

"And he never did it again?"

"Or did it somewhere else very far away. I don't know. The hardest cases are the ones with no connections between the people who did it and the people they did it to. But Jibb now, I don't think that's the kind of case this is. There's a connection somewhere; we just haven't found it."

Early the next morning, they left. Like Rosendrie, Ipsin was south of Cantercaster. The puddles from the storm were soaking into the earth; the sky was blue and the world washed clean and bright. The streets were busy, repairmen replacing windows that had broken and city workers chopping fallen trees and ferrying them away. The autohorse stopped once and sharply, Jesco and Scoth almost unseated inside. A little boy chasing after a ball had run heedlessly into the road. His father bellowed from the porch of a house and sprinted to retrieve him. Knocking on the carriage door once he had his son in arms, the man called, "Sorry, gentlemen!" and retreated to the sidewalk.

Otherwise, the road to Ipsin was uneventful. The autohorse drew them on to the Hall of Records, where Scoth went inside to see if he could get any information about Tallo Quay. He came out with an address and went to the autohorse to program it in before returning to the carriage. As they pulled away, Jesco said, "Is his home close by?"

"They only had an approximate address for a man named Michum Quay, his wife Shadra, and unnamed children close to majority age. It was old information. But Tallo must be related in some way to them. Quay isn't a common surname and these are the only ones in the area."

"An approximate address?"

"Turn left at The Donkey Inn, past the four patches of trees, down the road to Shackton, and then five-skip on the left. I couldn't program that last part into a destination card since I have no idea what it means, and neither did the clerk who gave it to me. The horse will only take us to the inn, and from there on, I'll have to drive it manually."

In due time, the carriage was slowing for the inn. Jesco stayed inside as Scoth hoisted himself up to the seat and called for Horse to go on. They rode past the patches of trees and turned for a narrow dirt road that cut down a sharp slope. The ground was spotted with shadows from the trees, which rose up like dappled white poles far overhead and only bore branches and leaves at the very top.

Shackton was a shantytown. Every piece of rusted sheet metal and plank of splintered wood in all of Ainscote seemed to have rolled down this slope and gathered precariously into homes at the bottom. All of them were propping each other up and a few had collapsed from the effort. Struts held up the ones built upon the slope itself. Clothing and dead fowl hung from lines between the trees, and crude barrel fences had been erected to outline yards. There were no addresses or street names, and the dirt lanes were very narrow.

Eyes turned to the autohorse and carriage. The only traffic here was on foot. Jesco could hear Scoth's muffled voice asking for directions to the Quay home. He was soundly ignored until he produced a coin. Then a young girl led them on, running ahead through the maze of tight alleys and beckoning to the autohorse. She stopped before a shanty with rusted red sides and a barrel fence missing many of its barrels. Scoth gave her the coin, the girl slipping it into her pocket and running away.

The detective got down as Jesco opened the door of the carriage. Raised voices were ringing out from the shanty, a man and woman yelling at one another in anger. Something crashed and their shouts only increased in volume and temper. Alarmed, Scoth said, "It might be better if you stayed put."

Jesco closed the door and retook his seat as Scoth knocked and went inside. Uncomfortable minutes passed in the carriage with dirty faces pressing up against the windows to look in. A boy of fifteen or sixteen shouted, "Are you a lord? Are you a lord, sir?" His jaws were crenellated parapets, each merlon of a tooth separated by a gap so large that the tip of his tongue could protrude through. Jesco shook his head repeatedly to the question, but there was a dull look to the boy's eyes and he continued to ask. Finally, other people knocked him away so that they could look in. Some were obviously scanning around for anything to steal, and the humble insides of the carriage disappointed them.

Scoth came out of the residence, his trench coat dripping. The people about the carriage faded away at a fast clip. Hoisting himself up to the seat, Scoth pushed the autohorse forward. He was trying to find a place to turn around, but the alleys were so tiny that that was not possible. At last he shouted to another child, producing a coin for a route out of Shackton, and they were duly led back to the main road. Scoth stopped there to fiddle with the autohorse, and let himself into the carriage. The horse drew them on alone.

"Offered you a drink, did they?" Jesco asked. The splash on the trench coat was one of alcohol.

"Roaring drunk, Michum Quay, and his lady friend who is not his wife," Scoth said in aggravation. "Drunk and screaming their heads off about nonsense as they threw glasses at each other. I couldn't understand half of what they said. But I got it out of him that he hasn't seen his son Tallo in years."

"How many years?"

"He was incapable of specifics. Tallo went to work for a brothel, he said with disgust. That had to be the escort agency. His father wanted nothing to do with him after that. But he knew that his son was living in town with a woman some time later."

"Can we speak to the woman? Where is she?"

"We're headed her way now and we've already seen the establishment. She works as a maid at The Donkey Inn and the father says that she still does. The employees keep rooms there and that was where Tallo lived with her."

It did not take long to reach the inn. The autohorse swished its tail as they disembarked and entered. Raucous but good-humored voices were bellowing within the barroom, the noise coming and going with the swinging of the door. The entryway was otherwise demure, a stout woman at the counter checking in a guest and two men reading papers in armchairs.

"Help you?" she asked tersely when Scoth and Jesco came to the counter.

"We are seeking the whereabouts of a man named Tallo Quay," Scoth said, showing his identification.

"Put that away!" the woman exclaimed in a horrified hiss. "Chase off good business with that, you will. Tallo hasn't set foot in this inn in years, so whatever business he's mucking about in, it's not here. Get out with you!"

Unperturbed, Scoth leaned on the counter. "Who is the maid that he lived with when he was here? We must speak with her."

The woman lifted the counter and beckoned them in frantically, her eyes on the men in armchairs. They were looking up from their papers. She escorted Jesco and Scoth to an office space behind the counter to have the conversation there. "That's Merlie Jonkins and she's not mixed up in anything! The girl barely has a brain in her head to call her own."

From the inner pocket of his coat, Scoth withdrew the hand drawn picture of the nervous blonde. "Would this be a fair rendering of Merlie Jonkins?"

The woman paled. "See here, I don't want any trouble-"

"My partner and I are not here to cause trouble," Scoth said smoothly. He had slipped in referring to Jesco as his partner, but Jesco didn't mind. "We simply want to ask Ms. Jonkins some questions. Where can we find her?"

"Upstairs in her room, chances are," said the woman with an anxious look around them to the entryway. "It's her day off but she took a wrench to the shoulder last night spotting for Ellna in the bar. I haven't seen her come downstairs so she must be resting. Just go up and knock on the fourth right-side door nice and quiet-like, don't scream what you are and barrel your way in!"

"She speaks as if from long experience," Scoth said flatly once he and Jesco were going up the stairs, and Jesco snickered under his breath.

Merlie Jonkins answered the knock. Her left arm was wrapped up in a crude sling made of towels and pins. Except for that, she looked better than she had in Jesco's visions of her. Although still a slender woman, she had been eating better.

The room she was within was the same as in the thrall. The wallpaper was peeling, and there was the spindly wooden table. Upon it were stacks of coins. Following his gaze, Merlie said, "'S my tips." She took a chair by the window. "Police, you said? Here about Beddam?"

"No, we're not here about Beddam," Scoth said.

She didn't hear him. "You can't hold those bunnies against him! He didn't know he was in anyone's backyard. He thought he was trapping in a field, not someone's pets." She nodded, convinced of Beddam's innocent mistake. "Who keeps bunnies for pets no-how? Fur and meat, that's what they're good for. But these were wearing little blue coats."

"I'm not interested in the bunnies," Scoth said. Jesco could not help but wonder why a man would then think that they were wild bunnies in a field.

But Merlie Jonkins did not possess a discriminating mind. "If you're not here for Beddam, is it Sprout? He didn't mean to-"

"We're here about Tallo Quay, Ms. Jonkins," Scoth interrupted.

She both blanched and wheezed in laughter. "*Ms.* Jonkins. Like I'm a proper prat, huh? Nobody calls me that. I'm Merlie. What do you want about Tallo then?"

"We're attempting to locate him."

"He didn't come back. He went out that day, two years ago, maybe three now, and didn't come back."

"Where did he go?"

She began to look extremely nervous. "I told him not to get messed up in rich folks' business. But he was dead set on getting his pound of flesh from her."

"Who do you mean?"

"I don't remember her name. That rich woman who had a different man in her bed every night of her life. Even women she had in her bed on some nights. That's what Tallo told me. Sometimes she had two men at the same time, or a man and a woman, like her bed was a party and everyone was invited. Indecent." She adjusted her sling.

"Can you tell me how you met Tallo?" Scoth asked.

"Here. He came in for a drink one night all downhearted. He was on fire. A man on fire! Not real fire," she clarified for them. "Fire in his heart. Passion. But she doused his fire with cold water and sent him away. After she took what she wanted of him, she gave him that little clock and told him to go. Go back and sell yourself to someone else. But he didn't want to do that. He cried at me. All the world wanted from him was his body."

"Did he stay with you after that?"

She flushed. "Yes. He had nowhere else to go."

"He sounds like he was very angry at that woman," Jesco said when the stain in her cheeks grew brighter in anticipation of their judgment. The two of them must have started a sexual relationship almost immediately for her to be so ashamed about it.

"He was!" Merlie agreed. "He was furious. He wanted to make her sorry for not giving him a little something after he'd given her everything."

"And how was he going to do that?"

"Poor people, see, they got dirt on the outside. I'd rather that, dirt you can't hide. Rich people, they have dirt on the inside. They look clean but they're not. He knew some of her dirt from living there in her big house. He'd spied on her when she had visitors. And he'd gone through her papers when she was playing with her other men and women. They aren't supposed to do that, go into her little home office that she keeps. She locks it, but he lifted her keys. He was real careful, put everything back the way it was so she would never know anyone had been in there. And that's how he got the dirt on her."

"Did he tell you what it was?" Scoth asked.

"It wasn't so dirty to me. Some of the royal blood, generations past the throne, the ones who have hu . . . humanitarian interests . . ."

She enunciated slowly and went on. "Those ones, they pulled strings to get her the ground in Lizziner over the competing mines. That's rich ground, Lizziner, he said. They made sure that she was the one buying it. Some are in Parliament and they aren't supposed to fund interests like that. It's against the rules. But everyone does it, and there are Parliament people slipping favors to the other mines in exchange for things. I didn't really understand all that Tallo was saying."

"That's all right," Scoth said. "Did he say anything else you remember?"

"He knew some names. The names of the people giving her favors. He was going to tell someone who worked in another mine so they could make a scandal. But everyone in politics and business is rolling in a mud puddle so what was his little bit of dirt? The game of it is that everyone is filthy dirty and everyone knows it, Tallo said, but everyone pretends to be squeaky clean. You got to show the world how dirty someone else is but still look like roses yourself, or else you're called a hypocrite. But I told him these are rich people's games and he should keep his nose out of them. He didn't, though. He was going to get himself hurt or something,

I told him, the only one that gets hurt in the games of the rich are the poor. He was hunting that man."

"What man?"

"The one with the strange name. I can't recall it. Colomo? Co . . . Cadelmo? It was something like that. Tallo thought the man would be very interested in his information. And then this man could give Tallo a little something in return. The problem was that it was hard to get to the man to tell him. It was hard to find out where he was, and then he never stayed there long. It was like hopscotch. Tallo would find out the place where he was and take a carriage there to find him, and the man would have just left for somewhere else. Then Tallo would find out the next place and go *there*, but the man was gone again and Tallo didn't have the money to keep chasing him around the country. Tallo couldn't work when he was chasing, so I gave him my money. And often the man wasn't even *in* the country. He would travel for months at a time around the world. Tallo sent him letters but never got a reply. It was rude. If I get a letter, I take the time to write back. But this was a very busy businessman, so he didn't."

She stretched her good arm to the table and turned over a coin in her fingers. "Then he found out where the man was going to be again. It had been two years of waiting and chasing and waiting some more. It was in the papers that the man was going to be attending a play in Cantercaster. Tallo got a lot of papers. He knew that this was his moment. He took the little clock and his booklet where he'd copied down the dirt from the papers in her office, his coat and gloves since it was getting cold, and left. He never came back here. I figure the man put him in a theater company somewhere as gratitude."

*And he never contacted the woman who had supported him for two years?* Jesco didn't ask the question on his mind. It seemed cruel.

Scoth showed her the timepiece and she touched it longingly. "That's it. She was rich, rich, rich, and this was all she gave him. She should have been ashamed."

"Did he leave anything behind when he left?" Scoth asked.

"Just a pile of clothes. I gave them away a year ago. He didn't have much when he came to me. Why are you looking for him?"

"His name has come up in an investigation of a murder. Tell me: do you know a man by the name of Hasten Jibb?"

"No."

"Did Tallo ever say that name to you?"

"No."

"Did he say the name of the play?" Jesco asked.

She shook her head. "He might have at the time, but it was years ago. He was always talking about plays and the parts he wanted to have. That was his passion. I couldn't tell them all apart. I've never been to a play. It's a waste of money to me. The man was going to be at one that wasn't performed much." She brightened as her memories came back. "A tragedy. It was a tragedy. People want to laugh these days, or they want romances that end all happily, but this was a sad one."

As Scoth spoke with her more, Jesco looked around for something to touch that would put him in the mind of Tallo Quay. The clothes would have been best. Then there was the table, but it was too small to dine at or work upon. It was just decorative to hold some knick-knacks, or coins. Would he have touched that table for any length of time? Jesco didn't think so. The wallpaper wouldn't contain much either.

Then there was the bed. "Did Tallo sleep here?" Jesco asked in a pause of their conversation. "In this same bed?"

"In that bed? No," Merlie said, finding nothing odd about his inquiry. "It's new. The last one got the rot in it last winter and was only fit for fire, sheets and all." The new bed was someone else's old bed, and was fairly battered.

He would have touched the doorknob with his bare hand, but when he looked at it, Scoth caught his eye and shook his head. The detective removed a bag from his pocket and said, "I'm going to need to take your doorknob."

"You need to take *what?*" Merlie asked in bafflement.

Once they were back in the carriage, Jesco said, "Why don't you want me to touch it yet?"

"Because it will land you in bed for days," Scoth said. "How old is this knob? Eighty years old or more? How many hands have touched it? How long would Tallo ever have touched it except for opening and closing the door? Let's look at the other information we've received before you land in my bed again."

"Your spare bed," Jesco corrected.

He loved that waning smile. "My spare bed," Scoth amended. "Drool on yourself later. I think we went about this the wrong way at the start. This isn't about Hasten Jibb but peripherally. This has more to do with Kyrad Naphates, even though she's innocent of the murder."

"Should we see her again?"

"Not yet. I want a little more background on her, more specifically, the people around her. Who would have a need to involve her in a police investigation?"

*. . . they hated her . . .*

"They wanted to take the mines away from her," Jesco said. "It was a fleeting moment in the thrall. She inherited her husband's company and refused to sell it to the heads of the other companies, or to marry their sons so they could gain control that way. She broke the wall they had set up to government regulation . . ."

"And she's trying to gain a Parliament position that would further her reach," Scoth said. "Then look at that article to appear all of a sudden, just days before she gets voted on. Someone wants to bring her down."

"What is the next step?"

Scoth sat back in his seat. "We need to speak with the journalist who did it."

# Chapter Eight

It did not take long to get in contact with Noran Gordano, nor was it difficult to get information from him. Meeting with them at a pub near his publication's office, he motioned to a booth in the shadows at the back. He was an older man with a large gut packed impeccably into a fine suit, and his eyes were livid. As they sat down, he said, "That was not my article."

"But it was your name," Scoth said as the server delivered three ales. Since the place only carried one kind, there was no need to ask what they wanted.

"And that's a damned *crime*, but that's how it has been these last years," Gordano spat once the server was gone. "Word comes down from on high about how they want the stories skewed, and if our articles don't come across skewed in just the right way, then up top rewrites them and publishes them with our names. I've had six articles mutilated beyond all recognition of what I'd written, and this is the second time something has been published under my name without any of my input whatsoever. South Press used to be a respectable publication. Now it's becoming as trashy as the Freetie. But no more. I've accepted an editorial position at the Cantercaster Bulletin. I'm a trusted name in journalism. I've been around a long time and written a lot of big pieces. I'm respected. But I won't be for much longer if it goes on this way, and I'm not going to stand to the side and watch my legacy be ruined."

Before Scoth or Jesco could inquire further, he burst, "I've always done society-related pieces for South Press. Not that society always is appreciative of what I write. Running charities that can't account for donations since the money's gone into their pockets, their overindulged, demonic children who get legacy bids at Nuiten and University of Archangels even though they can hardly read and are drunk from morning to night. Yes, they were very upset about that last piece, especially Lord and Lady Mascoll. Their five children are the bane of Ainscote."

He grinned evilly as he remembered the dust-up from that article, and cut off Scoth's question. "The paper changed ownership and it took a nastier turn. I could write what I pleased before, but it had to be accurate. Fact-checked. So we didn't get a fleet of solicitors pound-pound-pounding on the door with court dates in hand. Oh, yes, the Mascolls wanted to sue, they threatened fire and brimstone, but I had the police records on each of their children, I interviewed everyone connected to those cases and I had admissions officials from both schools talk to me anonymously about how the legacy applications of fire-breathing, ale-swilling, money-burning, dog-kicking brats are given a wink and nod. The universities get huge donations for accepting them. Lord Dollar who fails every test will beat Polly Pennypockets and her perfect grades every time. Not a single word of my piece was imaginative, if you follow me, and they had to live with it."

"You said it took a nastier turn-" Scoth said.

"Yes, yes, I'm getting to that. It used to be owned by the Armex family, but they sold it to the Tralonn Corporation. A good lot of the employees were let go; I weathered the turn and the desks filled up with new people. And then I started getting suggestions on what to write. Go after Mr. Pom Fanli, the superintendent of schools. Go after Lady Collia Rotham. The problem I had was that there wasn't much for stories there in the way the paper wanted. I chase real news. I write stories about matters that impact people's lives. What I *don't* do is give an angel's fart about a superintendent who wears women's undergarments beneath his suit, or a lady whose true parentage puts her title in question. That's the kind of news you'd find in the Freetie, scurrilous, scandalous, stupid, a waste of ink and paper."

"Were you ever told to go after Kyrad Naphates?" Scoth asked rapidly as the man paused to breathe. Jesco poured his ale into his own personal cup and sipped it.

"Of course I was!" Gordano roared, taking in Jesco's cup swap without interest or comment. "There's a whole list of people that we're supposed to go after any chance we get. I wanted to write a piece about her trying to get that liaison position just a month ago and my editor said not to bother since it wouldn't get published. Why not? It's newsworthy. Other journalists in other cities wrote about it, but not here where she lives. He said it wasn't of interest. But a man wearing silk drawers is? I can't fault a fellow for liking a bit of silk against his skin. The reason an article about her going for liaison was deemed not of interest was because it was positive. The paper's gone negative as can be, and especially on all those people it doesn't like. She's just one of a bunch and that article to come out days ago . . . I won't make nice about it. I saw *red*. I didn't write a single word of that article. I don't know where it came from. I haven't ever written an article about her. I actually refused two years ago when they asked me to do a little piece about her getting drunk and dancing on a table at a private party, and how it isn't dignified at her age and someone saw her brassiere when her dress slipped off her shoulder."

He slapped the table with great offense. The cups bounced. "*That isn't news*. Somebody else did it. And Kyrad Naphates herself wrote a letter to the editor saying there's no age limit for a woman to get drunk and dance on a table, and she's only sorry there weren't photographs of it because she has on good account since she can't remember it that she did a hot cha-cha." He waved away their questions to finish his story. "That didn't work out how the up top was hoping, I'd wager. She laughed, so all of Rosendrie laughed with her. The paper wanted to make her look like a fool, but she made the paper the fool for reporting on it. Of all the letters we got about that article, nine out of ten took her part and told the paper to get back to reporting real news."

He sighed gustily. "But that's what they've reduced me to: underwear stories. And that's why I'm going. If I wanted to write underwear stories, I would be at the Freetie."

"How does one get on this list of the hated?" Jesco asked.

"The Tralonn Corporation is headed by a board of rich old men who take a spite to certain people for various reasons. I don't sit in on their meetings and I don't know. But the superintendent was embroiled in a controversy about allocating more money to the poorer schools. It's been put off for years and those children sit in termite-ridden shacks while people dither about the budget. Fanli cut some things to fund it and all hell broke loose. The pampered, preening little princes and princesses at Ford could make do without the newest whirly-gigs in science class for a year while those schoolhouses went up. That was what got him on the list, I daresay, and Rotham was on it for fighting a gentlemen's business club to gain admission and winning. Naphates is probably on it for her style of mine practices and she made S. Pecost & Sons look like the greedy demon seeds they are in that great collapse a decade ago. Remember that?"

Jesco shook his head and the man said, "They had gotten what they wanted from the area and walked away before the bodies were even cold. She swept in with all of her charity agencies to bring food and start funds for the orphaned children, and to see if they could pull out the bodies. They couldn't, not more than a few nearer to the surface, but at least they tried and she paid for the funerals. Every last one. That meant the world to people. She's made good in life but they still see her as one of them. She *is* one of them. She did that same work long ago. She can pull up a chair right at their sides and share stories with them about relatives lost in collapses, downed by mine dropsy. She treats people like they're human beings, not cogs in a machine, and there was a huge backlash against S. Pecost & Sons. Every bit of kindness she showed to those miners and their families who weren't even her problem made stark how vicious and cold S. Pecost & Sons was being. They had to come back and make some recompense to save face, and there's still egg on it all these years later. South Press reported on that, back when the paper was reputable. It wasn't my story, but I remember it very well. Excuse me a minute." He got up and went to the lavatory.

"Well?" Jesco asked Scoth, who was scribbling in his pad of paper. "It doesn't sound like this is anything. Any one of her servants or escorts could have walked into that office, asked to speak to a journalist, and talked all about our visit. They would publish it without caring if it was the whole story, or even true."

"No," Scoth said as he wrote. "Why didn't that journalist publish it under his or her own name? Why use this man's instead? Someone who couldn't admit to it wrote this article, and slapped the name of a respected journalist atop it so people would give it more credibility." Underlining so fiercely that he almost punctured the paper, he looked troubled. "This may be nothing. But I'm curious about who is on the paper's board and the nature of the spite against her. I also want to know what man Tallo Quay was so desperately seeking."

"We don't know what play it was, or which theater, or even a firm time period."

"But we do know that this man worked for a mine, and in a significant position. He was significant enough as a person that his social engagement was printed in a newspaper. A regular fellow would not be of note."

Gordano returned to the table and resumed speaking without delay. "I'll tell you something that gets my goat about how the paper has changed. Go after a fellow for his underwear choices, but don't go after a fellow who skimmed money off the poor twenty-five years ago to build up the empire he has today. Celebrated as a man of the people when he used them up and spit them out, when he beats prosties, when he has a dozen children off a dozen women and refuses to acknowledge or support them . . . oh, no, don't look into him! There's a list of people we're supposed to go after and a list of people we aren't, most of them top drawer in business. I know for a fact that a member of the board is a friend of Self Bly and he's the biggest criminal on the wrong side of the bars in Ainscote. If I were to write a word about him, it would never see the light of day."

"Naphates aside, are there any mine owners or mine workers upon either of those lists?" Scoth asked.

"It's not a physical list but a mental one that you hit time and again when you try to write about people. I don't usually write about the mines, so I don't hit it. Davia Oard, she's hit that wall repeatedly in trying to write about Corey Wiffleman and his shambles of an operation that's got more citations than ore. But no, better to spend time smearing Naphates! It's a shame. She's a decent person, and there are scant few of those."

"Perhaps someone doesn't want her to get that liaison position," Jesco said.

"Who cares if she gets it?" Gordano said in exasperation. "In the end, it isn't going to make much difference. She broke the wall decades ago when she made her mines have standards. The other mine owners were mad at her then, mad that the government pressed harder and made them comply. It isn't going to hurt them to make a few small changes now. The big changes are long in the past. That cabal of old men is going to the grave as we speak, the mines passing on to their feckless, pompous, spoiled, soft-handed progeny that have servants wipe their arses and chew their food for them."

Scoth was out of questions, and they parted. The autohorse clopped faithfully away from the pub as Scoth said, "It did not seem prudent to mention to him that I grew up in a wealthy family."

"I didn't know there was any humor in you for years," Jesco said in amusement.

"I'm a riot," Scoth said flatly. "And I'm taking you to the asylum. I'm going to be in various Halls of Records doing legwork tomorrow and you can't help with that. If it all comes up dry, we'll resort to the doorknob."

Jesco was rather sorry to be returning to the asylum. This had been a most interesting trip, and if he was honest with himself, a most interesting companion. "Will you keep me up to date if you can?" he asked once the carriage was parked in the asylum's driveway and his belongings were unloaded. "I know I'm not truly your partner, but I'd really like to-"

"A fair sight better of a partner than Ravenhill's been," Scoth grunted. Calling to the autohorse, he swung the door shut and nodded to Jesco as the carriage pulled away.

Jesco's disappointment at a reprieve from the case could not be sustained for long. He was swarmed with shouting children upon his entry, smiles and greetings from the nurses and attendants, and Matron Beebee called over the hubbub that he'd received a letter from Isena and to stop at the nurses' station so someone could read it to him. Older othelin invited him to join a game of chess in the garden later on, and though this was a very odd family to have, it was Jesco's and he loved it.

His dirty clothes were borne away for special cleaning. Two of the children had tried to enter his room in his absence to play with his whirly-gigs. They'd been soundly scolded at the time, and scuffled their feet in embarrassment as a nurse gave them a second scolding in front of Jesco. "But we'd brought our winter gloves!" one protested when the indignity became too much. "We weren't going to touch them bare-handed. We know!"

So then Jesco took a few of the whirly-gigs to the drawing room and any child who wanted to could wear gloves and partake in a demonstration. Sfinx had a short thrall at one. It did not scare him but make him smile, and he said, "Sir! Sir! This one is going to be in a museum! Property of the late Mr. J. Currane, seer of the Cantercaster Police Force, it says on the card, and people are looking through the glass to marvel at it."

"But it's new!" someone exclaimed. "New whirly-gigs don't go in museums."

"But it's old then!" Sfinx said happily, coming back to the present. "One hundred and fifty years old and we'll all be dead, and people not even born today will be staring and gawking at it." Everyone swarmed around that particular whirly-gig, trying to peek into the future through it just as those future people in the boy's thrall were trying to peek into the past.

There was dinner to be had and a nurse read Jesco the letter from his sister. She and the children were well, and they were planning a trip for the end of summer to visit him. The hotel room had been booked for five days, just a quarter-mile from the asylum so they could pick him up every day and take him along on their sightseeing. Jesco could hardly hold back his smile. Included in the envelope were shorter letters from his nephews, and little Gemina had sent a picture she had drawn of two identical horses, one helpfully labeled an autohorse so that he could appreciate the difference.

He would go shopping in the meantime and buy all of them gifts. Taking the letters back to his room, he returned the star to the wall and readied for bed.

. . . she had been a very bad girl . . .

Of all the memories to haunt him, this one was quite benign. It just put him in mind of Collier, which was never a bad place to be. But when he went to sleep, he dreamed of Scoth. Scoth at home, stubble on his cheeks and his hair a mess, tools in his pockets and the tension of work subdued within him. Jesco sat in the chair in the upstairs workroom as Scoth fiddled about, people appearing in the skylight to peer in. Hasten Jibb with a bloody chest, a mother and daughter with ribbons in her hair . . . Jesco didn't mention them and Scoth didn't look up, and the dream went on in that fashion with Jesco vaguely aware that it *was* a dream.

The next morning passed in idleness, and in the afternoon, one of the rucaline patients died. The man's heart had given out. The very large family stormed in on waves of grief and fury, their shouts filling the corridors when they refused to be contained to the presiding doctor's office. At first they attacked the doctor and nurses for incompetence, and then their anger turned upon one another. It was Cousin Nammie's fault for giving him the rucaline and his mother's fault for not caring for him at home and his brother's fault for not taking him in when his mother couldn't do it anymore. They fought about what little inheritance the man was leaving behind, should it go to his mother or his siblings or his wife of two months at the time he overdosed. She was now raising his ten-year-old daughter that he had never met, and she was the only one of the lot with any common sense. No one could speak without screaming and the child was getting upset, so the mother ushered her out the front doors and did not return.

The rest of them fought about what should be done with the body, burial or cremation, where and when, and on and on it went in chaos for the better part of two hours until the attendants threw them out. Peace was restored to the asylum, though the nurses grumbled at one another that Doctor Haskins was too soft and should have expelled them much sooner. Then Nelle toddled over to Jesco, who was sitting upon a sofa in the drawing room. She was crowing about her toy and clambered up beside him, and pressed it to his cheek when she lost her balance.

He hadn't had time to move, and suddenly was in thrall. Someone yelled, "No, no, no!" and yanked the girl with her toy away. She burst into shrieks and the collar zapped her.

"Be glad to put this day to bed, all of us," a nurse said with a tired shake of her head as she brought the wheelchair to the sofa. Jesco's strength was returning already. It had been a fairly new toy and the touch brief. But he did not trust himself to walk, and let the nurse steer him to the dining hall.

"Her shoes are starting to pinch her feet," he said from being Nelle temporarily.

The nurse had known him for a long time, and took his word for it. "I'll pass it along. What I wouldn't have given to have you around when my children were small and couldn't explain to me why they were fussing!"

They said a prayer for the deceased man that he might find a home among the angels, and dinner was served. The children ate quickly and fled the room, since an attendant had promised to show them a magic trick if they bathed and dressed for bed without delay or complaint. The adults filtered out in twos and threes, and Jesco had just finished a refill of his soup bowl when Scoth appeared in the doorway. His eyes went over the patients and stopped upon Jesco, and then he strode in, snagged an empty chair, and plunked it down on the other side of Jesco's private table.

"Why are you in the wheelchair? What did you bloody well do to yourself this time?" he snapped in disapproval.

"It was an accident, and a small one," Jesco said. "A child touched me with her toy. She only wanted to show it to me. What brings you here?"

"I was coming back from the Hall of Records on Cornice Street and it takes me right past the asylum."

"Sure, right past it if one goes completely out of the way."

Scoth's lip quirked. "You know what I named the destination card for the asylum? Prick Pick-up. Now be quiet and listen to this. I looked up a lot of things today, starting with the Tralonn Corporation. It's a wealth management branch of a bank, handles billions of dollars in client assets. It seems that the Rosendrie South Press wasn't doing well financially, which was why the Armex family put up a part of it for sale. Tralonn owns half of it and took over the daily operations; the family owns the other half and stepped back."

"The paper became the mouthpiece of a bank, or a division of it."

"There are twenty-five members on the board. Eight of them have ties in some way to Ainscote mines. The ones that interested me most are two men named Ivan Camso and Torrus Kodolli. Merlie couldn't remember the name, but all of her attempts had similarities. Camso's father-in-law owns Shayner Gems, an operation at the southernmost tip of Ainscote. Now, Kyrad Naphates' mines do precious little in way of gems. Oil shale, limestone, rock salt, potash for fertilizers, those are the larger chunk of her gigs and they're spread out all over this country and abroad."

"They aren't competitors," Jesco said.

"No, they aren't. Then I looked into Kodolli and things got more interesting. He's got competing interests in his company named Agrea, and Agrea makes S. Pecost & Sons look like sweethearts who care. Half the mining deaths in the last one hundred years were in Agrea-owned mines. Fought or flat-out ignored every regulation in all that time, and only conceded reluctantly when the government started to fine Agrea outrageous amounts. That was after Naphates changed her mines. It was a domino effect, really, what she started. She increased the wages, made it safer, recognized the union, let government officials inspect, and all of that. Miners at other companies began to agitate for the same treatment, walking off the job and costing the owners money. I can see why the heads of the industry would have a grudge against her. They were doing things exactly how they pleased and one of their own betrayed them. Old Cluven Naphates let the fox into the henhouse when he married a former miner, and I mean it as a compliment to the fox."

Gavon stopped at the table with a bowl of ice cream and Scoth interrupted himself to scold, "You can't give that to him! You're touching it with your bare hands!"

"It's all right," Jesco said. "For some reason, Gavon doesn't impart memories to my belongings. Gavon, could I have a second bowl for the detective here?"

"Oh, sure," Gavon said placidly. Even the stern homicide detective was five years old in his head, and he asked, "Do you like chocolate or vanilla?"

"I don't need-" Scoth started.

"I'll get you a scoop of both and you can decide."

"I don't need-" Scoth repeated helplessly to Gavon's retreating back.

"When's the last time you ate?" Jesco asked. "Oh, that's right, you haven't yet today. You've been working, and hunger is for the common man."

"I had something at breakfast," Scoth grumbled.

The attendant returned with a bowl and spoon, which he handed to Scoth. "Now, mind you, don't touch Jesco's table. He's a seer."

"I am," Jesco confessed.

"Ruddy insane, the whole lot of you," Scoth mumbled, and pushed a heaping spoonful of chocolate into his mouth.

"Did you learn anything else today?" Jesco asked.

"I'm getting to it," Scoth said, swallowing ravenously on a second spoonful. "Kodolli is a very old man with homes and business offices all over Ainscote. He also maintains a home and office in the Sarasasta Islands."

"Is he of such influence that a newspaper would mention him attending a Cantercaster play?"

"Don't skip ahead. He married his wife Cliya Burne when they were in their thirties. Burne is a well-known acting family in the theater world.

She acted herself when young, never top-bill but she didn't have any trouble getting cast in smaller roles. Whether that was talent or her family name, I can't say. She retired upon her marriage and bore two sons, Morgan and Flike, and one daughter Sherra. Flike fell off a cliff at a party and killed himself at fifteen."

"How did he manage to do that?"

"Bunch of young fools being daredevils and it cost him his life. So that was the end of Flike Kodolli. Sherra took her mother's maiden name of Burne when she became an adult and is still acting today under it. She's married to another actor, no children, and her company tours in northern Ainscote."

"And Morgan?"

"Morgan Kodolli is a vice-president of Agrea. Married and with two children, both of who are now in their twenties. It makes sense that this family would be mentioned in the papers for attending performances. I looked into their charitable contributions and there are several playhouses that benefit from them. Then I pulled up the papers in the cities where they're located and yes, the Kodolli name comes up here and there, especially on Benefactors' Nights, where a special dinner and performance is thrown in honor of the people who donate large amounts of money. Torrus Kodolli attends often. Not every one, of course, since he's constantly traveling between his offices. It's not evidence of anything, but it's reasonable to assume this could be the man that Tallo Quay was chasing." Scoth dribbled the melted drops at the bottom of the bowl onto his spoon to consume those as well.

"Kodolli could be very bitter at Kyrad Naphates still," Jesco said, stringing it together as he spoke. "And Tallo Quay could have known that from living in her home as an escort. He could have heard her talking about Kodolli, and other mine owners who were angry with her for how the industry changed. And when she angered Tallo, he went snooping and found out who in Parliament was secretly helping her business along. Would that information be valuable to Kodolli?"

"They get voted in," Scoth said. "Know your enemies and then pull every dirty political trick you can to get them voted out. Or simply go to the press and accuse them of slipping her favors on the sly. Ruin reputations, start investigations . . . yes, I can see how Quay would think he was holding the jackpot in those names. And what did he want for himself? He wanted an acting career. Ivan Camso has no connection to the theater, but Kodolli! Who better to approach than Torrus Kodolli, married to a former actress, the father of a current actress, and with a possible grudge against Naphates? Sadly for Quay, Kodolli is a very hard man to track down."

"Did you look up what play it could be?"

"I searched for tragedies that don't get put on very often. I wish Merlie Jonkins could have been more specific. But I did find, at Luthen Playhouse, a run of Scarred Crest. That fits the bill, if you pardon the pun. It's a famous play, but it's run only twice in the last ten years. It was playing in autumn three years ago. Merlie said Quay took his coat and gloves because it was getting cold. I thought she meant the showing was at night, but perhaps she meant the time of year. It was mentioned in the Cantercaster-Oftow News that Torrus Kodolli would be attending the Benefactors' Night. There was a long list of benefactors printed on the back page of the community section. His wife wasn't mentioned, but I learned from another source that she is an invalid. Her health is poor, and she stays in their island home. The warmth does her well."

The dining hall had cleared out considerably while they talked. Only two women were left at a far table, one casting admiring glances to Scoth. "Do you know where Torrus Kodolli is now?" Jesco asked.

"I do, in fact. He's in Somentra currently, up in the hills miles away where he rents space in Cable Holding. We'll be going to his office tomorrow, unless you have somewhere else to be."

"Still, nothing in this connects to Hasten Jibb. Anyone could have lost a timepiece there. We're only assuming it has something to do with the body."

"What are the odds that not one but two people went down that alley in Poisoners' Lane, and at roughly the same time?"

"Does Torrus Kodolli own a home in Melekei? Or anywhere on the route that Jibb would have taken that day to get home?"

Deflating a little, Scoth said, "No. But this is the only lead we have. The only other piece that's new to this is what a courier saw on the road Jibb was taking home."

"You didn't tell me about that."

"I had flyers put up around Melekei and in the streets around his home, asking the public for information. A response came in just this morning. I stopped at the station before I went to research and found a letter on my desk. A courier from another company, Stanley Moss of Post on Wings, claims that he saw Hasten Jibb in late afternoon picking up his bicycle off the side of the road in that stretch of farm country outside Melekei. He slowed and asked if Jibb was all right, and Jibb said that he'd hit a rock going too fast on his way to Chussup and went flying. But the bicycle was undamaged, and Jibb wasn't hurt. Landed in tall, thick grass and that cushioned it. Moss rode on and left him behind, picking up the packages that had fallen out of his satchel." Scoth shrugged. "Nothing queer about that, and there wasn't even a bruise from it on Jibb's body the next day. Moss said there's a sharp, pebbly turn there that he's taken too fast himself, and nothing was amiss about the scene, so he'd forgotten all about it until he saw the flyer. Maybe Jibb was embarrassed about the fall, so he wasn't in good spirits when he got home."

"But what were the packages?" Jesco wondered. "He had already taken the whirly-gigs to that old woman and that was his last delivery of the day."

Scoth's mouth flapped wordlessly. As a kitchen worker came out to wipe down the tables, Gavon returned and said, "Do you want a roll to your room?"

"I'll roll him!" Scoth said almost in a yell, ripping the pad of paper from his pocket and flipping through the pages rapidly. "Why the *hell* did Jibb have packages at that point? He had taken the lord's jewels to the bank hours before and Mrs. Cussling didn't mention giving him anything to deliver." He came to the page where he had copied down the letter from the courier. "'He was unharmed, not even a tear to his trousers at the knees, from landing in that river grass. There's no river there but the grass grows thick and soft as a pillow.'"

"Because they have to clean the tables now," Gavon said obliviously.

"'I left him collecting the little packages that had fallen out of his satchel and rode on,'" Scoth concluded. Stuffing the pad away, he stood up and came around the table for Jesco's chair. At the last moment he remembered his hands, and swiped two napkins from another table to cover them. He pulled Jesco away and rolled him to the doorway.

"He was doing courier work on the side," Jesco guessed, motioning to the hallway that led to his room. "Wassel said something about that. The company doesn't approve of its couriers taking side jobs, but it's hard to prevent. Jibb must have picked up those packages somewhere in his day."

Scoth opened the door to his room and pushed him inside. Standing with care, Jesco used the desk and chair for support and made his way to the bed. He sat down and pulled up his legs one after another. Scoth rolled the chair to the wall and parked it there, saying, "You would have made a fine detective."

"Thank you," Jesco said.

"Are these all yours?" Scoth asked about the whirly-gigs.

"Yes. I love to collect them."

Scoth bent down to take a look at one. "A sunner? I've never seen one of these up close. Is this the kind that gives you a dose of sunlight on cloudy days or winter months?" Jesco nodded. He didn't fall into a slump with the reduced winter light like others did, but it had been enjoyable to take apart. Keeping his hands covered with the napkins, Scoth picked it up to inspect it. He bumped the controls on the side and the golden disc grew brighter.

"Just leave it," Jesco said when the detective tried to turn it off. "It'll go off on its own."

Scoth set down the sunner, which was filling the room with an intense golden light. "There's an annual whirly-gig convention over in Sprogue. Have you ever been to it?"

"No. I've never even heard about it."

"Companies bring out their newest. So do individual inventors, most hoping to get picked up by a big funder. There are marvels, there's junk, and everything in between. Contests and demonstrations and little tent shops, too. It takes place at the end of next month and lasts for a weekend. I was just about to send away for my ticket of admission."

"That sounds like wonderful fun."

"If I can get away, that is."

"You can't work all the time, Scoth. They walk with you, that's true, but they can wait for a weekend to let you rest and recuperate."

Scoth was looking directly into the sunner. The light radiated upon his handsome face and illuminated paler strands in his dark hair. Though it was not winter, something in the blaze was relaxing the detective, and he did not look away from it. "These cases," he said ruefully. "These are the ones that get to me the most. People like Hasten Jibb. No one cared much when they were alive. No one cares much now that they're dead. Someone should care. Someone should give them a little respect by finding out what happened. I'm the last stop for someone to care, and I'm just a stranger. If the captain had his way, Hasten Jibb would vanish into the cold files and no one would spare him another thought. When the captain's got relatives weeping and wailing in his office, then the victim is important because other people deemed him so. But if the victim didn't count to anyone, then he doesn't count to Whennoth either."

Scoth closed his eyes but kept his face turned to the sunner, letting the light beat through his lids. "It wasn't a brother or cousin but a friend," he said. "Back when we were boys. He was part of a frivolity circuit that went up and down the Razille in boats. They rarely went back to Lotaire. We got to be friends, he and I. They always stopped in Korval where there are fairgrounds. One of those people that you could not see for almost a year, and then pick up exactly where you left off. He was murdered when we were ten. And they never caught who did it. They never wrote to an asylum or a proper police station to see if they had a seer around. He was just another dark-haired Asqui brat on the circuit, and it was sad but . . ." He shrugged to show the lack of interest in pursuing the case.

"But he was much more than that to you," Jesco said.

After a long, drawn-out breath within the beam of the sunner, Scoth said, "We just got on well, the two of us. Such good friends that we could finish each other's sentences. His parents were dead, and he'd been taken in by the gamma. Usually circuits have a gamma or a gappa, an older person who minds the orphans. The gamma had eight or nine children to look after, too many to pay much attention to any one in particular. He had me, his summer buddy that he went swimming and fishing with, and I'd say I was the only one broken up about his murder. So sometimes it's hard for me to see you do your work. Not you in a personal way, but any seer, that's how I mean it. You could have given him some respect after he died, but none of you were there. No one sent for you. He didn't count for enough. He wasn't a businessman, or someone who lived in a big city where a seer is right at hand. He just vanished in pretty much every mind but mine."

"What was his name?" Jesco asked.

The intensity of the light was fading, and Scoth glanced at him. "You would be the only one to ask that in the few times I've told the story. His name was Ramono, but he went by Ono. The Asqui word for zero. Even his name showed how he counted for nothing."

"There were no leads on his case? Nothing at all?"

"I was supposed to meet up with him that day, but my mother had kept me behind for shirking my chores. I couldn't leave until I finished them. A woman who'd gone to fish found Ono at the riverside, his upper body pushed into the water. It looked like he'd gotten into a fight, and someone held him under until he drowned. Towns like Korval don't have official police like they do here. I've told you that. It's just a bunch of privileged fools who like to wave clubs and homemade badges around to feel important. No witnesses, no motive, no interest, so no case. Now that I'm older, I have a better idea of what happened. There are different kinds of frivolity circuits. Some are a carnival of wonder, gymnasts flying through the air, wild animals jumping through burning hoops, and some are a carnival of contests. That was the kind Ono was on. Testing strength, speed, smarts, agility, luck, talents at singing and spelling and such. And some are racier. Do you know about those?"

"I've heard about them in passing."

"They're banned in most places. Sexual feats, orgies, there aren't too many of those types of frivolity circuits and they're smaller than the other kinds. But some people think every circuit is that sort, and that every Asqui there is going to entertain that way. All of them carry knives as a precaution, even the children. You might go the length of a carnival and never get propositioned, but you'll never go the length of your life in a frivolity circuit and never have it happen to you. Ono was bothered for the first time when he was eight."

"That's terrible."

"It's disgusting, that's what it is. I can't stand when we've got someone in a cell at the station with those proclivities. Usually men, occasionally a woman, all of them waiting for trial and thinking it's just fine and dandy to have an attraction to a child. Ono got propositioned at eight, and the summer he was ten, he'd had it happen by two men at different times. I remember him telling me about it. They were asking him how much for his body, showing coins and promising more, and getting mad when he said no. The first man was seventeen, which seemed quite old to two ten-year-old boys, and Ono said that his head was misshapen and he reeked. Some fellow out of the backwoods who had come to the carnival, that one, and he was going after all the boys and girls until a pair of Asqui men got him by the arms and threw him out of the fairgrounds. He sneaked back in days later, scooped up a little Asqui girl playing with her wooden animals, and tried to take her away. She was three years old."

"Angels save us," Jesco said, revolted.

"She screamed like the dickens in his arms and her grandmother, her mother, her aunts, and her older sisters came running. All of the women in that family worked the Ladies' Strong-Arm contest, and Ono and I laughed and laughed about that. Nothing but muscle, the whole lot of them. They beat him bloody, dragged him out of the fairgrounds, and told him never to come back or they'd kill him. And I believe they would have. So he was the first man that summer going after Asqui children, and the second was a man we called The Marble for his shape. He was old enough to be balding and he took a real shine to Ono. Offering flowers like they were beaux, dice and toys, he came every day to the carnival with a new gift and pleaded with Ono to take a carriage ride with him, have a picnic somewhere. He was getting pushy, and frustrated when Ono kept saying no. Ono had taken to hiding from him."

"You suspect that one of those two men followed him to the river on the day he died," Jesco said.

"All Asqui children are taught to hold their own. I think there's a fair chance that that's what happened. A man followed him over there, Ono said no again, and they fought. But he was a child against a grown man, and he died in that fight. All a seer would have had to do was touch his clothing to know. But there was no seer, or anyone with the sense to save Ono's clothing and write for one. There was just the mayor as the chief of police and his friends' adult children for officers, and they let a murderer slip through their fingers since the person he killed was insignificant. Maybe . . . I always thought that maybe if I'd just done those chores when I was supposed to, I would have been there. One to one, Ono didn't stand a chance. One to two, however . . . it might have ended differently."

"It might have ended in both of you dying," Jesco said as the sunner dimmed and turned off.

Scoth did not debate that with him. They had seen enough, both of them and in different ways, to know that that possibility was true. Bending down to the whirly-gigs, Scoth checked the weather-catcher. He said off-handedly, "I could get two tickets."

"Two tickets?" Jesco repeated, lost in the change of subject.

"To the convention. If you'd have any interest."

Astounded, Jesco tried to keep his voice even and equally off-handed. No man had ever asked him anywhere. "I might like that."

"You'll have to bring your sheets and spoons and things for the stay."

Jesco gave up on his efforts at nonchalance and smiled, feeling as radiant as the light from the sunner. "I can do that."

"And don't touch anything without your gloves on!" Scoth growled at him. "There's going to be a side-hall on the second day for Science's Greatest Failures. I want to see that one. I might enter my shoulder shooter in it sometime. And, just so you're on alert, there are always protestors outside from the Church dressed up like angels to hand out tracts against science and call everybody demons for going in. They throw things now and then, eggs mostly, and last year it was their haloes."

"I'm inured to being called a demon," Jesco said. "It's happened too many times before."

A perturbed expression came over Scoth's face, and he barked, "I'll see you tomorrow." He walked out the door and closed it behind him, leaving Jesco in a state of surprise and happiness upon his bed.

# Chapter Nine

The city of Somentra was tucked away out of sight in the quiet green hills to the west. There was a lot of traffic on the main road from Cantercaster, and it only grew worse when they reached the foot of the hills. Scoth rerouted the autohorse to another road that wound through the trees. It was narrow and unpaved, at times running alongside deep slopes that ran down to a riverbed that was nearly dry. The river itself had been redirected. Now only trickles of water slipped between the rocks in the bed's lowest point. Bright yellow birds splashed in the little puddles far below the road.

With the fall of industry in Wattling, some of it had moved to Somentra. Plumes of smoke rose into the air from the factories, dissipating in the wind. Those plumes were all the evidence of civilization that Jesco had until the road suddenly emerged from its green cover. Down in a valley was a sprawling city. The factories formed a necklace around the many lines of homes and shops, and the air was hazy from the swells of smoke. Chemical scents seeped into the carriage.

"I would not want to live here," Jesco said.

"Nor I," Scoth said. It had been a friendly ride between them, although most of what they spoke about was the case. "They don't ever stop. Three shifts a day, each eight hours long. The factory doors never close and they breathe that smoke night and day."

Cable Holding was a business center at the very heart of the city. It had two wings connected by a second floor walkway suspended over a garden and fountain. Carriages swung by the curb to release well-dressed men and women, all of them carrying briefcases and making beelines to the doors at either wing. A trolley full of window washers with brushes and buckets lifted into the air on one side, and when it reached the second floor, they got to work with swift, even strokes.

The directory guided them to the right wing and up a flight of stairs to a closed door labeled AGREA. Flowers in vases were everywhere, their sweet scents warring with the pungent chemical odors. Entering the office, they stopped at the secretary where Scoth requested an audience with Torrus Kodolli. The flabbergasted woman went through a door behind her desk and soon returned, saying coldly, "You must make an appointment. He has an opening next week."

"That will not do," Scoth said, keeping his badge out. "He can meet with us now, or I can involve a judge."

She went away again and was gone for fifteen minutes. Then she beckoned them through to a hallway. They walked past many offices with people hard at work inside. A courier burst from one office and almost ran into them, his satchel overflowing with ledgers and letters. Spinning aside at the last second, he raced away.

When they passed the office that was marked T. Kodolli, President, Scoth said, "Where are you taking us?"

"Mr. Kodolli will be meeting you in the conference room," the secretary said frostily.

That was the last room in the long hallway. It was wood-paneled, and three-quarters of it taken up by a massive oak table. Maroon drapes had been drawn back and tied with heavy bows, but sheer curtains still obscured the view of the street. The sunlight filtered in red through them. Although there were no flowers, the air was heavy with the scent of perfume.

There was not one man in the room but four. The oldest had to be Torrus Kodolli himself. Seated at the table and a jeweled cane beside him, he stared at Scoth and Jesco with affront. Age had wizened him. His suit was slightly too big on his frail frame but elegantly cut. Gems glittered within rings on two of his fingers.

Beside him was a starched and pressed fellow with thick spectacles, and the last two men were much younger, extremely muscled, and standing in the corners of the room. Their faces were expressionless, but their eyes were trained upon Scoth and Jesco. Then a fifth man with a graying comb-over entered the room and pushed past them to join Kodolli on the far side of the table. "Will this take long?" the new arrival asked querulously. "I've got to drive out to Carrin." Something about his tone made Jesco think that the man had only said it to show off how important he was.

"Now, now, Morgan," the old man chided. The younger man was his son. "Apparently, these detectives here have something very serious to question us about." His tone was polite but mocking.

"I am Torrus Kodolli's solicitor, Aveth Eemes," said the man with thick glasses. The two in the corners were bodyguards, Jesco presumed. Kodolli was a very rich man, and required protection. The name Eemes had been on the directory, explaining how the solicitor had arrived so quickly to sit in upon the interview.

Scoth dispensed with the pleasantries and pushed the photograph of Hasten Jibb across the table. "Do you recognize this man?"

Lifting a little from his chair to reach it, Torrus Kodolli gave it a casual glance. "No."

"He was found murdered in Poisoners' Lane roughly two weeks ago," Scoth said. "Have you been in Somentra long?"

"My client does not have to answer that question-" the lawyer started.

Kodolli waved him off and smiled meanly. "I'm sorry to disappoint, Detective, but I've only just arrived in Somentra five days ago. I have spent the last month south in Fyllyn, as an entire office of employees and my home staff can attest, as well as various friends, shopkeepers, and acquaintances. But why would you think that I had information about this murder?"

"Have you ever met a man named Tallo Quay?" Scoth asked.

"I asked you a question," Kodolli said with another mean smile.

"And I am the one investigating this case," Scoth responded. "Have you ever met a man named Tallo Quay?"

"I can't recall. Do you have a photograph?"

"I have a picture." Scoth pushed that across the table and Kodolli took it. The bodyguards watched, their eyes all that moved. The solicitor was stiff in his seat; the son looked at the picture with a furrowed brow. It was hard to see Torrus and Morgan as father and son: Torrus had sharp features and gleaming eyes while Morgan's face had all the definition of a bowl of pudding.

Torrus Kodolli turned the picture from side to side like he was taking it very seriously, and then he laid it down. "He doesn't stand out."

"You're saying that you don't know him," Scoth said.

"I didn't say that. I employ thousands of people. Is he one of them?"

"He spent two years trying to get in contact with you, and finally made your acquaintance at Luthen Playhouse. It was a showing of Scarred Crest." It was a bluff since they had no proof of the two men meeting there.

However, it appeared to work. The older Kodolli took another glance at the picture as the solicitor repeated that he didn't have to answer.

Again, his advice was dismissed. "Do you know how many people want to speak to me, Detective . . . Scoth, is it?" Kodolli mispronounced it, and probably on purpose. "I run a large company, a very large company. Journalists always want a word. Societies chase after me for donations. Members of Parliament plead with me to fund their reelection campaigns and give them endorsements. Total strangers approach me for jobs and favors; those idiot protestors hike their union signs in the air and picket outside my mines and a few of my homes and offices. Maybe this man did approach me at the intermission, come to think of it."

"What did he want of you?" Scoth asked.

"He said he had something of value to me. How many times have we heard that?" The old man looked at his son, who snorted with derision. His comb-over wafted in the breeze of the movement. "Just some gossip, it turned out."

"Which was?"

"I never got the specifics. He was playing cagey, and I didn't care enough to prize it from him. It was late. I'm an old man who wanted to enjoy my show, and go home to my bed and hot water bottle. I told him to go off and he did. I never saw him again."

Tallo Quay had dedicated years of his life to chasing down this man; Jesco could not believe that being told to leave would have succeeded in dissuading him so easily. Scoth said, "Do you know Mrs. Kyrad Naphates?"

Kodolli's lips puckered like he was sucking upon a lemon. "I have had the misfortune of meeting that jewel-swathed strumpet."

"Your relationship isn't a pleasant one."

"Relationship? Hardly a relationship. We met at her wedding very long ago and have seen each other sporadically at social events since then."

"Were you friendly with her late husband?"

"He was a business competitor, but we were pleasant. I would have absorbed his company into mine had he sold it, as he should have. He had no heirs, nor would he name some vice-president of the company his successor. He refused to consider that one day he might die."

Kodolli laughed. It was as dry a sound as sandpaper, and like his smile, full of mockery. "That was why he took such a young wife, young enough to be his great-granddaughter, to make him feel young as well. And it was why he did not have his papers in order so it all went to her upon his inevitable demise. *Weeks* after the wedding and that filthy trollop from a penny-pinching family became the head of a multi-million dollar business when she could barely read and still spoke in miners' brogue. I was embarrassed for old Cluven at the wedding, since he did not have the sense to be embarrassed for himself." Kodolli shook his head, his lips still pursed. "I'm afraid, gentlemen, that I fail to see any connection between a dead man, a man who interrupted my dessert at the intermission years ago, and myself. Would you care to enlighten me, or will you continue to waste my time?"

"Did Tallo Quay give you anything?" Scoth asked.

"Give me anything? I told you: he wished to give me information, and I did not wish to receive it. That happens from time to time, people thinking that I'm going to be fascinated to learn the peccadilloes of my competitors and that I'll line their palms to hear everything. From what I recall, his information had something to do with Naphates. I didn't want it. I didn't need it. I try to do as little dealings with her as possible. These companies are our legacies from our parents, and we pass them down to our children or loyal staff favorites should there be none. Cluven's blindness and denial led to his company going to a veritable stranger. Someone who did not understand how business is run, who feels no loyalty to our circle, who did nothing but lift her skirts to get where she is today!" The old man's voice was rising in fury. "What was this man going to tell me about her? That she was covertly helping my miners to unionize? That she sleeps around when rich ground is discovered to make sure it's sold to her, or plies a man or woman with escorts should her body not be to the seller's liking? I know what that whore of a woman does and I want no part of it! She's cost me hundreds of thousands of dollars since Cluven died with her shenanigans! Perhaps it's in the millions now; I would not be surprised!"

"It's all right, Father," Morgan Kodolli said.

"Be *quiet*, boy!" his father roared like his son was five years old and not five plus fifty. Morgan fell into a meek silence. "If you have nothing else, detectives-"

The solicitor gasped. He was looking straight at Jesco, and cried out, "This isn't a detective but a seer! That's why he is wearing those gloves. You do not have permission to touch anything in this room, or in the entirety of this office! This is an invasion of privacy!"

"A seer!" Already irate when the topic was Naphates, Torrus Kodolli came utterly unglued to realize a seer was in the conference room. He snatched his hands off the table, taking the photograph of Hasten Jibb and the drawing of Tallo Quay with him. Thrusting them at the solicitor, he shouted, "Have these destroyed! You! You!" He had turned to his bodyguards. "Get them out of this office! If they resist, call more guards to help!" The pair of men stepped menacingly from their corners and started around the table.

"Put your hands on either of us and I will see all of you arrested!" Scoth bellowed. "We will see ourselves out, and return if we have more questions."

The guards followed them out of the building, and all the way to the carriage. As Scoth and Jesco entered it, the two heavily muscled men retreated to stand at the doors of the wing. Jesco took his seat and said, "That went well."

"They were afraid of you," Scoth said. "Terrified. Involved in Jibb's case or not, there are memories in that room that they don't want you to pick up upon."

"What did you think?"

Scoth directed the autohorse to take them to the nearest place that sold food and sat back as the carriage began to move. "If that old man killed Jibb for whatever reason, he can't be the one to have put him in that alley. Torrus Kodolli couldn't lift a sack of wet sand, let alone the body of a grown man."

"The bodyguards could have done it."

"But what we're still missing is *why*. And if Kodolli was telling the truth about where he was, all the way in Fyllyn, and when, then he couldn't have killed Jibb. Fyllyn is hundreds of miles to the southwest."

They stopped at a busy restaurant, Jesco pulling out his own utensils to eat and Scoth wolfing down two entire meals. It was difficult to talk with the racket all around them, and it took so long for the check to arrive that Scoth estimated the cost and put the money on the table. Evening had fallen outside and they wanted to return to Cantercaster. But the main road was even more throttled with traffic than before, so Scoth sent the autohorse back to the quieter route through the trees.

"My gut says he didn't do it," Scoth said. "I'm sure he's responsible for horrible things, I *know* he's responsible for horrible things from looking at his company's history, and that's why he panicked to find out what you are. But this one . . . I don't think Jibb's murder is his. I'll still contact the people at Fyllyn and see if I can get confirmation that he was there."

"I don't believe him," Jesco said. "The part where he said that he told Quay to go away and Quay did."

"No, I didn't believe that either. Tallo Quay was too obsessed."

"But Quay just falls off the map at that point. He didn't go back to Merlie, or to his father's house. Where did he go? He didn't like to be an escort, so would he return to it? He had only what money he'd gotten from Merlie, and I doubt it was much. Did he pawn the timepiece then, since it wasn't of any use to him? Was it stolen from him? The case was opened somewhere, a finger tapping on it, and above was a chandelier."

"If it was in a pawnshop, you would have seen people taking it out of the case for a look-see," Scoth said thoughtfully. "Stolen and you would have seen someone grabbing it, wearing it or giving it away. But you didn't see anything of the sort. It went from Merlie's room to the room with the chandelier, and then it was in someone's pocket at the crime scene."

This case was becoming a headache to Jesco. "Say Quay gave Torrus Kodolli the timepiece to prove the veracity of his information. Now Kodolli has it, but what does he do with it? Even if he were young and hale enough to drag that body into the alley, why in the world would he be wearing her timepiece? He loathes her. That was plain to see. If I happened to have a timepiece of a person I disliked that much, I wouldn't be putting it on. I'd get rid of it. And did you see the jewels on his cane? His rings? That timepiece is too modest for his taste."

"He could have given it to one of his bodyguards. Then it got dragged from the fellow's pocket when dumping Jibb's corpse. Yet if it's true that he was in Fyllyn . . ." Scoth rubbed at his eyes. "We should go back to Ragano & Wemill, take a look at more of the jobs that Jibb worked."

"To see if there's a connection to Kodolli?"

"I don't know what else to do at this point." Scoth frowned and looked out the back window. The carriage had just gone around a curve of a hill, and all that showed were green leaves shaking in the wind beneath a purple sky.

"What is it?" Jesco asked.

"I thought I heard-"

"Yah! Yah!" Six hooded men on horseback charged around the curve. They pulled to the side of the road to go around the carriage. But when the first of them drew level with the autohorse, he slowed and moved in, making Horse go closer to the edge. There was a long drop off it. The others bunched up behind him and ran alongside the carriage, shouting wordlessly in male voices.

"They're going to force us off the road!" Jesco exclaimed. Kodolli had been more than upset about their interview; he was trying to kill them to stop the investigation!

Scoth ripped open a side panel and jammed a button, crying, "Faster!" The autohorse picked up speed, outpacing the real horses, and the men kicked them to catch up. Reaching up to the ceiling of the carriage, Scoth dug his finger into a gap and pulled. The entire panel up there came down and he shoved it under their feet. Packed onto every inch of the ceiling was intricate machinery, which began to spin and click as Scoth flipped switches, tugged latches, and shouted instructions. "Glass, dim! Horse, combat!"

A man cried out as he lost sight of Jesco and Scoth within the carriage. Jesco turned to the horse. Its skin was separating along its seams, and scaled sheets of gray were coming out to wrap the body. They connected everywhere but in a circle in the mid-back. The long barrel of a shooter rose from the circle and pivoted upon a metal arm. Scoth yelled, "Fire!"

The projectile struck none of the riders, but the tremendous blast of it spooked the horses. They screamed and jerked away from the carriage, the riders shouting as they jerked on the reins. One panicked horse bolted into the trees but found the grade there too steep to mount. It fell, throwing the rider off. As the horse staggered upright, it stepped upon the rider's abdomen. He shrieked with pain.

The mounted riders caught back up with the carriage. Taking clubs from their belts, they beat at the windows. The glass did not shatter and the metal arm of the shooter pivoted to them. Scoth shouted, "Fire!" This time, a projectile struck home in a man's upper arm. He cried out and fell back, another man riding up and bashing at the shooter with his club. Just as Scoth yelled to fire again, the blow of the club broke a piece of the metal arm propping up the shooter and allowing it to pivot. The blast went wild and the shooter slumped down to bounce along the autohorse's scaled back.

The carriage was hurtling toward a curve. A blade appeared and a rider pulled alongside the autohorse to slash at the traces. Scoth grabbed Jesco roughly and forced him hard into his seat, shouting, "Brace the front seat!"

There was little for Jesco to hold onto, but Scoth had not been speaking to him. Wooden struts snapped out from the space between the top of the seat and the window. Clicking, they curled rapidly down Jesco's shoulders as another strut went around his upper legs, pinning him.

The carriage fishtailed as it broke free of the autohorse and threw Scoth. Scrabbling for purchase, he crawled away and heaved himself into the seat. "Brace the back seat!"

Then they were airborne. The world tumbled outside the windows, the deepening purple of the sky becoming the trees shaking in the wind and with another half-revolution it was back to the sky. The carriage struck the rocky hillside with a crack, caught air from the impact and cracked down again. Spinning and cracking and spinning . . .

The wheelchair was being thrown all around the inside of the carriage, into the ceiling, into the walls, and into them upon the seats. There was nothing they could do to hold it steady. Jesco was holding the struts around his shoulders in a death-grip; Scoth was doing the same.

The lower band had failed to activate over him. His legs were jouncing with each blow onto the rocks.

Everything was happening much too fast, yet every second of it lasted an eternity. They were going to plummet to the center of the world, Jesco thought, and then in another spin, he saw the dry riverbed. The carriage revolved and hit it with an enormous blast.

They were upside-down, the wheelchair landing upon the ceiling. Then the carriage overturned one more time and skidded. Striking Jesco's leg as it rolled past, the wheelchair hit the window and fell onto its side. Finally, everything went still.

"Don't move," Scoth whispered. Jesco let his head slump to the side and closed his eyes to slits. The door was now above him, and attached to the carriage only by the bottom hinge. A triangular jag of purple light came down where the door sagged from the frame.

Coming from high above them was the sound of voices. It was hard to make out most of the words at the distance, but one had a booming pitch that carried. They were discussing whether or not to climb down and look into the carriage. The prevailing opinion was to not attempt such an endeavor when night was dropping fast, and the slope so steep. "No one could have survived that!" exclaimed the loud-voiced one twice.

*Don't come down,* Jesco pleaded. *Don't come down.*

They talked up there for some time. And then, convinced that no one had survived the plunge, they rode away. The purple faded to black as Jesco listened for any sounds that someone was returning. All he heard was crickets. The machinery along the ceiling had gone quiet. Blood was dripping from his forehead. The wheelchair must have struck him in the head on the way down, though he did not remember it.

Fumbling behind his head, Scoth made the struts over his shoulders release. He staggered to a crouching position beside the wheelchair. "I'll see what's going on," he whispered, and slid the broken door aside. Hoisting himself up, he exited the carriage. It sounded like he was opening the lower compartment. Jesco looked up to starlight as Scoth thumped around. Then the carriage rocked. The detective had jumped down and landed heavily in the riverbed.

There was a crack in the carriage along the side pressed to the rocky ground. A little water trickled in steadily and made a pool around the wheelchair. Footsteps went here and there for several minutes, Jesco curious but dazed.

Scoth returned to the door above and rested a blazing lantern beside it. "Still got your senses?" he called in.

"More or less," Jesco said.

"See if you can't reach behind you. There should be a lever behind the seat. Flick it to the side and the shoulder bands will come off." Jesco did as he was told and the struts retracted. Scoth said, "Good. Now, hold out your hand to mine, and with your left foot, kick it back twice and hard."

Jesco put his gloved hand in Scoth's, and kicked. The leg band released and the lower half of his body slid to the bottom of the carriage. "All right," Scoth said, letting go of him. "Lift out your wheelchair, and then we'll get you out."

Within minutes, they were standing outside in the moonlight and Jesco was holding a kerchief from his belongings to his cut. His bag was at his feet. Scoth was moving about with a limp from the wheelchair bashing into his knees twice on the fall. The road was invisible above them.

"Should we go back to Somentra?" Jesco asked. "We're far closer to it than Cantercaster."

"Those men came from Somentra," Scoth said. "We need to get as far away from it as we can."

They had passed a few towns between the two cities. In the morning, they could walk to the nearest one and rent a carriage ride back to Cantercaster. But it was going to be a difficult journey when they could not climb up this steep slope to the road to walk along it, and beyond the riverbed were woods.

The trees were tall and looming, and their leaves chattered in the breeze. At a strange sound, Scoth slipped a jackknife from his pocket. Foliage rustled and a large shape emerged, coming to them with plodding steps.

It was the autohorse. The poor contraption was a mess of hair and scales from the slashes of that rider, and exposed machinery where its tail had fallen off. Scoth put away his blade and cried out in a glad, raspy whisper, "Horse!"

"How did it find us?" Jesco asked, equally happy to see the autohorse.

"Same way my mother made that bird find me," Scoth said. "I put in a lot of her old equipment. Good Horse, good Horse."

Horse stood there as Scoth made the shooter retract, and withdrew a hitch from the spot where the tail had been to attach the wheelchair. Leading the autohorse to a boulder in the dry bed, he had Jesco step onto it to mount. After passing up the bag, Scoth went to the chest flap to work with the destination cards.

"What are you doing?" Jesco asked.

"Making Horse take us straight to the station. Someone will spot that carriage down there tomorrow morning, send a crew to investigate and

# THE SEER

find no one inside. I won't be hard to track down when they come looking for me at home, if they do, and you won't be hard to track down either. We need a safe place to be." He closed the flap, clambered up the boulder with a groan about his knees, and mounted the autohorse behind Jesco. At a kick, it walked obediently into the trees.

Everything grew closely together in this wooded area. Many of the trees to fall over time had not struck the ground but ended up at a tilt against a neighbor or two, their foliage enmeshed. It was eerie to travel amongst them with only the light of the lantern. The trees looked like soldiers in a frozen march, with some helping wounded compatriots along.

Leaves rasped against their legs and night creatures flickered in and out of the light. Owls hooted. Jesco's head wound had stopped bleeding, but it ached. All of him ached from that crazed, whirling plunge down the hillside. Exhaustion made him sag into himself, and then an arm went around his waist to steady him and Scoth said, "All right?"

Jesco could not get himself upright. He leaned back and said, "I'll live."

"To someone's regret, I would say. Next time, I'll add a strut that binds the wheelchair to the wall."

"That's kind of you, but could there *not* be a next time that we go over a cliff, Scoth?"

Scoth rumbled with laughter. "It was my grandfather's name. Laeric. Teachers at school would call me Larrie and I hated that. I'd get all puffed up at seven and eight and explain in indignation that it was *Laeric*, thank you very much. Even then, I was highly protective of my dignity. There was no dignity in being called Larrie."

He was asking Jesco to call him Laeric, but without saying it directly. "Add the strut, Laeric, and I hope that we never have to use it," Jesco replied. "Those were quite some additions you made to your autohorse and carriage."

"I like to fiddle with things."

"That was far more than fiddling."

"It's just fiddling to me, to take my mind away from the ugliness. And now that those riders showed me the weak spots, I've got plenty more fiddling to do."

"Torrus Kodolli can never be accused of being a shrinking violet."

As the horse steered around a solid wall of leaves dropping down from shaggy trees, Scoth said, "That was the most brazen thing I've ever seen, if he's responsible."

"How could he not be?"

"Matter of proof. Did he order his bodyguards to hire up some street-rassel to run us off? Or did his bodyguards do it of their own accord? What about that lawyer? He must facilitate a lot of Kodolli's business affairs and Kodolli isn't an honest man, so I doubt the lawyer is either. He's just as thick in this as his client."

Something was wrong with the autohorse. When they came to a field and Scoth kicked it to run, metal clacked brokenly within the enormous belly. For a moment it faltered, and then it broke into a weary trot. That was as fast as it could go. It was better than nothing, Jesco told himself as he jounced bareback upon Horse. If not for the autohorse, he and Scoth would be on foot with their injuries.

A long time passed before the autohorse reached the road. Still the mechanical creature kept to its slow trot. There was no traffic but that of the moon in the heavens above, gliding meditatively across the sky.

They passed a quiet town divided in half by the road through it. The only people around were drunkards staggering out of inns and saloons, and carriages-for-hire offering to take them home. More were parked outside an opium den. Since the autohorse was still functional despite its damage, Scoth did not stop to rent another ride.

Jesco dozed a little, and roused to Scoth's voice some time later. "The attack wasn't Kodolli's style."

"It wasn't?" Jesco asked sleepily.

"Unless age is making him lose his faculties. The captain, Ravenhill, no one at the station knew where I was going today. But Kodolli didn't know that. If he had killed us, he would have to assume that the police would come investigating. The eye of the law would be drawn to him, detectives hunting around for clues and bringing a fresh seer to poke at his things. And what did he give us to incriminate himself? He never copped to knowing Hasten Jibb; he admitted to meeting Tallo Quay but said that he sent him away. Quay's disappeared and can't contradict that statement. He took away the photograph and drawing, so you can't get anything from them. You clearly weren't ever in a thrall from touching the table barehanded. This attack was an impulse act, rash, and a clumsy one. Torrus Kodolli ignores what he doesn't like until the fines get too high. Then he spits fire but eventually acquiesces. He would just ignore this investigation until someone really starts breathing down his neck."

Jesco sighed. "This case is going to go cold, but not for lack of trying on our part."

"It's too early to call it cold. Someone in that conference room, or connected to it in that office, was greatly alarmed by the two of us being there. If they had nothing to do with Jibb's murder or Quay's disappearance, then why would they care to silence us?"

"The packages," Jesco yawned.

"Yes, the packages that Jibb had! He collected those after leaving the old woman's house, I presume. We have to look at every inch of that ride home. Someone gave him packages to deliver, someone who didn't want to use a proper courier service. Bet they paid him under the table to do it. Then he fell off his bicycle and spilled them . . . did one get lost in that grass? Did he go back that night to tell the person that one package, or more than one, was lost or smashed? Or did he deliver what he had and a recipient killed him? All I want to know right now is *who* did he pass on that ride?"

"Torrus Kodolli doesn't have a house in Melekei, and he likely wasn't anywhere near the city at the time. Does his son live there?"

"The son does some of the traveling with his father, from what I gleaned in my research, and stays in one of two homes when he isn't traveling. Neither is in Melekei: the closer of the two is fifteen, twenty miles away. He and his wife own a third home in the north where she stays. They don't have much to do with one another. I don't know anything about the lawyer."

Jesco slept, dimly aware the entire time that he was upon an autohorse instead of tucked into bed. Horse trotted on and on, slowing to a walk on occasion and responding only with great reluctance to kicks. Eventually it could not trot any further and plodded. Jesco dreamed that the autohorse was coming upon a deep, dark pit that would send them plummeting down into the arms of demons. He was twitching from fear and talking in his sleep, and a voice said, "No demons, Jesco, just a road through the fields under a starry sky."

It was morning when they arrived at the station. Heads turned when they came in, Scoth at a hobble and Jesco with dried blood on his face and shirt. Then they were seated and everyone was bustling about to get food and water and a first aid kit. The cut on Jesco's forehead was not deep, so he did not require a doctor, and Scoth's knees were badly bruised but that was all.

Scoth told the story and a patrolman was sent out to move the damaged autohorse to the stables. Spurred to interest at last in this case, the captain cast about for somewhere to stow them for the time being. A few of the patrolmen drifted away at once, not wishing to house Jesco, and Lady Ericho declined with a gracious apology since she was currently hosting relatives. Ravenhill burped and sank into a chair with a stupid expression. Sinclair's wife had just had a baby, but they could stay with him if they didn't mind a night broken by bawling. Then Patrolman Tokol exclaimed, "Well, not me!" when the captain turned to him, and Tammie plunked her book of pieces down with a disgusted look to Tokol.

"If the station wants to spot me some money for rent, my roommate just moved out of her wing and I haven't found a new person to move in," she said. "I'm over at the Byway and who'd look for them there? They can hide with me until a handle's gotten on this situation. It's only got one bed, though one of you two can sleep on the sofa."

That decided it. A nondescript carriage was hired to ferry them and the wheelchair to her home. Scoth had been awake all night and fell asleep as soon as the carriage got underway. The patrolmen were divided into three squads, one to Scoth's home and one to the asylum to pick up essentials, and a third following along after Jesco and Scoth to make sure no one made another attempt on their lives.

Tammie rode with them and watched out the windows, but they arrived at her place unmolested. It was an old, towering box of a house but not without charm, wisteria hanging from an archway to the front garden. It looked exactly like the asylum with flowers running riot all through it, and Jesco felt immediately at home.

"That's yours there," Tammie said as they got out, Scoth yawning. "That one to the left. Looks two stories but it's not, just high ceilings. I'm here at the right, and there in the middle is a shared kitchen. I'm not going to be cooking for you or cleaning up your dishes, just so we're clear from the start. I wasn't clear enough with Nattia, it appears, and I got right sick of the princess complaining that there were no clean spoons when she was the reason they weren't clean, or that the dinner I'd made was only big enough for one. Her parents came to stay once for a week and it was true of all three of them: content to sit around and do nothing while someone else works to get them through the day."

The carriage driver was paid and duly went away, as did the carriage of patrolmen now that they had arrived safely. Tammie searched through her satchel for the key and let them into the kitchen. Herbs grew in pots along the counters, long overdue for pruning, but otherwise it was tidy.

In the left wing, Scoth crashed down onto the sofa and promptly returned to sleep. Tammie tiptoed out and Jesco settled into an armchair. He wanted to make up the bed and sleep, but he had not brought his bedding along to Somentra. Having covered the back of the chair with his jacket, he slumped there and faded into unconsciousness.

Neither woke until the patrolmen arrived at the same time with their belongings. By then it was well into the afternoon, and Jesco thought it wise to keep awake until night to return his schedule to normal. He made up the bed and pushed himself away from it to bathe.

The captain had given Tammie enough money to cover the rent and the food for a week, and she'd gone shopping. Neither Jesco nor Scoth were good at conversation from their fatigue, but she was well equipped to carry a chat for all three of them and did as they made a meal and ate it together at the table. A liberal amount of ale was poured in their glasses both during and after the meal, Tammie of the opinion that both of them needed it. Then she retired to her wing and they to theirs.

"Is the sofa comfortable to sleep on?" Jesco asked.

"It'll do," Scoth said indifferently.

"We can trade off on the bed if we're here for a while, change the sheets-"

"More trouble than it's worth." He sank into the cushions and tipped sideways onto the pillow. "I'm not drunk. It just looks that way."

Jesco laughed. He wasn't drunk either, but warmth and ease was pervading every limb of his body. "So to Melekei then."

"It'll just be me turning endless pages in the Hall of Records. Why don't you stay here for the day and let your head heal up?"

"All right. But I don't want to be . . ."

"Be what?"

"Pushed off to the side in this case."

"You're not. This is just a part of it that you can't do, Jesco, and I can. So I will, and I'll come back here to tell you what I learned. I'll stop at Ragano & Wemill as well and get a list of all Jibb's jobs while he worked there. Jibb's jobs." He paused and then snickered at how it sounded. "I'm not drunk. I swear it."

Jesco took off his gloves. He didn't mind a day of rest, yet he was reluctant to miss anything. But he could not deny that there was little he could do at a Hall of Records.

Scoth was watching him, and something about the stoic detective looked as disarmed as he had with the sunner. "What?" Jesco asked.

"You've got nice eyes. I noticed that years ago, even when I was about ready to punch you in one of them."

"Flirtation is not your gift."

"It wasn't a flirtation. You just have nice eyes."

It *had* been a flirtation, and both of them knew it. "Well then, I've always liked your hair. Even though you must spend a half hour on it every morning getting it to look perfect. I'm not flirting either."

"I've gotten it down to fifteen minutes, and it's not a matter of vanity. Left to its own devices, my hair looks like a flock of birds call it their nest. There were a few times in my university days that I just shaved it off entirely." Scoth tried to prop himself up, but only sank deeper into the pillows. "It wasn't right what you said."

"Which was?"

"That the only men to have you would be prosties. I've been thinking on that for days now."

"It makes things very complicated."

"Complicated isn't impossible. You act like you're damaged goods, but what you have isn't real damage. Not like the people I've caught, twisted minds, blood on their hands, no shame about what they've done, and no concept that they should be ashamed. That's damage to me."

"If I wanted to sit beside you on that sofa right now, I couldn't," Jesco said, in placid disagreement with the alcohol running through him. "If I wanted to lean against you, I couldn't. Because I can't touch that sofa and I can't touch your shirt, and I can't put my sheet over the sofa because then *you'll* touch it."

"How do you work it out with Collier?"

"He buys brand-new, factory-made sheets, pillowcases, and blankets, and makes the bed with his hands covered before my appointment. If I pay enough, he'll buy a new suit for the night, and if not, I'll keep my hands covered until he takes it off. He replaces the bedding each time I go, just in case he imparted something to it the last time we were together. Like I said, it's complicated."

Scoth glared blearily. Getting up, he swayed and wobbled over to the window where he unfastened the curtain. He brought it over to Jesco and held it out. "Touch that and see if you have a thrall. Tammie said they're new."

Jesco touched the fabric, Scoth at the ready to jerk it away. Nothing happened. "It's clean."

"Fine." Snapping out the curtain, Scoth covered the sofa. He sat down and picked at the buttons of his shirt. Jesco had been watching all of this in confusion and amusement, and the ease from the ale turned to a very keen interest in what Scoth was doing. The shirt came off and was chucked away. Scoth leaned back on the sofa.

It was an invitation. Jesco got up and Scoth said, "I don't want to wrap my hands in napkins."

Jesco took off his shirt. His blood pumping fast, he went over to the sofa and sat down beside Scoth. "Still not flirting?" Jesco asked.

"Nothing of the sort. Just two regular fellows sitting side by side on a sofa with their shirts off," Scoth said. Then they were fairly honking with laughter at how foolish they were being, and how foolish they had been since the day they met. Jesco leaned against Scoth, loving the hard muscles in his arm. Lips pressed to his hair, and when Jesco looked up, Scoth kissed him.

It was fire between them in that moment. Jesco needed to be careful that he didn't accidentally brush the wall behind the sofa, or put his hand upon Scoth's trousers. But it was very difficult to plan out these things when his mind was floating away and his arousal had taken over. Fastened together, they kissed and kissed until he was light-headed. Hands kept running down his chest and shying away from his trousers, Scoth also fighting to remember what he could and could not touch.

"Maybe you should take these off," Scoth suggested, and Jesco found that to be a very fine idea indeed. He had hardly started to lower his trousers and drawers when Scoth made an impatient sound and wrapped his hands. Getting down to his knees upon the puddle of curtain there, he jerked them off and hurled them away like they had done him a grievous and personal wrong.

"Something else nice about you," Scoth said. Jesco's erection had sprung free. Bending, Scoth took him in.

His mouth was hot and wet and soft, and far more intoxicating than the ale. Jesco was licked and sucked and fondled, pumped and sucked some more. Every time that he thought he might explode, Scoth stopped and let him wallow near the precipice in ecstatic agony. Jesco could not hold still and pumped his hips, seeking release. But the detective was taking his time about it, and Jesco had no choice but to let him.

In time Scoth pulled away, his hand still tight around Jesco's shaft, and leaned in to kiss him. "Mercy?" Scoth asked against his lips.

"Mercy," Jesco pleaded, and Scoth took him in as his fist rode up and down and up and down . . . Jesco shattered into his climax, crying out as his seed pumped into that teasing mouth. A profound relaxation came over him.

Looking pleased, Scoth settled beside him. There was a telltale bulge in his trousers, which he had loosened but not removed. Seeing the direction of Jesco's gaze, he slid them down to his ankles. His phallus was thick and hard, and when Jesco put his hand to it, Scoth jerked. The torment that he had inflicted upon Jesco had also been tormenting him.

Jesco wanted to give him the same relief. Commanding his brain to focus on where all of his body was in space, he concluded that none of him was about to touch anything but the curtain or bare flesh. He slipped down to Scoth's lap and teased at him until he heard that whisper of *mercy.* Jesco granted it.

For as much ale as he had had, Scoth was able to set up an intricate system of bedding that allowed them to sleep in the bed together. Jesco only touched his sheets, and Scoth was wrapped up in a blanket atop them that folded over him. His bundled arm over Jesco, they fell asleep entwined.

# Chapter Ten

Patrolmen from the precinct were sent to the hilly road outside Somentra to look for evidence, but reported back that the scene of the attack had been swept clean. All that remained was the overturned carriage in the rocky riverbed. No one had checked into the local hospitals for medical care, even though one had taken a projectile to the arm and another had had his mount step on him. Since they had all worn hoods, neither Scoth nor Jesco could describe them. And with nothing left at the scene, Jesco could not use his seer abilities to gain an identity.

The location had been out of the way, so no one had seen the attack happen. The only witness was hardly that: an old man who heard the crash of the carriage from his cabin. Peering out his window later at the sound of thundering hooves, he saw at a great distance a pack of riders going past. They were much too far away for him to provide a description, and night was falling.

Scoth received multiple confirmations that Torrus Kodolli had been exactly where he said he was at the time of Hasten Jibb's murder. Deep in the southwest to survey a new site, attending social events almost nightly, the fastest train could not have carried him north to kill Jibb, dump his body, and flee back to Fyllyn. Discreet inquiries also answered the whereabouts of the lawyer. He had been in court on the day of the murder, in a city far west of Somentra, and stayed there overnight.

All of Jibb's work orders were brought to the house, Scoth and Tammie bent over them one evening while Jesco made dinner. Tammie was working on the Iron jobs and Scoth the Brass, searching for any connection to Torrus Kodolli. It was a massive amount of paperwork to sort through, and dismaying when one considered that the connection hadn't necessarily been written down. Jibb could have encountered the man while delivering for someone else.

They finished at the same time, Scoth swiping Golden Circle from the pile and Tammie taking Silver. Setting down a bowl of soup beside each of them, Jesco took the third chair to eat his own. "Who ever knew that there was a town in Ainscote called Beans?" Tammie said.

"I knew that," Scoth said.

"A normal person, not an officer charged with knowing every place. Jesco, did you know that? Do you even know where it is?"

"I do," Scoth said.

"No and no," Jesco said. "What Silver job did Jibb do in Beans?"

"It's got the initials V. F. S. beside it, meaning it's related to Ragano & Wemill's contract for Varden Farming Supply." She rifled through paperwork about the company. "Ah, it's Varden's experimental fields. That's what's in Beans. What a stupid name for a town! Makes you wonder how it got stuck with that. He picked up several wagons' worth of farm equipment from their main office in Chussup and ferried it over there."

"And what's he doing over in Golden Circle?" Jesco asked.

Scoth turned a page and said tiredly, "Riding himself sore for the holidays delivering gifts to very rich people. Then it snowed and there's a notation that he switched to horses."

"Yours looks so sad-like in the precinct's stables," Tammie said. "All ripped up on the side, twitching its bottom like it still has a tail. I give it a pat every time I go out there."

"It's not a real horse," Scoth reminded her.

"I know that! But one day these mechanical creations might get so complex that they *do* become real, ever think of that? And if that happens, I want them to remember me kindly when they take over the world." She swallowed a spoonful of soup and went back to the Silver jobs. "I'm getting blisters just reading about all this cycling he did. East of Chussup, west of Chussup, Cantercaster, Melekei, Cantercaster, Melekei, Amon Hollow, Melekei, Demon's Mountain . . . Bearded Valley, that's another stupid one . . . Melekei again, back to Cantercaster, all about Chussup, here to Melekei, there to a bunch of churches shuffling their angel relics around. Oh, I remember when one of those came to my hometown. Everybody lined up to gawk and revel at the toenails of Archangel Stillwater and there I was in the lot of them, ten years old and wondering if I should save mine in case I ever became an angel someday. Why are you waving that pen at me, Scoth?"

"Circle the Melekei jobs," Scoth said.

"Would've been nice if you'd told me a few pages back."

"Would've if you'd corked it long enough for me to get a word in edgewise."

She took the pen and turned back the pages to circle the Melekei jobs. "Wait!" Jesco exclaimed. There was something that he could do after all. He wouldn't go into thrall from a printed map. Opening it up, he said, "Read me the addresses of those Melekei jobs. Maybe some of them fall on the way he took home his last day. A client could have stopped him for a job on the side."

Scoth added in the Melekei jobs that Jibb had done for Golden Circle. Unfortunately, there were a lot at both courier levels, and there had been one or two when he was down in Brass as well. His most likely route had taken him past dozens of current and former places of delivery. None of them were to anyone with the last name Kodolli or Burne, or to Agrea or any of the companies related to it.

"Think we're barking up the wrong tree?" Tammie said when she came to the last page of Silver.

"I think the answer lies somewhere in Melekei," Scoth said, noticing at long last that he had soup. He nudged Jesco's knee with his own under the table to show his gratitude.

"Shame if Naphates truly isn't involved at all since it lost her the position," Tammie commented.

Jesco looked at her sharply. "What?" Scoth was surprised as well, his spoon wavering in the air and broth leaking over the side.

"I figured you knew. Didn't you look at the evening edition of the paper?" Tammie asked. "There was a copy left in the carriage I took home. I just left it there, seeing as I didn't put it there in the first place and it didn't seem right to sneak it out. But there was a little piece under Parliament News that they voted someone else to liaison. There were three vying for it: Naphates that the miners liked, Udusa that the mine owners liked, and Parkandeer that no one likes and now he's liaison."

"Maybe Parkandeer is responsible for all of this to bump Kyrad Naphates out of the running," Jesco said.

"For the love of angels," Scoth swore, swallowing hard on what soup remained upon his spoon. "Killing a random courier and leaving a timepiece there by the body on purpose in the hopes a seer would trace it to her so the paper could release a spurious article to ruin her chances of getting it? For a liaison position that Gordano said isn't going to mean all that much?"

They groaned at the difficulties of this case and returned to the papers, Jesco getting up now and then to refill their soup bowls until the entire pot was drained. It was nearing midnight when Scoth rattled through the pages he had copied in the Hall of Records about the Kodolli family. "Here's the closest I can place any of them to Melekei. Twenty years ago, there was a blind item that the wealthy son of one of the richest mine owners in the country was having an affair with a socialite in Bearded Valley. It was rumored to be Morgan Kodolli."

"The socialite did it," Tammie said in exhaustion. "In Beans and with farm equipment. But that's nice. Wasn't he married and with children by then?"

"He was," Scoth said. "Two young children, a son named Yvod, and a daughter named Grancie. But it didn't stop him from attending plays and parties several times a week. Lonely for the wife; I can see why she has little to do with him now."

"Jibb delivered to an Yvod Shurtan in Melekei, but he runs a sweet shop, so I don't think it's the same fellow unless he changed his name."

"Yvod Kodolli is a feckless playboy," Scoth said, rattling the pages again so they knew his information was coming from rags, "who travels about causing scandal. Mostly up and down the western seaboard, but occasionally he ventures inland to wreak havoc in dancehalls, saloons, and brothels. He does like to pick a fight. I've got seven mentions of his activities over the last five years. It's said he's had to pay off some people to keep from getting sued."

"What about Grancie?" Jesco said.

"She leads a much quieter life. There was only one item about her that I've found so far. She married a fellow named Dircus Dolgang, whose family a few generations back and over to the side started up a carriage empire. He's not a direct descendent, well-off but never to inherit . . . what's wrong?"

Jesco had gone for the Silver papers. Remembering that he shouldn't risk reading them, he pushed everything over to Tammie and said, "There was a Dolgang in Melekei, wasn't there?"

"Probably nothing," Scoth said.

Tammie flipped through the papers and stopped at the second to last one. "Here it is. This was from right before Jibb got his promotion to Golden Circle. He delivered a spanking-new autohorse, black and with one white sock, to 64 Ambria Lane, Melekei, care of D. Dolgange. Oh! And it was signed for by one G. Dolgange." She pushed it over to Scoth.

It wasn't precisely the same spelling, but they stared at one another around the table. And it still didn't mean anything, yet Jesco couldn't help a flicker of hope from taking root in his heart. He looked at the map. Beginning at the street where the old woman who'd received the whirlygigs lived, he followed Jibb's most likely path. It led him straight past the address on Ambria Lane.

Jesco let out a shout and shoved the map to Scoth and Tammie, who crowded around to see where he was pointing. Then they were all talking at once. Was the rag in error or was Dircus Dolgang not the same person as the D. Dolgange in the Ragano & Wemill paperwork? What did the G stand for and if it was Grancie, was she related to the Kodolli family? And what, under the moon and stars and sky, could she have had against Hasten Jibb? It wasn't like he could have been sexually involved with her or the man she had married. She wasn't in any way involved in Agrea, to Scoth's knowledge, so what was her connection to Kyrad Naphates, if any? How had the timepiece ended up in that alley and *why*?

They could do no more without rest, despite their jubilation at finding even the barest thread between Kodolli and Melekei. But then Jesco got in bed and felt a hand slide onto his thigh, and it was much later than that when he finally went to sleep.

His cut was healing well when he looked in the mirror the next morning. For such a small place, it had an enormous bathroom and a counter with two sinks. Scoth was standing over the other one and flattening his hair, which was as unruly as he had claimed when it was left to its own devices. "Why are you getting ready too?" Scoth asked as Jesco washed his face with a cloth. "It's just Melekei's Hall of Records today."

"I will stare at the wall if that's all I can do, but I won't be left behind," Jesco said. This case was wringing him dry and he wanted to see it brought to a resolution. "All I'll end up doing is staring at the walls here."

Scoth concentrated on his hair and didn't put up a fight about it, and Jesco got dressed. The three of them shared a carriage to the station. Tammie went in to start her day and Scoth headed for the precinct's stables to see if there was an unused police carriage and autohorse. Following him in, Jesco stopped at the stall to look in at Horse. It came forward to have a nose rub. Jesco complied and Scoth yelled back, "I *programmed* it to do that!"

With the Shy Sprinkler's case gone quiet, there were several unspoken for carriages and autohorses. Scoth selected an unlabeled carriage used for undercover work, the windows shielded in curtains rather than one-way glass, and a shabby old autohorse model. It stood there like a statue as he reset the destination cards. Another carriage came in while they were there, someone yelling his head off incoherently inside, and two patrolmen exited with a drunken and cuffed man destined to cool his heels in the tank. One nodded to Scoth and said, "Got ourselves a statute four-sixteen here."

"Nothing good comes of a four-sixteen," Scoth said, and the patrolmen hauled the yelling man away.

"What's a statute four-sixteen?" Jesco asked when they were on the road.

"It's a police code, not official," Scoth replied.

"That doesn't explain what it means."

A grin tugged at the corner of the detective's lips. "Got to be an officer of the law to know a four-sixteen."

"Sure, *Larrie*, I'll sign up now."

Scoth traded his amusement for affront, and then he touched the tip of his shoe to Jesco's. "Fair's fair."

The Hall of Records in Melekei had once been a church. Flying buttresses with white pinnacles led up to the nave roof, and when they walked inside the vast building, their footsteps upon the tiles echoed. "I hate these things," Scoth mumbled, an autolibrarian spinning in place to come their way. At a passing glance, an autohorse could be mistaken for a real one. The same was not true for an autolibrarian. The mouths did not move with the same dexterity as a human's, their skin was too glossy, and they had wheels instead of legs to reduce the sound they made. To hide this, they were all female so that the wheels could be hidden under long skirts.

This one had a pink-cheeked, youthful face beneath a gray wig, and one of her wheels was squeaking. She stopped before them and opened her mouth after a delay. A recording welcomed them to the Hall of Records and asked what they needed. Scoth told her and then they followed to the stairs going down to the basement. The steps were narrow, halved for a ramp that the autolibrarians could travel upon.

She rolled down it beside them and said at the bottom, "This way, please!"

No human ever could have remembered where anything was in the towering sheaves of papers, books, and newspapers that filled the basement from end to end. Another autolibrarian was down here, without a wig, and she was flipping rapidly through an old, battered book as she read and recorded the information. Then she turned the last page and dropped the book into a wastebin. Giving a polite smile to the newcomers, she said, "Hello, Marjorie."

"Hello, Julena," the gray-haired autolibrarian said. She rolled all the way to the back, her skirt brushing on tables and chairs, and stopped. "You will find all the history of a particular address here. Look up the street name first, and please do not remove anything. I will be happy to make copies for you. And no smoking."

"Thank you," Scoth said, already moving his finger along the bindings of the black books that filled the shelves. He pulled one out and sat down at a table. There was only a tiny space not taken over by stacks of dusty books.

"How can I help you?" the autolibrarian asked Jesco.

"I'm fine," Jesco said.

"Would you care to visit the common room for refreshments?"

"No, thanks."

"Would you care for something to read? We have a wide variety of-"

"I can't read."

"Would you like me to teach you?"

"No. I can read, you see, but I have trouble seeing the letters."

"We are proud to serve the seeing-disabled. What can I read to you?"

"Go away!" Scoth whispered, his nose in the book.

Jesco retreated with the autolibrarian on his heels. "Can you look up Ainscote rag pieces?" he asked.

"Of course. Julena would have that information. What rag do you have in mind?"

Jesco didn't know. He hadn't expected the answer to be in the affirmative. "I don't have the name. But the articles were about a man named Yvod Kodolli."

She rolled ahead of him and went to Julena, who was reading a new book. The autolibrarians repeated the same greetings and Marjorie informed her what Jesco was looking for. Then Marjorie rolled back upstairs, and Julena's mouth opened and closed as she processed the request. At one-minute intervals, she delivered assurances that she was accessing the information and thanked him for his patience. Light glinted off the white skin over her skull.

At last, she recited a date from several years ago, and a rag called The Mighty. "Socialite Yvod Kodolli, 23, has been charged with assault for beating a barkeep at The Egalantine Inn who refused to serve him alcohol when his behavior became disruptive. Pleading not guilty, Kodolli appeared in court ever in style, wearing a Burbell suit and a yellow aviator's cap. He was sentenced to community service."

The autolibrarian paused to access another article from the same rag. "Grandson of mining magnate Torrus Kodolli, the dashing Yvod Kodolli attended the Royal Remembrances Ball with the noted singer and songwriter Ruza Belk on his arm. Putting aside his legal woes, this most eligible bachelor danced the night away . . ."

Jesco waited as more information was accessed about Yvod. It was all the same. He did nothing but attend parties and court dates. His crimes never graduated beyond bar fights, and his sentences were paltry punishments of community service and restitution to those he injured. In a gossip column was a rumor that his family had severed him financially.

When Julena ran out of her stored information, he asked her to look up Morgan Kodolli. Very little of it was legal matters. He might have had an affair long ago. He cut the ribbon at the opening of a new hospital wing that had been funded by Agrea. Reams of plays and parties were listed with him noted as attending, but unlike his son, he didn't commit any crimes while there so nothing more was said. When the autolibrarian finished in her recitation of his small doings, Jesco asked for Grancie Kodolli. There was less than either her father or brother. She had been born and married, and that was all except for sporadic mentions of her attending plays and other social events. Jesco said, "Will you look up Dircus Dolgang?"

"It's a Dircus Dolgange with an –e who currently owns 64 Ambria Lane," Scoth yelled from the back. "His business is listed as carriage sales."

"Shhh!" the autolibrarian hissed, her eerily smooth face forming an approximation of a horrified expression as she put her finger to her lips. Lowering it when Scoth quieted, she returned to accessing. All she had in her data banks was his marriage to Grancie Kodolli, and a mention that a Dircus Dolgange owned Fast Ride stores in six cities. Melekei was one of them. The business was luxury carriages, and it was expanding with a seventh store next year in the Sarasasta Islands. Dolgange and his wife Grance maintained a summer home there.

"Laeric!" Jesco called as the autolibrarian shushed him with a duplication of her horrified expression from earlier. Scoth came over, brushing dust from his hands, and Jesco said, "The autolibrarian just read me an article where Dolgange's wife is referred to as Grance. It has to be Grancie. She just goes by Grance as an adult."

They decided to go to Fast Ride first since it was on the way to the house upon Ambria Lane. The autohorse pulled them to a fine store, showpieces of carriages at rest beyond the large windows. A man in a suit was speaking to a couple looking over one. Saying that Jesco still looked like he had come out for the worse in a bar fight, Scoth went in alone.

Jesco could see him through the windows talking to an employee. His body was still tingling from their bed games. Scoth was not too openly affectionate outside of the bedroom, but Jesco did not take it as a lack of interest. There were occasional nudges and glances, all of which made his heart beat a little faster. This was just how Scoth was. One had to appreciate the subtle with him, and trust that once the door closed on the world, a different side would emerge.

Ten minutes later, Scoth was back in the carriage with Jesco. "It's Dircus and Grance Dolgange, definitely, and Dircus has been gone from Melekei for the past three months. His grandmother is ailing and it looks to be terminal, and they were very close when he was young. He hired a manager to oversee all of his stores and he's gone to Deleven to be with her. He stays in contact through couriers. The last note came just a few days ago, relaying that his grandmother has slipped into a coma. The employee in this store had nothing bad to say about Dircus. Polite, even-handed, pays fair wages and runs an honest business. People like working for him."

"What about Grance?" Jesco asked.

"No love lost there, on the other hand. He hinted that she doesn't like the little people of this world. He only sees her now and again because she stops in to handle the books."

"Did she go to Deleven with her husband?"

"The fellow didn't know."

The autohorse took them to Ambria Lane. The houses were beautiful, and the big gardens around them ranged from staid to rollicking. The Dolganges lived beside a house with a garden covered in statuary of fairies and gnomes and exotic birds. But theirs was much tamer in trimmed bushes and stone footpaths that wandered all through an expansive lawn. The windows were closed and curtains pulled on both stories of the grand house. "It doesn't look like anyone is home," Jesco said.

Since Scoth had not expressly told him to stay in the carriage, he climbed out after the detective. They let themselves through the gate to the garden, where Scoth looked to the ground and said, "It's all been newly planted, relatively speaking."

He indicated the rose bushes, each of which was cupped in a ring of freshly overturned earth. They went to the front door and he knocked. No one answered. After several minutes had passed, he said, "Maybe someone's in the back."

Of course no one was in the back, but Jesco nodded like that was perfectly reasonable. They walked down the driveway. The stables were empty, and it was evident that only an autohorse lived here. There was no hay or water bucket or stalls, just an empty room big enough to hold two carriages and an autohorse or two. "I could touch something," Jesco offered.

"But what?" Scoth asked. "We don't know if Jibb touched anything, or was even here at all."

"Just *what* do you think you're doing?"

Past the stables were a lawn and a fence, and on the other side of it was a matronly woman wearing gardening gloves and an apron. Scoth and Jesco retreated quickly from the stables, and Scoth proffered his badge. "We're with the police, ma'am."

"Well, it's about damn time!" the woman exploded. Despite her age and bulk, she scooted over the fence and stalked angrily through the grass. "How many complaints has my husband lodged at your station? Three? Is it four? And just *now* you are getting around to responding."

They had no idea what she was talking about, and Scoth said, "The police are very busy, ma'am."

"Don't you give me that busy bull-cocky of yours! I'm sick of it, just sick of it, going on all night and into the morning."

Scoth withdrew his pad and paper and said solicitously, "Tell me the problem as you see it."

"As I see it?" the woman echoed. "As any reasonable person would see it, I have to live next to a party that keeps me awake once every season! These properties aren't so big that the noise doesn't carry, and these people aren't so respectful that my garden goes untouched in their carousing. They tore up this yard last time, and they stole statues from mine and destroyed the flowers! Carriages all over the road! Horses left to wander! It starts at sunset and goes on near to sunrise."

"This would be Grance Dolgange you're speaking of?"

"Yes! There's the Autumn Revels and the Winter Revels followed by the Spring Revels, and thank the heavens that she takes her summers away from Melekei so I don't have to listen to yet another one."

"When were the Spring Revels?"

"Just a few weeks ago. I'd have to get my calendar to tell you the exact date. I saw the carriages and horses and bicycles start arriving and said to my husband to get the earplugs, because there's going to be another one. She never thinks that she might let the neighbors know beforehand so they can make arrangements to stay elsewhere. Well, my husband Ocel has had enough of this, too. We happened to have our three great-nieces and a friend of theirs staying over that night, and their eyes were as big as saucers to hear the drinking and shouting and swearing in the garden. Ocel asked them to keep it down and they told him off so he turned the hose on and pointed it over the fence. You've never heard such foul language! They went inside but we knew it was just a matter of time. At least we had a few hours' respite, and then I smelled smoke and they'd started a bloody *bonfire*." As Scoth took notes, the woman calmed down. "I went over there last year after a party to *talk* about this nonsense. This isn't the country. This isn't a dormitory at a university either."

"What did they say?" Jesco asked.

"Mr. Dolgange wasn't there; he almost never is and I've never seen him at these parties. It's only Mrs. Dolgange and she's a piece of work. She's still young, I'll give you that, but old enough to know better. It's just a little get-together, she whined at me, a few friends come to talk and have a mug or two of ale. More like thirty to forty friends, all of them yelling and laughing, and vomiting, yes, *vomiting* when they've imbibed too much. Right over the fence and into my shrubberies! They smoke those stinking cigars and sing the crudest songs at the top of their lungs; the men get into fistfights on occasion and someone could get very hurt. They'd damaged the inside of her house as well, I saw when I was there. Drawers dumped out, holes burned in the sofas, her clothes strewn everywhere like they'd tried on everything in her closet for a fashion show. But she didn't take a word I said seriously. She just threw some money at me to cover the damage to my yard and expected that to be the end of it. And that's what she's done ever since, just had one of her servants come over and ask how much the damage was and pay it. But it's not about the money! It's about being respectful. Do you know how long it took the gardeners to put this garden of hers back in shape? It was *trashed*."

"It sounds terrible to live beside," Jesco said, since Scoth was writing.

"Yes, it is terrible. The bonfire had me in fits. I could see them out there from my second story back window, dancing all around it like heathens and throwing things in. Clothes, shoes, and two of them were so drunk that they stripped down to their drawers and burned up the rest. They laughed like it was the funniest thing in the world. And there was Grance, going back and forth from the house with furniture to let them burn."

"Who are her friends?"

"I don't know any of them except her brother has come once or twice and I've heard her introducing him, and there was an older man one time she said was her uncle or cousin. I don't remember. Most are young, but not all; I've seen one fellow bring his *baby* along. He didn't come with his child to this one with the bonfire, or I'm sure it would have toddled straight into the flames and burned itself to a crisp. No one would have been minding it, least of all the father. I just wanted to cry in the morning when the sun shined down on all the destruction. Every inch of the yard here was in tatters, and a part of mine, too. The bonfire pit was still smoking, twisted metal bits jutting up from it. I can't imagine what the inside of her house must have looked like: splattered with vomit from end to end, no doubt, and holes kicked in the walls. Her guests had all gone by then. The girls were agape to see the aftermath. They spied some of my statues tossed about over in Grance's yard and rounded the fence to bring them back. Then Grance came out and pushed some money on the girls to give to me, and that bicycle."

Scoth's pen stopped. He looked up. "A bicycle?" he asked pleasantly.

"They'd been betting on cards on top of everything, and a friend had lost his bicycle to her. But she didn't want it. She said the girls could have it. Molly declined but Grance insisted, and they were a bit frightened of her so they just brought it back here with the statues."

"And is it still here?" Scoth asked, his shoulders tense.

"They took it home with them. It's much too big for Patty, she's only eight, and Cordelia. She's ten. Molly could just about manage it. She's thirteen and a leggy girl, and her friend Sonora is even taller. I told them they should sell it and split the proceeds four ways to make up for that broken night of sleep."

"What color was it?" Jesco asked, his heart pounding.

"Blue. A beautiful sapphire blue. It was a very nice bicycle, but I wouldn't expect any less from a friend of Grance's. They're from well-off families, judging from their clothes and jewels and carriages. But why are you interested in that specifically?"

Scoth came clean about their purpose, and then they were in the woman's living room as she hunted down her calendar. "Enza Elveig, and that's Ocel," she called by way of introduction. Her husband was sitting upon an armchair, looking stunned as he considered the replacement photograph of Hasten Jibb and picture of Tallo Quay. He was not one to be rushed, and Scoth was letting him peruse the pictures as long as he liked.

Mrs. Elveig bustled back, her gardening gloves removed, and paged through a calendar. Her husband motioned to Jesco, who went to the chair and said, "Yes?"

"This is the fellow killed?" He pointed to Jibb.

"Yes, that's him. Do you recognize him?"

"No. There are so many couriers that go down this lane. I don't pay them any mind. She gets a lot of deliveries, the Dolgange woman. I heard her complaining to her husband once about how she wanted to buy something, and he said that she spends too much. Money slips through her fingers like water. He's a nice fellow, Dircus. I've only spoken to him a few times, but always nice. I can't say the same about his wife. She's one of those sorts that only has something to do with you if you've got something she wants. At least that's how I read her. Since I don't have anything she wants, she's got no reason to be pleasant. Not even a wave over the fence. And she wasn't at all pleasant when her husband said no about what she wanted to buy. It was a painting she was after. And then I saw it being carried in not three weeks later, so the lady found her money somehow." He set down the photograph to examine the picture of Tallo Quay. "No, not this fellow either."

"It was the same night," Scoth said to Jesco with intensity. The party and Hasten Jibb's murder had happened at the same time.

"And you think the bicycle belonged to the dead man?" Mr. Elveig said.

"Yes," Jesco said. "Was there anything you noticed about it?"

"I helped the girls to ride it a little, before my nephew came to pick them up and take them home. It took us a while to figure out how to fit it in when the carriage was full of girls and bags and what-not. But we finally squashed it in there. Lovely color, that blue. There were silver letters on the side of the seat reading Fleetman."

That had been the brand of Jibb's bicycle. It *had* to be his. He had left his home and ridden back to Melekei, right to the house next door and proceeded to lose his life. And for some reason his body was transported to Poisoners' Lane and dumped there. Scoth showed the timepiece to the Elveigs and neither recognized it. They gave him the Cantercaster address of their nephew's family, and the information that they had not seen Grance Dolgange for several days. They'd figured she had left early for her summer in the Sarasasta Islands, and were relieved to have her gone.

In the carriage, Scoth could hardly sit still. "We're going to put this together."

"What if he walked into that drunken party?" Jesco asked. "They sound like they could be prone to violence. What if a few fellows were picking on Jibb, goading him to fight, and killed him? Carriages were coming and going all night long, the husband told me. One could have had Jibb's body inside."

"And they dumped him far from Melekei," Scoth said. "That still doesn't explain the timepiece."

"If Tallo Quay gave it to Torrus Kodolli to prove himself, and Kodolli gave it to his granddaughter . . ."

"But it was nothing special. Why would she want it? Unless she gave it to one of her friends, a friend who ended up dumping the body for her or with her, and then it got caught on the nail and dragged off. But then why were none of that man's memories in the timepiece for you to see?" Scoth looked out the window. "We need to track down that bicycle!"

They rode to Cantercaster. The younger Elveig family lived only two miles from the asylum, in a small but sweet home with a picket fence around the garden. Janos Elveig answered the door, a trim man with a friendly disposition, and welcomed them in for a chat. The daughters

# THE SEER

spilled down the hallway to see what was going on, and their father said soberly that the detectives had come to talk about the night of the party and the bicycle.

They were adorable girls, each a head taller than the one before, and all with long brown curls and bows of different colors atop their crowns. All three sat down upon the sofa, the oldest straightening her dress and the younger two imitating. Gently, Scoth said, "I understand there was a noisy party when you were visiting your great-aunt and great-uncle. Could you tell us everything you remember?"

"Very noisy," Molly said, her sisters nodding vigorously. "They were shouting and screaming-"

"And burning things!" the littlest girl interrupted.

"And burning things, yes, but let me finish and you can have your turn," Molly said. "The burning didn't come until later."

"Did you see a man arrive at the party upon a blue bicycle?" Scoth said. Jesco sensed that he was reluctant to show the photograph of the body or even talk about the murder to these girls.

Molly shook her head. "No, sir. A lot of carriages came in the evening, and a bicycle that was green as a shamrock. We were out in the yard playing hide-a-penny when the people showed up. And then they stood about in the front and side garden saying . . ." She looked to her father, suddenly in desperate emotional straits.

Watching from the doorway, the man said, "It's all right, love. The detectives need to know exactly what happened for good or ill."

"They were saying very rude things to each other, and laughing as they drank. Cursing, kicking at the plants and picking the flowers, cursing again when they got thorns in their fingers. It wasn't just *whispered* curses, like it's all right when you're alone and there's no one to hear. It was loud. They called each other . . . demonic assholes." Her eyes slid back to her father, who gave her more encouragement to keep going.

Mortified, the girl said, "One man was going about to look at all the women's breasts and saying what sizes he liked and who had the best, and a woman shoved him in the fountain for it. Everyone laughed as they screamed swear words at each other. She said she'd seen what he had in his trousers and it wasn't anything to brag about. The whole lot of them got fouler and fouler, even the oldest people, and my great-uncle turned his hose on them. It sprays out far. They went inside, yelling at us for getting them wet, and we went inside, too. It was getting too dark to play out in the yard anyway. Auntie and Uncle and all of us went to the kitchen. Do you want to tell the detectives what we did then, Patty?"

"We made beaded purses," said the youngest proudly. Cordelia was the middle child, and only nodded now and then to confirm what her sisters were saying.

"We listened to music and made our purses," Molly said. "Sonora's was the prettiest, but all of them were quite nice. Sonora is my friend."

"And mine!" Patty insisted in umbrage.

"Sonora is a good friend to all of us," Molly amended. "We cleaned off the table and had our dinner, read the comics in the paper and it was bedtime. We didn't have to sleep if we didn't want to, but we had to be up in the spare room and quiet since it was night. But *they* weren't being quiet. They'd come out of the house, mostly in the backyard. It was dark but they had lanterns. It was still hard to see anything. We watched from our window and there's a tree blocking a lot of the view. But we saw that orange flame go licking up into the sky. Patty fell asleep, and Cordelia read a book. She couldn't sleep with that noise. Sonora and I sat by the window and watched what little we could. We made a solemn pledge to never get drunk."

Jesco held back a smile as she went on. "I've never seen adults acting like that. They were . . . without decorum. Kissing and dancing, screaming curses, pretending to summon demons, and the fire would throw sparks into the air when something new was tossed in. Cordelia fell asleep around midnight. Sonora and I did some time after that. The noise still woke us up over and over. In the morning . . . it was awful. Cordelia screamed."

"Can you tell me about what you saw?" Scoth asked the middle child.

Nervously, Cordelia said, "I woke up first and got dressed, sir. I wanted to see if those people were still there, and the view from the window in our room wasn't good. So I went downstairs and outside to look over the fence. The carriages were all gone, and so was the green bicycle that had gotten propped up atop the fountain and the horse they'd been letting wander around the garden in the evening. But those people had come in my great-aunt and great-uncle's yard at some point and torn a part of it up. I helped to decorate that garden with the statues, and they were all messed up. The flowers were stomped to bits and I knew my great-aunt was going to cry. She loves her flowers, sir. Everyone came out and saw it."

"They were in the other yard, some of the statues," Patty said, about to burst from being quiet for so long. "We went to get them and the lady gave us a blue bicycle."

"She wouldn't let us *not* take it," Molly said. "She said, 'Here, here, a brand-new bicycle! I don't need it. Take it, take it! Have fun!' She rolled it at us and I didn't know what else to do so I took it."

"Did any of you hear a man shouting sometime in the night?" Scoth asked.

"Sir, they were always shouting."

"And what did you do with the bicycle?"

"We brought it home. It was much too big for Patty and Cordelia. I could just about ride it, but I already have a bicycle and it's purple. I like purple better than blue. We let Sonora have it all to herself. She doesn't have a bicycle, and she's tall enough to ride it with the seat adjusted. She took it home with her."

"Do you know if she still has it?"

"Yes. She rides it to school everyday."

"And where does she live?"

"She lives just around the corner. Turn left at the door, pass three houses down, turn and that's Sonora in the white house. Are you going to have to take her bicycle away? Is it evidence of a crime?" Anxiously, Molly said, "Sonora needs a bicycle, sir. Her family can't afford one." The littler sisters were aghast.

"We may have to take it, since we believe it was stolen," Scoth said.

"But she will be reimbursed for its cost," Jesco said. These girls were darling, and he hated to see them so distressed about their friend losing her bicycle. He had plenty of money to cover it.

"Is there anything else you remember, even something that you think might not be important?" Scoth asked.

Molly and Patty had nothing more to say, but Cordelia spoke hesitantly. "She wasn't happy to see it there, sir."

"What do you mean?"

"The lady. Mrs. Dolgange wasn't happy to see that blue bicycle when she came out of her house in the morning. It was parked below her porch and had tipped over into the bushes. I saw her face when we were over there picking up the statues. I thought that she was going to yell at us for being on her property, or be upset at how her friends had destroyed her whole garden and broken the fountain, but she just stared at that bicycle like she couldn't figure out how it had gotten there and then . . . then she didn't look happy about it. She covered her hands in her shawl to get it out of the bushes. Then she saw us there, and she gave it to us. Molly is telling it right, sir. She wouldn't let us say no. She said that a friend lost it in cards to her, but what was she going to do with it?"

"And it smelled," Patty said. "Just a little, like someone had spilled ale on it. We cleaned it off. There was ale spilled on just about everything, even the statues and we had to wash those, too."

Scoth thanked them, and he and Jesco went outside. It seemed foolish to ride in the carriage such a short distance, so they started for the corner on foot. "He was naked," Scoth said. "I bet that was some of the clothing that Mrs. Elveig saw getting tossed into the fire. It was Jibb's. I wonder if his satchel went into it, too. But Grance Dolgange didn't think about his bicycle, so she pawned it off fast on those girls. She knew they were just visiting her neighbors and would take it away home."

Sonora Khessmyn was a tall and slim girl, the only child of two aged parents. All of them were polite but intimidated at the badge of Scoth's, and again he and Jesco listened to a story about the party. Sonora could not even bring herself to repeat the obscenities, and she took them into the backyard to see the bicycle in the shed.

It was a sapphire blue Fleetman, lovingly tended, and with green and lavender ribbons twined around the handlebars. "I added those," Sonora said. "Those weren't there when Mrs. Dolgange gave it to us."

"We'll have to take it," Scoth said.

Her eyes filled with tears, but she kicked the stand and pushed it to him. Jesco promised to have the money sent to her so that she could buy another, and that made her brighten a little. Scoth got her address before they left.

The bicycle was too large to fit in the compartment beneath the carriage, so they parked it between the seats. It made a tight fit with the wheelchair. "Didn't you want me to touch it there?" Jesco asked, overcome with uncertainty. "It might not be his-"

"It is," Scoth said with intensity. "This is Jibb's bicycle, I have no doubt. The thrall might land you on the floor, so let's get you back to the house where you can land on the sofa instead." He gave the autohorse the destination and they drove away.

They did not speak for most of the drive. There was nothing to say with the bicycle between them. At the house, Tammie gasped to see it come out of the carriage. She cleared space in the living room for it to be parked, and sat in a chair to watch.

Scoth covered the sofa in one of Jesco's spare blankets, and stood to the side. Removing his glove, Jesco approached the bicycle. Here were the answers that they had been searching for, locked in the cool metal skin and padded seat. They would know, and this could come to an end.

"Go on, Jesco," Scoth said. "Let's bring Hasten Jibb some peace."

It would bring all of them peace. Jesco touched his fingers to the handle.

# Chapter Eleven

-he was-

-he was-

He was Ansel and he loved this bicycle but it cost so much so much *so much* that he was going to have to get an Arkkadian instead but Fleetman was the best and everyone would go wild at school to see it and he just wanted to touch it one more time before he chose a lesser bicycle . . .

-he was-

-he was-

-she was-

She loved her son, her pride, her joy, but if Nini didn't pick a damn bicycle in this store soon then she was going to have to ask for a chair to sit down while he dilly-dallied, her feet ached and this blue bicycle was so pretty . . .

-she was-

-he was-

-she was-

-he was-

-he was-

He loved this bicycle and he had it, he had the money at last, he had the money! It was perfection, lightweight and fast as a bolt of lightning. Crack! Gone! There was no better bicycle anywhere, nothing and here it was and here he was and here was the money and *sold*!

He was Hasten Jibb, and he owned a Fleetman. Pride filled him to walk the bicycle out the door and a man asked even before he mounted, "Is that a Fleetman?" And Hasten said *yes*. Quality, he loved quality, he was no pirate and he had no treasure chest but this was what he had instead and it was no less to him than rubies and emeralds and diamonds. Why did people want those things so much? They didn't do anything but sparkle. At least clothes covered a body and he had fine duds, the finest duds, and now the bicycle, too. He rode it home, his pirate booty, but he had earned this and not looted it. People craned their necks to see the brilliant blue and he was so proud that he could burst.

His favorite tale had been Snake of the Seas, one installment published every month that he grabbed up with the ink barely dry. Mama called them junk but no! No! Hasten forgot to breathe when he was reading them! How they'd battled over control of the Ribbons, Captain Vannen Chank of the dreaded pirate ship Mormodune and Lord General Viscey du Spelwether of the Ainscote Sea Guard! They fought and fought, winning and losing and betrayals and lost cargo, and then they came to the last battle and found out they were twin brothers separated at birth . . . *amazing* . . . That story had ended but he was rereading them, one installment a week so he could lose his breath all over again.

His Fleetman was flying, flying over the watery gray ribbons of the roads with stolen cargo in his satchel and the Sea Guard coming up fast behind him to reclaim it and cast him in irons . . . He was the Sea Guard storming the deep blue ocean after pirates . . .

Jesco was both Hasten Jibb, and himself watching this joyous man-child pedal about on his new bicycle. He knew the cities, he knew the streets, only the slimmest part of him had to mind where he was going in his deliveries and the rest of him was lost in thrilling fantasies and pleasant memories. The love of his bicycle was the love of a captain for his ship; he loved to stop at Worthing's to see their new jackets and trousers all smart upon the racks because he and Dochi had always done that together, they'd pretend to be pirates and loot the store of what they wanted in whispers after Mama went to bed . . .

He'd had the fever and something was missing in him but Dochi said *don't you mind it, Hassie*, and Hasten rode past a group of young women and knew that he should feel something but *don't you mind it* . . . he didn't mind it . . . he was on top of the world when he flew down the roads, he was free and he loved to be free with the sea winds in his hair . . . even the sun was laughing with him and he was happy . . .

He had money for stylish clothes, money for stories and his bicycle, a roof over his head and food on the table and he was aware that other people strove for more, but *more* was a nebulous quality and quantity in his head. Mama wanted *more* but Hasten was never quite sure what that was. *More* was what the couriers talked about and he retreated because *more* was what they pressed on him, what kind of *more* did he want, a woman, a fellow, children of his own, a mansion, an autohorse and carriage with leather seats . . . he did not understand . . . was *more* working Golden Circle? He liked the *more* he got in tips. There was something here he did not grasp, something always far away and hard to see . . . something they were all hungry for, and when they got it they only grew hungry for something else, but he already had everything he wanted . . .

. . . don't you mind it, Hassie, I like you just fine this way, you're still my brother and I'll always talk pirates with you . . .

Jesco nudged. A monotonous stream of deliveries peeled past him, but at its center was always Hasten who found them not monotonous at all. It was summer and winter and spring now, Hasten glad when the snow melted so he could climb back onto his bicycle. Some deliveries needed a horse and carriage or a wagon but on rural stretches he'd let the horse fly and that was almost as good as his Fleetman . . .

Nudge . . . nudge . . .

The appalling hoards within Lord Ennings' mansion scandalized and delighted the boy within him, but the part of him that was a man pretended to see nothing amiss, moved things here and there as the lord wished, smiled and used his manners and accepted his tip and left. On the way home, he thought about a ship sinking from too much weight, and towering piles of extra furniture getting thrown over the side to be swallowed up in the blue.

He took the jewels to the bank . . . these he would not throw over the side, these he would clutch to his chest as the ship sank . . . he had them admitted and took the receipt to the office where he picked up a Silver job. It was an excuse to ride his bicycle, which had gotten sick of sitting in the corner waiting for winter to end, sick as Hasten had gotten sick of it. He flew to Melekei with the whirly-gigs filling his satchel and did not say no to lemonade since he was also sick of rum and hard tack from traveling the high seas.

She knew he didn't understand *more* quite in the right way so she talked to him about bicycles and whirly-gigs and the stories that Hasten and her grandchildren were reading . . . he liked delivering here because she never made him feel badly about what he didn't grasp . . .

Jesco gave the scene another push, and Hasten was riding away. He swooped from street to street and came up on his favorite house with all the statues. Fairies! Dragons! Even a mouse in a pirate hat! They would chase him back home in his head, shouting and throwing ropes to catch him with Captain Mouse sailing the roads in a ship.

A woman in the next yard waved and shouted, "Ragano? Are you with Ragano & Wemill?"

The statues fell back to wait. Hasten squeezed his brakes and coasted over to the sidewalk. He bumped up the curb and the woman came to the fence. She was somewhat pretty but that was where it ended . . . *don't mind it, Hassie* . . . and he said, "Yes, I'm with Ragano & Wemill." He had been to this house once before. It was the first autohorse he had ever delivered, which was why he remembered it so well. "I brought you your autohorse some time back."

She smiled. Hasten had not been interested in the particulars of the woman, but Jesco paid them close heed. She was in her twenties, tall and narrow, with small breasts and her shape as straight down as an arrow beneath her housedress. Her wedding ring was large and garish. Four connected bands of strawberry gold went around her finger, all of them bearing streams of tiny diamonds, and the centerpiece was a massive diamond surrounded by a circle of smaller ones. Her earrings were just as eye-catching. From each ring hung thin bars of gold that extended halfway down her neck and clacked when she turned her head.

Her hair was dark blonde and pulled back with a clip. A pretty face but her smile was a grimace of bared teeth, and the deep blue of her eyes was also pretty yet the insincerity of her smile was matched with a flat gaze. She was examining Hasten Jibb with piercing intensity that he did not find intrusive, or even notice.

*Look at that horse!*

That was what Hasten was noticing. Parked in the driveway was a pale green carriage with a brilliant purple lily painted on the back. The autohorse was also purple, though paler than the lily, and not the one that Hasten had delivered. Hasten had never seen a purple autohorse before, and neither had Jesco. Nor had Hasten ever seen this carriage, and he came down this road all the time. She had a visitor.

"I remember you!" the woman was saying. "Look, I'm having a terrible problem. My autohorse is at the mechanic, I'm having a party tonight, and I ran out of time to mail some packages to Chussup and Cantercaster. They must get there today, or tomorrow at the very latest. Do I absolutely have to go through your office, or can I offer you money to deliver them? There are twelve packages and I'll pay you five dollars each."

Five dollars each! When he paused from surprise, she said, "Ten dollars. I must get these delivered!"

"I'll deliver them," Hasten said. He had taken side jobs plenty of times and pocketed extra cash that way. He didn't know why couriers got in trouble for that if Ragano & Wemill found out, but he never said anything and they had never caught him.

Straddling his bicycle, he waited on the sidewalk while she ran into the house for the packages. It took some time for her to return since they had to be addressed, but he didn't mind. He wheeled back a little to see if there were any new statues in the neighboring yard. There was! Under the broad leaves of a fern was a gingerbread cookie man with a bite out of his head. That was funny.

The woman returned several minutes later with all of the packages in a basket. She looked anxious as he slipped them into his satchel. "I'll get them where they need to go," Hasten said reassuringly. "I can do the ones in Chussup tonight since I live there, and I'll take the Cantercaster ones early in the morning."

"Thank you! It's a load off my mind to get them out of here."

"Did you want to put on a return address in case they don't get accepted?"

"Oh, no. I've wasted enough of your time, and I know all of these people will accept them. I've mailed them little gifts many times." She counted out his money, her earrings clacking as she nodded to herself, and the boy within him was dazzled. Golden Circle! He'd been lucky to get a penny tip in Iron, or a few pennies in Brass. Silver was where he started pulling in dollars, and Golden Circle was golden. That was a joke to him.

"Hope your horse feels better!" he said as another joke when he put the money in his wallet.

"I do, too," the woman said, and waved as he prepared to ride away. He'd made more from this side job today than he had from his hourly pay! More than he would make all this week! After he delivered in Cantercaster in the morning, and he would have to leave at the crack of dawn to get it done, he would go to his favorite restaurant and splurge on the Royal Platter. Sausages and pancakes and eggs and cut fruit with whipped cream . . .

The statues gathered in the next yard, mumbling mutinously and staring at him, and then they besieged the streets to chase after his bicycle. He knew that there was nothing actually there, but the furious stampede of one-legged flamingos, squat gnomes, sparkling fairies, and hopping toads made him soar. Added in the mix was a purple autohorse that breathed fire, Captain Mouse in his ship and the gingerbread cookie man brandishing a sword in fury since Hasten had taken a bite out of him. *Chomp.*

They were gaining on him! He went too fast around a curve to get away. The front tire hit a rock and the handlebars jerked. Truly was he flying then . . .

When the memories resumed, Hasten's happy chase fantasy was gone. Rucaline! There was rucaline in the packages! Or at least there was in the one that had come apart in his fall. But the packages were all the same shape and the same weight. The only difference in them was the addresses. So he thought that they all contained little white cakes of rucaline.

Patrolmen had arrested three people who lived across the street back in his Iron days. He remembered them standing in the front yard, their hands cuffed behind their backs, their heads hanging, and Mama said, "Look at them! Look at them in their shame!" They had gotten in trouble for buying rucaline, and one was in even more trouble because he had given some of it to his friend, and she'd lost her mind on it. Once Mama went into the house, Hasten crossed the street. He had gone to school with one of the patrolmen. That was Levi Linski, a friend of Dochi's when Dochi was alive, and he explained all about rucaline to Hasten.

If Hasten delivered these packages, he could be arrested. Then he was giving it to people who could lose their minds on it like that woman had. The police would take away his bicycle and his job in Golden Circle and he would go to prison and not feel the sea winds in his hair ever again.

*Go to the police*, Jesco thought to the man in turmoil wheeling home. But still alive within this man was a child, a very frightened child who did not know what to do. He was going to get in trouble, and he gripped the handlebars more tightly so no one could take his bicycle away. It never occurred to him to tell his mother, or to go to the office and hand over the packages to his boss. It never occurred to him that he was carrying a treasure trove in drugs that he could sell on his own. Rucaline was a drug and drugs were bad, so he had to get away from drugs.

The memory stopped, and the next one began. It had come clear to him in his room. In his mind's eye was Dochi, and Dochi was telling him to take those packages back to the woman. Yes! He would give them all back, including the one that had gotten smashed, and the money on top of it, and say *no thanks*. She could find another courier to deliver those, or wait for her autohorse to come back from the mechanic. She could even borrow her visitor's carriage and purple horse to do it. Hasten would not. He didn't want to go to jail.

A boy. Angels above, a boy.

He swept through the darkening roads and arrived at the house. It was early night. There were carriages parked carelessly up and down the sidewalks, autohorses waiting patiently. Some of the carriages jutted out into the road and others had a wheel or two propped up on the sidewalks. All of the lights in the house were blazing behind the sheer curtains. That was right! She had said that she was having a party. The driveway was full of carriages, too. Black and tan and parked haphazardly so no one could get out.

He would have parked his bicycle on the sidewalk, but a stray horse was clopping up it. Dismounting, Hasten walked the bicycle through the garden. Everything had been tidy when he was here in the afternoon, but now it was a mess. There were cups on the ground, flowers ripped up and tossed aside, and someone had balanced a bicycle atop the fountain. Water coursed down the bars and dripped from the wheels. The air smelled of urine and ale.

There was laughter and shouting from the first floor of the house. More cups and puddles were on the porch, so he turned at the hedges and parked his bicycle there. He was going to knock on the door and ask to see her-

-he was-

-he was-

-she was-

She reeled over her own two feet and tripped on a bicycle, knocking it over and falling on top of it. Stoman shouted *the carriage is this way, Lyza, you damn drunk*, and she clambered out of the bushes and off the bicycle to tell him what she thought of him . . .

-she was-

-she was-

Such a pretty color! But it was big, a grown-up's bicycle, and it was sticky!

The lady smiled at Patty. She had a lot of teeth like a shark, and she smelled. It was an ale smell when a shark should have smelled like fish, and a shark didn't wear hoop earrings with diamonds either, or any kind of earrings at all.

"Fun, fun, fun! You can ride it everywhere!" the woman said. Her smile was a shark smile, all teeth and no lips. Patty looked up to Molly, who did not want the sticky bicycle, and could not take it with both hands. She was holding the flamingo statue so Patty was helping to keep it steady . . .

Jesco took his hand off the bicycle. Tammie and Scoth helped him down to the sofa, where he told them everything he had seen with Scoth writing it in his pad of paper. A dull throb was in Jesco's stomach. "We still don't know anything for sure," he said when he finished.

"We know so much more than we did," Scoth said. "We can place Jibb for certain at Grance Dolgange's home in Melekei within minutes to a couple of hours of when he was murdered. We've got proof that she's involved in the distribution of rucaline!"

"Horrible and no two ways about it," Tammie said, having gone to the kitchen for a drink and flopping into the armchair. Liquid spilled over her fingers. Wiping off her hand, she said, "A real adult in his head and he wouldn't have gone back. He would have gone anywhere but back. Any of us would have told him that. He could blow her whole operation, to her way of thinking, if he opened his mouth to someone. He could have demanded she pay him to keep his silence. That's what she would have considered when he showed up on her porch. He's going to want money to shut up, or to be let in on the business, or he's got principles that will land her in hot water. She couldn't see into his head that he just wanted to hand back those packages with the money and go home on his bicycle."

Scoth spoke as he wrote. "She wanted to get that rucaline out of her house before the party, a party that has before damaged or flat-out destroyed portions of her property. Maybe she was worried that her friends would find it. With all the cakes that were in those twelve packages . . . that had to be a million dollars in rucaline. If she were ratted out for it, she'd spend the rest of her life in prison."

"There had to be somewhere safe in that big house of hers to stow it," Tammie protested.

"But I can see her being nervous about it. What if it was destroyed or stolen, and even more worrisome, what if a person found it and took some? Had a bad reaction and had to be taken to the hospital? That would gain the interest of the Drug Administration, whether she was involved or not, and there would be agents dispatched to speak with her. They'd start digging around in her life and her friends' lives. Also, the neighbors had already complained to the police about her parties and what if they stopped by? It's understandable she wanted that rucaline gone, and saw an opportunity when a courier went past her house. Also, the unusual carriage and autohorse that Jibb saw on his first stop there! Yvod Kodolli was described in a rag as owning a purple autohorse. But it doesn't sound like that carriage was still there on Jibb's second visit. Was it, Jesco?"

"If it was, it had been moved. Or else he left," Jesco said. "There wasn't anything special about the rest of the carriages. They were quality, but regular colors and styles."

"You think the body got dumped in that carriage, Scoth?" Tammie asked.

"That's quite a conspicuous carriage to take around for someone doing something he or she wants to stay hidden," Scoth said. "We canvassed the streets of Wattling immediately after the murder-"

"I was part of it, remember?"

"And not one person reported seeing a horse and carriage like that. Those are details that would stick out, especially so soon afterwards. That couldn't have been the vehicle that got the body to Poisoners' Lane."

"Can't assume he was dead then. He could have died in the carriage on the way, whatever carriage they took."

"If only that bicycle had had eyes," Scoth said. "But still, we've got him at that house now. He had the intention of walking up to the door and knocking on it. Who answered, and what happened then?"

"He got himself poked, that's what," Tammie said. "And not one of those loads of people thought to take themselves to the Melekei police and report it. Nice lot of friends she has. And one of them knew enough about seers to strip him naked."

Jesco shifted to see what parts of his body worked and what didn't. He was weakened but functional, and the dull throb was gone. "And burn his clothes and all of his belongings so no seer could ever lay a finger on them," he added. "They could all be in the rucaline trade with her, those friends at the party. They wouldn't have gone to the police then. They were protecting their business."

"If they were all in it with her, then she wouldn't have been so desperate to send it away with a courier," Scoth said. "So Jibb takes it, but he's back within hours when she has a house full of guests and there's the rucaline."

"Bet it comes to her from the Sarasasta Islands where she's got her summer home and her grandmother lives," Tammie said. "That's where they grow it, hidden in the wild places where no one lives. Maybe she grows it herself on her property. Then it gets sent to her in Melekei, and she mails it on to people in Chussup and Cantercaster who will sell it in those places or take it elsewhere. But she's already gone, the neighbors told you? It's a little early to leave for summer yet."

"She might find it in her best interest to be gone if she learned a homicide detective and a seer showed up at her grandfather's office in Somentra with questions about Hasten Jibb." Scoth looked from Jesco to the bicycle, which was still parked in the living room. "The Sarasasta Islands have a different idea of law enforcement. If she's gone there, it will be difficult to have her extradited back to Ainscote."

"But we never would have gotten this far without the timepiece," Jesco argued. "We would have found a naked man and nothing for us to go on. It was the timepiece that led us to Naphates, and then to Quay's girlfriend who led us to Kodolli."

"Basically we're moving ahead in the case," Tammie said, "yet still have no idea what's going on. You've got to contact all the stations, Scoth, let them know to be on the lookout for Grance Dolgange. She could have joined her husband in Deleven, what with his sick relative, if not the Sarasasta Islands. And maybe there should be a lookout for the brother. He's six kinds of trouble. Isn't so far to think that rucaline might be the seventh in his pocketbook of general mayhem and menace." Scoth was already standing to take his leave of them.

Lifting a leg, Jesco stretched it out back and forth. Just a cane would see him around for the rest of the day. Tammie shook her head in amazement at him. "What you see, Jesco! I felt like I was right there with Hasten on his bicycle when he was riding around, and like a child again with a problem too big for my brain. Did he notice any of those names and addresses on the packages so that you know them?"

Three-quarters of them had gone into the satchel without any more examination than Chussup or Cantercaster. "There was a P. Delgoda, Box 54 in Cantercaster Post Building Twelve. And two for Chussup: Submissions c/o Shaune Shaver, Last Times Print, and O. Levec, Enterprise, 5th Floor, Statesbury Lane."

"Those aren't home addresses. She was mailing them to post boxes and people's place of employment. I guess if I were receiving something like rucaline, I wouldn't want it going to my home either. Nattia opened my mail in addition to helping herself to my food. I would take out a post box and never bring it here. And Last Times Print!"

"Never heard of it," Jesco said.

"That's a religious newsletter, that is. I've seen them handing it out for free on street corners, pages full of nonsense about demon armies planning an attack and we've all got to pray hard and send money to keep them back."

"And no return address, so it couldn't be traced back to Grance Dolgange," Jesco mused.

"Wonder how she did it on the regular. Something went wrong that day she gave all those packages to Hasten. Maybe her usual gig was to give them to a different courier in on it who didn't show up for his side job, or else she delivered them in person on her autohorse that broke. But she's too sly for that. She doesn't want them associated with her. Maybe she drops them in the normal post and lets them fly that way. You can do that with small packages that aren't too heavy; you don't have to take them in and see someone personal at the counter to have them weighed. Or else she works with a courier company like Ragano & Wemill, but she couldn't take them in for delivery without her horse and when she's busy trying to set up for a party. And she recognized the green jacket when poor Hasten was going past her house. Good courier for a reputable company; he's most likely Silver or Golden Circle if he's in Melekei so she felt confident that he wasn't going to open the packages or steal anything. Scarce jobs for Iron or Brass in that area."

"He was just in the wrong place at the wrong time."

Tammie whistled. "Can you arrest a person for being intended to receive rucaline when the delivery was intercepted? I suppose not. They can just play dumb, say someone crazy must have done it. But the police should investigate all three of those people. Are you hungry for dinner, Jesco? I'll cook for you in this instance; you look wrung out as a dishrag."

Scoth returned during their meal and joined them at the table to eat. "Every station in Ainscote is being notified to be on the lookout for Grance Dolgange, Dircus Dolgange, and Yvod Kodolli. Hopefully the news will reach the port before she sets sail, if she's trying. The time of year might be to our benefit. The sea will still be a little too tempestuous for a trip to the Sarasasta Islands. The heavier freight ships will set out around now, but the recreational cruises won't start for another few weeks."

There was nothing more to be done with the case for the night, but Scoth's mental list grew through the meal and continued to grow ever longer when they were side by side in bed. "We'll get a warrant in the morning to search the Melekei property. I'll order the station's background investigator to pull up everything on the Dolganges and the Kodollis as well. I'll contact the Drug Administration, so I can talk to their agents who work on rucaline eradication. Will you be able to go?"

"I can go," Jesco said. "We need to stop on an errand of mine, though. I have to send the money to Sonora Khessmyn for her lost bicycle."

"We can do that on the way to the station to turn the bicycle in as evidence. We can also take your wheelchair along just in case."

Jesco turned to him in the darkness. "You sound happy."

"We're getting somewhere at last. I almost want to get a pint to celebrate after all this rigmarole we've gone through. Grance Dolgange is going to get hauled in somewhere and then we'll have quite a lot of questions for her." He jerked and said, "And her jewelry! I want to confiscate all of the jewelry in that house. It was a party. She had to be wearing plenty."

"If she was smart enough to burn his clothes, she was smart enough to destroy her own."

Scoth stroked Jesco's side. "But jewelry? That's harder to part with than a dress. If she didn't destroy it, then she probably hid it somewhere. But she must have a lot of jewels. You can't touch all of them. We'll need more seers. I can contact the asylums and see who we can get." His hand drifted lower and cupped Jesco's buttocks. "Could buy some more sheets if there's a problem." Flailing about in the bedclothes, Scoth liberated himself and rolled Jesco onto his stomach. Then he lay down atop Jesco, kissing his shoulders, and straightened to massage his back. It didn't stop there, the massage going lower and lower and getting more interesting by the inch, and soon it became so interesting that he forgot about the case that was dominating every moment of their lives.

The next days passed in a blur. Every meter of the Melekei property was inspected. Nothing of suspicion was found within the house, and while nothing appeared amiss in the stables at first glance, chemical treatment revealed traces of blood upon the floor that were not visible to the naked eye. Everything in the gardener's shed, which was located directly behind the stables, was inspected and dismissed as the instrument of death. Only one could have made the wounds in Jibb's chest, but there was no blood on it, and Jesco touched the blade to confirm its innocence. His thrall contained nothing more exciting than the grumpy ponderings of the old man who gardened for the Dolganges, and relatively few of them.

Dircus Dolgange was still in Deleven when the police of that city went to speak with him, and his wife was not there. He had not heard from her in some time and reported that their relationship was distant. Claiming to have no connection to the rucaline trade, he was horrified at the very suggestion. When he offered to have a seer verify the truth of his statement, Jesco mentally dismissed him from involvement in drugs or the murder. There was no chance that the man had attended the party that night. His alibi was watertight. Nurses, doctors, and attendants had seen him at his grandmother's bedside every hour.

Sightings came in for Yvod Kodolli. As of a week before, he had been in Radmark. That was forty miles south of Cantercaster. Attending a birthday party for an up-and-coming actress, his photograph was printed in the local paper. The actress was duly located and interviewed. Yvod's appearance at Celia Swanne's party had been unexpected. She hadn't even known who he was. He arrived without invitation, downed flute after flute of champagne before posing for the photograph, and was forced to leave when his flirtations with the seventeen-year-old girl and her friends became lewd. It was apparent that he'd come to get drunk and have a rip-roaring good time, but it hadn't been that sort of party. Many parents were present, and none of them were remotely amused to see a man in his late twenties hanging on their teenaged daughters. The Radmark police also interviewed the friends, and one remembered that Yvod said he was traveling south. He'd offered to take her for a ride on his purple autohorse. When she declined, he loudly suggested moving the party over to a local brothel where there was an orgy room for rent. That was when several enraged fathers got him by the arms and showed him the door. He thrashed and argued drunkenly to stay; he demanded to be released; he asked imperiously if they knew who he was and shouted that he would ruin the birthday girl's career. All he had to do was send a handful of letters to do it. Ejected regardless, he swore and wobbled away. The fathers stood outside to ensure he didn't attempt to slip back in, but they never saw him again.

"But Grance wasn't at the party," Jesco said when the information came to the station. "Perhaps she's not with him."

"She maintains a lower profile and always has," Scoth said. "She throws parties at her own home where she's in control. She doesn't tend to go to affairs like these, or call attention to herself if she does."

A more recent sighting of Yvod came from Lanfolli, where he had toured breweries. His mood was jovial though subdued compared to the party in Radmark, and no one remembered much about him. After that he was spied in Four Coves, where he visited a brothel and became so intoxicated that he could not perform with the prostie he'd selected for the night. She recalled him well, since he could not afford to pay and had had to leave to get money from his sister back at the inn where they were staying.

*She was with him.* Jesco and Scoth took out the map one evening and Tammie gave them a checker piece to put on every place that Yvod had been sighted. He and Grance *were* going south, in a general fashion that made it hard to anticipate where they would turn up next. Their pace was an ambling one. Drawing his finger down to Port Adassa, Scoth said, "Here's where the ships leave to the Sarasasta Islands."

"They're certainly taking their time about it," Jesco said.

"They may not think anyone is after them yet. And they have to know that the only ships leaving are freight. This could be killing time, if that's their destination." He slipped up the map to a blank space between Lowele and the port cities. "They have to take the train through the Squasa Badlands. There's no other way to the port. If we left in a carriage tomorrow and cut straight south, we could be at the train station in two days."

"Two extremely long days, going from dawn to dusk," Tammie said.

"We're supposed to clear it with the captain when we take trips that far away," Scoth said, irritated. "And he'll tell me to bump it all over to the Drug Administration so they can handle it, or leave it to the Lowele police when everyone knows that bunch of fools let anything slip by them for a dollar! They're as bad as what passes for law enforcement in Korval."

"Unless you and Jesco just went, and gave me a message to deliver to the captain," Tammie said with an evil glint in her eye. "Sometime tomorrow afternoon, say, seeing as I forgot it in my pocket. He can be mad and you can come back with an apology and a dumb comment that Lowele wasn't as close as it looked to be on the map. Better to be stupid than defiant. Your problem is that you stomp in all righteous with him, that you're the hammer *and* the nail and he's just the dumb post where you hang your hat, and it gets his back up."

"Let's go," Jesco said as Scoth thought about it. "Let's just go."

Tammie tapped the last sighting on the map. "Look at where they were just three days ago! Spotted in Corsingdale. They've got a long sweep west to get to Lowele, and if they're still messing about as they have been, you might get there some days before they do."

"Or if they drove hard and straight, they're there right now," Scoth said.

"Be stupid, Scoth. I know it's hard, but it's for the best."

Scoth stared at the map as they waited. Then he looked very faintly amused. Crossing his eyes and letting his tongue loll about at the side of his lips, he said in a thick, witless voice, "You know, Lowele didn't seem so far at the time, Captain."

# Chapter Twelve

The rented autohorse pulled them at great speed south through Ainscote. Beyond the windows of the carriage was rolling farm country with quaint towns scattered through it, and less often, cities. When the traffic upon a road grew too busy, there was an audible clanking sound from within the gut of the autohorse. It changed destination cards to find side routes that would allow it not to slow. Scoth had paid top dollar for this horse and the luxury carriage with a seat that pulled out and flattened into a bed.

They did not stop at restaurants to eat or drink, having provisions in the carriage, nor at an inn to sleep when they had the bed. There was a second compartment behind the main carriage that held a waterless toilet. It was hard to reach with the wheelchair taking up space, but they managed. Speed was of the essence.

Only once did they stop, and that was when something went wrong with the autohorse's left hind leg. It instantly rerouted itself to a service station in the nearest city. Since Scoth had paid for a fast journey, two mechanics left another repair job to respond to theirs at once. They were welcomed into a lounge to sit and have a drink, and watched through a window as one mechanic rapidly detached the leg and the other hurried to the stock room to get a fresh one. In less than twenty minutes, they were back on the road.

They arrived in Lowele a little more than a day after leaving Cantercaster. It was late morning, the autohorse ferrying them toward the train station at the southernmost point of the city. Lowele was a rough place: the roads unpaved and without streetlamps, and it had more saloons per block than any other kind of business. All of the wooden buildings bore false fronts that rose to peaks and overshadowed the streets.

The sidewalks were raised and passed directly in front of the shops. Crowds of people were upon them. They could get nowhere quickly when employees of the shops had set up tables on the sidewalks to promote the best of what they were selling within. Children shouted for candy pinwheels and adults ogled whirly-gigs, families clustered together to pose for photographs, and older people sat upon benches and rocking chairs with their feet out in the way of everyone. Carriages stopped at the sidewalk outlets to offer rides or release travelers to inns and restaurants. Jesco searched in vain for Grance and Yvod, but it was impossible to see every bobbing head in the throngs. "What will you do if we find them?" he asked.

"Hire a suspects' carriage to ferry them back to Cantercaster," Scoth said. He was looking out the window to the other side of the street. "I don't know that we can hold Yvod for long, but at least we'll get to hear what he has to say in an interrogation or two first."

They disembarked at the train station and Scoth gave the autohorse the destination of the closest service station to check itself in. With a programmed whicker, the autohorse bobbed its head and drew the carriage away. Jesco placed his bag in the seat of his wheelchair and pushed it along.

The station's platform was an absolute madhouse, due to the train arriving from the port only minutes ago. People clutched their hats at a breeze and hefted luggage and small children into their arms. All of them were speaking at once to hire carriages, get rooms at inns, find a place to eat, and asking where they picked up their autohorses. A school trip had been on that train, and two wavering lines of children in blue uniforms marched past Jesco and Scoth with satchels over their shoulders. They were singing, and the matron with them waved to four large carriages that could not find a place to park and had stopped directly in the road.

Hard-muscled freight workers were unloading heavy crates from the four back cars of the green and black train. Wagons were waiting for the crates, drivers sitting in the seats and shouting the names of their businesses to the freight workers if it was not already printed on the wagon sides. Another car was opened and autohorses came out, travelers shouting to them. "Ya-ya! Come here, Ya-ya!" "There she is, Carcey, step lively now!" A worker directed the horses to a slim avenue that ran alongside the far end of the platform.

"First class, prepare to board! First class, prepare to board!" someone shouted in a ringing baritone beside three cars near the front that had their windows gilded in gold.

"They would ride in the first class cars with their money," Scoth said. He forced his way through, Jesco following closely in his wake with the wheelchair. It wasn't nearly as crowded where there was a queue of well-dressed travelers. Separated from the second and third class people by velvet ropes, they were waiting as the interior of the first class cars was cleaned. The work was almost done, maids with rags and sacks of refuse stepping out and going to cars further back.

Neither Yvod Kodolli nor Grance Dolgange was in the clutches of people behind the ropes. Jesco and Scoth circled the group twice. The last maids exited and a station worker let the people board. All of them looked relieved to escape the hubbub, one old man saying to his wife, "Still some time until it leaves, but we can have a nice sit-down and order a cider."

"How many trains are there each day?" Jesco asked.

"Just one," Scoth said, turning to stare out into the crowds. Those who had just arrived in Lowele were all mixed up with the people aiming to leave it. "It takes almost six hours to pass through the badlands, so it leaves the south just before sunrise to get here, and leaves here at midday to get back by evening."

A station worker went by with a scrawny, squalling pickpocket of tender years in his grip, the boy twisting to free his collar as he was marched implacably to an office. Scoth motioned for Jesco to come, and they stepped in behind the worker and boy. "It isn't stealing if she dropped it!" the boy said. His face was smudged with dirt and his clothes were more patches than whole. "Let go of me!"

Scoth showed his badge and was let behind the counter to speak with someone. Jesco took a seat in the tiny waiting area. The office let out into the ticket exchange, which had three long lines of people waiting in aisles between benches to make their purchases. Vendors sold drinks and snacks along the sides. Turning away from it, he propped his foot upon the wheel of his chair and glanced out the window to the platform.

Had Yvod and Grance already made it here and taken yesterday's train? Or were they still dawdling about on their way to Lowele, if that was even where they were going? They could not be going anywhere else if their plans were to quit Ainscote. This was the only route out unless they were going to sweep back through the country and charter a boat to the Northern Ice.

Something caught his eye and he looked down. A bit of air was going through his pocket. It was the boy, who had been shoved into another seat and told to stay there until someone could deal with him. His finger twitched as he stared innocently away from Jesco. An othelin child, obviously a manipulator, and homeless. He couldn't have been more than nine. Jesco put his hand casually over his pocket, pinning his wallet there. Scoth was not yet back, so Jesco pushed his chair into the ticket exchange and bought a cup of lemonade and a giant, salted pretzel. The warmth of it bled through his glove. Returning to the office, he offered them to the boy. "Go on."

The boy took them warily. Then he ripped a hunk from the pretzel and shoved it in his mouth. "Oh, don't feel sorry for him," called the man at the counter. "He's sneaking onto the trains and stealing all the time, dirty little demon spawn."

"Not the only demon spawn in this waiting area," Jesco said. The man looked disgusted, since Jesco was the only other one there, and dropped his gaze to rifle through a ledger.

"Where are you from?" the boy mumbled with his mouth full.

"Cantercaster," Jesco said. "You?"

"Dorset, down by the port."

"Isn't there an asylum in Dorset?" Jesco was sure there was. One of the Cantercaster nurses had worked there before moving north. "You'll get all the food you want there, a warm bed and clothes."

The boy was offended. "An asylum! I don't want to get locked in an asylum when I've got my brain about me."

"I've got my brain and live in the Cantercaster asylum, yet I'm not locked in or else how am I here doing my job for the police?"

The boy had no answer for that, and gobbled up the whole pretzel. He was downing the lemonade when Scoth returned and gestured to the big room where tickets were being sold. Feeling like he had to say one more thing to the child, Jesco bent to him. "I was scared when I was taken to an asylum as a boy, too. But do you know what happened to me when I got there?"

"What?" the youthful manipulator asked uncertainly.

"I found my home." That was all Jesco could do. The rest of it was the boy's decision.

Jesco rolled his chair into the ticket exchange after Scoth. Profound aggravation in his eyes, Scoth guided them up to the front of the line while saying, "Yes, they received notification to be on watch for Dolgange and Kodolli. They hung it up on their wall. But that's all they did. No one's been keeping an eye out for those two. I *knew* it would be like this."

"So they could have strolled onto the train without problem," Jesco said. "But maybe they haven't showed yet. They haven't done any of this trip with speed."

Scoth displayed his badge at the counter and held out money. "Two second class tickets to Port Adassa, preferably a quarter compartment, if there's one available." The startled clerk nodded.

"Get back in l-" a man began to complain. Seeing the badge, he cut himself off and found somewhere else to look.

"We're going down there?" Jesco asked once Scoth had the tickets. The wheelchair marked as special handling, the clerk pulled another worker aside to ask for packaging to wrap the chair in. After that, it would be taken to freight.

"We've got to go there," Scoth said. "If they're already down in Port Adassa and feeling antsy, I'm sure they could slip enough to the captain of a freight ship to buy themselves passage."

Freight was still being unloaded from the back cars when they stepped out onto the platform. Dozens of station workers were there to get it done fast. As soon as one car was fully unloaded, crates and oversize luggage were rushed inside. A line of autohorses waited patiently for their turn, one real horse among them stamping his hoof in dislike at the manufactured horses to provoke a reaction. They soundly ignored him.

In the first class cars, people were reclining in comfortable chairs and accepting drinks. The doors were opened occasionally to admit more wealthy passengers. The platform was still in a hubbub, although calmer than before since the new arrivals to Lowele had left. There were people going south for business, evident by their dress and briefcases, and others were headed there for a holiday. Five dark-haired girls and boys in red vests were entertaining upon a mat laid out on the platform, juggling and doing gymnastics beside a hat for money. They were part of a frivolity circuit, adults standing near them holding large cases all printed with Top Line Tricks. A sixth child was doing pratfalls beside the five experts, and the people watching the routine chuckled and donated pennies.

Scoth was watching them as well. "I used to do that. Ono always said genuine clumsiness was as good as talented fakery, and I certainly was incompetent at standing on my head and juggling. I learned their routine and did my pathetic best at their side." Just then, a woman dropped a whole dollar into the hat. All six children clapped hands to their foreheads and fainted. The audience roared with laughter and produced coins.

"Five minutes, boarding! Five minutes, boarding! Second and third class, five minutes boarding!" the man with the booming baritone shouted. Seats were assigned in second class, and third class was a free-for-all. They moved away as people queued up noisily for the third class cars, Scoth checking the tickets for the number of their quarter compartment. Jesco made a rueful sound and said, "The captain is going to suspend you for the money slipping through your fingers."

"Let him. I'll take those days off to patch Horse back together. A quarter compartment is wiser for you. The last thing we need is a bit of luggage falling on your head, or the car attendant coming up behind our seats and thinking she's being helpful by putting a neck pillow around your shoulders."

When boarding started, they joined the back of the group for second class and moved up slowly to the cars. Then Jesco stepped in and climbed three steps, giving a nod to the car attendant as she greeted him. He had only been on a train once before, so this was still a thrill for him, and this train was finer than the first. Polished wood on the walls and burgundy seats, there were latched compartments above for small luggage and carpet all down the aisle. People sat two to each side. Behind him, Scoth said, "I read it wrong. We need to go up one car to our compartment."

The attendant opened the door, and they walked across metal plates to get to the car. There were chain handrails, but a careless step could spell disaster on a moving train. The attendant in the next car let them in and pointed out their compartment, which was only steps away. Jesco rolled open the door to a tiny room with two cushioned chairs facing a grand window. Between the chairs was a slim dresser bolted to the floor. Sitting down, he undid the latches and opened all three drawers. The first held snacks, the second chilled bottles of fizzy drinks and water, and the last had napkins and the newspaper. "You are *so* suspended, Laeric."

"First class and it would be champagne and shrimp," Scoth said, sitting in the other chair and swiping the newspaper. "But this isn't bad."

Out the window was a view of the empty land beyond the train station. There wasn't much to see but grass waving in the breeze, a distant curve of the track, and miniscule farms far beyond that. The train would loop around on the curve and head into the Squasa Badlands. The scene would not be so bucolic then. While Jesco had never been to the badlands, he had seen desolate pictures of its craggy peaks and sandy sweeps.

People filed past the compartment as a stream of shoulders through the window in the door. Realizing he had to use the lavatory, Jesco stood. It would be easier to do it now than when the train was moving. "I'll be back shortly."

"Don't touch anything," Scoth said grumpily as he turned a page.

Jesco started up the car. The platform was visible through the windows on his right side, and it was clearing rapidly. The only people still there were waving to others already on the train, all of them shouting, "Goodbye! Goodbye!"

The small gymnasts were gone. A family rushed for the train from the ticket exchange, a mother snatching the hand of a toddler girl who had stopped to pick up something from the ground. The child wailed to be dragged along, her older siblings shooting out ahead with bags tucked under their arms. They came to the same car Jesco was on, and the attendant said, "You made it!" The children filed in past Jesco, calling out their seat numbers and pointing to them, and the mother climbed in with the shrieking girl and went straight into the lavatory, a pungent scent trailing after them.

Jesco waited for a minute, but the girl was crying and the mother scolding, and it didn't seem that they were going to be coming out any time soon. Noticing him, the attendant said, "The next car up is also second class. Why don't you try there?"

He crossed the metal plates to the other side and walked through the car. No one was in the lavatory or waiting for it. Going in, he made use of the facilities and was out in seconds. Everyone was laughing in their seats at a man in a pinstriped suit and top hat. Even though the train had yet to move, he was sprinting for the first class cars like they were already pulling away. His hand was clapped to his hat to keep it from flying off.

Jesco laughed as well and watched him go. He vanished from the windows beside the seats and reappeared briefly in the one within the door. First class was just ahead of the car that Jesco was currently in. He looked through the window and across the metal walkway to the gold-lined car on the other side. As grand as he was finding second class, first was that much grander. He could see a bar at the back of the car, and a bartender wiping off the counter. A man came down the aisle to order a drink, and Jesco's merriment died upon his lips.

It was Morgan Kodolli. Looking unhappy, he loosened his tie and spoke to the bartender. Then he bent down to peer out the window to the platform as his drink was fixed. Backing away, Jesco turned and hurried down the car to the far door. They weren't here for Morgan Kodolli, but Scoth still had to know that he was a passenger. The train whistle blew as Jesco was crossing the plates between cars. He almost ran through his own, the mother and young daughter still having a row in the lavatory, and flung aside the door to their quarter compartment. "Laeric, I saw Morgan Kodolli!"

Scoth pulled down the newspaper. "Are you sure?"

"Absolutely. I had to go to another car to use the lavatory, and I saw him plainly through the window-" The train lurched and began to move. Through the walls of the compartment, he heard people cheering.

Scoth got out of his chair and joined Jesco in the aisle. "Where?"

"No, not in here," Jesco said, holding onto the wall to steady himself. "He's up in first class, the last of the first class cars . . ."

Suddenly, Scoth stepped away and dove toward two pairs of seats facing one another. None of the four were occupied. Sitting upon the edge of a seat closest to the window, he lowered it and exclaimed, "It's them!"

Jesco took another seat and looked out. Latecomers were running desperately for the train, two women grabbing hold of a railing and heaving themselves up into a second class car. Much farther back was a man whose luggage opened and spilled his clothes everywhere. He stopped running to pick it all up, two more people swerving to go around him.

Grance Dolgange. And the fellow at her side had to be her brother Yvod. She had her skirt gathered in one hand and a heavy bag swinging in the other; he carried nothing and pulled out ahead of his sister. He was a good-looking man, his hair the same dark blond as Grance's but rakishly shaggy, and his features were finely chiseled.

The train was gaining speed. The man who had dumped the clothes waved at it in dismay, a station worker coming out to help him gather his things. Grance and Yvod were still running, car after car passing them by. Some of the people in Jesco and Scoth's car cheered for them to make it.

It looked like they were aiming for the second class cars, but those were sweeping past. They changed course and headed for the third. Then Jesco couldn't see them anymore, the train curving away from the station. Standing up abruptly, Scoth got his arm. "Come on."

They returned to their compartment and Scoth pulled the little curtain over the window. "What are we doing?" Jesco asked.

"They're likely to come through here to get to first class," Scoth said.

"They don't know what we look like."

"But Morgan Kodolli does, and if he saw them running, he might head back. I've got to find train security. I want all three of them detained and ferried to the police station in Port Adassa for questioning. Wait here."

Jesco waited impatiently in the little room. The train went around the broad curve of the track and picked up much more speed as it straightened. Out the window was a sea of grass rolling in the wind. It lifted along a slope and plunged down steeply, the train going down a smooth cut beside it.

They approached the badlands rapidly, the grass turning more pale and thin by the minute. Pools of earth appeared between the thatches of it. Still Scoth did not return, and Jesco had just made up his mind to leave the compartment in search when the door opened. Scoth closed it and said, "The train guard has a private compartment beyond first class, and I can't get to it without Morgan Kodolli seeing me. He's sitting right on the aisle."

"Can an attendant get the guard?" Jesco asked.

"I asked one to carry a message to the front for me. But when the angels were doling out brains, some demon slipped by and stole his. He went ambling up there and still hasn't come back. I never saw Grance and Yvod go past. Maybe they've decided to try and lose themselves in the morass of third to escape the ticket punchers if they didn't have time to buy them." Scoth leaned on the back of his chair, his brow furrowed. "I don't want to tip them off prematurely. They can't jump off once we're in the badlands-"

"Do you honestly think they would jump off a speeding train?"

"I can't speak for Morgan or Yvod, but Grance? Her father must have mentioned that a couple of detectives came to the office asking questions about Jibb. A murder at her home, her rucaline involvement, that's why she left for her summer holidays early. She's got to get to the Sarasasta Islands or she's going to land in prison."

"But the timepiece," Jesco said tiredly.

Scoth met his eyes with equal exhaustion. "I can't even begin to tell you why that was there, and I won't try. But we need to have her restrained well before the port."

Time dragged by. When the train guard finally knocked on the door and hobbled in, Jesco's heart fell. This was no burly, well-trained man or woman of the law but a spindly, bald old man with a mild hunchback. He wasn't much taller or heavier than the homeless child that Jesco had given a pretzel. Shrunken within his clothes, which were trousers and a polkadot shirt with a star badge attached to the pocket, he was the least imposing authority in imagination. "I'm Cheffie, guard of the Blazing Star. Help you fellows?" he asked in a reedy voice, and covered his mouth to yawn. His breath revealed that he'd been drinking.

Scoth showed his badge and explained. Blinking, Cheffie said, "Well, we can stow the fellows in the brig. That's past third class. And the lady I can keep up front with me. Nicer accommodations." He tipped his head in a chivalrous move as if he were wearing a hat.

"I'm not worried about supplying her with nicer accommodations," Scoth snapped at the guard. "She is a suspect in a murder. Do you carry handcuffs? I only have two pairs on me."

Cheffie reached around to his back pocket and freed a pair from his belt. "I got a pair. Look, why don't you fellows sit tight for a bit? First things first is that I have to see if the brig is freed up. Sometimes the freight workers stow luggage in there if they run out of room. Can't stick three people in the brig if there's already an autohorse standing there!" He slapped his chest and laughed. "I'll look for this man and woman on the way so I can come back and tell you which car they're in."

Scoth described them in detail. Then they stuck their heads out of the door when the guard left and watched him hobble between the cars to the one traveling behind them. Once the old man was safely inside, Scoth said, "This case. This *case*. Not one part of it has been easy, and all to culminate in Cheffie the drunken, demon-damned train guard."

"It hasn't been easy, but we've still gotten here," Jesco said. "If they do jump for it, are you intending to go after?"

"In the badlands? No. I'm not going to die by the venom of a click-clack snake, or in the claws of a mountain cat, or the hundred other dangerous creatures out there. There's a reason this train doesn't run at night, and why nobody lives out here. If Grance jumps, good luck to her." They sat down. The thatches of grass had turned to naked ground, and it was cracked like a giant pane of brown glass to fall from the heavens. Coming up were massive, scattered boulders and towering crags, and they too looked like they had been dropped from the stars to shatter upon the earth.

Every time footsteps went by their compartment, Scoth got up to see whom it was. An eternity passed before Cheffie returned, and he was shaking his head as he entered. "They're not on the train, your people."

In exasperation, Jesco said, "We saw them running for it!"

"But you didn't see them make it, did you? I walked every car on the way to the brig, and had to walk them again to get back here. Plenty of ladies and plenty of gents, but none matching your descriptions."

This was absurd. Jesco wondered if the old man's vision was failing. With dangerous calm, Scoth said, "Is the brig free and clear?"

"Oh, yes, they didn't put anything in it this time. I got on them after the last. Are you going to arrest the man in first class then?"

"Not at the moment. I'll walk the cars and have another look."

"They're not there. I checked real carefully both times. They're back at the station, I tell you, and planning to ride the train tomorrow. If you swing back on the morning train from Port Adassa, you can arrest them on the platform."

"Thank you," Scoth said, and the guard went away.

"Well?" Jesco said.

His lips thinning, Scoth said, "This is ridiculous. He must have missed them. I'm walking each car. Stay-"

## THE SEER

"No." Jesco followed him out the door, and they crossed the shifting metal plates to the next car. Scoth gave him a dirty look and Jesco understood that it had much more to do with this new problem than anything Jesco had done. They turned to the passengers and got to work.

No one was in the lavatory when Scoth opened the door, and Jesco proceeded down the aisle. There were men and women reading newspapers and bouncing babies in their laps, sleeping with their hats tilted to shield their eyes, and gazing out the windows. Old and young, dressed everywhere from demure to brazen, a few of them looked at Jesco and Scoth in disinterest and most didn't bother to look up at all. The car was only three-quarters full, and some had stretched out over the unoccupied seats with jackets for blankets and pillows. One had covered himself up from head to foot, and Scoth lifted the jacket off the sleeping man's face to peek at him. It wasn't Yvod.

There were many cars in the train, and the wind was very strong in the times they were crossing between them. It made Jesco nervous, and he was always relieved to get inside the next car. They went from one to another, waiting outside lavatories to see who exited, and knocking on quarter compartments that had the curtains drawn. There were only two of those, and when people answered, Jesco apologized for disturbing them accidentally.

When they came to the third class cars, it became harder to search. The seats were smaller and all of them were occupied. There weren't nearly enough to go around, so dozens of people were standing and holding onto bars for balance. Anyone who got up for the lavatory or to retrieve luggage from overhead had their seat stolen, and several voluble arguments were going on as Jesco and Scoth walked through. A child of about eight was whining to his father that he couldn't stand for six hours, and when he was ignored, he punched his father's side in a tantrum. A white-haired woman exclaimed, "Aren't you a great big baby? For shame!" Outraged, the child shrieked, "I'm not a baby! I'm not a baby!" The father still did nothing. The boy's shrieks only cut off once Jesco got to the end of the car and closed the door behind him.

The little gymnasts were a sharp contrast in the next car. One was holding up another on his shoulders, and the child on top was holding the bar. People chuckled at the picture they made. The children smiled and waved. The others were squashed onto two seats, eagerly trading postcards, and one was minding a watch so that they could trade off with the children who were standing. In the back of the car, several women were singing and holding onto a stretcher, where an extremely aged woman was laying down under a woolen blanket. She looked over to Jesco when he passed and cried with joy, "Arlen! You're Arlen!"

"No, I'm not," Jesco said, but in a gentle voice.

Eagerly, she tried to take his hand. Seeing that she had on no rings, and not wanting her memories in his glove, he removed it and let her grasp his bare fingers. Hers were very cold, but her eyes were warm and full of recognition. "You come to the shore with me. Come to the shore, Arlen, with these girls. We're going so I can watch the tide come in one last time." The women smiled at Jesco. They were hospice workers, according to the blue bands on their arms.

One leaned forward and said, "Tell me about Arlen, Mrs. Kamb."

She let Jesco go and faced the woman. "He was my beau in university. I was in the first class of women admitted to Nuiten and he couldn't take his eyes off me." Another worker motioned for Jesco to move on while the dying woman was distracted. He slipped away to the door, putting his glove back on. There were few attendants minding the cars in third class; each appeared to have several cars to oversee and strolled about between them.

They had gone through a dozen cars now, and there was still no sign of Grance or Yvod. The thirteenth was the car reserved for people traveling with small animals. It was packed, and the noise was deafening. Dogs were barking, cats hissing and meowing, birds tweeting and flying about in their cages, and there were even little pigs on leashes. A woman was feeding a tiny black lamb that had been outfitted in a diaper. It sucked greedily at a bottle and butted it for more. Milk splashed all over its face.

Posted at the back door of the car was a sign. No passengers were allowed past this point, and the door was locked when Scoth tried it. He looked back through the car and waved to an attendant stepping out of the lavatory. She came to the back.

As Scoth took out his badge, she said cheerfully, "No more passenger cars back there! Got to move up the cars if you're looking for seats."

"Let us through, please," Scoth said. "Police business."

"Oh!" She took out a ring of keys and searched through them. "Looking for someone? There's nothing back there but our supplies car, snacks and such, and the freight cars after that."

"Could anyone board the supplies or freight cars?" Scoth asked.

She stared at her keys in confusion. All of them looked completely alike. "I keep a bit of string on the one to the door but it's fallen off. Bloody help there, eh?" Picking one out, she inserted it in the door. It didn't turn. "The supplies car can be boarded, that's the next one down, but we shoo people out of there if they climb in by accident. Sometimes we get a person down one car further where we stow the post and some luggage. Everything beyond that is freight, and those cars can't be boarded. They're fully enclosed. But we get people now and then clinging to the bars for a free ride. Some of them fall off in the badlands."

The fourth key turned and she pulled open the door. Raising her voice to be heard over a furious gale of wind and the sound of the train clacking on the tracks, she said, "But I had a quick look-see in those cars once we'd pulled away, and Cheffie did afterwards. There's no one back there." She didn't lock the door behind them, assuming that they would be right back. Jesco and Scoth crossed over to supplies as the woman walked away into the last third class car.

Both stopped to rub sand out of their eyes once they were inside. It was being carried by the wind. Then they took a look at the car. Big buckets were bolted to the floor, all of them covered and labeled, and there were shelves likewise bolted to the walls with their contents barred in. Food and water, medical supplies and pillows, it was so well packed that nothing even rattled as the train hurtled on.

The brig was a small, barred room without any feature but a bench. A sign warned to place a bucket inside if the person happened to be drunk. "They missed the train," Jesco said, having no choice but to accept it. "It doesn't matter. We can camp out at the Port Adassa station tomorrow evening when it's due to come back. They'll just take a room at some inn at Lowele for the night."

"I'm going to check the post car," Scoth said, his voice heavy with defeat.

They passed between the cars. The train was shooting through sandy hills. An old wagon wreck was out there, the tongue down in the sand, two of the wheels gone and the ragged bonnet waving in the breeze. Then it was out of view. Scoth opened the door to the post car and let Jesco in first.

He heard the loud laughter of a man, although he could see nothing through staggered banks of shelving units. Pivoting, he squeezed Scoth's arm hard. Scoth closed the door quietly and stood still beside Jesco.

The laughter was coming from the back of the car. An exasperated sigh replaced it, and a female voice said, "Stop trying to break into that! Who cares to read a bunch of strangers' mail?"

"We should swap it all," the man responded. "Open them up very carefully, slip out the letters, and stuff them into other envelopes before sealing them up again."

"Because that's amusing to you?"

He grunted over metal scraping. "Why . . . are these . . . all locked?"

"So people like you don't get into the mail and have a lark with it," the woman replied. Jesco knew her voice from Hasten Jibb's memories.

He gave Scoth a small nod and mouthed *it's her*. Slipping around Jesco, the detective peeked down the aisle. Jesco crouched and did the same.

In the staggered banks, boxes were stacked and restrained with wires on the shelves. Many of them held tabloids and special editions of newspapers, with their final destination printed on the side of Port Adassa, Dorset, or Thilian. Beyond the shelving units were giant buckets filled with oversize luggage, some of which belonged to Top Line. One of the bags was open and had spilled juggling balls on the floor. They were rolling about within the car. Past the buckets were individual compartments, and it was from those that the voices were coming.

Sounding even more exasperated, Grance said, "Will you *stop*? Let's just go up to first class and see if Papa is-"

"Oh, come on! We have alcohol and we have each other. What else do we need? He must think we missed the train and is right now working himself into a jolly good temper. Imagine his face when we step out onto the platform and he can't shout at us about anything. Besides, this way we ride for free." The metal scraping had ceased. Now there was an unsteady slapping sound. A ball ran out of one compartment and the man said, "Think I should take my show on the road, Grancie? I'll call it Yvod's Bouncing Balls."

"What'll the horse do?" Grance asked. "You realize you left it right there in the middle of the road with the carriage?"

"It'll just stand there until the train brings me back in the fall."

"It'll be stolen by then."

"Then I'll buy another one."

Scoth pulled back and Jesco whispered, "Should we get Cheffie?"

"He won't be any kind of help," Scoth hissed. "There are only two of them. I can handle it." Removing a pair of cuffs, he rounded the shelves and started for the compartments briskly.

Neither Grance nor Yvod heard him coming. The train was making noise and the balls were rolling and thumping into everything. Jesco crept after Scoth, stepping warily so he wouldn't trip on the balls. It was more than one bag that had been opened, he saw when he passed the luggage in the buckets. Several had been rummaged through, and so had the boxes of newspapers in the banks.

Suddenly, Yvod stepped out of the compartment. He was walking backwards while juggling three balls, his eyes fixed upon them. Catching one, he noticed Scoth and Jesco coming. The others fell to the floor as he smiled gallantly. His color was high like he had had quite a lot to drink. "Can you show us the way to first class? I think we boarded the wrong c-"

"Yvod Kodolli, you are under arrest," Scoth said, whipping out and grasping Yvod's arm. The cuff was slapped on faster than the man could react, but he began to struggle when Scoth attempted to take his other arm.

"What is this?" Yvod yelled, breaking away and backing up. "We're just on the wrong car! You can't arrest us for that."

"You're under arrest for the murder of Hasten Jibb and for the illegal distribution of rucaline," Scoth said. To the first charge, Yvod gave Scoth a look like he was insane. But to the second, the color drained out of his face. His free hand dove into his pocket and he pulled out a switchblade.

"Grancie!" he shouted as he lunged for Scoth. Scoth moved lightning-fast. Grabbing Yvod's forearm, he slapped the back of the man's hand with a hard blow. Yvod lost his grip on the switchblade, which flew away and hit the wall. Scoth whirled him around and tried to get the second cuff on.

Grance Dolgange appeared in the doorway to the compartment, her eyes wild. "Get him, Yvod!" she shouted.

Then she saw Jesco's gloves, and she understood without a word exchanged between them. Losing color just like her brother had, she turned away from Scoth and Yvod as they wrestled. She ran for the back of the car, her fingers flying up to the side of her head where she removed her hoop earring with a frantic jerk.

*Her jewelry.* She wanted to ensure that Jesco didn't get hold of her jewelry. Those were the earrings he had observed through Patty when Grance was giving over the bicycle. She had to have worn those at the party and Jesco would see what had happened through them!

Yvod dove for the switchblade and Scoth landed bodily on top of him. Leaping the struggling pair, Jesco sprinted for the back of the car where Grance was rolling open the door. She took several steps onto the shifting walkway and cried out when she realized that she could not board the freight car behind this one. There was no door, only a flat, featureless wall. Jesco passed the compartments and made it to the doorway.

Wobbling on the metal plates that connected the cars, Grance hurled her earring over the side. Her hands went to the second earring and she fought to remove it while staying balanced. Jesco stepped out after her and reached for her arm, shouting, "Stop!"

She twisted away, blinking hard at sand in her eyes. Both of them reeled as the plates shifted with the turning of the train. He grabbed hold of the chain as the second earring dropped from her fingers.

From her dress pocket came a blade. Slashing it through the air in warning, she yanked off her necklace and hurled it away. As it vanished into the sand, Jesco said, "The police will comb every inch of the ground along the tracks to get it back, Grance!"

She laughed harshly and slashed a second time. As he moved back, she yanked off her huge ring of diamonds. Then that was gone too, and she said, "Let them search! By the time they find anything, I'll be far from Ainscote."

Something slammed in the car, and dimly came Scoth's cry of warning. "*Jesco, watch o-*"

It happened too fast. Yvod seized Jesco from behind and propelled him forward onto the walkway, Grance lunging forward with her blade. The metal plates squealed under their feet and rotated with the train as it went around a curve. Pain burned in his side and he'd been stabbed . . .

It was not the first time that he had been stabbed, no, not with all the memories he had taken in from others, and the shock of it gave way quickly. Grance withdrew the blade and flailed for the chain as the train kept turning. Jesco fell back onto Yvod, who tried to push him over the side. Clinging to him, Jesco refused to be dislodged. Yvod lost his balance and they tumbled back into the car.

As the two fell, Jesco had a split second view of Scoth pounding on the locked door of a compartment, his face frantic as he stared out the small window. Metal grating had been placed over it. The floor rushed up and Jesco had no time to catch himself on anything. His head cracked against it and the world went black.

-he was-

-he was-

-he was washing this nasty mess on the floor-

"Stuff him into that one," Grance was commanding when Jesco returned to himself. He had touched something that sent him into a thrall, but he was no longer in contact with it. Still too stunned to move, and feeling warm blood pumping from his side, he remained limp as he was dragged into a compartment.

"Let's toss him off the train, and that one, too," Yvod said. Scoth was still pounding in the other compartment.

Sarcastically, Grance said, "And if the driver or someone looks back and sees them? If the train has sensors along the roof attuned for that kind of thing? The train will stop. *The train will stop, Yvod.*"

"Then what do we do?" Yvod said. They were arguing out in the aisle that ran between the compartments. Jesco stayed very still.

"We need to get higher in the train. Go back into that suitcase and take out those wigs you found earlier, and a shawl for me. That one is locked in and this one will bleed out. And keep your hand in your pocket so no one sees the cuffs. We'll take care of that later."

"We should strip him, or else some other seer will . . ."

"Don't be such an idiot! In three hours or so, we'll be at Port Adassa. We'll book passage on the next ship leaving and be gone. Let a fleet of seers peep through his clothes for all the good it will do them. Now come *on*! Close the door to that compartment. No one will find him until the postal worker goes in for the mail. I'll get the back door."

Jesco kept his eyes closed and held his breath as footsteps neared. One set went past the compartment that he was in, and the second set entered. "Nice gloves," Yvod said mildly. Jesco felt a tugging at his hands as his gloves were slid off.

"Damn!" Grance said.

Yvod returned to the aisle. "What is it?"

"You busted the door to outside somehow when you two fell in. Every time I close it up, it just slides back open."

"The catch must be broken. Leave it. Who cares?" As Grance continued to fiddle with the back door, Yvod rolled the one to the compartment shut. After several seconds, they walked back through the car to the luggage buckets. Yvod laughed at Scoth, who was shouting in panic for Jesco.

For a long time, Jesco slumped in silence. The only movement he made was to stiffen his left arm against his wound to lessen the bleeding. The blow to his side had not been a killing one, he gathered, and attributed it to the turning of the train as it had been dealt. They had all been thrown off-balance.

Scoth stopped banging. Yvod and Grance rustled through the luggage to disguise themselves, their voices coming through the wall to Jesco as dull burbles. A sharper sound came from the door to the walkway. Every time the train turned, it opened and banged shut.

Once the voices were gone, Jesco dared to move. First he inspected his wound. His shirt was sodden with blood. The blade had gone deep but missed his vital organs, so far to the side that it was less serious than it looked. Getting up with a groan, he went to the door and pulled off his shirt to cover his hands. He rolled it aside and staggered over to the compartment where Scoth was ensconced. Appearing at the window, Scoth said in relief, "You're alive!"

Jesco pressed at a keypad lock, blood smearing from his shirt to the numbers. Tapping the door, Scoth called, "You can't. This is a bank compartment. He jammed the numbers and it responds by locking on both sides. It should have triggered an alarm for the train guard, but . . ." Only the angels knew how long it would take for Cheffie to hobble to the back of the train, if he responded at all.

A twinkling attracted Jesco's eye at the back of the car. The train was going around a curve, the door having opened and now sliding shut. As Jesco wobbled away, Scoth called, "What is it?"

Gasping from pain as he opened the door, Jesco spied the cause of the twinkling. The second earring hadn't gone over the side. Hanging precariously by part of its hook, it had gotten caught in the chain along the walkway. The wind was edging the hook up the link, and the sun was reflecting off the diamonds hanging from the hoop.

It was about to fall, the wind and the weight of the bejeweled hoop working together to free it. Jesco dropped upon the walkway and thrust out his covered hand. The train squealed and turned, the wind kicked sand into his eyes and pulled at his shirt, and the earring fell.

The wind ripped the shirt away only a moment before the earring fell directly into his palm. He clapped his other hand over it, rocked backwards, and launched himself toward the car as he went into thrall. Crashing down to the floor between the compartments, the door rolled shut on his feet.

-he was-

-he was-

"*Jesco!*"

-she was-

-she was-

That son of a demon had brought it here, angels above, he had brought the delivery here! To the house! She stared at him dumbly and he smiled, smiled, smiled like the fool he was . . . he had no idea what he had done and she wanted to slap that stupid smile off his face . . .

"Jesco, let go of it!"

He didn't release the earring. He couldn't. He had to know. Moving aside in his mind, he let it sweep him away.

# Chapter Thirteen

And with the party starting in only hours! The delivery shouldn't have arrived for another *week*, coming with the shipment to the store and concealed in a box marked for the books manager! Then it would have been placed in the back office like normal, the employees warned not to open her mail and just to send her a message that it had arrived. She'd never worried about them getting into the delivery. Dircus hired honest people and they did as they were told. Once she received the message, she would have gone in for the day and locked herself into the office. The books were easy to manage and took only a little time. After that, she addressed the packages of rucaline to each dealer, dumped them into a bag mixed in with outgoing shop mail, and drove everything to the postbox on her way home.

There was a *procedure* for this, a strict procedure that had the rucaline in and out of her hands in a matter of hours. But Yvod had upended it with no more thought than he put into anything else.

Now he was sprawling on the couch, his dirty shoes propped up on the armrest and she hated him . . . she wished that she'd never had to involve him but half of her initial contacts were through him and hadn't he remembered what Farron *said* when they first got started? You *don't* have it on your person and you *don't* have it in your home and for the love of the angels you *don't* ever swallow it, you stay clean, clean, clean because the smallest whiff of involvement in rucaline will bring down the whole of the Drug Administration on your head.

"Why did you bring it here?" she exclaimed, pushing in her new earrings.

He didn't care, he never cared, and still he was smiling. His eyes had a telltale vacant look that told her he'd tried the smallest bit of rucaline himself. Kicking off his shoes, he said, "I was already coming this way, Grancie! It was no problem. The Four-fingered Man brought it to shore-"

"You shouldn't have been there to take it! What happened to Kobbes?"

"I gave him a wad of cash and told him not to worry about it! Why should he have to hide it in boxes of carriage parts and send it to-"

She was so angry that she cut him off again. "I have everything sent to the store so it doesn't come *here*! To my *home*! You can't stay for the party. You need to take it away!" Even as she said that, she had the dismal realization that he was in no condition to do so. His eyes drifted away from her, off into the distance where he was being crowned king or falling on a bed in a soft tumble of feminine limbs. Damn! Most people would mistake him for drunk but Skorla . . . Ailie . . . oh, they would recognize his look and Ailie would whisper to Yvod to share . . .

. . . and he *would* . . .

There could not be rucaline at this party. There could *not*. She had condemned rucaline after involving herself in it, left parties if it turned up in someone's hand, made up a frightening and utterly false tale of a strange man high on rucaline who slugged her in the street and swiped out for her purse. For years she had built up a reputation as a person who wouldn't have anything to do with rucaline or those who did it. She was careful not to pound the drum too hard or too frequently, but they knew, everyone acquainted with her knew that she was frightened of it. None would ever think that she'd been deep in the business all along.

Her mind was spinning in fruitless, agitating circles. She'd invited the newly married Lord and Lady Eddpra and they loved a party, the wilder the party the happier the two of them were, but not rucaline, never rucaline, Ivan had lost his girlfriend in university to a bolus dose and Nysta loathed Yvod. He had promised her a wedding and enjoyed her body but the ring never came . . . of course it hadn't come, Yvod would say anything to get a woman in bed . . . Nysta was vicious in her spite to those who wronged her and if she saw him high on rucaline tonight . . . a chance at long last for her to lash out at him, to hurt him as badly as he had hurt her . . . all it would take was an anonymous message that could never be traced back to her but would turn the eye of the law to Yvod . . .

And then to Grance.

The unaddressed packages were on the table. She thought to pack up the delivery and her brother back into his carriage and send him to the nearest brothel for the night. But she couldn't trust him with the rucaline!

If she hid it in the house and he stayed for the party, his high would wear off and he'd bother her for more, catching her to whisper about it every five minutes, dogging her and getting mad when she refused, and then he'd upend the house to find it! Involve a trusted friend or two in the search! She could not control him and he never listened to reason because he was just so *stupid.*

She had to stop panicking. First, she would get rid of her brother. Stalking over to the couch, she went through his shirt pockets and slapped him when he dully tried to push her away. She claimed the packet of rucaline from his vest and threw it on the table before she moved on to his trouser pockets. It occurred to her that she could flush it all away, or grind it up and pour the powder down the sink, but this was so much money and everyone was waiting for the rucaline! No, she wasn't going to destroy it. She wanted the money, needed the money that this delivery would bring. What she would do with it, well, she would figure that out once Yvod was out of her hair.

He had *taken* it. She should have anticipated that he couldn't resist it forever. If there was ale nearby he had to drink it; a woman and he had to charm her. Now he'd gotten into rucaline and he wouldn't be able to stop. He'd want more and more and more and soon everyone would see what he was doing and *damn!* She didn't want this blasted for her!

It wouldn't be. Once they were in the islands over the summer, she'd supply him with a heavy dose when they went out sailing. Drive him out of his mind and push him over the side to drown in the late afternoon. If she did it in the rough waters off Rogo Peak . . . yes, that would be the best place. People went under there every year, even the strong and sober. She would sail back to shore, sob and demand a search and fall into hysterics when they couldn't start at once since it was now evening.

If his body was recovered in the following days, no one was going to suspect rucaline. They would believe what she said: Yvod drank too much and fell over the side, and she'd never seen him come up. All of the authorities knew what Yvod was like. Even in a lenient island culture, he went too far. They tangled with him every summer. In retrospect, this demise of his would seem inevitable.

Grance's problem would be solved. When she determined that no more rucaline was on him, she heaved him up and said, "I'm sending you to Baker's Dozen." That would keep him occupied for the rest of the night, stuffing his mouth with doughnuts and stuffing his manhood into prostitutes. There were loads of brothels in Melekei, but Baker's Dozen was a deliberate choice on her part. It was the seediest of the establishments. Even if they suspected he was on rucaline, they were likely using it, dealing it, or at the very least turning a blind eye to it.

"But the party . . ." Yvod said dreamily. "I like your party."

"Papa is coming to the party this time. Do you want to see Papa?"

That was the right thing to say. No, Yvod did not want to see Papa! Not after Grandfather had cut off Yvod's allowance for his behavior, and Grance's with it though she had done nothing wrong. Papa had given them a little since then but not too much. He wouldn't go against what Grandfather wanted. Grandfather had the final word on everything, and he could not be cajoled, persuaded, or threatened to change his mind once he'd made it up. Yvod had been punishing them both with frequent absences from family events. His tantrum was upsetting no one. He overestimated his importance greatly.

She got Yvod to his feet and walked him to the front door. Down the stairs to his carriage, and she settled him inside. It was a mess from his travels, newspapers and clothes and food strewn everywhere, and it smelled of perfume. A woman had been within here recently, and fresh anger overcame Grance. Had that woman seen the rucaline? Was she going to talk?

Everything was going to explode if Grance did not get a handle on this. She went to the autohorse, feeling a flicker of annoyance at its silly color, and searched through the destination cards. She found the one for Baker's Dozen, installed it, and closed the flap.

The carriage rocked. Her brother had fallen to the messy floor inside. His head poked out the open door and he said, "Want to come along with me? They got men there, too! I'll bring them back here to party!"

She didn't go over to slap him. She didn't scream. Her blood was running cold at how he'd so blithely interrupted her means of income. She had married fast when she was cut off to get some security back. But it wasn't enough. This was, and she would preserve it through any methods necessary.

Yvod was still babbling about the prosties he could bring. If Grance was angry when she sent him away, the risk was too great that he would come back to aggravate her further. That was how Yvod worked, unless he was too drunk to remember who he was currently agitating. She had to play this a different way. Going to the open door, she assisted him back into the seat. Sweetly, she said, "You have a good time. I heard they've got several new women since the last visit you had there."

"But you could come. Forget the party!"

"I'll come tomorrow night. We'll rock the walls."

Now he was staring at her earrings in entrancement. The rucaline was fixating him upon something else other than arguing with her. "Go on, Yvod. I will see you soon." She closed the door. He smiled vaguely at her through the window.

# THE SEER

The autohorse didn't move. Of course it didn't move! She'd switched the destination cards but hadn't inputted Yvod's identification number. Opening the door again, she asked him what it was. He stared at her blankly.

He would just have to sit in there until he roused a little more and remembered it. She wasn't going to drag him back into the house. Going to the garden, her mind worked on what to do with the rucaline.

Minute after minute passed with Yvod failing to stir. A Ragano & Wemill courier turned down the lane and hope rose within her. She'd throw money at him and get all of it out of her house. Frantically, she waved. The caterers would be arriving within an hour to deliver and she had on some of the jewelry but still not the dress she wanted to wear . . . her hair had to be done and the ale glasses brought down from the top shelf . . .

Jesco watched the exchange of packages and money from the other angle. After Hasten Jibb rode away . . . all of the statues chasing after him in his merry boy's mind . . . Grance went to the carriage and opened the door. Slightly more cognizant, Yvod gave her the number. She programmed it into the autohorse and was relieved when it began to move. Pulling past the house, it circled at the stables and backtracked to the lane. Her idiot brother was borne away.

She'd gotten rid of him. She'd gotten rid of the rucaline. All was well.

Jesco nudged through the next hours. There was nothing in them but preparing for the party and the start of the party itself. Figuring the problems were solved, Grance had put Yvod's visit and the courier out of her mind. The sky darkened as the party progressed from outdoors to indoors, guests getting towels to dry off and threatening to march next door and teach that old man with the hose a lesson or two. But the ale was flowing freely and music was playing, so the neighbor was forgotten. Someone had brought two escorts in tight gowns, and they danced together lasciviously. Papa drank as he watched them. The blonde cupped the redhead's buttocks as they ground against one another. Her fingers slipped down to the hem of the dress and she flashed her dance partner's bare buttocks to their attentive audience. Papa laughed at the naughty peek he'd gotten and called to Grance for something stronger to drink. She got it for him. The doctor had told him to cut back to save his liver, but tonight was for enjoyment, not good sense.

. . . she was having such a good time . . . she threw parties, *true* parties where inhibitions were checked at the door. If her guests wanted to fight, they fought; if they wanted to have sex, they found a room; if they wanted to eat to the point of vomiting and eat some more, there was a feast in the kitchen and dining room with which to glut. People were playing cards and swilling drinks and kissing wherever she looked as she wandered through the house. One couple had gone farther than that, almost naked on a couch in the parlor with half a dozen voyeurs cheering them on. They were friends of friends and she didn't remember their names, but she'd find out and invite them again. They weren't shy about putting on a show.

She left the man bending down to the woman's lap to kiss the dark hair between her thighs, everyone hooting and hollering, and passed to the front of the house. Bryna staggered around the corner of the entryway, giggling and drunk, and fell on Grance. Laughing, Grance caught her. Bryna swayed in her arms and said, "There's someone at the door."

. . . sweet love of the angels, it was the courier . . .

Bryna had staggered on down the hall, and for the moment, nobody was in the entryway but Grance. She stared in blind fury at the man there holding one of the packages . . . he had brought it back, *he had brought the rucaline back and she had a house full of people* . . . Stepping outside and closing the door swiftly, she said, "What are you doing here?"

"It broke when I fell off my bicycle," the man said. "I know what these are. I know what these are and I won't deliver them. I'm sorry."

The package in his hand was busted open, the rucaline visible inside. She felt dizzy at how badly this day was going. Pinched between his knuckles was the cash that she had given him. He opened up his satchel to show her the rest of the packages. "I don't want anything to do with this. Drugs are dangerous. I came to give these back to you." Something crashed from within the house, a lamp or a mirror shattering.

She didn't believe for a minute that the package had opened by accident. He'd gotten curious and gone nosing. "Name your price," she said flatly.

He looked at her in bewilderment. She was dealing with someone even less intelligent than Yvod. "A hundred per package?" she asked, switching to a coy smile to charm him. "Two hundred?" Perhaps he wanted a regular cut, to be the courier for every delivery. He wanted more money. It was always about money. "Three hundred? Your own courier company? Or would you like something else?" Her smile grew even coyer. She'd sleep with him if that was what it took, give him the time of his life and wrap him around her little finger so he'd do anything for her. Sex didn't mean a thing to her and he was handsome enough.

It was apparent that he preferred men from how he didn't react to her flirtatious smile. He tried to give her the busted package. When she didn't take it, he said, "I'll put them on the porch for you. Good night."

"No!" she exclaimed. "Isn't there any amount of money-

"No, thank you," he said.

He placed the broken package on the banister and reached into his satchel for another one. Voices boomed in the entryway. Stepping to the courier as he put down a second package by the first, Grance said in panic, "All right. But, please, will you put them in the stables for me? I would appreciate it very much."

Jesco did not want to watch, but he had to. A little of Collier's star burned within his inner eye, and part of his mind trained itself upon the shifting beams as Hasten Jibb returned the packages to his satchel. He went down the stairs to the garden, and Grance went back inside the house. She cut quickly through to the kitchen and dropped a casual reference to the couple having sex in the parlor. The two people eating shrimp snorted with laughter and went to see.

Grance's hand . . . Jesco's hand . . . went out to the spare knife in the side drawer. She slipped outside and headed for the stables, the blade hidden up her sleeve. Letting herself in, she closed the door for privacy. No one had parked in here, or could when the Eddpras had left their carriage in front of it.

The courier was looking for a place to put the packages down when there was no table or counter to hold them. She motioned to the corner, where he bent to stack them up neatly. When he was done, he turned and offered the cash. "And here's your money."

"Thank you," she said, taking it, and stabbed him.

She did it twice, deeply and viciously with her mind as blank as the sky. She was just handling the problem. He cried out but no one heard. Everyone was in the house, the windows and doors closed. When he fell, she waited for him to still and let the blade drip on his shirt. Then she wiped it off on his trousers and checked herself over for blood spatter.

There was none. Now for the rucaline. She gathered up the packages and slipped out the back of the stables. In the gardener's shed? Not safe. In a flowerpot? That could be smashed and the contents discovered. Snagging a spade from the shed, she covered her hand in a rag and hastily dug shallow holes in the soft earth beneath three of the bushes along the fence. There she buried the rucaline. Afterwards, she rid herself of the spade and rinsed off her hands with the hose.

Now for the body. She didn't know what to do with that. Burying packages was one thing; a body was quite another. And the clothes . . . she had to do something about his clothes and satchel or else a seer could . . . She stripped him and hid everything in the shrubbery behind the stables.

Getting her father from the house, Grance brought him to the stables to see the naked body. She'd gone out for air, heard an odd sound from the backyard and headed over to identify the cause . . . sob, sob, clutch Papa's arm . . . this crazy, naked man had appeared out of nowhere, came at her with that knife . . . no, she had never seen him in her life, Papa, he was a mental case and she'd managed to turn the knife back on him as they struggled . . . Papa, was she going to go to *prison? . . . No, baby, no . . . Papa, we can't have the police here tonight. We can't! I thought I saw Ailie with rucaline in there! I wasn't sure; he was hiding it from everyone. Papa, what do we do? If the police search my house and find Ailie with any of that . . .*

Papa had never been hard to play. She had seen through him since childhood. He liked to be the hero but those chances were few for a man who lived under the thumb of his father. Torrus Kodolli filled the room with his presence, dominated conversations and demanded everyone be his reflection or else he decimated them. Papa bridled beneath his outward compliance. That was why he fought so often with Yvod, who also filled the room and could not bear a pair of eyes to look elsewhere. Grance went to Papa with messes for him to fix and he leaped to the occasion, loving an opportunity to step from the shadows of both his father and son.

He could not resist a chance to be in charge, to call the shots, to be the big man. As she had calculated, he did exactly that. She hurried to fulfill his commands to go out to the road and make sure that no one had blocked in his carriage, and to find a spare rug, blanket, or tarp.

His carriage was at the curb and free to move. The party was still carrying on within the house but it would not be long . . . no, they did not have much time . . . She went inside and was thankful that everyone was still engaged in carousing. Taking her oversize throw from the back of the sofa, she sneaked back to the stables.

They wrapped up the body and blade together, Papa whispering that she was never, ever to invite Ailie to a party again. Grance shook her head fervently. *Never, Papa, never.* Then they cleaned up the blood with the gardener's rags and carried the body out to the carriage. Darkness had fallen and no one was around but a wandering horse, which was grazing upon a neighbor's lawn. No sooner had they shoved the body inside than the front door opened and two of her friends spilled out. "Grance, there you are! Grance, you've got to see what they're doing now!"

Papa smiled tightly and hugged her. He hissed in her ear, "Go in there and pretend everything is fine. I'll take care of this."

. . . thank you, Papa . . .

. . . oh no, he has to go, my father is so sorry to be leaving, he wants to stay and have a good time, but he's overtired . . . yes, the doctor thinks that he will be fine if he just takes it easy . . . he got his jollies from those trollops dancing and is that couple still going at it in the parlor . . . it's three couples now? . . .

. . . laughter . . .

Jesco nudged to the bonfire, which Grance had set up as a cover to get rid of the bloody clothes and rags that she had tucked into the satchel. When they went up in flames, she was filled with relief. Nobody was interested in going into that dark corner behind the stables except to relieve themselves. The packages were not going to be discovered. That was where she should have put them in the first place!

But everything had worked out fine in the end. Drinks were pressed on her and burning down her throat and she danced . . . tomorrow morning she'd dig up the rucaline when everyone was gone, wipe off the dirt and get it in the post. Before she did anything, that had to get done. Not at your home, not on your person, and most assuredly not *in* your person . . . she'd been warned long ago how to stay safe in this game and she'd taken all of it to heart . . . the people who got caught always tripped up on one or more of those three rules.

Not her, however. Yvod and the courier had tried to trip her up, but she was still standing. The courier wasn't, and Yvod wouldn't be for much longer. He'd be wise to enjoy himself while he still could. The problems were being solved, and she gave herself over to revelry. Dancing and drinking and blindfolding a man before she pulled him away with her for play . . . he didn't know who she was but her body excited him, his hands on her breasts, between her thighs, he pushed himself inside her and she lost herself in the crackling of the fire, the singing of the crickets and rhythmic grunting of her lover . . . as soon as he spilled his seed, she would fade away and he would always wonder which woman at the party he had been with . . . that was as pleasurable as the sex to her, to deny him her identity . . .

Jesco nudged. She had worn the earrings three times since the murder, her new favorites, but the memories held nothing of interest and then . . . she disappeared.

He blinked and trembled, Scoth pulling the earring away. Jesco was on the floor of the car, his hands crossed over his chest and his head balanced on Scoth's knees. Scoth was being vigilant that his trousers did not touch the back of Jesco's neck. Beneath Jesco was a blanket, presumably a new one from the supplies car. His bare skin upon it was not triggering a thrall. Crammed beside them in the narrow aisle was Cheffie. He was putting a sterile bandage over the stab wound, his hands in gloves.

"I saw her do it," Jesco said, weak from his wound or the thrall, or a combination of the two. A spare pair of gloves was resting on his chest, and he put them on shakily. "Grance Dolgange murdered Hasten Jibb in her stables during the party, and Morgan Kodolli took the body away in his carriage."

"And Yvod?" Scoth asked.

"Yvod Kodolli brought the rucaline to her house that afternoon. He wasn't supposed to do that; the delivery was supposed to arrive within a shipment of carriage parts at her husband's store. But he was not present at the murder, nor did he have prior knowledge of it."

"Tallo Quay? Anything about him? Or the timepiece?"

"Nothing about Tallo Quay, but she hasn't owned these earrings long. And there was nothing about the timepiece. That must have come from Morgan."

"I want your ablest men and women working on board this train," Scoth said in a stentorian voice to Cheffie. "We will search car to car and take them into custody. As soon as we arrive in Port Adassa, I want their police station notified and a barred carriage sent to transfer them to a holding cell. Do you have a nurse or doctor on board?"

"That's me, too," Cheffie said apologetically. "I don't think he'll die from this, but I'll call over the medical carriage at the port station to take him to the hospital."

Jesco could feel his legs, but could hardly crook them at the knee. Still, he could turn his head just fine and raise his arms. He would need his wheelchair for a short time, but that was back in freight and inaccessible until they arrived. He closed his eyes as Cheffie said, "We can get Brant from the third class cars, Margo too, they're the closest. If they're not in those cars, the next attendant up will be Hankum. He deals with a lot of our drunks-"

-he was-

-he was-

-he was Laeric-

Jesco looked so pale and it was stupid, *stupid* to have brought him along, to involve him in a fight when one touch could flatten him . . . if something worse had happened then Jesco was going to walk with Laeric and that would sting more than all the rest put together . . .

The thrall broke as Jesco was heaved upwards. He found his feet, though they would not hold his weight, and the two men helped him through the post car to the luggage buckets. Clearing a space between the last bucket and the shelving units, Scoth set him down and said, "I'll be back. I promise. We're going to throw all three of them in the brig and then I'll find you a better seat than this one."

"Don't let me walk with you," Jesco said, pulling the blanket around his chest. "Let me go, Laeric. When it's time, no matter how it comes about, just let me go. I won't be leaving with regrets, so don't have any for me." Scoth looked stricken as Cheffie vanished around the staggered banks.

He pressed a rough kiss to Jesco's forehead. "You'll walk with me always," he said, and backed away to go after the train guard.

Jesco was not worried. He had every confidence in how it was going to play out, Scoth and a fleet of train employees searching the cars, descending upon Grance and Yvod and cuffing them. Hauling them to the brig with their father to wait out the last of the journey to Port Adassa. This case was ending at last, even if there were still some loose ends to tidy up.

. . . she had been a very bad girl . . .

. . . a scholar! Doesn't it feel fine! Go to school today, Taniel, go to . . .

. . . Hold on tight to my back and I'll swim across! . . .

. . . chase! They were catching up, the fairies and flamingos and . . .

. . . everything in the world is a bloody menace to you . . .

No, that last one was Jesco's. That was a real memory. The world shifted all around him, whirling pools of memories rising from the floor and all of them wanting him to look in. He stared ahead to the image of Laeric Scoth and the world steadied as he slipped into sleep.

# Chapter Fourteen

He woke up in a hospital bed, the sheets so new that they had creases. Still dressed in his trousers but with an equally new gown for a shirt, he blinked blearily. The table beside him held a glass of water in his personal cup. Pushed up beside the bed was his wheelchair. He had scant memories of getting from the train to the hospital, or any idea how long ago it had been, and his stab wound had somehow gotten stitched with him unaware.

Out the window, the sky was gray. It was very early morning, and he was in need of the lavatory. He got out of the bed, tested his legs, and found that they held. Going to the door, he saw the lavatory straight across the hallway. No one was inside.

When he stepped out, he went to the nurses' station to quietly ask what was going on. Every room he'd passed held sleeping patients. There was a message for him, which one nurse read out loud. "All three suspects have been detained. Will stop by when I can. Signed, Laeric. Postscript: don't touch anything." The nurse put down the message. "Well, that's not very nice, is it?"

Jesco had taken it very differently. "He's just brusque. It isn't meant poorly." The nurse did not look convinced. Since there was nothing else to do, and his legs were weak, he took himself back to bed.

By morning he was feeling much better. After breakfast he walked to the hospital's common room and took a seat. The view from the big windows was of the sea. He had seen it many times through other people's memories, but this was the first time as himself. Waves rolled in, their crests white as they crashed to the sand. Seagulls called and swooped through the sky as holiday-goers walked along the beach with umbrellas over their shoulders to keep off the sun. Children crafted sand castles and darted in and out of the shallow fans of water to spread over the shore with each wave. It was a beautiful, entrancing scene, the beating of the waves coming through the glass as a steady, soothing rumble. Jesco could not look away. When he was stronger, he wanted to stroll down to that beach and watch the ships trailing along the horizon.

That was where Scoth found him sometime later. The night had been long and it didn't look like the detective had spent much of it sleeping. The products he used in his hair had lost their control, so he was a rumpled yet riveting mess. Falling into the armchair beside Jesco, he said, "We got them. We got them on everything."

"I'm glad," Jesco said. "Do you need me to touch a belonging of Morgan Kodolli's to get his memories about Hasten Jibb's body?"

"No. He confessed. He doesn't want a seer touching him. The demons know what else you'd dig up. I'm sure you've got a thousand questions, but I'm too tired to think so just let me ramble as it comes to me. How about I start with Kyrad's erstwhile escort Tallo Quay? So the fellow went to the theater to talk to Torrus Kodolli, who sent him away. That much was true. Morgan was there that night, and saw it for himself. What the old man failed to mention was that he arranged to meet up with Quay at Agrea's Cantercaster office later that night. It isn't far from the theater, and they don't use that office. Most of what's in it is storage, years of old paperwork and the like that nobody needs but hasn't gotten rid of yet. One room is still set up as a conference space, and that's what you saw, the chandelier hanging over the table. What you didn't see was how much dust was all over everything, and that there were heaps of boxes, stacks of ledgers, and old file cabinets lining the walls. Quay came in and shared his dirt, and he pushed that timepiece over the table to prove he had a real connection to Naphates.

"But Torrus Kodolli doesn't play those games, his son told me. If Quay would sell out Naphates, he'd sell out Kodolli once something better came along. Kodolli hates disloyalty, even if it hasn't happened yet. He wasn't about to help a turncoat. The old man had his bodyguards strangle Quay and take his body away in Morgan's carriage. The remains were buried in the fields behind the home Torrus Kodolli keeps in Cantercaster. Apparently, Quay is not the only one out there. Missing union organizers, prosties who saw too much, people threatening to cause the old man trouble . . . we're going to be digging up those fields real soon."

"Was it Torrus Kodolli who sent those riders after us in Somentra?" Jesco asked.

"No. That was Morgan. Don't ask questions," Scoth groused.

Jesco smiled and let him continue. "The bodyguards forgot to take the timepiece along when they went off with Quay's corpse. It had gotten knocked off the table, still in its case, during the struggle. Morgan found it when he was going over the scene to make sure nothing of Quay was left. Since the place is storage that no one goes into, the old man just kicked the case with the timepiece in it behind the boxes. Then they left in his carriage and the affair was done."

"They should have thrown it out!" Jesco exclaimed.

"It didn't seem pressing to them. No one was going to find it there. The low-level employees of Agrea don't have keys to that office, nor do most of the high-level employees. None of them had any reason to take a carriage over to that office. Like I said, all that's in there are reams of old paperwork, broken equipment and extra furniture. It's junk. Junk that needs to get sorted through, trashed or donated, and no one's bothered with it in many years. The company just pays for the space rather than put in the time to discard everything. It was very late at night by that point and the old man wanted to go home. So that was the end of Tallo Quay, and how the timepiece transferred to Torrus Kodolli."

Beside the nonstop hurly-burly of human activity, the waves rolled in peacefully and had all along. Every breath that Jesco had taken upon this world had been with this lovely, tireless ocean curling and uncurling its rippled blue skirts unseen. They watched it, Scoth stifling a yawn.

Pulling off his glove, Jesco put his hand over Scoth's. Fighting off another yawn, Scoth said, "I think, in a strange way, that Morgan was happy to rat out his father. He has lived in that man's shadow all his life. Taken his orders, bent over backwards to please him, and all to be told that the deceased brother Flike had showed a lot more promise for business. Morgan is a petty, jealous, vindictive man. But then you look at his father, and you understand why. Anyway, Quay was buried, and his timepiece forgotten in that office. Life went on. The old man kept his company going and pried a little into the background of the Parliament members slipping Naphates favors. But Morgan thought his father was hesitant to go on the attack. Naphates is well liked, and he's got so much dirt of his own that he doesn't want pried into and dug up. An attack would have to be elegantly designed, and Torrus Kodolli is getting on in years. Losing some of his fangs, Morgan said. But perhaps his father *is* designing something, and hasn't thought to inform or involve Morgan. That's also possible. Torrus doesn't confide in his lesser son. That's neither here nor there."

"But the article that went after her . . ."

Scoth gave him an irritated look, but turned his hand over and interlocked their fingers at the same time. "There was a family kerfuffle going on around the same time as Quay's murder. The old man was sick of seeing Yvod's name in the papers for acting like a hooligan, and was tired of paying all his court fees. Yvod couldn't go three months without getting into fresh trouble, and his grandfather was shelling out left and right to shut people up and lower his sentences. What was printed in the papers was nothing compared to what the old man paid to keep out of them. He wanted Yvod to show initiative, get involved in the family business or take a job elsewhere. Just do *something* more than drinking and fighting and whoring, and costing his grandfather money. Torrus Kodolli has worked every day of his life for well over sixty years, and he can't stand that his own grandson hasn't worked a single day ever. He cut off Yvod and Grance both. They were receiving extremely generous allowances on a monthly basis."

"Why Grance as well?"

"Same reason minus the trouble. The old man makes money and those two do nothing but spend it, whether it's on court fees or jewelry shopping or ritzy vacations. He wanted them to take some pride in themselves, learn the value of a dollar, because one day the company will pass on to them. But Yvod couldn't even graduate from university, he failed out of three different schools, and Grance graduated but she's never shown any interest in picking up the torch. They don't want to work like they see their grandfather and father do. They're spoiled rotten since the cradle. Anything they've ever wanted, they've gotten. Up until their grandfather cut off their allowance in the hopes that it would propel them to become adults."

"It didn't," Jesco observed.

"It didn't," Scoth repeated. "It was too late for that. Until he brought down the hammer on their allowance, Grance had just been handling a little rucaline. It was something she got involved in when she and Yvod were at Nuiten. It wasn't so much about the money for her as it was the thrill. The thrill of outwitting law enforcement; the thrill of getting away with it. She slipped it into the country and gave it to the dealer, who did the dirty work on the streets and handed back a stack of bills. After she lost her family money, she got married fast to the wealthiest man she could convince to put a ring on her finger. That won her a beautiful home in Melekei and plenty of money to spend, but not the exponential amounts that she was accustomed to living upon. She expanded her rucaline business greatly as a result."

"The neighbor heard the husband complaining about how much she spent."

"The Dolganges are a rich family, but they live rather on the modest side compared to how they could. She'd run through the money Dircus gave her, run through her rucaline money, and be at loose ends until more came in. She has entire storage spaces around Melekei and Cantercaster filled with clothes and furniture and jewelry. She has to eat at the best restaurants and stay in the most expensive rooms at the finest hotels. She grew up like that and that's how she intended to keep living. That was how she went from one dealer to twelve, and she had plans to take it further than that. And no, the husband doesn't know a thing about the rucaline, before you ask. She kept him in the dark, as well as her father and grandfather, and everyone in her social circle save her brother. Rucaline was the perfect business to her perspective: she did very little yet made money hand over fist, just as long as she didn't get caught. And then Yvod interrupted the system of delivery to bring it to her house personally the day of the party."

"She panicked," Jesco said.

"She adores the thrill, but she's no fool. She knows damn well what happens to rucaline distributors. She and Yvod were looking at life imprisonment. She wanted it gone and paid Jibb handsomely to take it away. But then he came back and she killed him." Scoth shook his head. "She's one of the cold ones. Stone cold. There's no heart beating behind that breast, that's for certain. Her father was distraught at times in his interrogation; her brother showed some worry, although most of it was for himself. He didn't know that Hasten Jibb got murdered that night. But she was flat when she talked. Completely flat. Committing murder was nothing to her. She doesn't care a whit about who Jibb was. He just got in her way. That people lose their minds on rucaline is nothing to her either. Then they shouldn't have taken it. That's how she thinks. It's not her problem. She wrapped up the body, sent it off with her father in the carriage, and that was that."

"Mercy," Jesco pleaded. "Tell me about the timepiece."

Scoth sighed and acquiesced. "As she went back into the party to suggest a bonfire, Morgan Kodolli went off with Jibb's body. He had no idea that Hasten Jibb was actually a courier. He had taken his daughter's word for it that this was just a homeless, crazed bum wandering naked around Melekei who had attempted to assault his daughter. Melekei has had a lot of problems with miscreants, problems that they've been trying to quash with more security at the outskirts of the city. Morgan rolled out of Melekei, looking for a place to dump Jibb and not wanting to take the body to those fields and bury it. Then he'd have to involve his father in this. And as he was sitting within the carriage, he had an idea."

Scoth took a moment to stretch and Jesco glowered at him. "He knew that Kyrad Naphates was up for that liaison position, but it was a lot more personal than that. After Cluven Naphates died all those years ago and she inherited, the old man offered to buy the mines and she refused. So he ordered his son to bedazzle her. Morgan was a strapping young buck at the time, and his father didn't think it would take much to sweep a silly girl off her feet."

Kyrad stirred within Jesco's memories. She adored her entertainments, that much was true, yet there was nothing silly about her. "But she was quite determined to not get married again."

"And that doomed him to failure in his attempt to woo. He pulled out all the stops: flowers and gifts in the post, poems at a party and a fancy dinner just for two. She was the most beautiful woman in Ainscote, she had the company his father was after, and Morgan wanted her badly. He thought they would be the sharpest couple in the country, splashed on the front page of society papers, and invited everywhere to meet the best people. But his dreams came to nothing. She didn't want him back. As the son of the man who owns Agrea, he's not used to women who say no. All he's ever had to do is flash his last name and his wealth, and women fight to be on his arm. He was handsome once but nothing to look at now, yet that's true to this day. *Kodolli* is a magic word. He's proud of who he is.

"Still, for all his pedigree and money, he couldn't catch Kyrad. He confessed his devotion at that fancy dinner and she laughed in his face. She suspected what he was about and she wanted no part of him either in her bed or in her company. Decades later, Morgan Kodolli is still hearing her laugh. He hates her for so much more than business. Some trashy girl from a miner's family turning him down! That's been cutting at him for all these years. He got married, had children, hasn't seen Kyrad in years, but he's still burning with rage that she rejected his proposal."

Jesco had been within minds like that, fuming over slights long after everyone else had forgotten about them. "She was under no obligation to marry him just so he could fulfill those fantasies about being in the papers and rubbing elbows with former royalty."

"That's how a normal person views it, Jesco. That isn't how he views it. He was doing her an honor. She was nothing; he was everything. He was going to win his father's approval through wedding her as well. She was the ticket to his future. For everything that he hasn't accomplished in his own life since then, he lays it at her feet. The moment she laughed was the moment everything went wrong for him. He was practically spitting on the table in the station as he spoke, and I had to pretend it was all very logical to keep him going. He's the reason the Rosendrie South Press published that nasty little article about her partying a few years ago. He hadn't attended the party himself, but heard about it from someone who did. The article was his way to draw some blood, to get his pound of flesh from her, but that didn't work out. No one cared. That infuriated him. She holds a supremely important position in his head-"

"Yet in no one else's," Jesco finished.

"He doesn't see that. It was a bit rich to hear him savage her in the interrogation room for accidentally showing her brassiere when he himself attends sex parties at the home of his own daughter."

Finally, *finally*, it was coming together. "Morgan got the timepiece from the storage office!"

"Yes. He was almost to Cantercaster and still looking for a place to dump the body when it came to him. How to get a real revenge on her all these years later. He reprogrammed the autohorse to go to the office, where he let himself in and dug around the boxes to retrieve the case. It was still there, exactly where his father had kicked it."

"But it was that timepiece that led us to him and his family! He may as well have drawn us a map to him!"

Delicately, Scoth said, "There's a reason that the old man hasn't handed over the reins of the company to him, I'd say. Morgan . . . it became clear as we were talking that he just doesn't have the same horsepower." Scoth tapped his forehead. "He isn't a clever man. This was his logic: he and his father had never touched the timepiece, so what was a seer going to get from it? Quay even said that he had barely touched it himself. It had sat in the case with the lid closed since it was given to him. What would a seer see except Kyrad Naphates and Tallo Quay, who was now dead and no one had ever come looking for him or reported him missing? Morgan got the timepiece and thought about where would be best to leave the body. Rosendrie is south of Cantercaster, and that was why he took the body all the way down to Wattling to be within a few miles of her home."

"Did he know that he was in Poisoners' Lane?"

"Not at first. It was night, and all he had for light in that area was the lantern he keeps in his carriage and another embedded in the chest of the autohorse. He wandered around Wattling, driving the horse manually and seeking a block where no one was hanging around, and eventually ended up in the dead zone. By the time he figured out where he was, he thought it might work to his advantage. There was absolutely no one around to witness him get the body from the carriage. He dragged Jibb into the alley and hung the timepiece from that nail to make it look like it had been dragged from a pocket by its chain. He never let it touch his bare skin."

"Which was why I only had vague impressions."

"He thought he was being brilliant with where he left the body. Anywhere else and someone likely would have swiped the timepiece. But in Poisoners' Lane? Very few people go in there, and pretty much always just to walk through. *No one* is going to pick up a timepiece from there. He was guaranteed that it would still be in that alley near the body by the time the police arrived.

"As for Jibb, he had been clumsily wrapped in a throw from Grance Dolgange's house. It was saturated with his blood and came off while he was being dragged. Morgan took it further down the alley, put a heavy rock in it and tied it shut with a cord left on the ground. He threw it in the river. The blade, too. Then he drove away into the night unobserved, passed back through Wattling and went home. There's nothing remarkable about his autohorse or carriage, so he didn't stand out to anyone. The timepiece would be found in the police search, he trusted, and the police force with a seer would link it to Kyrad Naphates. He had one of his bodyguards stake out the road going to her home. Once we went past and the bodyguard got confirmation from a servant of hers that it was the police, Morgan had that article run in the South Press. It did what he wanted: blew her chance of getting the liaison position, associated her name with an unsolved murder, and reminded everyone how she runs through escorts."

Jesco was astonished. "That was an awfully big risk he took all to settle an old score. An old score that didn't even matter to anyone!"

"It mattered to him. He'd also been drinking at Grance's party, and drank more in his carriage. Something too risky when sober can seem like a great idea with a respectable amount of alcohol flowing through the veins. He wanted to make problems for Naphates, and he did. But he made a lot more for himself. In fact, in his efforts to stir the pot a little for Kyrad, I'd say he just brought down his entire family."

"Did you ask him about the attack outside Somentra?"

"I did. Morgan recognized the photograph of Hasten Jibb and went into a blind panic that we were linking them. The timepiece, too, and Tallo Quay. He sent those riders after us with orders to kill, and believed it would be several days before the wreck was noticed. That isn't a heavily traveled road. He informed Grance that the police were drawing lines between the body and their family, and they decided the best thing to do was to quit Ainscote. The sea is against them for a little while longer, however, so they took their time in getting down to Port Adassa. They've got homes in the Sarasasta Islands and also in Brozzo, lots of money in foreign banks. We don't have an extradition agreement with Brozzo, and the island authorities won't be in any rush. Yvod and Grance started south, and Morgan wrapped up some loose financial ends, packed up his things to get mailed to his foreign homes, and did the same. They traveled separately and arranged to meet at yesterday's train. He intended to find the next freight headed for Brozzo or the islands and purchase passage. It never occurred to them that the police might be on their tails. Hasten Jibb was just a courier, after all."

Scoth settled back in the chair in satisfaction. "We'll dig up those fields behind the old man's house and get him and the bodyguards on multiple counts of murder. We've got Morgan on multiple charges of being an accessory, and attempted murder in our two cases since he hired those riders. We've got Yvod on rucaline distribution, and Grance on that plus the murder of Jibb plus attempted murder of you. All the money and lawyers in the world won't save them now. It's a good day."

"It really is," Jesco agreed. "Maybe Kyrad will make an offer on Agrea."

Scoth laughed. "Maybe she will. And maybe my suspension won't be too long. I'm about to hand the captain a stack of arrests that will rock all of Ainscote. Every newspaper from coast to coast is going to have this story on the front page. It will be a storm."

It was hard to imagine that when everything here was so tranquil. "But not yet."

"Not yet," Scoth said, tipping his head. His eyelids were drooping shut from fatigue. All of the tension was gone from him, as so rarely happened. In moments he was asleep, his hand still in Jesco's.

Jesco watched the waves come in, fully within his own mind and memories, and all of his strength returning. Within each crest before it broke, the sun was reflecting upon infinite stars.

# Epilogue

Jesco slipped back into the calm rhythms of the asylum, where life moved at a slower, more reflective pace. The gardener continued his never-ending battle with the flowers and foliage, doomed to lose in the loveliest way. The children circled around Jesco for attention as they always did, Nelle wanting to sit in his lap and the older ones requesting tales of murder and whirly-gig demonstrations.

A letter came from Isena, who had been shocked and proud to see his name in the papers connected to the case. His nephews had taken the article to school to show their friends, and now all of the little fellows wanted to meet this seer who solved crimes. Her postscript reported that she had visited their parents and siblings recently. While nothing had changed with their mother and father in South Downs when it came to Jesco, and she doubted anything ever would, she wanted him to know that Lyall sent his well wishes.

Lyall. They had been the best of friends until Jesco's seer abilities came over him. That changed them into enemies. To have well wishes from an older brother who used to beat him was an extraordinarily queer feeling. Lyall had told Isena that he was sure Jesco wouldn't want letters or a visit to the asylum from him and his wife, and Isena offered to pass along Jesco's answer should it differ.

The world was changing. Some people changed with it. Yes, he would like to hear from Lyall, to know what kind of man he had become. Jesco still longed for his roots, and if his brother was extending a hand in friendship, then Jesco was going to take it. They could not help how they had been raised, and they were not who they had been long ago. Jesco would give him a chance. He would come out no worse than he had been before if Lyall still rejected him. If not, he had another member of his family back.

He would never step out of the asylum's front doors to see his whole family arriving for a visit. That was a dream that would not manifest. But how rich he felt when a carriage disgorged Isena and her children, and one day Lyall might be there, too.

The storm had descended just as Scoth predicted, and all Jesco had had from him were terse though affectionate notes. The murder of Hasten Jibb was solved yet only gave birth to further cases. A fleet of seers was brought in for the bodies in the fields outside Torrus Kodolli's Cantercaster home. Jesco was not one of them. His knife wound needed to heal. He hoped the cases wrapped up tidily and Scoth could step away when it was time to attend the whirly-gig convention.

He received a visit from Tammie one day. She had brought along a framed plaque that the station received from Parliament. Scoth had received one for merit, as had Tammie, and this one was for Jesco. His name was printed in tall letters, and hanging underneath the glass was a medal. In their struggles to solve the murder of a courier, they had ended up taking down the largest distributor of rucaline in their region.

Sitting beside him in the drawing room, Tammie was nonplussed about the plaques. "It beats a kick in the pants, but it's not something we can use to pay the bills, is it? I suppose I can impress the ladies with the medal, take it from the plaque and wear it when I go about my day, but most will just think I look like a prat and secretly I'll agree. I didn't do so much on this case anyway. I do miss having you two as roommates, though, but I would like to ask why I came out that one morning and the curtain was down in the window."

"You don't want to know," Jesco said, and she grimaced. "How is Laeric? Have you seen him?"

"Barely. Now he's got those bodies in the fields to work. He was there at the station when they brought in Torrus Kodolli, however. That man! I heard his buttoned-up lawyers had a hissy fit at the judge for him being denied bail. He's old, he's frail, he's not dangerous, they bleated. It was all the bodyguards' fault and not his! But the judge considers him a flight risk, not to mention the corpses still coming out of the soil, so he can cool his heels in a jail cell and wait for trial. Also, Dircus Dolgange filed for divorce. He's looking at the ruin of his business, his wife distributing rucaline right under his nose. But Kyrad Naphates is coming out of this smelling like roses."

Jesco had seen her picture in the paper, though he had not read the article. "I'm still sorry she lost that liaison position."

"Don't be. She's not. She said that she would just go for it again next time. That's politics. And now she's got a legion of women who know her name and are outraged on her behalf, because Morgan Kodolli gave a statement before his lawyers muzzled him that it was basically all her fault for spurning him ages ago. She *owed* him. So a woman has to accept a proposal from any man who offers one just because she's afraid that he might try to implicate her in a *murder* far off in the future? Should I walk around all worried-like that the lordling with the squashed nose is even now plotting against me? That's insane. Funny, that man."

"The lordling?"

"Morgan. He looks so mild-mannered on the outside but you delve into his brain's workings and see that he's missing a heap of gears. His sentence won't be as long since he didn't stab you or the courier personally, or kill Quay or order him killed or have anything to do with the rucaline. But he's ruined all the same, his son and daughter and father will be in prison for the rest of their lives, and good riddance to the whole lot of them." She wrapped her hand in her sleeve and swatted Jesco's covered arm. "You owe me curtains, the two of you. Ugh."

He hung the plaque on the wall in his room but got tired of the sun reflecting off the glass. Removing it to his desk drawer, he forgot about it. Three weeks had passed since the train when there was another murder for him to work. Neither detective was Scoth. The thralls upon the evidence at the crime site were so intense that they landed him in his wheelchair for several days. Gavon tended him well until he could get about with a cane.

He had only just graduated to walking about on his own when Sfinx hurtled down the hallway early one evening. "Sir! Sir! A carriage is here for you! There must be another murder, sir!" He sprinted away, shouting to a friend.

Jesco had been on his way to the dining hall for dinner. He was sorry to have another case when he had just gotten back on his feet. Looking down the hallway to the front doors, he saw a regular carriage parked there instead of a police carriage. Then his heart jumped. Scoth was coming inside. He was just using his new personal carriage for the case.

He looked good, as he always did. But he wasn't in his usual garb for work. Dressed in a casual suit, he'd warred with his hair yet could only claim a partial victory. A cowlick had sprouted up above his left ear. Whatever the case was, it had caught him out while doing something else.

"Is the destination card for the asylum really named Prick Pick-up?" Jesco called.

"It is," Scoth said irascibly. His smile waxed and waned, and he stopped before Jesco. Strangely, he looked a little nervous. "It's new. It's all new. I made sure of it."

"The carriage? I should think so. The old one was smashed in the riverbed."

"No." Scoth ran his hand through his hair in agitation. Cowlicks sprung up all over. "We've got a table reserved at The Seven Temptations' restaurant, so hop into something more presentable and let's go."

There wasn't a case. He had come to the asylum to take Jesco out. Just as he began to answer, Scoth said, "And you should bring some of your things for the next few days, too. I've got it all set up at my house, new sheets and everything else I could think of. And there are these . . ."

He pulled out a pair of theater tickets from his pocket. The showing was tomorrow night. "It's a private box. You don't have to worry about people touching you by mistake while getting to their seats. Then I thought the next day we could drive out to Whenx to see the autohorse races in their brand-new stadium. Place bets, have a mug of ale and a bag of popcorn." His nervousness intensified. "You don't have to do any of that. It's only if you want to. I just have some days off and I thought . . ."

Jesco loved this man. "I want to go."

"You don't have to say that only to placate me-"

"I'm *not*. Laeric, I really want to go." Jesco laughed, having never wanted to do something so much in his life. Taking off his gloves, he cupped Scoth's cheeks and looked straight into his eyes. "I can't wait."

"Sure?"

"Very, very sure." He tipped Scoth's head and pressed a kiss to his cowlicks. Then Scoth offered his arm and Jesco took it, and they walked away together.

More M/M Steampunk Titles by Jordan Reece:

The Hunter

The Tracker

Hexed

Jordan Reece also writes M/M romance as Octavia Zane:

Love and Werewolves

The Alpha's Captive Omega

Mr. Pretend

# About the Author

Jordan Reece is an independent author who enjoys writing fantasy, especially steampunk. Reece also writes fantasy and science fiction under the name Macaulay C. Hunter.

Printed in Great Britain
by Amazon